EVIL
REINCARNATE

LEIGH CLARK

TOR

A TOM DOHERTY ASSOCIATES BOOK

NEW YORK

EVIL REINCARNATE

A Tor Book
Published by Tom Doherty Associates, Inc.
175 Fifth Avenue
New York, N.Y. 10010

Tor® is a registered trademark of Tom Doherty Associates, Inc.

Library of Congress Cataloging-in-Publication Data

Clark, Leigh.
    Evil reincarnate / Leigh Clark.
      p.   cm.
    "A Tom Doherty Associates book."
    ISBN 0-312-85723-3
    1. Women psychiatrists—Fiction.   2. Psychopaths—Fiction.
  I. Title.
PS3553.L28615E95   1994
813'.54—dc20   94-30176
                                            CIP

Design by Lynn Newmark

First edition: November 1994

Printed in the United States of America

0 9 8 7 6 5 4 3 2 1

For Sherry Robb,
who made it happen,
and Natalia Aponte,
who made it work.

Say, maiden, can thy life be led
To join the living and the dead?
Then trace thy footsteps on with me,
We are wed to one eternity.

John Clare
"Invitation to Eternity"

These things are full of dread:
the past,
the present,
the passage between both worlds.

Prologue:
The Malediction

Venice. 1594.

He could smell the evil now as he approached the narrow doorway, and his heart grew cold with the fear of it.

He stopped and looked once more at the world outside, the Grand Canal in the distance, gondoliers and boatmen calling to one another as they passed in the night, the water a dark mirror under the stars. He listened to the church bells ringing out across the city. Then he moved through the doorway, and into the room.

The light inside shone dirty gold. A thick candle sputtered atop a human skull. Melted wax dribbled into its hollow sockets and grinning mouth like the corrupted flesh of a Plague victim.

The bearded young visitor thought of the Plague and crossed himself, then turned to the room's sole inhabitant.

He seemed old beyond understanding or belief, his skin withered parchment, his hands spider's claws. He scratched at a faded manuscript unrolled across the top of a narrow writing desk. He looked up with his yellow cat's eyes at the bearded young man standing before him.

"There is blood on your hands," he said, in a hissing whisper.

"Another one is dead," the young man said. "I did with her as you commanded."

The yellow eyes narrowed. "Do not come into this house

with blood on your hands. I do not wish to have the Doge's men question me about such things."

"But what about me?" The young man's voice rose. "What will they do to me? *There were those who saw tonight. I had to flee for my life. I did not choose to come here!"*

The old one smiled. "You serve me of your own free will."

"My will is no longer my own." The young man lowered his dark eyes. "I am damned in what I do for you."

The other raised a raven's quill to his lips. "Fine words, coming from the mouth of a hired murderer, a common assassino. *You kill eagerly enough for the Count Ludovico Contarini, noble member of the Doge's* Signoria. *Your tender conscience does not shrink from that."*

The old one's eyes glittered with malice. "And yet, you feel reluctant to do the bidding of a humble scholar, such as myself."

"Contarini is a vicious pig. But at least he is human."

The old one laughed then—a high, sinister sound, like the breaking of glass inside a tomb.

The young man drew back from the evil laughter. "Besides, Contarini possesses that which I desire more than anything else in this world!"

The laughter stopped. "He pays you gold for blood. A common exchange. But I—" A spider's claw pointed to the ancient books and manuscripts about the room. "I offer you something more rare and wonderful than all the gold of all the ages."

The old one leaned forward, dark robes falling onto his desktop. "I offer you—the secret of immortality. The transmigration of souls from one life into the next, throughout all eternity. You give me the blood of others. I give you, in return, eternal life."

"I do not want," the young man said, "your eternal life."

"Ah?" The old one's yellow eyes regarded him with curiosity. "What could it be, this object that you so desire?"

"You know what I want."

The old one smiled, pointed teeth glinting in the dirty

golden light. "*Ah, yes.* La contessa. *The lovely young Countess Contarini, the fair Alessandra, wife of the man whose murders you so willingly commit.*"

The smile vanished. "*A man who sits on the* Signoria, *and the dreaded Council of Ten. A man who could condemn you to a slow, agonizing death in the Doge's torture chambers with a mere nod of his head.*"

The young man paled beneath his dark beard. "*I cannot fight Contarini and his great power. I cannot take her from him. But* you *can. You can give her to me!*"

The old one sat motionless as a mummified corpse.

Then he said, "*For her sake you commit his murders, and mine?*"

"*For her sake, I would do anything.*"

The spider's claw laid down the raven's quill.

"*Then you shall have her.*"

He nodded. "*My thanks, Master. I will do your bidding with a glad heart.*" *He looked up into the old one's yellow eyes.* "*And I will never again enter your house with blood on my hands.*"

He bowed and left the room.

You shall have her indeed, *the old one thought, watching him leave.* In this life, and the next.

He folded his spider's claws together.

And when the time is right, the fire will have you both.

I

*dreams
of
darkness*

1
The Beast in Chains

Los Angeles. 1994.

The iron door slammed shut behind her.

Connie Stallman stepped into the main corridor of the Los Angeles Police Department, Hollywood Division, over an hour late.

She had never learned the fine art of hanging up on patients, not even those as irritating as Jennie Hodges.

The uniformed officer beside her introduced the two detectives standing in the middle of the corridor.

"Lieutenant Ed Dormer, Sergeant Mike Salazar, Homicide. Dr. C. M. Stallman, psychiatrist at the Beckford Clinic in Hollywood."

She nodded to them. "Sorry about being late—"

Ed Dormer stopped her. "We have our delays. You have yours."

"I'm sure you want to get this over with."

"Take your time. He's not making bail. But he *will* be leaving us soon."

"Transfer," Salazar said. "We don't have facilities for holding dangerous suspects like Tod Jarrow long-term."

Dormer nodded at the black carrying case in Connie's hand.

"For the interview?"

"A small camcorder."

Salazar asked Dormer, "Lathrop have a problem with that?"

"Captain Lathrop might like to know just how Dr. Stallman plans to use this particular videotape."

"For diagnostic reference only," she said. "It becomes part of the patient's confidential file."

"No chance of its being broadcast at some later date?"

"No."

"Or handed over to reporters for selected sound bites?"

"I'm a doctor, Lieutenant, not a tabloid journalist. The Beckford Clinic's in Hollywood, but we're not part of the media scene any more than you are."

"We have to be careful about these things," Salazar said, trying to smooth it over. "We don't want Tod Jarrow getting any more free publicity than he already has."

"He won't get any from me. That's not why I'm here."

"Why *are* you here, Dr. Stallman?" Dormer asked.

"The court requires a fair and complete evaluation of the defendant's mental fitness to stand trial. I'm here as a public servant, Lieutenant Dormer, just like you."

"Sure. But why are *you* here?"

"You want my credentials? Or a personal statement of faith?"

"No offense intended, Doctor." Dormer tried to come up with a smile. "We're both playing the same game here, from different sides of the court. We each have an interest in Tod Jarrow. I want him put away. For keeps, if I'm lucky. Fifteen to twenty-five years, parole in seven, if I'm not. You, on the other hand, want him rehabilitated, put back into normal society."

"I don't need anyone to tell me what I want, Lieutenant."

"Like I said, Doctor, no offense. But we might as well lay all our cards down face up."

"Not if you're dealing yours from the bottom of the deck."

Dormer almost smiled, a real one this time. "You know, the hardest part of my job isn't catching these bastards. It's making sure they stay caught. You're a nice lady, Dr. Stallman. But you and me, we're natural enemies. You have to understand that."

Connie accepted the truce offer for what it was worth.

"I understand," she said, "but I don't agree. I think we're on the same side."

"Really?"

"You want to keep Tod Jarrow locked up. So do I. But not the whole person, just a part of him. I want the dark side locked up, the side that's hurting him, and other people. Your way destroys everything, the good with the bad. My way, if it succeeds, gets rid of the bad and lets the good survive."

Dormer glanced at Salazar. "She wants to save his good side."

He turned back to Connie. "Lots of luck, Doctor."

As they started down the corridor toward the interrogation cell, Connie said, "This might go faster if I'm alone with him."

Dormer smiled his forced smile. "Believe me, you don't want to be in a room with Tod Jarrow by yourself."

"Look, Lieutenant, I know something about him, okay? I know he was arrested at the scene of one mutilation-murder. I know he's been charged with others."

"You know the details?"

Before she could answer, Salazar said, "Jarrow blinded one of his arresting officers while they were trying to restrain him."

Dormer added, "He's good with a knife. Likes to use it for creative surgery on certain delicate body parts. Most of his female victims were still alive when he started cutting on them."

"If you think you're scaring me, Lieutenant—"

"Not at all, Doctor. Just thought you might like to know what kind of person you're trying to save."

"Jarrow's mutilation patterns seemed to follow the old Nightstalker MO at first," Salazar said. "We thought there might be a similar tie-in to the Satanic rituals and devil worship that we found with Richard Ramirez. But so far, no fit."

"Of course, Ramirez made things easy for us," Dormer admitted. "Walking into the courtroom screaming 'Hail Satan!'

Our friend Jarrow's a bit more tight-lipped than that. He won't talk."

"About the mutilations?" Connie asked.

"About anything."

They stopped in front of another iron door.

"You have any kids?" Dormer asked her.

"Two."

"The man who lost his eyes to Jarrow has four kids. He gets state and department disability. But it's tough for a blind cop to see the light at the end of the tunnel."

"I'm aware of the risks that go with my job, Lieutenant."

"We'll be inside the cell with you," Dormer said, "watching Jarrow the whole time. If he tries something, that's our problem. You take care of the interview. But do not go near him. Do not touch him. Do not try to render any kind of assistance, *no matter what happens.* These types can be very tricky. We want you to keep both your big brown eyes, Doctor."

Connie stared at the iron door in front of her for several seconds before asking, "He's in there now?"

"Ready and waiting, whenever you are."

2

The Interview

The room held little more than four gray walls.

The air inside hung hot and close, heavy with odors of stale sweat, cigarette smoke, body waste. The only light came from a ceiling bulb encased in wire mesh.

A long metal table cut the room in half. On the side nearest Connie, a straight-backed chair had been drawn up close. On the opposite side, in a chair at least five feet back from the table, Tod Jarrow sat and waited.

From where Connie stood, she could not see his face. He sat dressed in a dirty white T-shirt and faded jeans, dark-haired head bent forward, elbows on his knees, wrists cuffed. On either side of him, two uniformed officers stood alert and motionless.

"All yours, Doctor," Dormer said.

Gripping the leather handle of her camcorder case, she walked over to the chair on her side of the table.

Connie pulled the chair out from the table. Its metal legs scraped across the concrete floor.

Jarrow raised his head.

She felt it then, like a dead weight on her lungs.

Fear—a deep, irrational fear.

She could see that, on the surface, there was nothing to be afraid of. Tod Jarrow appeared to be somewhere in his late twenties, early thirties, lean and muscular, with a face that might have been good-looking, except for the ugly bruises and hastily stitched cuts, the souvenirs of his recent violent arrest.

But when she looked into his dark eyes—

The eyes, she thought, *of someone returned from the dead.*

Aware of the dampness beading her upper lip, she turned her back on Tod Jarrow and began to remove the camcorder from its case.

Even as a child, Connie had been trained to act calmly under pressure. *In an emergency,* her late father Andrew MacKendrick used to tell her, *you want your body to be your ally, not your enemy.* Dr. Jacob Abraham Mauder, her great friend and psychiatric residency mentor, always told her she had nerves of steel.

Sure, Jake, she thought to herself now. *Nerves of steel.*

She tried to ignore the feeling that Tod Jarrow's dark eyes were staring at her back as she adjusted the tripod's height, and checked the sound-recording level.

Throughout the camcorder setup, Connie did not look once at Tod Jarrow, although she sensed that he was there, watching her, flanked by guards. When she glanced briefly through the viewfinder to adjust the framing, his dark eyes stared back into hers, glittering sharply through the ground-glass lens.

I'm watching, they seemed to say, *and I'm waiting.*

She moved away from the camcorder, and walked over to the chair on her side of the table. Sitting down, she placed her pen and notepad to one side. Across the table, Jarrow leaned forward slightly. Connie could see the guards on either side of him tense.

She folded her hands on the tabletop and forced herself to smile into Tod Jarrow's dark eyes.

"Hello, Tod," she said, her voice even, well-pitched. "I'm Dr. Stallman, but you can call me Connie. I've been asked to talk with you. But the real reason I'm here is to listen—to whatever you have to say."

The dark eyes watched in silence.

"There are no restrictions," she went on. "You can say whatever you want to say."

The whole room was silent now.

Connie sat with her hands folded, watching Tod Jarrow. Over the years, she had learned to wait in interviews, to sit and wait and say nothing, to let her patients know that she would continue to wait as long as necessary—until they felt it was the right time for them to speak.

Tod Jarrow, watching her with his dark eyes, leaned forward and said, "Why should I talk to you?"

He spoke softly, not much above a whisper, but it echoed like a gunshot in that silent room.

A sense of relief washed over Connie. Jarrow's eyes suddenly looked less dark. They seemed bright, faintly mocking, with a go-to-hell cockiness that made him look likable, even attractive, beneath his bruises and stitches.

"Why should I talk to you, cunt?"

"Watch your mouth, son," Salazar said.

The dark eyes shifted to him. "Fuck you and that son shit."

Salazar moved forward. Each of the flanking officers grabbed one of Jarrow's arms. His body tensed, and Connie could see the trust she had won vanishing before her eyes.

She turned to Dormer. "Stop it!"

He said nothing.

"I won't stand for this!"

Dormer's hard eyes seemed to say that was fine with him.

"I'll stop this interview," she said, "and file a complaint charging you and your officers with obstruction of a medical examination required by law in the State of California."

A certain uneasiness entered Dormer's eyes.

"He has to be allowed to say whatever he wants to, Lieutenant. If you're going to censor him, I'm wasting my time here. You might as well conduct this interview yourself."

Dormer looked over to where the two officers held Jarrow, as Salazar moved in on him. Dormer shook his head. They released Jarrow and resumed their flanking positions. Salazar stopped, then withdrew slowly.

Dormer said to her, "We *will* censor the prisoner's actions, if that's okay with you, Doctor."

Salazar gave Jarrow a hard-cop stare. "Call *her* whatever you want, pretty boy. Just don't get started with me."

Connie looked at the dark eyes that had been watching everything silently, with no visible response.

She started over again, repeating his question for him.

"Why should you talk to me, Tod? No reason. You don't have to. But if you want to, you can. If you want to, I'll listen."

She stopped talking then, and waited.

She was prepared to wait a long time. After that stupid macho move by Dormer's men, Jarrow would almost certainly pull back into his snug, psychopathic shell and sit there, glaring out at a world that he could always trust to turn on him, always.

Don't start labeling him a psychopath, she cautioned herself, *before you even finish the interview.*

But everything pointed to it. Connie knew more about the murders than she had told Dormer. She had read the police files, the news accounts, the various coroner's reports.

She could imagine what it must have been like for his victims, all of them young women, alone with him somewhere, seeing the sudden transformation in his dark eyes, realizing then what they had picked up tonight, what they were in for now.

"So I can say whatever I want?"

Connie looked up at him.

"So what?" His dark eyes shifted to the camcorder running silently on its tripod. "You're taping all this shit for the DA."

"No I'm not. The tape becomes part of your patient file at the clinic. It's not admissible evidence in court."

He glanced at Dormer, who said, "What she says is true."

"So? You just tell the DA whatever I tell you, right? Big fucking difference."

"I have to report on your mental fitness to stand trial," she said. "That's all."

He smiled at her with a thin, mirthless grin that stretched his stitches. "You got to decide whether I'm crazy or not, right?"

His voice dropped almost to a whisper. "You can decide that anytime you want, Connie. You can decide that right now."

"No, I can't. That's not how it works. I don't just make a snap decision. I have to get to know you, how you think and feel. I don't know you yet. I don't know you at all."

Tod Jarrow's lips were closed, but his words came to Connie's mind with all the intimacy of a lover's whisper.

You know me, yes, Contessa, you know me well.

The fear that gripped her then made any earlier fear of him seem trivial, a mere muscle spasm. This fear was old and distant, incredibly ancient, but terrible as Tod Jarrow's blood-fresh crimes, and real as his dark eyes, watching her from the far side of the table.

You know me, yes, Contessa, you know me well.

The gray walls of the cell seemed to turn into damp, rotting stone. She could actually *smell* the dampness, and the brackish water that made the stones damp. She could even hear it now, dark water lapping against cut stone. She saw the colors of other stones—pink marble, alabaster, porphyry. And gold, golden domes and towers and doors. More stones now, stones set in walls, smaller stones, brightly colored, making pictures, mosaics, patterns on the walls. Blood, war, plague, death. And again, the smells. Dampness, incense, spice. Gold and spice, stone and death—and everywhere the water, like the fluids of the womb.

It ceased. The smells and visions, delicate and terrifying, vanished like a stray thought. Her mind snapped back into focus.

She looked away from Tod Jarrow. She knew it was a mistake to break eye contact like that. It shattered the ever-tenuous trust between doctor and patient. But she could not go on with the interview right now. Not after what she had heard him say.

You know me, yes, Contessa—

Not after the sudden terror it had released inside her.

But Tod Jarrow said, "Why the fuck do you care whether I'm crazy or not anyway?"

Connie turned back to him, forcing herself to stare straight into his dark eyes. The smells and images were gone now—stone and water, gold and death. But the echoes kept reverberating inside her mind, like aftershocks from an explosion.

"You're the one who has to care whether you're sick or well, Tod," she managed to say. "You do care, don't you?"

"Shit, no," he said quietly, his dark eyes dropping from hers.

"You're the one it happened to." She felt some sense of her own control returning now. "It was your experience. Nothing can change that."

You had to be careful with someone like Tod Jarrow. You could not push him too far, or he might close up on you and never talk again. But at this point, she felt he was slipping away from her anyway, withdrawing into his own dark world. So she took a chance, and pushed hard.

"The things you did, Tod, you wanted to do them. No one else forced you. It was all your choice. You know that."

She waited, heart pounding with anticipation.

He raised his head, dark eyes angry now.

"I had a choice, huh? *You think I had some kind of choice?*"

"Easy," Dormer warned him.

A thread of saliva trickled down from Jarrow's mouth. His dark eyes glittered like black diamonds.

"You know there was no goddamn choice about *any* of it!" he whispered to her, air rattling in his throat.

"No choice at all!"

He moved with a speed and fury that took them all by surprise.

Dormer and his men had been expecting something, but nothing this fast. Jarrow leaped forward, crashing down belly-first onto the table, grabbing at Connie's hands as she raised them in front of her in stunned, slow-motion response. His cuffed hands clamped her right forearm and jerked it toward him. She was dragged to her feet, screaming now, chair tipping back onto concrete, pen skittering wildly across the tabletop, notebook pages fluttering in the air.

Salazar brought the edge of his hand down hard on the cuffed wrists, right above the metal. Jarrow's head snapped back and his teeth clenched tight. But he did not let go of Connie's forearm.

By now the two flanking officers had him. One drove a fist into the back of his neck. Jarrow's mouth dropped. He collapsed across the table, still gripping Connie's arm. Salazar pried the strong fingers loose, one by one.

Connie stepped back, eyes dull with shock, cradling her right forearm, shaking her head, crying, "Wait—*wait!*"

Dormer moved in front of her. "Interview's over, Doctor."

3
Real World

Connie drove her dark blue Acura Legend through the traffic along Sunset Boulevard, hitting the brakes more often than the gas.

She did not even listen to the music from her tape deck, some harpsichord thing by Bach that she played for her patients when their nerves went bad. She was thinking about Tod Jarrow, what he had said and done, what had been done to him. She did not need the videotape to bring that back. It was locked inside her head, playing over and over like an endless loop.

She remembered the smugness in Ed Dormer's hard eyes.

"Thanks for coming by, Doctor. You tried your best."

A superior smile flickered over his face.

"Some types just can't be helped. They won't permit it."

"I'm coming back later, Lieutenant, to finish the interview."

He looked at her then as if she had made a bad joke.

"Once would be enough for most people, Dr. Stallman. Besides, he's being transferred soon. He's not our problem anymore."

"He's *my* problem now. I'm going to talk to him again."

"Whatever you say, Doctor."

In truth, she did not want to talk to Tod Jarrow again, ever. The mere thought of it terrified her. But whatever he had done, he was suffering for it now, trapped in a world of pain.

That's why I got into this kind of work, she reminded herself, waiting for an endless red light to turn green, *so I could help the Tod Jarrows of the world.*

She had wanted to be a doctor ever since, at age seven, she first helped inventory her father's pharmacy. The late Andrew MacKendrick never let the fact that his only child was a girl keep him from teaching her everything about the pharmacy business he would have taught a son. He taught her the names of the drugs, how they worked, what they did. When she asked him who decided to give which drugs to which people, he told her about doctors, and gave her a dream.

Three years later, when Andrew MacKendrick dropped dead from a heart attack one summer evening, an important part of her world died with him, but not her dream of becoming a doctor.

Connie's eyes filled with tears. She missed her father so much—would always miss him.

She did not decide to become a psychiatrist until her internship at Cedars Sinai, where she first started working with teenage suicidal schizophrenics, abused children—all the rejects of Southern California's high-glitz, disposable society. At the end of her four-year psychiatric residency with Jake Mauder, she turned down an offer from a lucrative private practice in Beverly Hills and joined the staff of the John Harris Beckford Clinic, a community mental-health center in Hollywood.

She parked in the space marked RESERVED FOR DR. STALLMAN, and shut off the car's engine.

The aftershock of the Jarrow interview hit her then. She raised a hand to her forehead, late-afternoon sunlight streaming in through the tinted windshield.

You know me, yes, Contessa, you know me well.

She could hear Tod Jarrow whispering to her again, making her blood run cold, his soft voice hissing slightly on the *s* sound.

But he had never actually said that.

She sat up straight in the front seat, staring out the windshield at a scruffy royal palm beside a pink stucco building in the distance.

Pink marble. Dark waters. Gold towers.

"No!" she shouted, scattering the disconnected images.

She sat there in her car, thinking. He had not said that. She could always check the videotape to be sure, but she *knew*. Jarrow had been looking at her with those unnerving dark eyes of his, but his lips had not moved. He had said nothing.

But she had heard it anyway—clearly, distinctly.

You know me, yes, Contessa, you know me well.

Contessa? What the hell was that supposed to be? Some Spanish version of her given name, Constance?

Contesssssssa.

Overwork, she thought simply, opening the car door and putting the whole business out of her mind.

Inside her office waiting room, she found her receptionist, Rebecca Martinez, a fourth-year UCLA pre-med student, going over appointment instructions with a frail elderly lady.

"Connie! You okay?"

"Just fine, Becky. Thanks."

"I heard what happened at the police station. My God, it sounded so awful!"

"Well, it wasn't quite as bad as it sounded."

Back in the office lunch area, Connie opened the refrigerator door and hesitated over a choice between organic carrot juice and Diet Pepsi. Feeling guilty, she took the Diet Pepsi and promised herself carrot juice tomorrow.

Rebecca poked her head into the lunch area.

"All your messages are in on your desk—and Ken called, just to see how you're doing, but he didn't leave a message."

Remembering his concern for her safety at work, Connie wondered what Ken would do if he knew of Jarrow's attack.

"Did he say anything about—you know?"

Rebecca shook her head. "*I* didn't tell him."

Connie started for her private office, then stopped.

"Becky? Do you know what the word *Contessa* means?"

"*Condesa?*"

"No," Connie said, remembering clearly the way she heard Jarrow say it—the way she *thought* she heard him say it. "With a hard *t. Contessa.*"

Rebecca shrugged. "*Condesa* means like, you know, a countess or something. I don't know about the other."

Contessa, Connie thought, walking into her office and looking at the neat stack of phone messages on her desk. The more she thought about it, the less sense it made.

But you never heard it anyway, she reminded herself, *except in your head, so forget about it, okay?*

She sorted through her messages. There were five from Jennie Hodges. She felt a twinge of guilt, and put those in a separate stack. She also set aside one from Benjamin Simmons's foster parent, Mrs. Amanda Baker. It did not have a call-back number. The message consisted of only two words: *No progress.*

The phone rang out at the reception desk. Rebecca got it.

"Connie, for you! I'm transferring. Then I'm outta here!"

"Dr. Stallman speaking."

"Doctor?" said a deep, easy-going male voice. "I've got this serious problem. I'm married to a beautiful woman. I'm crazy about her, our kids are crazy about her. Only problem is, she spends all her time working with people who really are crazy. So she's never home for dinner. Any suggestions?"

Connie smiled. "I love you and I'm sorry I'm late. I just—"

This is not the time to tell him about it, she thought, *not over the phone.*

"I got sort of delayed with that interview at the police station," she said. "I'll tell you about it when I get home."

"And when will that be? Reason I ask is, I've got two mighty hungry kids here. They don't want to see you that much, but—"

Their daughter Stevie started yelling in the background.

"Looks like I'm wrong about that. Guess they do want to see you after all. Here's one of 'em to say hello right now."

"Mommy!" Trent gushed into the phone. "Hi, Mommy!"

"Hi, baby," Connie said, imagining Trent held in the crook of Ken's arm, grabbing onto the cordless phone with both pudgy hands. "How's Mommy's big boy?"

"Mom!" Stevie came on the line. "Dad says I pushed Trent into the pool, but I *didn't,* okay? He fell in by himself, 'cause he's such a dork!"

"He's not a dork, Stevie. He's just littler than you."

"Do you love him more than me?" Stevie asked.

"I love you both the same. And that's a whole lot. I'll be

home real soon. Let me talk to Daddy again, okay, sweet-heart?"

When Ken got back on the line, Connie asked, "Hasn't Galina given them their dinner yet?"

"She's been helping," Ken said. "But tonight's specialty is the world-famous Barbecue á la Stallman. I know you health-food nuts aren't into barbecue. But, hey, at least it's fish."

"I'm not a health-food nut!" she protested playfully. "But that's sweet of you. The kids love barbecued anything. I'll be home right after I return these calls, okay?"

"End-of-the-day phone calls can be a real bitch," Ken agreed. "Any that couldn't wait till tomorrow?"

"Just one," she said, thinking of Jennie Hodges. "I guess I could take care of that, then hold the others."

"Sounds good to me."

"Okay. It's a deal. See you soon."

"You'll be—Stevie, keep your hands *off* the fish, please?"

Ken turned back to the phone. "You'll be making three hungry people who love you very happy."

She was still smiling as she dialed Jennie Hodges's number. She let it ring sixteen times before hanging up. Then she checked her patient directory to make sure the message number was correct.

Her phone rang again.

"Whenever they jump you like that," said the slightly nasal voice with the New York accent, "you're supposed to play dead. All those years, and I taught you nothing?"

"Jake!"

"Bad jokes aside." His voice lost its banter. "You sure you're okay now, *bubeleh?*"

"Jake, you must be the fourth person to ask me that today."

"What's with this fourth person bullshit? You okay or not?"

"I'm fine, Jake. I'm completely fine, okay?"

"Between you and me, you don't sound so fine."

"Well, I am. And it happened to me, not you."

"True. So, what happened?"

"Nothing important, Jake. You want the boring details?"

"No, I just called to sell you some junk bonds. Yes, I want the boring details. Talk."

Connie told him what had happened. As she did, she could imagine Dr. Jacob Abraham Mauder sitting there in his paper-cluttered office, heavy face pensive, thick-lensed black-frame glasses perched low on his nose, thumb flicking absently at his bristly salt-and-pepper moustache while he listened silently and carefully, the way he had trained her to do.

When she finished, she was the one who broke the silence. "Well?"

"I'm sure you left things out. They'll be on the tape."

"Sure," Connie said, remembering Tod Jarrow's dark eyes. "You want to see it?"

"Later." Jake cleared his throat. "Not to waste time, it sounds wrong. He's double-tracking you. He knows what he did. He knows why. But about the why part, he's not talking."

"Which wouldn't be unusual for a psychotic personality—*if* we can assume at this point that he's psychotic."

"We can assume. But there's more to it than that. This schmuck tells you he had no choice about what he did, implying that someone else made him do it. Then, he attacks you. I don't like that, Connie."

She saw where this was leading. "I'll learn more when I finish the interview, Jake."

"Learn what? How maybe to duck faster the next time? He's got a problem with women, right? And for some reason he seems to have made a transference with you. You know what that means."

"You think I should turn it over to someone else."

"Did I say that? I think you should give it some very careful thought. And if you do go ahead with it, you should ask yourself whether it's real empathy or maybe a transference problem of your own. Like I always told you—"

"—empathize, never identify," Connie finished the Famous Mauder Insight for him. "Yeah, Jake. I know."

"If you know, do. And if you're really as fine as you claim, why don't you go home to your husband and kids, Lady Doctor?"

"I was just getting ready to leave when you called." She smiled. "Thanks for calling, Jake. You didn't have to."

"Some *meshuggener* jumps my best student and I'm not supposed to call and see how she is?"

"Yeah, well, you're a sweetheart. Give my love to Esther."

Then she asked, "Jake? Does the word *contessa* mean *countess?*"

"What do you think it means? Don't you ever watch old movies? *The Barefoot Contessa*. 1954. Humphrey Bogart, Ava Gardner. Not a bad flick. Catch it on cable, or rent the tape sometime."

"What language is it? *Contessa?*"

"Italian. What else? Finnish? You studying languages now?"

"No, it's just—"

"Something to do with that schmuck, Jarrow? Turning you into a linguist?"

"Goodbye, Jake."

She was clearing off her desk when the phone rang.

"Me again." Jake seemed to be talking over a mouthful of something chewy and delicious. "Another Famous Mauder Insight, long as we're talking languages. Guy's first name. Tod. Only one *d* you said, right?"

"Right."

"Funny way to spell it. Usually has two. Anyway. Means *death* in German, as in *Der Tod in Venedig*. You know, *Death in Venice,* Thomas Mann's story? Great film by Visconti, by the way."

"Thanks a lot, Jake. Bye."

Screw it, she thought, getting up from her desk, and putting Tod Jarrow firmly out of her mind.

His dark, burning eyes.

Contessssssaaa.

4
Dangerous Visions

The traffic thinned out as Connie drove up into the Hollywood Hills. The grades got steeper, the curves sharper, the views more breathtaking. Some of the side roads, although paved, grew narrow as bicycle paths.

Connie loved it up there, the next best thing to living in the real mountains, Arrowhead or Big Bear. If Ken had made the choice, they would be in one of the beach cities, close to his beloved ocean and boats. But Connie had grown up in Long Beach, and had no fondness for the flat, close-packed life-style of seaside L.A. Besides, this way she was only a few miles from work, with no freeways to worry about. Ken, who had a commercial real estate office in downtown L.A., proved a good sport about his own longer commute, as he did about most things.

As Connie pulled into the driveway, Ken waved to her from the barbecue grill on the redwood deck, his blond hair dark in the late-afternoon sun. Stevie came running across the grass, her own blond hair flying out behind her, blue eyes alive and happy. Trent toddled far behind, outdistanced from the start.

"Hey, Stevie!" Connie called.

"Mom!" Stevie panted, clutching her in a round-the-knees bear hug. "Dad won't let me help with the fish!"

Connie brushed back her daughter's blond hair.

"Have you been a good girl?"

Stevie nodded solemnly. "Can we go swimming after we eat?"

"Not right after. But maybe we can do something else now."

She handed Stevie a video game, still in its maroon plastic bag, with The High-Tech Connection's keyboard logo on one side.

Stevie's blue eyes widened. "Wow! Zorena! Mom, I love you!"

Connie bent over to receive a quick kiss, then called to Stevie, who had almost reached the front door by now, "Don't get so wrapped up in the game that you forget about dinner, okay?"

"Mommy! Mommy!" Trent cried, struggling toward her with one chubby arm raised in the air, the other held firmly in the protective grip of Galina Marenkov, their housekeeper.

"Always he is running," Galina said, a little out of breath from the chase. "I tell him, *walk* to see your Mama, don't run. But, he runs. So?"

"Thanks for keeping after him, Galina," Connie said, picking up Trent and getting covered with wet, eager kisses. "But you should be home now, fixing dinner for Vladimir and Tanya."

"Is no big deal to wait for you, Connie."

"That's sweet, Galina." She bounced Trent in her arms. "I understand it's my fault no one's eaten yet."

"This is not true. Tonight Ken"—pronouncing it with the Russian *ye* sound—"makes his grand barbecue of the fish."

"Let's go see if he needs any help."

The fish on the grill, New Zealand orange roughie, was fragrant with fresh herbs and olive oil. Mesquite glowed in place of charcoal.

Ken looked up and smiled. "The lady of the house returns."

She kissed him, wedging Trent in between them.

"Sorry I'm so late. But I see your fish isn't done anyway."

"Almost." He nodded at her elegant navy blue suit. "Going to eat in that? Or change into something more comfortable?"

"Sounds okay to me." She put down Trent. "I'll go change, then help with the salad while you finish up here, Master Chef."

"There is no need," Galina announced. "The salad and the mushrooms and the rice, all is ready."

An hour after dinner, Connie and Ken sat on the redwood

deck, sipping at a light Chablis as the sky faded slowly to a dark, pinkish orange. Galina had gone home. Down below, Stevie and Trent sailed a toy model pirate ship across the shallow end of the pool. A soft breeze moved over the deck, barely noticeable in the gentle afterglow of the day.

"Why did Jarrow attack you?" Ken asked quietly.

Connie's fingers tightened around the stem of her wine-glass.

The children's laughter floated up to them from beside the pool, along with the sound of splashing water.

"I wasn't hurt. It sounds worse than it was."

"I didn't ask that."

Down at the pool, the pirate ship sailed the choppy waters of the shallow end.

She turned to him. "Who told you?"

"Jake."

A frown creased her forehead.

"We both share this concern for your well-being."

She took a quick swallow of wine.

"Now that I've answered your question, how about mine?"

She lowered the wineglass. "I said something that fright-ened him. Maybe it made him mad. I think it frightened him."

"What was it?"

"I told him he was responsible for what he had done. I wanted to get him to talk. I tried to push him. I guess I overdid it."

"He tried to kill you for something you said."

"Ken, that's overstating it."

"What do you think would have happened if you'd been in that room alone with him?"

She felt the fear from earlier in the day pass over her again, and saw Tod Jarrow's dark, staring eyes.

You know me, yes—

"It wasn't that simple," she said. "You can't just take one action out of context. You have to understand what hap-pened."

"What did happen?"

"Ken, I don't want to keep reliving it forever. It was just something that happened, okay? I didn't get hurt. It's over now."

"Does it bother you to talk about it?"

"No, it does *not.*" She was growing irritated with him now.

"If it doesn't bother you, I'd like to hear about it."

For the second time that day, she recounted the incident, leaving out, as she had with Jake, the part about what she heard—what she *thought* she heard Jarrow whisper to her, as he stared at her with his dark eyes.

You know me, yes, Contessa, you know me well.

It was full evening now. The pool lights were on. The toy pirate ship cast a large and sinister-looking shadow, like the past reaching out into the present, across the pale blue cement bottom of the shallow end.

"What did Jake think?" Ken asked.

"That I should forget about the case, let someone else take it over. The same thing the cops at the station think. The same thing you think too, I'm sure."

She set down her wineglass on a side table, making it rattle.

"Nobody's trying to tell you what to do, Connie."

"No? Then they're sure as hell making a lot of suggestions."

She hunched her bare shoulders against an evening suddenly too cool for just a tank top and shorts.

Ken came over and crouched down beside her, taking one of her hands in his.

"Have I ever tried to run your professional life for you?"

She shrugged. "Not really."

"Played backseat driver? Monday-morning quarterback?"

She shrugged again, and said nothing, staring down at the lighted pool.

"I didn't fall in love with you just because you're beautiful. Sure, that's part of it. But there's more. I love your stubborn independent streak. The way you go after something you want." He paused, looking at her. "I still love it. No way I'd ever try to change that, any more than I'd try to remodel a perfect house."

"Thanks for the flattering comparison."

His eyes turned serious. "You know what I mean. I'm not trying to tell you what to do. There's always some risk involved in any line of work. But this Tod Jarrow thing, that's an *added* risk, above-and-beyond. It's like stacking the odds against yourself on purpose."

She shook her head slowly. "It's not just Tod Jarrow. We've had this conversation before, Ken."

"You could've got yourself *killed!*"

Stevie looked up from the pirate ship down below.

Connie let out a deep breath. "Like you say, there's always some risk."

Ken rubbed his chin thoughtfully as he stared at the distant lights of Los Angeles, spreading out forever into the night.

He turned to her. "You're right. It's not just Jarrow. It's—a feeling. A premonition. I don't know what it is. That's your specialty, not mine. But I know I feel it. And I know it scares the hell out of me."

He squeezed her hand. "Don't get me wrong, babe. I'm not wimping out on you. But I'm scared. I don't know why. I love you and I'm really scared something bad's going to happen to you."

Cars leaned whining into curves on nearby Mulholland Drive. Stevie's loud, confident voice echoed out across the swimming pool. Music drifted up from one of the houses down in the canyon. Brakes squealed suddenly on Mulholland. The muscles tensed in Ken's face.

She smiled at him, and raised his hand to her lips.

"I know what I'm doing, Ken."

"Then you must be doing the right thing."

She ran a hand through his dark blond hair.

"Guess we could always sleep on it, couldn't we?"

He smiled up at her. "Soon?"

"Soon as we get the monsters to bed."

While Ken put out the last of the dying mesquite embers in the grill, Connie walked down to the pool in her bare feet, stepping on a plastic dinosaur that one of the kids had left in the grass.

"Mom!" Stevie pointed. "Look at my pirate ship!"

She looked out at the water, Trent pulling on one hand, Stevie the other, and thought about Ken and his fears, about her own fears, wishing suddenly that she was very young again, with almost no past and not much sense of a future, able to lose herself completely, at least for a while, in the sailing of a toy boat.

She heard the faint, hollow slapping of water against concrete, tiny ripples kicked up by the pool's circulation system, and by Stevie splashing her hands in the water, trying to make the boat go faster. She smelled the water in the pool, heavy with chlorine, and heard the water slapping against cement.

Water against stone. Dark water. Slime-covered stone. Dampness in the air above the water. Fog in her lungs. Hurried footsteps on flat stones. Lights bobbing, weaving in the fog. Torches. Water. Darkness. Light. Footsteps. Running. Faster. Voices. Screaming.

"All'assassino!" Screaming, louder. *"All'assassino!"*

Gold. Water. Blood. Plague. Death.

"Mom!"

She felt Stevie's fingers digging into her wrist, saw the small face turned up to hers, blue eyes sharp with fear.

"You almost fell into the water," Stevie whispered.

"Connie?" Ken came over to the edge of the redwood deck and looked down at her. "You okay?"

It's nothing, she told herself. *The water in the pool just reminded me of Long Beach.*

She had planned to visit her mother in Long Beach tomorrow morning, a journey she both wanted and did not want to make. But painful as some of her Long Beach memories were, they were nothing like the terrifying rush of sounds and images that had just assaulted her.

Dear God, she thought, *what's happening to me?*

"Connie?" Ken asked sharply, halfway down the deck stairs. "Are you okay or not?"

She nodded. "I'm fine."

But for the first time that day, she began to consider the very real possibility that she might not be fine at all.

5

Hunters in the Dark

Tod Jarrow hovered in the half-world between sleeping and waking, past and present, life and death.

After they hit him a few more times and kicked him in the ribs and kidneys, hard, as a warning—all this after the court shrink and top cops had left—they dragged him off to the isolation cell, the one with the padded walls and the big drain in the middle of the floor, so if you shit or puked yourself they could just come in and hose you off. They injected him with some kind of sedative then, like Thorazine—shot him full of the shit, so it felt like his hands and feet were over there on one side of the cell and he was on the other. Floating. Some dickhead came in and checked him out, to make sure nothing was broken inside. He poked around, asking him if this hurt, or that hurt. Jarrow said nothing. Fuck, it all hurt. The dickhead went away, and left him alone.

The fear came then, seeping into his drug-numbed body like a fatal chill, a deadly spreading contagion.

He knew where that would take him. Oh, shit yes. And he fought it, forcing himself to turn the fear into anger, to rekindle the rage that had seized him there in the interrogation cell, a rage that now seemed as strange and distant as some half-remembered story heard in childhood.

Her. Of all the thousands and thousands of doctors in this great stinking shitpile of a city, which one comes to him? *Her!* He had not even recognized her at first. But he had *felt* her, the way he felt everything now, on the ends of his senses, along the nerves that threaded together the then with the now. What the fuck was *she* doing here? Here, now, with him? She couldn't be here!

But she was.

He drew in a deep breath and let it out with a groan, arching his back up off the cement floor where they had dumped him, close to the drain.

"Hey, fuck face!" the dickhead called in through the communications panel. "Gettin' it off dreamin' about all that pussy you chopped up? Fuckin' pervert!"

He turned and looked at the dickhead's face, pressed against the wire-mesh glass in the cell door, sneering at him.

He had done enough killing, then and now. But him, the dickhead, him he would like to kill as a purely personal pleasure. But he would prefer to do it the right way, with true Damascus steel honed sharp as the razor's edge, slicing through flesh and gristle and bone like a heavy cleaver sinking into a side of beef. None of this blowing him apart like a game bird at close range. No. The swing of the sword arm, strength against strength.

"Sweet dreams, fuck face. That's all you're ever gonna get from now on."

The panel slid shut.

Sweet dreams! He laughed. But it sounded lost and haunted in the padded isolation cell, like someone weeping in the distance.

He stopped laughing, and willed the hate to return. What did that piece of shit at the door know about dreams? No doubt fell asleep drunk or drugged every night of his life, and slept like one of the dead.

Like the dead in their graves on San Michele.

The fear came back, strong as the taste of blood in his mouth.

He thought of the cemetery island, covered with low-lying fog, dark waters lapping round its shores. It was dangerous even to think about such things. He knew better. He felt his breathing, still suppressed by the drug, begin to accelerate. If you allowed yourself to think about any part of it, even for an instant, you would start to *see* it.

See them with their torches, faces muffled by cloaks, rushing down the *calli* of the city, footsteps echoing off damp flagstones, hunting for him in the darkness.

"No!"

He choked back the word, because he did not want them, the ones here and now, to come in and shoot him up again. He did not want to start floating any worse than he already was. Because if he kept floating, drifting down the dark river between then and now, they would come after him, the ones from then. They would find him, sooner or later, hunting for him in the darkness. Or *he* would, with his yellow eyes and withered skin, long spidery claws holding the power of life and death, lives within lives. *Stregóne.*

Il stregóne morello. The Dark Sorcerer.

Transmigrator of souls.

Tod Jarrow jerked his head to one side, the movement slow and dreamlike under the drug, and forced himself to stare hard at the padded wall, at some dried blur of puke or shit or blood someone forgot to get with the hose. He forced himself to concentrate on the minute physical realities of where he was right now, in the here and now. Because the other way, floating backward soft and easy down the dark river, would deliver him into the arms of death.

He forced himself to think of *her*. She looked so different now. But that was to be expected. The long, dark reddish brown hair he knew so well, shining down her back, had been replaced by shorter, shoulder-length hair, light brown now, streaked with gold, like one of her own silk robes from fabled Byzantium or far Cathay.

She had been wearing such a robe the first time he took her.

White silk, damasked with threads of purest gold. Torn open by trembling hands, his own, to reveal a body rich beyond the dreams of mere avarice. Dark nipples against alabaster skin, throat of ivory, brown eyes moist with wanting, lips soft and pink as a summer rose. And falling down around her face, and onto his own, thick brown hair tinged with red, like dark fire.

They had met, that first time, in a private room at the house of one of the richest and most influential courtesans in all Venice. She had arranged for it in secret through a close friend of hers, the wife of a powerful merchant. She came to her meeting with him wearing a domino, the black mask of Venice, and a hooded black cloak, for fear of discovery by her husband, Ludovico Contarini. Beneath her cloak she wore the robe of silk and gold.

On a night table next to the canopied bed, a single candle flickered in a silver bowl. He took her in that bed, their first night, seizing her warm flesh, making it one with his. To enter her was ecstasy, like possessing the heart of the world.

Afterward, when they lay spent beneath the canopy, damp flesh pressed together, she had whispered to him of love, her soft breath caressing his throat, making the flame of the candle dance in its silver bowl. He held her to him, so close that the beating of their hearts became one sound, one passion.

"We are wed to one eternity," he told her.

And this was true. He had known it from the moment he first caught sight of her, coming down the broad stone steps at the entrance to the House of Contarini, holding the skirts of her velvet gown in her right hand, her lapdog following on a silken leash, held in attendance by a maidservant. She herself held a white dove perched upon the slender fingers of her left hand, and she whispered trifles to the bird, pursing her rose-pink lips to blow kisses at it. How he had wished himself that bird! To rest forever on her hand, and be the object of her adoration.

He stood watching, like a man transfixed, as she and her maidservant stepped into the black gondola bearing the crest of Contarini. Even after the gondola departed, gliding like a dark ghost down the canal, he still stood watching, because he knew then that they were one. And he knew that he would do whatever was necessary to possess her—even if it meant giving his immortal soul over to the powers of darkness.

Il stregóne morello. The Dark Sorcerer.

He raised his head and dropped it back against the cement floor of the cell, sending a sharp wedge of pain through his skull. He could *not* stray from the here and now! The *here,* the *now.*

She had not responded to him today, of course. But she knew. She sensed it somehow, felt it deep within. That much he could see, looking at her as she sat there in her expensive suit, the gold and diamonds glittering on her left hand. Always *la contessa* with her gilded finery, always.

But it was not safe to think of her like that. He had done so once, there in the interrogation cell, and he had seen the alarm in her deep brown eyes. Yes, she knew. They had been brought together, once again, and it was always the same. The honored and the despised. The powerful and the powerless. The innocent and the guilty. It went on and on, from world to world, but it never changed. The *innocent* and the *guilty!* He laughed out loud, but this time it was bitter and echoing. The innocent! The guilty!

"Hey, fuck face. Need another needle up your ass?"

He faked a blank, staring daze until the dickhead at the door went away. Control. He must exercise control. It was his one weapon against *him. Stregóne.* Sorcerer. Transmigrator of souls.

Control. He had shown perfect control when the police came for him, there in the alley, when he knew beforehand that it was going to happen, and still, the girl's blood warm on his hands, he had turned and looked at them piling out of their patrol cars, turret lights flashing red and blue and amber against the alley walls, and he had thought, *Let them come.* He had struck out at only that one, blinded him like a Turkish dog, then had given himself up to them, surrendered himself to their abuse and torment.

He had shown control then.

He had shown none when he attacked *her,* there in the

interrogation cell. But was he proof against all temptation? A saint in mosaic on the wall of the Basilica? She had mocked him as she sat there, arrogant, conceited, beautiful—beautiful as always, and vindictive. *No one else forced you,* she had said to him. *It was all your choice.* And she had smiled as she said it. How dare she? How *dare* she! He felt the rage start to swell again, even in his drug-deadened limbs. He had not wanted to kill her then, oh no. Not even hurt her. But he had wanted to grab her, and shake that mocking, superior smile off her beautiful face. Her scornful face. Scornful of him, and his love for her.

He felt the fingers of his hands, big and clumsy as cucumbers, flex and curl into claws, then uncurl and fall limp again. His heavy breathing gradually subsided into the slow, even rhythm of drug-induced sleep. He drifted back into the past. But this was a different past. His past in the here and now, his own past as Tod Jarrow, instead of as—Let it not be said.

He was a boy again, barely into his teens. Summer in Wyoming. A cold summer, as they always were, the air so crisp and clean it felt like breathing pure white light. The afternoon thunderstorms had turned the meadow from brown dust to a field of orange and yellow wildflowers. The river ran full ahead of them, swollen with snow melt, tumbling over polished boulders, jagged rocks. In the distance stood the mountains, sharp and blue, crevices carved down their sides, peaks shining bright with snow. They were on horseback. Had anyone asked, they would have said that they were hunting. But real hunting was not part of his life back then. It was only an excuse for being out there, the whole world before you, stretching as far as you could see, and that was forever, the mountains standing watch like the sentinels of the gods.

He dreamed of being a boy again, and forgot her for a while. Forgot the rage, the hopelessness that she could arouse in him so easily, so carelessly, always. It had been that way, it was that way now, it would always be that way, through all the worlds, until the end of time—if there was, ever, an end to time.

6
The Iron Chair

Connie reached the top of the ridge soaked with sweat.

She ran a few more lengths, savoring the physical pleasure of it. Then she slowed down her pace, and stopped. She looked out at the hills around her, and saw the edge of the distant Pacific, glittering in the morning light like a river of diamonds.

She glanced at her watch. Time to head back. She had things to do, places to go.

Like Long Beach, she thought, and some of the brightness seemed to go out of the day. Not that she dreaded it, driving down to Long Beach to see her mother. *I love her,* she told herself defensively. But going home was never what it should be. Even after she had come to terms with the bad memories of Long Beach—her father's sudden death, the long years of no money and harsh struggle—she still did not feel comfortable about going to see her mother. Part of it was her mother's fault. Alice MacKendrick could be a hard woman, hard on herself, hard on others.

But part of it's my fault, Connie thought, *my attitude toward her, and her sickness.*

Before leaving for Long Beach, she wanted to stop by the office and try Jennie Hodges's number again. She had tried it just last night—

Last night, she thought, remembering, and the world seemed to come to a stop.

She stood on top of the ridge and stared into the distance, seeing nothing but the dark outline of her troubled thoughts. Fugue. A brief but recurring period of mental dissociation, a flight from reality. Connie knew that most fugue states were associated with an amnesic reaction on the patient's part and, while disturbing, were not always serious. But fugues could cross over the dark borderline into psychosis. They could become hallucinations that blocked out the light of reality forever.

That's not *what's happening to me!*

She had never felt any concern for her own mental stability, and she was not going to get started now. No sense looking for trouble. *People who look for it,* her father used to say, *usually manage to find some.* The fugue states, if that's what they were, probably had nothing to do with anything—except maybe overwork, combined with the Tod Jarrow mess, and some guilt about not wanting to go see her mother.

But the visions themselves, random and disconnected, were nothing to worry about.

Water. Stone. Blood. Death. Plague.

By the time Connie came panting back home, Galina was already there, fixing breakfast and helping Stevie get ready for school. Connie took a quick shower and got dressed. She kissed Stevie and Trent goodbye. Walking out to the garage with Ken, she tried to make herself appear calm and steady, business as usual.

"Still going to Long Beach?" he asked, as they unlocked their cars, the garage door lifting up automatically behind them.

"After I stop by the office for a minute."

"Don't want to talk about whatever bothered you last night?"

"Nothing bothered me. I'm fine."

"You're walking around like someone carrying a pressure-sensitive explosive device."

"I'm fine, Ken."

"Okay. Give my love to Alice. Tell her I know I'm overdue for my own visit."

"She doesn't care about things like that."

"Maybe not. But I do." He got into his Mercedes-Benz 280 SEL, then looked up at her. "Take it easy on yourself, okay?"

At her office, she tried Jennie's number again, and got nothing but an endless series of empty rings.

Then she called the Hollywood Police Station to check on

Tod Jarrow. She felt the pit of her stomach grow tight as she waited for the officer on duty to transfer her.

"Not a word out of him," Lieutenant Ed Dormer said. "Still sleeping like a baby rattlesnake. Of course we did have to top him off with a little medication the other day. Worked so well we may hit him with it again before we try to move him, tomorrow or the next day. Doctor?"

"Yes?"

"He's not worth your time."

"Why don't we let me be the judge of that, Lieutenant?"

Connie's mother, Alice MacKendrick, lived on the second floor of a fading pink stucco apartment building two blocks back from the beach, near downtown. A large flowering jacaranda tree grew in the middle of the courtyard. Alice did not get out to the beach much these days, not since suffering a massive stroke two years ago that left her a paraplegic, partially paralyzed on her upper left side. The illness hit Connie hard, haunting her with unresolved guilt. A father dead of a sudden heart attack. A mother crippled by a near-fatal stroke. Both of them good, hard-working people. What had they done to deserve it? What had she done to escape?

Emilia Santos opened the door. She was a short, dark young woman with a timid face and kind-looking eyes. She wore stone-washed denims and a T-shirt bearing the legend BEACH CITY, U.S.A.

"Hi, Connie. How are you?"

"Fine, thanks, Emilia. Mom asleep?"

"Watching TV."

Alice MacKendrick sat in a chrome-metal wheelchair facing the television in the small living room of her two-bedroom apartment. She was a thin, angular woman with short gray hair. A cigarette burned in her right hand. The stroke had affected the left side of her face, making her mouth droop a bit and slurring her speech on certain words. But it had left her mind intact, sharp and agile, critical as ever of herself and others.

Seeing Connie, she did not smile. Alice was not an easy smiler. She put the cigarette in her mouth and fumbled for the remote control with her right hand, snapping off the television.

"It's just shit," she said, taking the cigarette out of her mouth. "But you find yourself watching it anyway."

"I wish you'd let me buy you a VCR," Connie said.

"So I could watch prerecorded shit? No thanks."

Connie kissed her, a part of her own heart contracting, as always, to see the drooping mouth and feel the thin body in her arms. "You're looking very nice today."

"Not looking so bad yourself. But I was starting to think maybe you chickened out about coming down."

"Of course not," Connie said, feeling guilty. "I had to stop by the office first. I love seeing you."

"One of those things you look forward to the whole week long."

"Don't always make fun of everything I say to you."

"I don't." Alice stubbed out her cigarette in the ashtray attached to the wheelchair, then patted Connie on the cheek. "I like seeing you too. Emilia? Go get a Pepsi for Connie and yourself, would you?"

"Pepsi? Sure, Alice." She pronounced it *Ahleese*.

When Emilia left for the kitchen, Connie asked, "Do you think she knows very much English?"

"She knows the important stuff," Alice said. "Marlboro. Bathroom. Beer. TV. Telephone. I wouldn't want anybody around who spoke fluent English. She'd talk to me all the time, day after day. After a while, I'd find myself thinking about ways to kill her and make it look like an accident. Emilia speaks just the right amount of English."

"Does she even have a green card?"

"I think so. I only saw it once. Might have been a library card for all I know."

"If she doesn't have a green card, you could be the one who gets in trouble for it."

"What are you all of a sudden? An immigration inspector?"

"Mom, I just don't want any extra problems for you."

"Darling, we all have problems. But that's not one I'm ever going to lose any sleep over, trust me."

She took out a cigarette and lit it with a trembling hand.

"Speaking of sleep, you don't look like you've been getting much lately."

"Thanks."

"Or maybe you've just been dragging your work home with you."

Connie thought of Tod Jarrow and the images from last night.

"I've been thinking of taking some time off. Ken's been after me about going off on the boat, just the two of us."

"Sounds good to me," Alice said. "That's a hell of a man you have there. Enjoy him while you can. They don't last forever."

The shadow of the dead Andrew MacKendrick seemed to fall across the bright, modestly furnished living room.

Neither woman spoke.

Emilia came back with the drinks. Pepsi for her, Diet Pepsi for Connie, a Coors for Alice. Emilia took her Pepsi and went over to a chair on the other side of the living room to look at a magazine called *Astrología Romántica.* Connie shifted in her own chair and looked at the can of beer resting on the small side platform of her mother's wheelchair.

"Isn't it a little early for that?" she asked her.

"Actually—" Alice glanced at her watch. "It's a little late. I was waiting for you to show up." She took a sip, then said, "I'm giving you a chance to start in on one of your lectures about the perils of alcohol for older stroke victims."

"No one listens," Connie said. "I'm not giving them anymore."

"Good. I don't mean to tread on your professional turf, Connie, but you look a little depressed to me."

Her mother had always been good at that sort of thing, pinpointing her exact mood through some kind of strange mental telepathy—almost as if she could read her mind.

"This neighborhood is getting so awful," Connie said. "I wish you didn't have to live here."

"I know what you mean. It's tough having a low-rent mom, especially for a Yuppie from Hell like yourself."

"Yuppie from Hell! Thanks, Mom."

"I don't mean it in a bad way. Nothing wrong with being what you want to be. Every generation has its own crazy ideas about the good life. Take your father and me. Your dad got his first peek at Long Beach on his way back from Korea in '52. To a kid from the wrong side of St. Louis, it looked like paradise on earth. Looked pretty good to me too, having lived in Bakersfield for a while when I first came out here. I know you don't think much of Long Beach, but Bakersfield is *really* shitty, believe me."

Alice stubbed out her cigarette and coughed. "We thought we were pretty cool, living in Long Beach, although we wouldn't have used the word *cool* back then. Same idea. Not so different from your and Ken's feelings about where you live now. Your dad loved Long Beach. And because he did, all those years ago, I still do. It's changed. I've changed. The love part hasn't changed."

"But you could live wherever you want to now," Connie said. "We have the money."

"The money." Alice lit another cigarette. "You're still young, Connie, but not that young. Not so young you really think it's all about money."

Connie started to say something, but Alice waved it aside with her right hand, scattering smoke. "We didn't have much money after your dad died, and I know it bothered you. Well, you've made up for lost time. Has it changed everything?"

"Money makes life a lot easier," Connie said. "It gives you a kind of power, and that's important."

Alice shrugged. "If you're into that, I guess so. Gives you power over shop clerks, bank vice presidents. Enough of it gives you power over politicians, but that's about as far as it goes."

"You're just saying that to justify all this—" Connie swept her arm over the small living room with its cheap furniture.

"I don't know if I can justify it," Alice said. "But I wouldn't trade it for your kind of power. Because I've got something better."

She blew a stream of cigarette smoke toward the open window.

"What I want to say may sound a bit religious, and you know that's not me. Your father was the Scotch Presbyterian in the family. I'm a Welsh pagan. But I think old Saint Paul was right on target when he said that love is stronger than death. Not the way he meant it, because God is love and all that bull. But because human love *is* stronger than death. I loved your father when he was alive, but at the time I thought our love was just a part of the whole happiness picture, along with being young, healthy, fairly successful, living in a cool place, doing cool things—"

She turned to Connie. "And having a beautiful, above-average daughter, of course."

"You don't have to say that just to be nice."

"I wouldn't. It's true. You were part of the happiness picture. When your father died, that picture started to crack. Eventually, almost all the pieces fell out, the way they do with most people. I didn't make much money. I got older. You left home. I got sick. And here I am today, small apartment in a bad part of town, alone and not in such great shape. I know you think I'm a martyr to put up with it. Either that or a masochist."

"I never said that."

Alice MacKendrick looked carefully at her daughter.

"I don't like everything that's happened to me. Who the hell does? I don't like being old and stuck in this iron chair, dependent on some nice young girl to help me every time I have to go to the bathroom. I don't like what's happened to Long Beach either. But when all the pieces of my happiness picture broke apart and fell on the ground, I learned that the one piece I had left was all I ever really had in the first place. Your father and I were not the most romantic people who ever lived, but our love was very real. It was strong. He's been dead a while now. My love for him is as strong as it was when he was alive, maybe even stronger. Part of it may die when I do. But part of it's going to live on in you, even if you don't know it now. That's what I've got here, in this shitty apartment you hate so much. That's what I've got while I sit in this iron chair and smoke my life away. I've got a love that's stronger than death. That's a hell of a thing to have."

Connie looked into those quiet blue eyes and said nothing. Then she laid her head down on her mother's arm and began to cry.

Alice put her cigarette in the ashtray and smoothed back her daughter's light brown hair. "You see, you waste too much time feeling sorry for someone who's happier than you know. Happier than I have any right to be, really."

The laughter of children playing in the street below drifted up through the purple blossoms of the jacaranda tree.

Out beyond the breakwater, a ship sounded its horn.

7
Pressure Points

Connie looked paler than usual and her eyes were still red when she returned to the clinic that afternoon. Inside the waiting room, she saw Rebecca hang up the phone.

"That was the caseworker about Blair Renley. The runaway? She's still at the shelter. But it looks like you'll have to go there if you want to do the interview. They can't talk her into coming over here."

"Any word from Jennie Hodges?"

"I called her again for you. No answer."

Connie took a swallow of the carrot juice in the refrigerator.

"God!" She made a horrible face. "This tastes like shit!"

"Probably gone bad," Rebecca said. "It's been there a while."

"What's the shelf life, anyway? One day after you buy it?"

"How was your mom?" Rebecca asked.

"Fine, thanks. We talked about—things." Connie took a deep breath. "Any news from Benjamin Simmons's foster parent?"

"No progress, the usual."

"Anything on Tod Jarrow?"

"No. You had lunch yet?"

"I don't feel very hungry today."

"Bad for the blood sugar," Rebecca chided her.

Inside her office, Connie checked the appointment schedule, trying to find time for an interview with Blair Renley at the shelter. She could always move up the interview with Mr. Kazmajian by one hour.

Her phone rang.

"Connie," Rebecca said, "I'm transferring Jennie Hodges."

Connie heard Rebecca's "Go ahead," then an uncertain, high-pitched, "Connie?"

"Hello, Jennie. I tried to call you back last night, but you weren't in."

"You didn't call me back yesterday," Jennie said accusingly. "And I called you five times! *Five times.*"

"I was at an interview, Jennie. I tried to call you after I got back."

"That witchy girl in your office wouldn't even tell me where you were!"

"She couldn't, Jennie. I was with another patient."

"Was that other person sicker than *me?* Did they need to talk to you *more* than I did?"

Connie remembered Tod Jarrow, the lives he had so brutally taken, the dark confusion that still held sway in his tormented mind, and she wanted to tell Jennie yes, that patient was a lot sicker than she would ever be.

"I know you needed to talk with me, Jennie. But so did he. And I couldn't talk to both of you at once."

"So did he!" Jennie mimicked her with disgust. *"He* was more important to you just because he's a *man!"*

"Are you feeling better, Jennie?"

There was a long silence, during which Connie could hear Jennie breathing irritably into the phone.

"There's still nothing there, Connie. Nothing for me." Her voice trembled. "There's no reason to go on. No reason at all."

"Is that why you needed to talk with me, Jennie? To tell me you can't go on?"

"You don't care." Jennie's voice broke. "I have nothing, nothing at all, and you *just don't care!"*

Connie took a deep breath.

"Can I come in and get some more Valium?" Jennie asked.

"I'll transfer you to Becky. She'll make an appointment for you, okay?"

"You really *hate* talking to me, don't you?"

Later that afternoon, before leaving for home, Connie called the Hollywood Station one more time. It did not take Ed Dormer long to get on the line.

"He's still here, Dr. Stallman. We'll let you know when we move him. You have my word."

"Is he awake yet?" Connie asked.

"Still out to the world."

"That's a long time for him to be under sedation."

Dormer hesitated. "He had some bad dreams earlier today. Woke up and started screaming. We had to hit him with a little more winky-bye."

"Why wasn't I notified?"

"Doctor, this is a police station, not a hospital. We did what we had to do."

She clenched her hand into a fist. "Did he say anything?"

"Not much, except for a few words in Italian. *Fottuto."*

"What?"

Dormer spelled it for her. "Italian for *fucked.* But it means more like *damned* or *ruined*. That's what Detective Joe Lupone tells me, anyway. I don't speak the language myself."

"Does Tod Jarrow?"

"Not as far as we know. Grew up in Wyoming. Scotch-Irish on one side of the family, German-English on the other. Never went to college, or traveled anywhere outside the western U.S."

"I want to be notified when he wakes up again."

"That may not be possible, Doctor. What if it's the middle of the night?"

"I don't care what time it is, Lieutenant. I want to know when it happens."

"We'll do our best."

"Did he say anything else? In Italian or English?"

"We didn't videotape him like you did," Dormer said. "There was some more Italian. Only one other word we could make out. *Contessa*. As in *countess*. Said it several times. Really shouted it out. He's got a halfway decent pronunciation, according to Detective Lupone. Maybe something he picked up from a teach-yourself-Italian cassette. Anyway, we'll call you, even if he wakes up and needs to—Dr. Stallman? You still there?"

Connie focused with difficulty on the voice at the other end of the line. "Yes. Yes, I am."

"I'll be glad when this one's history," Dormer said.

As she hung up, she noticed a message Rebecca had left for her. *Jennie Hodges. Valium refill. Tomorrow 9 a.m.* She could hear the humming of the refrigerator in the lunch area down the hall, the buzzing of fluorescent lights overhead.

She grew afraid then, alone in her office, but not of Tod Jarrow and his dark eyes. What she feared now was something she could only sense, not see, a malevolence without apparent form—real, deadly, but unimagined, coming over her like wind blowing off dark water, carrying with it a whiff of rotting stone, a glimmer of gold, the faint smell of blood.

8
Lords of the Night

He fought against the second injection.

He tried to move away, quietly at first, as they bent over him, readying the hypodermic syringe. But when they forced out his right arm, inside up, so they could tie on the tourniquet, he fought against them with everything he had, lunging helplessly in their solid grip, shouting at them, screaming that he didn't need any more fucking dope, that he was already shot full of enough shit to knock out a whole fucking Tijuana whorehouse—

It was a mistake to fight. But he did not want to sleep again. They had almost got him this last time, as he drifted out of the dreams of boyhood in Wyoming, drifted backward, saw again the muffled faces, the torches in the fog. They saw him too, and came after him. Had he not been able to break free of the pull—

He had come back screaming, as he struggled up out of the darkness and into the light. The others rushed in then, the ones in the here and now, to shoot him up again.

They plunged the needle into his vein.

And now Tod Jarrow lay alone on the cement floor of the isolation cell, his head near the drain, hearing some kind of liquid gurgling and sloshing from the dark sewer pipe down below, looking up at the padded walls as they moved in and out with the pumping of the drug through his system. He fought against the sleep he knew would come now, and with it the reversal, the turning backward, the great transmigration.

They knew nothing of this, his captors. They would see it as dreams, drug dreams, nothing more.

Bad trip, hey, fuck face?

Not even *she,* who should know as well as he because she was part of this with him, wed to one eternity, now and forever—not even *she* would understand it, any of it, in her present state, as anything but dreams.

Dreams! he thought, and would have screamed it, mocking the padded walls and his captors. But his voice was going, almost gone now, fading with his sight, and when he tried to shout the word, *dreams,* what came out was a sound inside his mind, slow and draggy, echoing like the hollow crash of something dropped within a cavern.

D . . . R . . . E . . . A . . . M . . . S . . .

He was at the end of fighting now. The world was dark, the darkness a river. He rode that river, rushing through the darkness, dragged backward into its depths, swept along by its currents, everything within him stretching, transforming, suffering a sea change.

Tod Jarrow turned—and, turning, left Tod Jarrow far behind.

The first part came to him as memory. The memory of his first meeting with Count Ludovico Contarini, one of the six members of the powerful *Signoria,* advisory council to the Doge of Venice. That night Contarini had not worn the scarlet robe of his office, but a shapeless dark cloak, pulled tight around his heavy face, concealing as much as possible his thick gray hair. He did not loosen the cloak until they were safely behind the locked doors of the House of Contarini.

They stood inside the cavernous front hall of the ancient *palazzo.* A fire fed on the remains of oak stumps in the oversize fireplace. Two hunting dogs growled at them from beside the hearth. He and Contarini stepped forward to warm themselves before the fire. Its light cast their shadows in gigantic form against the far wall.

Contarini spoke in a deep voice, echoing off the marble floor.

"You come to me highly recommended by this *stregóne morello,* this Dark Sorcerer—this mountebank."

He said the last word with contempt. The mountebanks were the flamboyant street vendors of Venice, sellers of elixirs rare and wondrous, guaranteed to cure all ills.

"He is no mountebank, my lord. His powers are real."

Contarini smiled coldly at him. "The Republic is filled with posturing would-be magicians. I doubt that your master differs much from the rest. However, they say that he has a reputation for keeping his side of a bargain."

He shuddered at Contarini's words, remembering the yellow eyes, the hands like spider's claws—the power that bound him.

"You are chilled," Contarini said. "Step closer to the fire."

Contarini held his own large hands before the flames, and looked over at him. "Do you know what I want of you?"

He hesitated. "To do your bidding, my lord?"

"My *bidding!*" Contarini's voice lashed out at him.

He blushed beneath his dark beard, and stared into the fire.

"My servants do my bidding, or die! And I pay them nothing. But to you, I am prepared to pay a sultan's ransom. For such payment I expect more than mere obedience."

He did not answer, but waited for Contarini to go on.

"Your master says that you are skilled at drawing blood, quick with the Damascus blade, and the Turkish dagger."

"I know how to use them to good advantage, my lord."

Contarini nodded his approval. "A man in my position has many enemies. Foreigners, some of them, in league with the Pope, or the Turks. Enemies of the Republic, who deserve to die. But others are men I greet every day on the Rialto—or convene with often, in the inner chambers of the *Signoria.*"

Contarini paused, firelight flickering on his heavy face.

"Some of these may have to die, enemies of mine who hold high office. Perhaps even those who hold the highest office."

Contarini looked closely at him. "Have you the stomach for such work, *assassino?*"

"I will do as my lord commands."

"Heretofore, your master tells me, you have practiced your skills only on the whores of the *calli.* But can you kill men as well as strumpets? Men of power and influence? Or will you prove to have a girl's heart inside a man's body?"

"My lord will not find me lacking in courage, or skill."

A sly smile crept over Contarini's face. "We shall see."

He turned abruptly from the fire then, throwing his cloak back, and took from his belt a leather sack filled with *ducati*, the gold coins of Venice.

"This is a small token of my generosity. See to it that your actions merit such rewards, and many more will be forthcoming."

He took the gold from Contarini and bowed. "My lord."

"Of course I do not want it known that you are in my employ. I will communicate with you through messengers. If we must meet again, it will be in secret, as we have done tonight. No further meetings can be held here, in this house. My wife, the Countess Alessandra, is young and innocent, and easily frightened."

He hesitated, then bowed again. "As you wish, my lord."

"I cannot take the chance—Alessandra!"

He looked up from his bow, past Contarini, to the stairway at the end of the great hall, where he saw her, descending the stairs. She wore one of her silken robes from Cathay and held a lighted candle in one hand. The flame's brightness seemed to encircle her head, like the halo of a saint.

"Alessandra!" Contarini called to her. "Go back to your room! This does not concern you."

She turned in obedience to her husband's command, but hesitated for a moment on the stairs, looking through Contarini now, as if he had disappeared, and there were only the two of them, together in that great front hall.

Wed to one eternity.

He stood before the fire, watching her on the stairs, an angel of light in the darkness—

The memory of that night vanished suddenly, like a dream.

The fog lay damp on his face, cold in his lungs, heavy with the smell of the sea. He took a quick breath, one hand on the hilt of his sheathed sword, stepping back now as he looked down the *calle,* fog swirling along the narrow alleyway. Coming through the fog toward him were the bobbing torches, the burning eyes of the *Signori di Notte.*

Lords of the Night, security forces of the Doge and the Signoria, and the Ten.

Mother of God, he could not run forever! They knew the twisting ways of the city better than he knew the taste of fear in his own mouth. Fear of being taken alive, thrown into the Doge's dungeons, left to rot there in slithering darkness until he was handed over to the patient ingenuities of a Master Torturer.

"Alto!" cried a voice from the fog. Stop!

"Assassino!"

He turned and ran, the leather of his Córdoba boots slapping against damp flagstones. His sword jostled at his side, sharp blade heavy in its scabbard. He mounted the steps of a worn stone bridge arching out over a narrow canal. The chill fog burned in his lungs as he crossed the bridge. He could hear the cries of the *Signori di Notte,* the clanking of their weapons as they started up the steps behind him.

He stumbled coming down, slipping on slime-green stones near the water's edge. A starved cat sprang out of the fog at him, half its fur and one eye gone.

"By God and Saint Mark!" he gasped, heart jolting inside his chest as he reached for his sword.

Then reason returned. He began to run again, down another *calle,* alongside another canal, away from the stone bridge swarming with *Signori.*

A high-necked prow with six steel blades emerged from the fog. A gondola black as death glided down the narrow canal beside him, its passengers invisible inside a small cabin as the gondolier poled his craft silently forward, leaving only a swirl of dark water in its wake. He pulled up his cloak to hide his face from the passing boat, damp wool cold against his sweating skin. He could not afford to be seen. But there were eyes everywhere. Staring out at him from within the closed gondola. Looking down at him from the window of a grand *palazzo,* drawn by the noise and the pursuing lanterns, and the scent of death on the night fog.

He turned away from the narrow canal and into another *calle,* his lungs wheezing like a pair of old bellows now, more from fear than the running. Mother of God, he could not outrun them! Soon he would be at the edge of the Grand Canal itself. What then? Leap into the dark waters and swim? And be speared like a fish? Hail one of the hundreds of gondolas still roaming the great canal even now after curfew? Then overpower the gondolier and pole the vessel to some safe haven? It would not happen. The gondoliers were strong and wary. Even if he could catch one unawares, he could not outdistance the others, who would give chase at once under orders from the *Signori di Notte.*

Church bells sounded through the fog, tolling the hour with their deep iron throats. He fled across a small open square, empty except for the humble *ex-voto* shrine to the Virgin, its one candle flickering unsteadily in the darkness.

The fog lifted then—not entirely, but enough to let him see, in the distance, the high pale walls of a huge *palazzo* fronting the Grand Canal, its lighted windows and turreted roof, even its flaring, bowllike chimney tops.

He saw *her* again, standing high above him in a lighted upper window of the *palazzo,* like the Madonna Herself looking down from a gilded frame in the Basilica. Her dark reddish brown hair hung unbound, falling past her shoulders. Her silk gown was woven with threads of deep blue and bright gold in wondrous filigree. He looked up at her, all the beauty of the known and unknown worlds transfigured in her face, captured in the golden rectangle of light that burned above him now, more radiant than any sun.

She looked down at him, then turned her head, as if responding to someone in another room, and moved away.

They came upon him then, quietly, creeping up behind him. He turned to meet them. They stopped, torches raised.

I have passed this way before, he thought, and the back of his neck prickled, but not from the chill of the fog. He did not know why, but he felt that all this had already happened to him, somewhere before. The encircling *Signori di Notte.* The drawn weapons. The lights, yes, above all the lights. But in this strange sense of remembering that came over him now, he was certain that the lights, the first time, had been red and blue and amber. He had looked at the lights closing in on him then and he had thought, even as he thought now, *Let them come.*

The tall one stepped forward, the leader of the *Signori,* and drew his sword, crying, *"Guarda!"*

His hand tightened on his own sword hilt. How many were there? Seven? Ten? This was madness, truly. Then his face turned hard with contempt for his own weakness. It did no good to pray for deliverance, like a weak woman or a frightened child.

I am damned, he told himself, *and this is my damnation.* He drew his own blade and whispered, *"Guarda."*

A door opened at the back of the great *palazzo,* throwing a shaft of distorted light across the dimly lit *calle.* It cut through the fog that was now starting to come down again upon the *Signori di Notte* and the bearded young *assassino* standing with his drawn sword before them.

A large man stood in the brightly lighted doorway, his great bulk increased by a rich scarlet robe. He stepped out into the *calle,* gray hair hanging thick about a face heavy and saturnine, with full red lips and eyes quick to note the weaknesses of others. He cocked his heavy head toward the *assassino,* glancing at him with contempt, as if he were a dead dog sprawled alongside a canal.

Then he turned to the leader of the *Signori di Notte* and lifted his head with the lordly arrogance befitting a member of the mighty *Signoria,* which he was, and spoke in a deep, rumbling voice.

"Who dares to break the peace before the very door of the House of Contarini?"

9

Obsession

After they got the kids to bed, Connie and Ken made love.

Things were awkward at first. Sex had not been good between them for some time now. Connie blamed it on the pressures of their jobs, problems with the kids—the usual excuses.

But that didn't make it any better.

She winced as he entered her.

"Did I hurt you?" he asked.

She shook her head. "It's okay."

"I thought you were ready. Guess I was hurrying too much."

She smiled at him. "Just don't hurry now, okay?"

As he moved inside her with slow, deep thrusts, the familiar rhythms began to take over. She closed her eyes and moaned softly, turning her head to one side, her back arching off the mattress.

The images started then. Pictures in her head. Standard fare, especially when married sex begins to lose its savor. But so vivid were these fantasies, so detailed, that they seemed to eclipse the present reality, changing the shape of the bedroom, and replacing Ken with another lover.

A man about her age, maybe a few years younger, with dark hair and a short dark beard. And dark eyes.

The dark, haunted eyes of Tod Jarrow.

She cried out, in a voice mixed with arousal and fear.

Ken looked down at her again. "Are you okay?"

She nodded. "Don't stop, please."

The dark eyes returned. She had on some kind of silk robe, elaborately embroidered. The dark-bearded man, the one who looked like Tod Jarrow, pulled it open at her throat, then slipped it off her shoulders, his hands running down her back, letting the robe fall to the floor. Beneath the robe, she wore nothing.

He stared at her naked body, his breath coming hard and fast.

He crushed her to him. His mouth sought hers with a blind passion. He seized her breasts, stroking her nipples roughly, then reaching down a hand between her legs. She shuddered, standing there naked, locked in his violent embrace.

He picked her up and carried her over to a bed covered with gold quilts and silk sheets. She helped him undress, removing his velvet tunic and white silk shirt, touching the different parts of his body as she exposed them. He was big, much bigger than Ken. She took hold of it, closing her fingers around its length and thickness, feeling the heat of his flesh pulse through hers. She bent down to take it in her mouth.

He pushed her down on the bed and entered her with a sudden, violent thrust. She gasped in pain, then again with pleasure, her breath coming faster and faster as the rhythm of his thrusting mounted to a frenzy. Moaning, she wrapped her legs around his naked back, drawing him deeper inside her, digging her fingernails into his flesh, teeth clenched, eyes shut tight, as her moans grew louder, more desperate.

When they came together, the whole world seemed to come apart.

A roaring filled her ears. The light of a single candle blazed beside the bed with the brightness of a flaming torch. A deep sigh escaped her naked body, making her breasts rise, damp with sweat. She reached out across the silken sheets for the dark-bearded head. She pressed her lips against his, forcing her tongue inside his mouth, eager to taste him, wanting, in her hunger, to devour him.

But the face she caressed was beardless. The lips were Ken's.

She broke apart from him, embarrassed by her passion.

"Hey," he said softly, reaching out to touch her. "You were great. You know that? You were goddamn unbelievable."

She turned away. "Thanks."

They lay damp and naked on the bed, Connie resting uneasily in the crook of Ken's left arm. With his right hand he traced the contours of her large dark nipples.

"You are so beautiful," he whispered in her ear.

"It's just thelerethism," she said abruptly.

He looked up. "What?"

"Thelerethism. Erection of the nipple, as a result of sexual excitement or direct stimulation."

"Kills some of the romance, Doc."

She disentangled herself from his arms and got out of bed, walking naked across the thickly carpeted floor.

When she reached the window, she pulled back a curtain and looked out at the dark night sky and the lights of Los Angeles glittering in the distance. The images of a dark-bearded Tod Jarrow flashed through her mind, overpowering her still with fear and desire.

"Trying to give the guy down in the canyon a hard-on attack?"

"No one can see me way up here."

"After tonight, he'll be sure to buy a telescope. What are you looking at, anyway?"

She closed the curtain. "I'm thinking."

"About what?"

She said nothing.

"Tod Jarrow?" he asked.

She looked at him, startled.

"Just what every guy wants to hear. That his wife daydreams about someone else while they're making it."

"You think I'm having fantasies about sex with a serial killer? Thanks a lot, Ken!"

"Maybe *fantasy* isn't the right word for it. Maybe it's more like an obsession."

"I am *not* obsessed with Tod Jarrow."

"He seems to be on your mind a hell of a lot lately."

"He's part of my professional responsibility, Ken."

"Since when does that come home to bed with you?"

She saw the dark-bearded face looking down at her again, their bodies locked tight, moving together with desperate passion.

She took a deep breath, and ran a hand through her hair.

"Look. It's a tough case, okay? He's shut off, defensive. I'll probably lose him. They'll lock him up for life, or send him to Death Row." She folded her arms across her naked breasts. "You bring home some problems from work now and then, too. I've even heard you talk about them in your sleep."

"Sure. But if my problems had sexy smiles and big boobs, you might start to get a little worried."

"I'm worried already." She arched her back, thrusting her breasts forward. "Anything wrong with these?"

"Come here. I'll have to take another look."

10
The House of Contarini

Connie fell into a deep, heavy, dreamless sleep.

But it did not remain dreamless for long.

At first she felt an intense vertigo, like the aftermath of too much drinking. The ceiling started, slowly, to spin. The room tilted sideways. A rush of nausea flooded her gut. She tried to make herself wake up and go into the bathroom so she wouldn't vomit on the clean sheets. The spinning stopped.

Only to be replaced by a sudden sense of—

. . . d . . . r . . . i . . . f . . . t . . .

Drifting.

Floating, down a tunnel or a river in the darkness. It was peaceful, drifting with the darkness. But there was also a sense of hidden danger, as if the darkness had a meaning, and the meaning was nothing less than the balance between life and death.

She came out of the darkness with a jolt. Light hit her eyes. Soft orange, muted. Candlelight. She had fallen asleep naked. Now she was clothed in silks and heavy brocades, full skirts that rustled when she moved. She raised a hand in front of her face. Her fingers were adorned with gold rings and outsize jewels. A fine lace cuff trailed over the back of her hand. The tops of her breasts were bare, cinched tight and raised high by the low-cut bodice of a green satin gown.

She turned her head, and felt the weight of her hair. She reached back and drew out a length of curling, dark reddish-brown hair. By the weight of it, it seemed to be hanging far down her back. She stood there and stared at it, holding it in her hands, wondering at the thick-coiled richness of it.

It's only a dream, she thought.

But there was a tactile sensuality to this dream, a physical heaviness that made it seem more lifelike than reality itself.

She looked at the room around her. The walls were hung with richly embroidered tapestries. A window opened out onto cold night fog and a narrow street below. The salt smell of the sea pressed in upon her, dank and fish-flavored. Bronze lamps hung from the ceiling, lanterns with colored glass. A Latin prayer book rested upon a prie-dieu with a velvet-covered kneeler. High-backed chairs of carved walnut sat placed about the room. Small tables held statues of ancient gods and goddesses. A satyr chased a nymph, white flesh in headlong flight.

On a painted ceiling fresco edged with gold, Diana and her attendant nymphs bathed nude and unashamed. Candles flickered in silver sconces. Musical instruments rested delicately on sideboards: the many-stringed *cetera,* the bowl-backed *liuto,* the double-necked *tiorba.* A bed in the center of the room supported a canopy on four elaborately carved posts. The sheets were trimmed with intricate lace, the quilt damasked with fringe of gold. A thin dog with long legs and a pointed muzzle like a greyhound's lay on a carpet before the bed, gnawing at a large beef bone.

But her eyes passed by all this, moving toward the open window, drawn to the night and fog, and the one who stood in the *calle* down below, staring up at her now with a heart transfixed. Dark eyes in a dark-bearded face, blurred by mist.

Behind him, torches in the fog, cutting through the darkness. Voices crying out. The smell of blood on dank water. Church bells clanging like brass hammers through the cold night.

"Lei è pronta, madonna?"

She turned with a start.

A young girl stood before her dressed in black, hands folded, eyes lowered respectfully.

"Lei è pronta, madonna?"

She could understand what the girl was saying in her strange language, understand it perfectly, without translation, just knowing it somehow.

"Are you ready, my lady?"

She answered in that same language, *"Sì, adesso."*

It was no language she had ever spoken before in her life, and yet it was one she seemed to have been speaking all her life.

"My lord is at table," the girl continued. "The musicians are in attendance. The cook awaits your instructions."

"Yes," she replied, "of course," as if the girl had said the expected thing.

The girl left the room. But her eyes moved back toward the open window, once briefly and away.

Then she followed the girl.

They came to the second floor of the grand *palazzo,* down a long hallway, past flickering candles in golden sconces, rich hanging tapestries, gilded mirrors, solemn portraits of ancestors who had helped rule the Republic almost four hundred years ago, back when old Dandolo, the stone-blind Doge, had looted the treasures of Constantinople for the glory of Venice and Saint Mark. They descended to the *piano nobile,* the main floor of the house, a full story above the Grand Canal's water-line.

As they passed the great dining hall, adorned with gold-trimmed wall and ceiling frescoes, hanging lamps and massive high-backed chairs, she saw a huge man in a red velvet robe lift his head in her direction. His great bulk carried a gross sensuality, heavy with the weight of corruption. The servants and musicians in attendance looked up anxiously, their glances following his.

"You are late," he said to her, his voice deep and full, rounded at the edges with contempt.

"I was at my evening prayers," she said, feeling certain that the serving girl would support her in this lie.

"You are pious enough for the convent at San Zaccaria. But you have other duties of a more pressing, earthly nature."

A lewd smile spread over his face.

She felt the disgust rise within her. The knowledge that he was her husband in the eyes of God and before the laws of the Republic made no difference to her at all.

But he's not my husband, a part of her wanted to say. *Ken—*

But that name sounded distant to her, foreign, whatever meaning it once had now faint and far away.

The leering smile vanished from her husband's face.

"The cook awaits your instructions, my lady."

So I have heard, she started to say, but something made her only nod and murmur, "Yes, my lord."

"See that you do not starve us while you are about it."

He waved a hand in dismissal, turning his attention back to the musicians, who began to tune their instruments with self-conscious precision.

Inside the kitchen, a suckling pig roasted on a spit above an open fire. Choice cuts of fish and meat grilled on long racks over the flames. Scullery maids grated sharp cheeses and rare spices. Fragrant soups and sauces bubbled in iron kettles. Wines from all over—*malvasia* from Cyprus, *chiarello* from Saluzzo—decanted in bottles on shelves. Plates heaped high with fresh oysters, crabs, apples, pears, and onions lay spread out across the main worktable.

The cook, Giuletta, a hunchbacked little woman with dirty gray hair, came forward and bowed deferentially. She had been with the family for generations, first serving the present master when he was nothing more than a small, unpleasant titled child of five.

"Everything is ready, my lady." She tipped her gray head forward. "Do you wish us to serve the *torta con uccelli?*"

The *torta,* a pie with live sparrows baked into it, was to be cut open at the banquet table, where the half-dead birds would try to fly away, only to be caught by delighted dinner guests.

"Yes," she said. "Please do that. It might amuse him."

Giuletta smiled a mostly toothless smile. "It will amuse him, my lady."

"He is in a bitter mood of late."

"He is often that way," the cook agreed pleasantly, as if remarking on nothing more important than the recent bad weather, or the continuing stench of the back canal.

A scullery maid, Tulia, looked up from her duties at the main worktable. A year earlier she had provoked the master's wrath by being discovered naked in the arms of a gardener from Chioggia, the two of them rutting like pigs in heat in an unused bedroom on the second floor. So went the official version. Whispered rumors claimed that she had been too free in boasting of her master's favors on those nights when her lady mistress attended Mass or visited friends. Whatever the real reason, she had been punished. The master himself had cut off her ears and nose with a jewel-hilted Turkish dagger.

"The wages of whoredom," he had said to his wife at the time, bursting unannounced into her bedroom, terrifying her serving girl, fresh blood dripping from his hands onto the intricate weave of her fine carpet from Cathay.

"Remember this well—" He had raised the bloodstained dagger, a severed human ear dangling from it. "My lady."

Tulia lifted her chin, two ragged holes where her nose should have been. "How does it please my mistress?" she asked.

The question sounded innocent enough, but it concealed a lurking insolence, a suggestion that what pleased her mistress would not please her master at all, if only he knew of it.

"How does it please my lady Countess?" Tulia asked, hissing on the last word in that strange but familiar language.

Contessssa.

"Back to work, you!" scolded Giuletta. "Idle girl! You want to be missing your lips along with all the rest?"

The hunchbacked cook struck Tulia sharply on the back of the neck. The scullery maid muttered a dockside oath and turned back to the worktable, cursing the cook's ancestors and her eyes, her blood, and her bowels. Giuletta raised a hand to strike again.

Alessandra could see Tulia grinning at her now, showing her bad teeth and making the two holes in her face gape even wider. She felt a chill then more piercing than the night fog, for she knew that this girl would betray her. Whatever she had learned about the two of them she would tell, all in good time.

Alessandra turned away from the grinning noseless face.

Shouts burst from the *calle* in back of the great house.

Loud male voices raised in deadly anger came through the heavy wooden door that led from the kitchen out into the *calle*. Scullery maids dropped knives and spoons, and clustered around the closed door. Other servants hurried in from the great dining hall, some still carrying linen hand towels that they had been holding for dinner guests. A musician with a *liuto* in one hand stuck his head into the kitchen.

Then the master himself appeared, Count Ludovico Contarini, bullish silver head held low and menacing as he stalked through the kitchen. All the clustering servants fell back before him, awed by his physical size and the heavy red robe that signified his office, a member of the mighty *Signoria,* one of the six advisors to the Doge himself, one of the dreaded Council of Ten.

"Who causes this racket at my back door?" he growled at his chamberlain.

The chamberlain, Pietro, a thin, middle-aged man with a long neck and nervous eyes, murmured respectfully, "My lord, I do not know, truly."

A sharp *"Guarda!"* rang through the heavy wooden door and the servants drew back from it in fear. Whatever game was being played out in the narrow *calle* had death in its stakes now. Steel had been drawn. Flesh would be cut and blood would run. Such things were better left alone.

"Do I keep a house of cowards?" Contarini asked with disdain.

Pietro the chamberlain made a feeble gesture toward the door.

Contarini drew back the bar and threw open the door himself, thrusting his great silver head out into the mist that swirled along the *calle*. He stepped outside, glanced at the leader of the *Signori di Notte,* and at the dark-bearded, dark-eyed *assassino*.

"Who dares to break the peace before the very door of the House of Contarini?"

Now all the servants pressed forward to see, but Alessandra moved ahead in front of them and they drew back, grudgingly but instinctively, allowing their lady mistress full view of the drama unfolding outside.

Looking past Contarini's huge head and broad shoulders, she could see him, her lover Marcangelo, surrounded by the *Signori di Notte,* the Lords of the Night, their swords drawn and raised, pointing at him. Her heart skipped a beat. She had feared to see him wounded, even dying, wet with his own blood.

He stood facing the *Signori,* his sword drawn, the look of fearlessness on his face that had drawn her to him in the first place, and held her captive still. His dark eyes turned and sought hers, and a tremor coursed through her. She could feel the heat rise within her, burning through the cold night fog. She saw their bodies on the bed, locked together in a fierce embrace.

"My lord Count." The leader of the *Signori* stepped forward. "This man is a murderer. When we sought him out, he fled us."

At the word *assassino,* murderer, a gasp escaped her.

Contarini turned his head at the sound, his sharp eyes falling on her, but he said nothing.

He turned back to the leader of the *Signori*. "There is a witness to this murder? Or does he stand accused only?"

"My lord—he stands accused."

Contarini nodded. "Leave him to me."

"My lord, he is dangerous! He drew his weapon on us."

The *assassino* found his voice. "To defend myself! Or you would have cut my throat like a—"

"Silence!" Contarini bellowed inside the narrow *calle*.

The *assassino* lowered his head, defiance in his dark eyes.

Contarini nodded again to the leader of the *Signori di Notte*.

"There is no danger. Go. Leave him to me."

Raising their torches, they withdrew into the fog.

Contarini dismissed the servants. "Inside. All of you."

Then he looked at the young murderer.

She looked too, heart pounding inside her breast as she saw the muscular legs outlined in brightly colored hose, the high-necked velvet doublet, the feathered beret, the dark wool cloak falling from broad shoulders, the handsome face offset by dark eyes and a short dark beard.

"You are a fool," Contarini growled. "You deserve to die."

"I have—"

"You have *nothing!* Except what I give you." Contarini stared at him, and the murderer fell back under the weight of that stare. "I could turn you over to the dungeons, and there you would die horribly, up to your waist in stinking black water, gnawed by sewer rats, damning your own mother and the day she gave you birth."

The young man took a deep breath. "If I could but speak—"

"You cannot. You have nothing to say." Contarini lowered his deep voice. "You are not in my pay to act the part of a fool. To swagger up and down the city like one of the loitering, drunken *bravi*. If that is how you choose to carry on, consider yourself released from my service."

"That is not what I wish."

"Do you understand, then, the terms of our agreement?"

He nodded, hesitantly at first, then firmly. "I do, my lord."

"Then live by them. Go. Draw no more attention to yourself."

The young man turned to leave, and as he did, his eyes caught hers, and the whole world—the night, the fog, the church bells in the distance, the cries of the boatmen and the gondoliers—all seemed to come to a stop and hang suspended upon the look that passed between them. She felt her heart beating within her breast, the blood rushing beneath her skin. He was drawing her to him once again. It was more than love, more than mere desire. It was an all-consuming passion, a madness of the soul that drew her to him, the hunger of the moth for the flame.

Her husband's sharp eyes, glittering like those of a hungry ferret, fell upon them both and took in the look that burned between them. It was as if for the first time the three of them stood there together, in shared recognition, an unholy trinity of dark desires.

Her husband spoke first, to the murderer, her lover.

"Leave. And guard your actions." He paused, his deep voice seeming to drift across the gathering fog. "Guard *all* your actions, *assassino.*"

The other turned, and the warning followed him into the night.

The fog shifted then, revealing stray cats prowling along the *calle*. They chased after rats that scavenged through piles of garbage and human waste littering the alleyway. In one dark corner, a swarm of rats scattered before an advancing cat, leaving behind them the half-eaten corpse of an infant lying in a puddle of filthy water. The cat approached cautiously, sniffing at the tiny corpse. Then it took up where the rats had left off.

She averted her eyes.

"The scavengers of the dark," her husband's deep voice murmured, then abruptly, "and now inside with you—you will catch your death of cold out here in the night air, exposing yourself to the dampness, and"—looking at her—"to the longing stare of a hired murderer."

She turned from him, but his large hand reached out suddenly, like a snake, and caught her face, turning it back toward his, then trailing his fingers slowly down her slender throat and across the tops of her half-exposed breasts, now chill to the touch.

"If you are not very careful," he whispered, "you will catch your death, my lady."

The voices in the distance interrupted them.

"Corpi morti! Corpi morti!"

They both recoiled in horror at the dread cry.

Corpi morti. Dead bodies. Plague victims.

The warning shouts came from the corpse bearers, whose grim job it was to transport the victims of the Plague, to carry the diseased and swollen bodies out of the city. Ever since its first outbreak almost two hundred and fifty years earlier, the Plague had visited Venice sporadically, coming without warning like the wrath of God, then subsiding, then coming back again. When the Great Plague first struck, it killed almost half the city's population. Fifty noble houses and their families perished from the face of the earth. Bodies piled up, rotting and unburied, spreading stench and contagion. The surviving citizens went about with scented handkerchiefs pressed to their faces, burning incense to ward off the Plague's black kiss. Some of the corpses were dumped onto ships and towed out from the city into the surrounding lagoons and left to rot, deadly carrion piled high in floating sarcophagi.

Even now, when outbreaks of the Plague were less frequent and less severe, the bodies of its victims were still hurried out of the city with shouts of *Corpi morti!* giving warning to passersby.

Contarini put a heavy hand on his young wife's shoulder and steered her back toward the kitchen door. She could feel that hand tremble slightly, and despite her own terror she was glad. He dealt in power, this brutal man she had wed against her will. He understood power and relished it, using it like a weapon to win what he wanted. There was little, with his power, that he feared.

But he feared the Plague. Feared its swollen lumps that appeared in the neck and the groin, then the fever and the delirium, and then the vomiting of blood. All of it happening so quickly that sometimes a doctor was found sitting dead and bloody in a chair by the bedside of a dead patient he had come to treat only that morning. Ludovico Contarini feared the Plague as something beyond the control of money or power, or even terror.

The Plague was terror incarnate.

"Corpi morti! Corpi morti!"

The corpse bearers were upon them now, pushing a wooden cart down the narrow *calle* behind the House of Contarini, wheels creaking noisily, rumbling over cobblestones, weighed down by the dead bodies, swollen and blackened almost beyond recognition, thrown in hurriedly on top of the cart, eyes open, mouths clotted with vomit and blood.

"Corpi morti!"

Contarini drew himself up against the wall of his own house.

"La pesta!" he cried, a note of terror leavening his deep voice. Then to his wife, "Alessandra! Come inside, quickly!"

He gripped her shoulder hard and drew her toward him. She resisted, struggling against his grip. She shared his horror of the Plague. But in all horror there is some deep fascination, and so there was in this. She could not take her eyes off the death cart as it rumbled down the *calle* toward them. The faces of the corpse bearers, covered with black masks, made them look like revelers at Carnival. A Carnival of the Dead.

As they came closer, she could see the bloated, filthy bodies of the Plague victims. One of them was a woman, an older woman, thin and frail, with a twisted body and short gray hair. Her dead blue eyes were glazed with a mucus scum. A large rat poked at bloody vomit crusted inside her mouth.

Whether it was the ministrations of the rat, or the rumbling of the cart wheels, something caused the corpse's head to turn.

And the dead blue eyes of Alice MacKendrick looked into the face of Countess Alessandra Contarini.

She screamed, and reached out for the cart as it rumbled past them. Ludovico Contarini jerked her back violently, sheer terror in his grip. She screamed again, and again, until the entire *calle* rang and reechoed with her screams, louder now, or so it seemed, than the iron bells tolling in the distance across the fog-shrouded city and its dead.

II

*dreams
of
corruption*

11
Back from the Dead

Connie came out of it still screaming.

She sat upright in bed, her naked body damp and glistening, sheets tangled. The lights were on. Ken had his arms around her, trying to calm her down.

She stopped in mid-scream and turned to him, her mouth open, breathing hard, face glazed with sweat, brown eyes dark with a terror more real than the bed she sat on or the arms that held her.

Corpi morti!

"Hey," Ken said. "It's only a dream, okay?"

She stared at him, still breathing hard.

"Okay?" He squeezed her shoulders gently.

The church bells of the dark dream world continued to ring.

"Want me to get it?" Ken nodded at the bedside telephone.

She shook her head slowly, and turned to the ringing phone.

She put one hand on it. With the other, she brushed back a lock of tangled hair from her damp forehead.

She picked up the receiver. "Yes?"

"Dr. Stallman?"

"Speaking."

"Lieutenant Ed Dormer. LAPD, Hollywood Division. Sorry about waking you up in the middle of the night."

The clock on her nightstand read 3:08 A.M.

"That's okay."

"You said you wanted to be notified immediately, if and when." Dormer paused. "Guy on night shift just woke me up. Jarrow came out from under the dope. Very bad mood. Tried to put somebody's eyes out with his thumbs. We had to restrain him."

Connie's fingers tightened on the receiver.

"Did you sedate him again?"

"Not yet. He asked to see you. Got pretty hot about it. We told him he'd have to wait till later on. He said he might not be alive by then."

Ken asked her, "It's about Jarrow, isn't it?"

She looked at her husband's face, pale beneath his tan, blue eyes sharp with concern.

And for one disorienting moment, she saw the other husband, the red-robed dream husband, cruel and corpulent, blood on his hands and in his voice.

You will catch your death, my lady.

She shook it off with a quick shudder, nodded yes to Ken's question, then said to Dormer, "I don't want him sedated until I get a chance to talk to him."

"That might be hard to arrange, Doctor. It's late."

"I want to talk to him, Lieutenant. Now."

Ken put a hand on her shoulder and made a signal to cover the mouthpiece. She pressed the mute button.

"This has to be taken care of tonight?" he asked her.

"Yes."

"Sure you're up to it? That was one hell of a nightmare you just woke up from."

"Like you said, it's only a dream."

"Dr. Stallman?" Dormer's voice came through the earpiece. "Still there?"

She released the mute button. "I'm leaving now."

"We'll be expecting you."

She hung up the phone. Ken was watching her.

She reached out to him, touching a hand to his cheek.

"It's my job, Ken."

A muscle in his face twitched at her touch.

"Sure there's nothing more to it than that?"

She withdrew her hand. "It's a job I agreed to do. I'm sorry I have to do it right now. I'll be glad when it's over."

She began to dress.

"Want some company?" he asked. "It's not the best time of night to go cruising around Hollywood alone."

"I'll be at a police station." She adjusted her collar in a full-length mirror. "I'll have lots of protection. You'd get very bored." She turned to him, putting on a leather jacket. "After coming out of sedation, he'll be a weeping, teary-eyed mess. Not real scary."

She went over and kissed Ken on the mouth, then traced the lines of his deep frown with her index finger.

"Hey, I'll be okay. Believe me."

"I'm trying."

Dormer met her in the main corridor of the Hollywood Station. His eyes looked tired. He held a Styrofoam coffee cup in one hand.

"This must mean a lot to you," he said.

"I don't do things halfway."

"No, you don't."

He pitched the coffee cup into a trash can.

"We'll have to sit on him while you ask your questions. He's in one very ugly mood just now. After what happened with you the other day, we're not taking any chances."

"As long as you let him say whatever he wants to say."

"We'll let him talk until you get tired of it, Doctor."

They stopped in front of a different cell from the one she had entered the other day. The door looked the same, dark and drab. Dormer said a few words to a uniformed officer, who nodded stiffly and unlocked the door for them.

She was not prepared for what she saw next.

Tod Jarrow rested on his knees in the middle of the floor, arms bound by a straitjacket. The cell stank of vomit. There had been a halfhearted attempt to hose most of it down the drain, but the aftertaste still lingered. Jarrow's eyes darted from side to side, mouth open as he gasped for air. Two uniformed officers stood over him. One held a nightstick in his right hand. A new bruise, dark purple, spread across the left side of Jarrow's face.

She turned to Dormer. "They're *beating* him!"

"Restraining him."

"I want that straitjacket *off*. Now."

Dormer, staring at her, said nothing.

Connie started toward the kneeling prisoner.

Dormer grabbed her arm.

"Sorry, Dr. Stallman. That's as close as you get." To the uniformed officers, he said, "Take the coat off him."

As they unfastened the straitjacket, Jarrow's dark eyes twitched to a stop, coming to rest on Connie.

"You," he whispered in a broken voice.

The dark eyes did not frighten her this time. But they seemed to be filled with a sexual longing so powerful that it made her mouth go dry. She looked into them, unable to look anywhere else, and swallowed hard, remembering her dream from earlier in the evening. Her nipples rose stiff and erect inside her bra, straining against the soft fabric.

"You," he whispered once more.

Then, screaming it at her, "Whore of the world!"

Except she heard it inside her head in that other language, the language from her dream, foreign yet familiar.

Gran puttana del tutto mondo!

That scared her worse than anything he could have done. She smelled the dank water of the canals and felt the cold tendrils of night fog curling around her like the fingers of the dead.

Corpi morti!

She saw the dead eyes of Alice MacKendrick and felt the heavy hand of Ludovico Contarini on her shoulder. She pulled her short leather jacket up close around her, suppressing a deep shudder.

"Whore of the world!" Jarrow screamed at her again.

He tried to stand up, but the two officers pushed him back down again, cracking both his knees on the concrete. The officer with the club raised it, glancing at Dormer for permission.

Dormer shook his head, and stepped in front of Jarrow.

"I'm going to say this once," Dormer said quietly to him. "The doctor here has agreed to talk with you. She says you can say whatever you want. Fine. But let's get one thing straight right now. You make any sudden moves, and it's over. Understand?"

Jarrow said nothing. One of the officers holding him tightened his grip. Jarrow gritted his teeth as the pain shot through his arm and up into his shoulder, but he said nothing.

"I want an answer," Dormer said. "Understand? Yes or no?"

Jarrow looked up at him. "I understand your wife pisses in your mouth, and you swallow it."

Connie could see the effort Dormer made to hold back.

When he could trust himself to speak again, he said, "You've been warned, asshole."

He moved away from Jarrow, back and over to one side. Then he looked at Connie. There was little sympathy in that look.

She glanced at Tod Jarrow's dark, sex-hungry eyes.

And saw the images behind them. Scenes of frenzied passion on a bed of gold and silk. Visions of the city itself.

Fog. Gold. Water. Plague. Death.

Your own mother's death, Contessssa—

Stop it!

But nothing stopped. Instead, everything picked up speed and intensity, like a roller coaster starting to tip slowly, then faster, and faster, and faster, down that first long hill—

She snapped her head up, and looked at Jarrow. The dark sexual hunger was gone from his eyes. They mocked her now, from where he knelt on the concrete, like the eyes of a perverse child doing penance.

Or the eyes of a massive, gray-haired man in a heavy red robe, running his hand across the top of her half-naked breasts, whispering into her ear—

You will catch your death, my lady.

She raised a hand to the side of her face and felt the trembling of that hand, and seemed to hear the hissing of her own blood through her veins. Then she heard the scraping of metal against concrete, and turned to see Dormer wordlessly offering her a chair. She nodded her thanks, her legs shaky as she sat down.

Jarrow watched from his kneeling position.

She looked at him, feeling her upper lip twitch.

Nerves of steel, Jake. Right.

She made herself say, "They told me you had a bad dream under sedation, Tod. Do you want to talk about it?"

For several seconds Jarrow said nothing. She heard no sounds inside that room, other than the beating of her own heart, and a distant ringing in her ears.

Not another silent standoff, she thought. *Not tonight.*

"Sure," he said, looking up at her. "Let's talk about it. Why not?" A smile flickered across his face, like a gleam of light on a razor's edge. "After all, it's your dream too, Connie."

You know me, yes, Contessa, you know me well.

One part of her, the part that loved her husband and her children, wanted to run from that stench-filled cell. Run and never look back. But another part of her was drawn obsessively to Tod Jarrow, like a shark to blood, locking in on his dark eyes.

"Tell me about your dream, Tod."

"Our dream, Connie." He smiled again, and the razor flickered in the light. "We were both there."

You were there, Contessa, and you wanted me, and I would have taken you again, had it not been for your pig of a husband.

Her physical desire for him overwhelmed her, a hunger so strong it ached like an open wound.

I'm in big trouble, she thought, *and I need help, Jake.*

But Jake Mauder was not there to help her. There was only herself, and Tod Jarrow. He had asked for her, and she had come to him, without hesitation. Leaving her husband and children, she had gone out into the night for him, and him alone. Was it because he had asked for her? Or would she have come anyway?

Because the desire was that strong.

She said to him, "Tell me about your dream, Tod."

"What's to tell, Connie? You were there." The razor smile flickered again. "You saw what happened. You saw me standing there, behind the House of Contarini. Outside, in the fog. You, inside, looking down at me from your warm golden window."

As always, Contessa, you above me, always.

Connie glanced at Dormer to see how he was reacting to this. He stared blankly at Jarrow, stifling a belch. She knew then that he was not really listening. Jarrow was crazy. Whatever he said would be crazy. Why bother?

"I was trapped like a rat in an alley by the Lords of the Night," Jarrow continued, his dark eyes staring into hers. "You saw me down there, trapped. But you did *nothing* to help me! You turned away."

Because my serving girl called to me.

She felt reality skew off into dark, dangerous unreality.

What in God's name is happening to me?

"You turned away because you just didn't care," Tod Jarrow said, his voice a soft, accusing whisper. "You never cared as much as I did. *Never!*"

She turned to Dormer. "Please have someone get a chair for him. He's talking now."

Dormer told his officers, "Sit him down, but stay ready."

One of them dragged over a stool and placed it behind Jarrow. They jerked him up from his knees, then slammed him down hard onto the stool. Jarrow rubbed his knees with both hands, as if he had been kneeling on the concrete for some time.

Connie saw that he had a huge and plainly visible erection bulging up through his prison denims as he sat there on the small stool. She looked into his dark eyes, where the lust burned even more fiercely than it did below.

"Tell me more about your dream, Tod," she said.

He flashed the razor smile at her. "But you already know what happened, Connie. You saw them circling me, closing for the kill. But you didn't do anything about it, because you didn't care."

Have you ever cared, Contessa?

"If it hadn't been for your fat pig of a husband, they would have cut my guts out and dumped them into the alley for the rats to feed on."

The image of the rats and the dead baby in the alley came back to her then with all the sharpness of a color photograph.

"Or maybe they would've just wounded me, cut off my nose and ears, as a warning."

Tulia, the mutilated scullery maid, two gaping holes where her nose should have been, floated up before her like a grisly three-dimensional holograph.

"Or," Jarrow went on, "they might have taken me to the Doge's dungeons to rot for a while, before the Master Torturer came down to visit me. Or maybe I would've caught the Plague first in my dungeon cell, and died swollen and black-faced, puking up blood. Would you have cared if I caught the Plague, Connie?"

Corpi morti!

She shut her eyes tight.

"Dr. Stallman?" Dormer asked her. "Are you okay?"

"She doesn't like thinking about the Plague," Jarrow said, "or the Plague ships."

Dormer turned to him. "Shut the fuck up."

Then, to Connie, "Dr. Stallman?"

She opened her eyes. "I'm fine, thanks."

"Want to call it a day and come back later?"

She shook her head. "I'm fine."

Then she said to Jarrow, "Tell me more about your dream."

He smiled at her, hands folded, arms resting on his knees.

"Sure, Connie. I could go on and on. But *you* could proba-bly tell *me* some things I don't know. After all, it's your dream too, Connie. You could tell me what was on the menu for dinner that night at the House of Contarini. When the back door to the kitchen opened, I could smell the meats and their sauces, the pies and the spiced wines. They smelled delicious out there in the cold fog! But smelling's never quite the same as tasting, is it?"

He leaned forward slightly on the stool, so easily that the movement did not alert Dormer or the two uniformed officers standing behind him on either side.

Jarrow's voice turned bitter. "I've never eaten one of your fucking fancy dinners at the House of Contarini. Because I've never been invited in!"

You share your body, Contessa, but not your power.

He leaned back on the stool. "But it doesn't matter, does it? Because it's only a dream. Just something for a tight-assed headshrinker like yourself to scratch and sniff at. Ain't nothin' but a little ol' dream, folks."

He started to flash the razor smile. But it vanished suddenly, and his dark eyes locked onto hers.

"Except"—his voice dropped—"it's not really a dream at all, is it, Connie? It's a different world, a different time. *But it's just as real as what's happening right now.* Isn't it, Connie?"

You know me, yes, Contessa—

The cell seemed to be slanting to one side behind him, as she sat there and looked into his dark eyes. The ringing in her ears grew worse. And that was definitely her own blood she heard now.

"I don't understand, Tod," she began, trying to keep the room in balance. "Tell me more about—"

"Tell you *bullshit!*" he snapped back, looking at her with the contempt of someone who's seen through a cheap trick. "You know what I'm talking about. *You* know what's real and what's not."

He leaped off the stool like a cat and stood over her before Dormer or his men had time to do more than shout warnings and shift their own slower reflexes into gear.

He caught her face in one hand, tilted it back, his own face on top of hers, his dark eyes on fire now, her own eyes wide and staring, like those of a night creature trapped beneath the glare of a blinding light.

"This," he said to her, "is real."

He kissed her fiercely, tongue thrusting deep into her mouth.

In her startled response, she almost swallowed it whole. An electric shock seemed to pass between them, mouth to mouth, obliterating the cell, the guards—everything except the joining of their flesh.

Then as now, Contessa, now as then. Wed to one eternity.

The officers pulled him off her, shouting threats, roughing him up more than necessary. He stood looking down at her, breathing easily, his bruised face cool and mocking, the dark eyes glittering with savage triumph.

Her own breathing was harsh, ragged, as if she had run uphill for miles and miles and could not get her breath, would not ever get her breath again.

12
Night Hunger

Connie drove back home through a night world of shadows.

She kept her eyes fixed on the winding road ahead. Her mind locked in on shifting images: the isolation cell, Tod Jarrow's dark eyes, their kiss, mouth on mouth, flesh against flesh.

She thought of the other women who had kissed him, and what had happened to them. Mutilation. Murder. She shuddered, raising the back of one hand to her mouth, wiping it hard to get rid of the taint left by a murderer's kiss.

But there was more. During the interview, an aching hunger had smoldered deep within her. Now it was set on fire, burning out of control.

A murderer's kiss.

She found Ken waiting up for her when she got home. He

sat alone at the kitchen table, an almost-empty bottle of vodka in front of him, a full glass over to one side.

He looked up at her with bloodshot eyes.

She shivered, hunching her shoulders inside the leather coat.

"It's cold in here! Have you got the heat turned off?"

He took a swallow from the glass. "Did you save him?"

"I listened to him talk."

About a dream he had—a dream we both had.

"Was it worth it?"

"I'm glad he got another chance to talk. But the job isn't over yet, if that's what you mean."

"I mean, was it worth it to *you?*"

She felt Tod Jarrow's tongue pressing against her own, and she said, "It's always worth it, to try and help a patient."

Ken looked at her with his bloodshot eyes.

She hugged herself and shivered. "I'm freezing. I'm going to take a shower. You shouldn't be sitting down here drinking like this. It's late."

"It's almost morning."

"You know what I mean." She felt her stomach tighten. "What's wrong with you, anyway?"

"I couldn't sleep."

"I'm sorry I had to go out in the middle of the night."

"Are you sorry you went to see him?"

Her face grew hard. "Not now, Ken. Just back off. I do *not* need this right now, okay?"

She turned and walked out of the kitchen without looking back, because she knew that if she did, she would see him still sitting there, staring at her with his bloodshot eyes.

Upstairs, she turned the shower on full. Stinging needles of hot spray pierced her naked flesh, drumming on her stomach and thighs, drizzling down between her legs, giving her sexual hunger a sharp, cutting edge.

She opened her mouth and let the hot water rush in. It filled up her mouth, dribbling down over lips and chin. She saw Tod Jarrow's dark eyes again, felt him grab her face roughly. A shudder coursed through her.

She raised a hand to her breast, fingers brushing against an erect nipple. The shudder came again, more intense this time. She took the stiff nipple between thumb and forefinger, squeezed it once gently, then again, harder. The shudder became a violent trembling that reached down deep into every part of her naked body. Her heart beat rapidly. She turned her head to one side, hot water falling hard against it.

She reached a wet hand down to the aching hunger between her legs, touched its swollen softness lightly. The shudder became a seizure. It threw her against the side of the shower stall and made the lights flash white overhead.

She saw Tod Jarrow's eyes again, felt his tongue probing deep inside her mouth, saw his hardness bulging up through his pants.

Stop it!

The water continued to fall. But it fell outside now, down from a gray Venetian sky, hammering against the windowpanes. They were inside another borrowed room, a poorer one this time, closer to the Arsenal, where the lowest class of whores serviced the shipbuilders. No tapestries hung from the walls. No damask quilt covered the narrow bed on which they turned and twisted. Only gray light fell into the room, through a small, uncurtained, rain-spattered window.

She had him in her mouth, his length and thickness. He stared down at her with his dark eyes, feverish in the gray light. When he came with a hoarse cry, the fluid leaked from her mouth, dribbling off her chin and onto her naked breasts. He rubbed it over her breasts and nipples, then pressed himself against her, their skin sticking together.

She caressed his trembling shoulders and whispered in his ear.

"Did you like that, my Marcangelo?"

"I like it better when I spill my seed inside you."

"And what if I conceive a child?"

"Then we will take you to one of the hags that wait upon

the courtesans. She will ease you of your burden. It is no great thing, to cut loose a bastard child."

She shuddered, and tried to move away from him, but his body weighed down hard on hers.

"My husband grows tiresome. He will suspect us before long. I want you to leave his service."

"I have no choice in what I do."

"Let him find someone else to be his butcher! I do not want you forever washing blood from your hands before you touch me."

"I do what I must do."

"If you no longer served him, he would have less cause to be suspicious of us. If you love me, you will do as I wish."

He grabbed hold of her naked shoulders then, in a way that made her cry out in fear.

"Alessandra! Listen to me. I have no choice in what I do. No choice at all. I do as I must, not as I will. Contarini is not my master. I serve him at the command of another."

"Who is he, this other master of yours?"

"Let it not be said," he whispered, and turned his face away.

She fell back against the shower stall, panting for breath. The air was thick and steamy, filled with fog, hot instead of cold this time, bright instead of dark. But the feeling was the same, and the images returned. She saw the two of them again, standing there inside the narrow *calle,* behind the great *palazzo.* Tod Jarrow with his dark beard and heavy wool cloak. The man she called her husband, Ludovico Contarini, huge and overpowering in his heavy red robe, silver head low and threatening, like that of a predatory animal.

Stop it!

Both men had known her nakedness. Contarini's rough, violent hands moving over her naked body, taking what was his by law and custom. This was no dream. This was memory.

Memories of what had been.

Stop it!

With a violent jerk, she turned the shower control from hot

to cold. She gasped as the burning spray turned suddenly to ice. Trembling, she shut it off, then stood there shivering, her naked flesh breaking out into goose bumps, water dripping off her body and running noisily down the drain at her feet like blood.

13
The Dream Path

Galina Marenkov stuck her head in from the dining room. "No one wants the breakfast this morning? Ken? Connie?"

Connie looked up from the steaming cup of coffee she was trying to swallow in one gulp. "Thanks, Galina. But I'm really late. I've got Jennie Hodges set up for my first appointment. Benjamin Simmons is scheduled for later on. Tough day."

"So much work! So little sleep!"

Connie glanced at Ken. "I didn't plan it this way."

Ken stared at her, his bloodshot eyes transparent as glass.

"Mom!" Stevie called from her bedroom. "Don't leave before you kiss me goodbye!"

"Hurry up, sleepyhead!" Connie called back to her. "I'm leaving now."

Ken looked up at her from the kitchen table. "You think we'll always be here, don't you? Like a VCR tape you can catch later."

She turned to him. "Ken, you're just picking at nothing."

"Sure." His voice rose suddenly. "I'm just talking *about our family and our life together! That's all!*"

He took a deep breath. "I didn't mean that, okay?"

"No problem." She glanced at his jeans and T-shirt. "Going into the office later?"

"Have to meet a client in Pasadena at ten." He rubbed his forehead. "I'll go in after that."

They could hear Stevie running down the hall toward them.

"Look, Ken. I don't take any of you for granted. I love you all very much. Okay?"

"Sure."

When Connie pulled into the Beckford parking lot, it was mostly deserted, except for Lou Pelham's slate gray BMW 920i and one weather-beaten wino sitting hunched over in the staff doorway, glaring at the two cars and their drivers. Lou Pelham, expensively tailored as usual, waved a greeting to Connie, then walked over to the staff entrance.

The wino, wrapped in a torn, filthy snot green all-weather coat, shifted slightly in the doorway and glared up at Lou Pelham with two rheumy gray eyes. Lou had a full ebony face with high cheekbones and commanding African eyes. That face could look kind and fatherly, as it usually did to patients, or thoroughly intimidating, the way it did just now.

He said to the wino, "Move outta here, man."

The wino muttered something, started to make a defiant gesture, thought better of it, then got up and left.

"You look like you've just seen a ghost," Lou said to Connie.

She saw Tod Jarrow again, standing over her. *This is real.*

"I got a call from a patient in the middle of the night—"

She was going to say more, but she knew it would not sound right—not to Lou Pelham, anyway—to admit that she had driven down to the Hollywood Station at 3:30 A.M. to talk with a serial killer.

"Off-hours calls are a nuisance," Lou said.

"Also—" Connie hesitated. "I had some bad dreams. Very disturbing dreams. The kind that leave you waking up more tired than when you went to bed."

"Nature's way of telling us to lighten up and take a little time off. I hope you're paying attention, Connie."

"You just want to get rid of me, Lou."

"On the contrary, dear lady. I want to make sure you stay with us here at the Beckford for a long, long time."

His face became somber. "Don't ignore obvious warning signs."

"I won't, Lou. But it's just a dream."

After all, it's your dream too, Connie.

Inside her office, she started to check her appointment book, still worrying over the dream, probing at it like a sore spot in the back of her mouth.

It's just a dream, she told herself.

But it would not go away. It cried out for attention. Professional attention. After all, dreams, and their psychological meanings, were part of her job.

After all, it's your dream too, Connie.

She went over to the bookshelf and took down her battered student copy of Sigmund Freud's *The Interpretation of Dreams*.

Sometimes, when faced with an especially stubborn case, Connie found herself turning back to Freud. Not that it always helped.

It didn't help with Benjamin, she thought, flipping idly through *The Interpretation of Dreams,* wondering if anything would ever help that isolated, silent child.

She stopped turning pages at the section entitled "The Significance of Dreams in Everyday Life."

And almost dropped the book.

The ordinary consciousness, Freud wrote, *of someone awakening from sleep assumes that his dreams, wherever they came from, have transported him into another world.*

She read over the passage again, mouthing the words silently, her throat dry, her body cold, the horrible dreams of Venice taking shape inside her mind once again.

—into another world.

She shut the book with a bang that rang out in the quiet office, startling her. She replaced the book on its shelf, trying not to notice that her hands were trembling slightly.

Nerves of steel, Jake.

She sat down at her desk and forced herself to think.

The options, when she considered them, were fairly obvious.

Either she was suffering from a phobia of an unknown kind and origin that caused her to experience specific, recurring dreams.

Or she was entering the initial stages of a serious personality breakdown. Psychosis.

The assumption of psychosis would help explain a lot of things, especially the way Tod Jarrow had seemed to make specific references to her dream. She knew the way that worked. Psychotic hallucinations begin by impinging on reality. Finally, given enough time, they become reality.

She got up from her desk and looked into the full-length mirror that hung from the inside of the coat-closet door. Her face seemed slightly drawn, eyes puffy from lack of sleep. Otherwise, it was the same old face, holding its own the way our faces always seem to—in mirrors, anyway.

Is this the face of someone suffering from psychotic hallucinations?

Before the mirror could answer, her phone rang.

It exploded inside the silent office like a bomb.

She hit the speaker button. "Dr. Stallman speaking."

"Connie?" Becky asked.

"Yes?"

"Jennie Hodges, here to see you."

"Fine. I'll be right out."

"Don't bother. She's on her way back."

14

The Empty Space

Jennie Hodges said, "You're trying to avoid me, aren't you?"

Connie looked up from her desk. "I got here early just to see you, Jennie. It wasn't easy. Not this morning."

"You wanted to make me wait," Jennie accused her. "You *always* make me wait!"

Connie looked at the young woman standing in front of the desk, immobilized by her own contradictions, unable to live her life or let it go. Five-five, not tall, not short. Average weight. Featureless, shoulder-length brown hair. Plain face, neither pretty nor unattractive. Jeans, light jacket, running shoes. Large, rimless aviator glasses that seemed, despite their largeness, to pinch her plain face.

"Always!" She snapped out the word.

Connie gestured to a chair in front of the desk.

"Have a seat, Jennie."

She plopped down into the chair, jacket collar bunching up around her face, hands gripping the armrests, everything making her appear much younger than her twenty-four years.

"I want my Valium," Jennie said.

"We're going to try a new drug, another benzodiazepine derivative. It's supposed to be more effective than Valium in dealing with depression."

"What's it called?"

"No brand name. It's a generic version."

"I have to know what it's *called*, Connie."

"No, you don't. The idea is to help you feel better, not make you drug dependent."

Jennie's voice flared. "You think I'm hooked on that shit?"

"No." Connie looked at her. "That's why I'm being very careful with your refills."

Jennie's hands flexed on the chair's armrests.

"I want my refill now. That benzo-whatever-the-fuck."

"You'll get it. After we've talked."

Jennie's voice took on a hard, querulous edge.

"I want my refill *now!*"

"So, how have things been since our last talk?"

"If you don't give it to me right now," Jennie warned, "I'm *outta* here, okay?" She made a show of starting to leave.

"Go ahead." Connie's voice remained pleasant but neutral.

"You won't be able to come back without another appointment. And you're not getting a refill until we've talked."

Jennie got almost to her feet, then sat back down.

"So," Connie started again, "how have you been?"

Jennie said nothing.

"Have you done anything interesting?" Connie asked. "Met anyone new?"

"There's no one for me, Connie. You know that. *I want my fucking medicine!*"

She started to leave again, but both women knew the gesture was empty. Jennie struck an armrest angrily with her fist. Tears came to her eyes. Her mouth twisted with misery.

"I want my *medicine,*" she sobbed.

"Does the medicine help?" Connie asked. "Does it help with the nothingness?"

Jennie wiped at her eyes. "It helps me not think about it."

"Tell me about the nothingness again, Jennie."

"I already *told* you!"

Connie nodded, reaching for a notepad. "Tell me again. Then we'll get your refill."

Jennie swallowed. "It's—you know, nothing. That's all."

Connie looked up. "Just nothing?"

"Not *just* nothing. It's like—there's something inside it, but it's empty. But the emptiness has a kind of shape to it."

Connie turned back to her notepad. "Tell me about it."

"I—can't."

"As soon as you tell me about it, we'll get your—"

"I can't tell you because it scares the shit out of me, okay?"

Jennie looked scared. She sat scrunched down in the chair, gripping the armrests like handrails. Her eyes behind the aviator glasses were desperate.

Like Tod Jarrow's eyes, when they had him in the straitjacket.

"What is it that scares you?" she asked Jennie.

"The emptiness." Jennie shifted in the chair, still gripping the armrests. "There's a shape to it, like you can almost see it. But you can't. Because there's nothing there. *Nothing.*"

"Is it real?" Connie asked. "Or just something that feels real, like a—"

She was going to say *like a dream,* but instead she said, "Like something you imagined?"

Jennie shook her head. "It's real."

"How do you know?" Connie asked.

Because this *is real,* Tod Jarrow said inside her head, and kissed her again, fiercely, his tongue thrusting inside her mouth.

Connie's hand twitched, knocking over a glass paperweight on her desk. It spun in circles, revolving pointlessly.

Jennie looked up at her. "You okay?"

Connie nodded. "Tell me more about the empty space."

"I tried to look inside it once," Jennie said, her voice flat. "But I couldn't. I couldn't make myself do it."

"Why not?" Connie asked, feeling absurdly that it was Jennie, and not she, who was conducting this interview now, leading it down the twisting path to wherever it was going.

"Because I was scared," Jennie said simply. "So scared I almost pissed myself."

"Scared of what?" Connie asked, scared herself now, scared that she knew the answer, sensed it, even before asking.

The fear cut deep into Jennie's eyes, making her pinched face behind the aviator's glasses look like a shriveled skull. "I was scared," she said, "that if I looked into it, I'd—disappear."

Connie stared at the young woman sitting across from her. But she did not see her.

She saw instead an empty space, in the form of a doorway. She stood on one side, Tod Jarrow on the other. She saw herself take a step forward, toward the doorway.

"I was so scared," she heard Jennie say from a distance.

Connie saw herself step into the doorway, and through it—

"So scared—"

—and disappear.

She gasped, and raised a hand to her mouth.

Jennie sat there, staring at her.

My God, what's wrong with me? What's happening, please?

"You shouldn't have gotten up so early," Jennie said. "Why don't you give me my refill and go back to bed?"

Connie tried to say something, but could not.

Jennie leaned forward. "You know, Connie. If you keep fucking around with my medicine like this, one day I am just going to go out and get it over with. No shit."

"Don't make threats," Connie managed to say.

"It's no fucking *threat!*" Jennie slammed her hand down on the desk. "I'll take the elevator to that restaurant on top of the Cal Pacific building. Tramonto? They have a stairway in there that leads to the roof and it's never locked. A friend of mine who works there told me about it."

Connie wrote out the new benzodiazepine prescription mechanically on a sheet of notepaper.

"I'll go up those stairs and out onto the roof before anyone can stop me," Jennie said. "Then I'll jump off the edge. *And I'll do it, Connie!*" Her pinched face seemed frightened behind the aviator glasses. "And I hope you're the one who has to come and identify me!"

Connie tore off the sheet of notepaper and handed it to her.

Jennie snatched it greedily, then stuffed it into her jeans pocket without even looking at it.

Connie said to her, "Before you think seriously of jumping off any building, call me first, okay?"

"Why? You don't give a flying fuck what happens to me."

No, echoed a cold voice inside Connie's head, *you don't.*

The coldness startled her and she blurted out, "Yes! I do!"

But Jennie was already gone, slamming the door behind her.

15
Transfer

"**O**kay, fuck face. It's bye-bye time."

Tod Jarrow started up from sleep—sweating, chest heaving.

Nightmare fragments. Withered skin. Yellow eyes. *Il stregóne morello.* The Dark Sorcerer. Transmigrator of Souls.

"Come on, *move* it!"

Jarrow shook his head to clear it of the nightmare fragments, free it from the drift back down the dark river. Shook it hard to bring himself back into the here and now. The *here,* the *now.*

"Get your sorry ass in gear, you fucked-up piece of shit."

It was the dickhead talking, the one with the sandy-colored moustache, the one who had taunted him through the door panel in the isolation cell.

Jarrow shifted on the lumpy mattress and looked around at the cell he was in now. Rust-stained sink. Open toilet with black slime crawling up the sides of the bowl. Compared to isolation, it was a penthouse suite.

"Hey, fuck face." The uniformed officer sauntered over to him. "You piss me off, okay? I tell you to move, you take fuckin' forever. I oughta snap these around your fuckin' balls."

He rattled a pair of handcuffs in his face.

Jarrow looked at him. "Shove it up your ass."

"Who the fuck you think you are?" He wrapped the handcuffs around one large fist. *"Who the fuck you think you are?"*

"Back off, Ambrose," Ed Dormer called from the opposite side of the cell. "Cut the shit and get him ready for transfer."

Ambrose said to Dormer, "Guy's a fuckin' butthole, okay?"

"Just get him ready."

Ambrose sighed, then said to Jarrow, "Hold out your little handsies, fuck face."

Jarrow kept his hands where they were.

"You understand English, you sorry piece of shit?"

Jarrow worked to control his breathing. He had drifted back again while he slept, drifted back to find himself face-to-face with the old one, the transmigrator of souls.

Yellow cat's eyes staring deep into his own soul.

You serve me of your own free will, assassino.

Ambrose turned to Dormer. "See what I mean? Is he a butthole or what? Somebody bring a needle and stick this fucker for me."

A male nurse with a hypodermic syringe looked at Dormer.

Dormer nodded. "Sedate him."

Mike Salazar said, "Our little girlfriend, the court psychiatrist, isn't going to like this much."

"She can shove it up her sweet pink crack," Dormer said.

Jarrow looked up at him. "She'll find me. No matter where you move me. She'll find me. Always."

Dormer stared at him and said nothing.

"Listen, fuck face," Ambrose said. "We do this however you want. You make it easy for us, we mainline it in your arm. You give us trouble, we shoot it straight up your fuckin' asshole."

The nurse strapped on the tourniquet, cinching it tight.

Jarrow's veins stood out inside his forearm like packing cords. He looked at the hypodermic needle as the nurse brought it in toward his arm.

Bringer of sleep and dreams, and drift.

And this time, death. Death and transmigration into a new life in the endless cycle of lives, at the hands of the Dark Sorcerer, transmigrator of souls.

"Just hold still, fuck face, and you won't feel a thing."

Ambrose stood close to him.

"You move any, it's gonna hurt like shitfire."

The nurse rubbed the inside of Jarrow's forearm with a disinfectant swab, then brought the needle down against his skin.

Jarrow grabbed at the hand with the hypodermic, caught it,

forced it up and back, jabbing the needle straight into the center of Ambrose's eye. Ocular fluid drizzled out onto the syringe.

Ambrose started screaming.

Jarrow slammed the heel of his hand into the nurse's face before the man had time to react and seized the hypodermic.

He turned to face Dormer and his men, rushing toward him now.

Dormer had his gun out.

Cowards! Jarrow thought. *More timid than a Doge's lap-dog!*

He made a threatening jab at them with the hypodermic.

Dormer and the others stepped back. Jarrow laughed.

He was still laughing when the nightstick caught him on the side of his face, cracking inside his skull like a gunshot.

His mouth fell open. Blood spattered a nearby wall.

The darkness gathered him up then, malevolent yellow eyes waiting patiently for him at the other end.

16

The Dark Man

The call came through as Connie was getting ready for her next patient, Benjamin Simmons.

"Dr. Stallman?"

"Speaking."

"Lieutenant Ed Dormer. I'm going to make this quick. Jarrow's been transferred to Terminal Island, a minimum-security prison near Long Beach."

Connie thought of Alice MacKendrick and her iron chair, and lost track momentarily of what Dormer was saying.

"I'm sorry," she began, "I didn't—"

"I said I don't know who's in charge of him down there."

"Lieutenant, I told you—"

"I know what you told me, Doctor." Dormer's voice took

on an edge. "You might check with the warden at TI. Or the DA's office. They're running this show now. I'm not."

The line fell silent.

"It must be nice," Connie said, "taking the easy way out."

The silence deepened on the other end.

Then Dormer said, "People like you make me sick, you know that? You want to save these monsters, but it's always the other guy who has to clean up the blood and the shit."

He took a sharp breath. "Jarrow injured two of my men. Broke one man's jaw. Stuck a hypodermic needle in the other's eye."

Connie said nothing.

"Jabbed it in good and hard. Man's going to lose the eye. Jarrow give a shit? Just before it happened, he said you'd always be able to find him. Wherever he was."

Wed to one eternity.

"So go find him. Hold his hand. French-kiss him again. Just don't look for any backup on this one."

"That was uncalled for, Lieutenant."

"Yeah, you're right. I apologize. It got to me, that's all. No hard feelings, Dr. Stallman, okay?"

"I'm sorry for what I said, about taking the easy way out."

"Sure. We're both sorry. Only one who's not is Jarrow."

Connie punched off the speakerphone and stared at her hands on the desktop. Well, it was true, wasn't it? She *had* kissed Tod Jarrow. She had responded to him, got turned on.

By a murderer's kiss.

A Famous Mauder Insight came to mind then.

Office romances may work for stockbrokers, Jake liked to say, *but not for psychiatrists. Never fall for another shrink. And never, ever fall for a patient.*

She thought, *I am not in love with Tod Jarrow—*

—not in this world.

Her phone rang.

"Connie?" Becky said. "Benjamin Simmons is here, with Mrs. Amanda Baker, his foster parent."

She did not want to see them, not right now.

"Thanks, Becky. Send them on in."

They took their usual places, Connie behind her desk, Mrs. Baker in one of the chairs, Benjamin in the other.

"Pissed himself again yesterday," Mrs. Baker said. "Threw one of his little fits. Had to go, but did he care? No. Just did it all over himself. Like a dirty little pig."

Benjamin, in the other chair, sat shrunken and silent, dark eyes staring straight into nothingness.

"You're supposed to call immediately whenever he has a seizure, Mrs. Baker," Connie said. "Why didn't you?"

"You ain't always here," Mrs. Baker said defensively.

"You can leave a message, and you have my home number. Benjamin's seizures can be very dangerous, Mrs. Baker."

"Didn't hurt him none. *I* was the one had to clean it up! He didn't do his little Jesus this time. Just laid there all curled up on the floor. Right in a puddle of his own piss."

Benjamin Simmons suffered from catatonic seizures. Sometimes he would assume a kneeling position, arms held straight out from his sides, and remain that way for hours. At other times he would get into a fetal position on the floor, knees tucked close to his chest, ignoring food, water, bodily functions.

"You can't blame Benjamin for his seizures, Mrs. Baker. He doesn't have any control over them."

"Easy for you to say! *You* don't have to wipe up his piss."

"Mrs. Baker, if you could maybe—"

"Leave you two alone for a spell?" She lifted her heavy body out of the chair. "Sure, for all the good it'll do. Nice to get a little rest from him now and then."

She turned at the door. "You send your report to the county?"

"Just like every month, Mrs. Baker."

"County don't get that report, I don't get my money."

When the two of them were alone, Connie smiled at the silent child. "Hello, Benjamin. How are you? Nice to see you again."

His dark eyes did not respond.

Like Tod Jarrow's eyes, she thought, then stopped herself. They were nothing like Jarrow's eyes.

The eyes of someone who has come back from the dead.

She got up from her desk and went around to Benjamin's chair, kneeling down in front of it. She took one of his hands in hers.

"I know it's not easy for you to talk. That's okay. I like you even if you don't talk to me. Even if you *never* talk to me. We don't have to talk to be friends, do we, Benjamin?"

She looked into his eyes. He did not respond.

Then, slowly, he turned his dark eyes and looked into hers.

She felt like calling up Jake Mauder, the L.A. *Times,* and CNN. Benjamin Simmons, after six long months, had *responded* to her!

She wanted to say something, reinforce the breakthrough, even though she knew that talking was not indicated, not right now.

She smiled, and looked into his dark eyes.

He did not smile back, but kept looking at her, his eyes deep, mysterious wells of blackness.

Night. Fog. Dark water sloshing against the banks of the canal as she walked quickly alongside it, the hem of her long velvet gown trailing across wet cobblestones, heart beating within her breast, fog damp in her throat. Church bells rang out through the night. A figure appeared in the distance, then came closer. His face materialized from out of the fog, dark eyes, full beard.

His arms encircled her.

"I risk my life to meet you like this," she whispered, speaking once again in that other language, foreign yet familiar.

"And I risk mine," he whispered in return, drawing her close to him. "But what is life without our love? If I must live my life without you, I do not want it. I cast it away as a thing of no value, like the ears of a Turkish slave."

She looked up at him, his dark eyes, dark beard. "I love you, Marcangelo," she said, "but I want my life." She tried to break free from his embrace, but his strong arms held her fast. "I want to live my life!"

A coldness entered his dark eyes. "It is not your choice alone, Alessandra. Your life belongs to me, as mine to you. You cannot live it apart from me." His embrace tightened around her. "You are mine, I am yours, always."

"Let me go!" she demanded, her voice rising above a whisper, echoing out over the canal.

"We are wed to one eternity," he whispered, dark eyes burning in the fog. "Always."

Always, echoed another voice—old, evil, hissing like a serpent inside her head.

She saw the face then, within the fog, the living skull that held the evil voice.

Yellow eyes. Withered skin. Hands like spider's claws.

The Ancient One. Transmigrator.

Marcangelo broke away from her, terror in his dark eyes.

Always, whispered the Dark Sorcerer once again, raising a spider's claw from the fog and pointing it at her. *Through this life and the next, through all the lives there are.*

Wed to one eternity.

The laughter came then, evil and high-pitched, drifting through the fog.

She found her voice. "Who *are* you?" she cried at the fog.

"The Dark Man."

The voice that answered her was rusted, squeaking like a door that had not been opened for a thousand years.

It spoke again. "The Dark Man."

Connie looked up, her face dripping sweat, drops falling like soft rain onto her wrists.

Benjamin was speaking. His mouth moved awkwardly with the unaccustomed labor of making half-remembered sounds.

"The Dark Man."

He looked at her again, but this time his dark eyes held a terror that mirrored her own, a fear of the evil that had appeared before them both.

"The Dark Man!"

Benjamin screamed, his voice breaking off, giving out on the last word, hissing like an empty tape.

Connie, on her feet now, stumbled and fell back against her desk. Papers spilled to the floor, fluttering in slow motion.

"The Dark Man," Benjamin whispered.

She wanted to comfort him, tell him there was no such thing.

But there was.

She had seen him, yellow eyes, withered skin, hands like spider's claws.

And somehow, beyond any sense of reason or reality, Benjamin Simmons had seen him, too.

17

Verdict

The Beverly Hills office of Jacob Abraham Mauder, M.D., looked more like an absent-minded professor's study than the consulting room of a prominent psychiatrist.

Books fought for space on overcrowded shelves. Loose papers lay scattered about. Connie sat in a chair that had been cleared for her. Jake leaned back in his own large desk chair, thumb flicking absently at his moustache as he listened.

When she finished, he raised his black-frame glasses and massaged the bridge of his nose.

Then he looked at her, blinking through the thick lenses.

"So, that's the whole *megillah?*"

Connie nodded. "Sorry to dump it on you like this." She looked at her watch. "It's late."

"Late-schmate. Esther's going to throw out my dinner because I'm a little late?" His eyes twinkled behind the thick lenses. "I should be so lucky. Then I could get deli take-out."

"Esther's a great cook and you know it."

"Sure, but you can get tired of anything, even perfection."

Jake's eyes lost their twinkle. "You having some kind of trouble at home, *bubeleh?*"

"No, not really."

"What's with the *not really?*"

"I mean, not any real trouble." She thought of her and Ken's dying sex life, and his fears about Jarrow. "Nothing serious."

"Nothing serious," Jake repeated. "But all this other *meshugaas* you've been telling me about—*this* is serious?"

"It's why I called you. I need help, Jake." Her voice slipped lower. "I don't know what's going on, but I'm getting scared. After what happened with Benjamin today—I almost lost it. I need a second opinion. You're the one person I've really been able to trust, ever since Dad died."

"I'm honored by your trust, Connie. But what about Ken? Shouldn't you trust him a little, too?"

"Jake, he's already upset by what he knows about this Jarrow thing. If he knew the full story, he'd go crazy."

"You think he's never going to find out, someday?"

"You want me to tell him, don't you? About the dreams, the fugues, whatever. About Jarrow—kissing me."

"I think it might be a good place to start."

"If I tell him, I'll have to drop the Jarrow case."

"Which might not be such a bad idea."

"Thanks, Jake. Everybody wants me to do that. You. Dormer. Ken. What is this? A secret men's club? You guys vote on it?"

Jake cleared his throat. "We can do many interesting things in our profession, Connie. But to help someone who doesn't want to be helped—that we can't do."

"Tod Jarrow does want to be helped."

"How do you know?"

She stopped, and looked down.

"Because you want to help him. Is that it, *bubeleh?*"

"You make it sound like I'm emotionally attracted—"

"Connie, it's nothing to be ashamed of. You know how it

goes with the conscious and the subconscious. The conscious—"

"—is like an adult, and does what it thinks is right. The subconscious is like a child, and does what it wants to do."

"Such a student! After all these years, she still remembers!"

Jake got serious again. "Consciously, you are responding to Jarrow in a mature, professional way, doctor to patient. But subconsciously—it's another story."

"Jake, what about the dreams? *We're having the same dreams!*"

"How do you know that?"

"Because he *told* me about things that happened in my dreams!"

"You didn't videotape that interview last night, did you? The one where he talked about the dream, then kissed you?"

"No, I didn't. I already told you that."

"So how do you know those things he said came from the dream?"

"You think I just heard it that way, Jake?"

His voice became softer. "When our mind doesn't like the way reality looks, or sounds, it makes a few adjustments."

"Okay, fine. I made the whole thing up."

"Bubeleh, please—"

"But what about the visions? The fugues? They keep coming back, Jake! And they keep happening in the same place. Venice. I think it's Venice. It's full of canals."

"Sounds like Venice."

"Jake, I've never visited Venice in my life! I don't know how to speak Italian. Why do I keep seeing a place I've never been to? And dreaming about it in a language I can't even speak?"

"Maybe they're someone else's dreams?"

"You're not taking me seriously."

"I always take you seriously, Connie. I think these fugue states are symptoms of conflicting stressors. On the one hand, you're feeling repressed hostility for your husband. On the other, repressed attraction for this Tod Jarrow bastard, the good-looking serial killer."

"Then you don't think I'm suffering from paranoid delusions? Psychotic hallucinations?"

"No. Nor do I think you are mysteriously time-traveling back to what sounds like sixteenth-century Venice."

Jake leaned back in his chair. "I do think you're under too much pressure with this Jarrow business. You can deal with pressure better than almost anyone else I know. I remember from your psychiatric residency. But *this* pressure poses special dangers. I think you should hand over the Jarrow case to someone else, as soon as possible."

She bit her lip. "What if I went down to Terminal Island, for one last interview? With armed guards inside the cell, of course."

"On a scale of one to ten, ten being worst, I think that idea rates an eleven, maybe a twelve."

"But Jake, what if I drop the Jarrow case and I still keep having these dreams, or fugues?"

"Try dropping it first, then see what happens."

"But what if they keep coming back, Jake?"

He looked at her for several seconds without answering.

Then he said, "In that case, things get more complicated."

18

Feast Day

As Connie drove home through the congested Beverly Hills traffic, she thought about what Jake had said.

Maybe he was right. She had no proof that Jarrow ever said any of those things last night. She had not taped the interview.

Maybe it was just the result of waking up from that horrible dream, and then going down to the police station with it still in her head, and letting her nerves play tricks with her mind.

After all, it's your dream too, Connie.

She turned off from the bumper-to-bumper crush on Santa

Monica Boulevard and headed up Laurel Canyon, into the Hollywood Hills.

The traffic around her picked up speed, engines straining on the steep grade. Cars zipped past. Headlights came on in the sudden darkness of a Southern California evening. Lights glistened from distant hillsides, like fairy lanterns moving in the night.

Looking again, she almost thought they *were* moving.

Like torches, moving across the hillsides. Lines of torches, held by servants dressed in livery. Incense wafting up behind them from swinging, hand-held censers. The solemn chanting of priests. The ringing of bells, growing louder in the distance.

The horn blared in her ear. Bright lights flashed in her rearview mirror. Adrenaline pumping, she hit the brakes and pulled over slightly. The angry driver behind her moved out and around, engine whining, horn blasting.

She swallowed hard, and gripped the wheel with both hands. A steady stream of headlights rushed down the twisting road toward her now, like a river of glittering white diamonds.

Or a line of torches, winding in formal processional across the huge open square of the Piazza San Marco, the domes of the Basilica outlined by their wavering light.

The blaring horns sounded in front of her. She turned the wheel just in time to stop from drifting across the center line, into the headlights of the oncoming traffic.

Shaken, she pulled off onto the shoulder and came to a stop.

Headlights. Torchlights. Hundreds of torches.

"No!" She shook her head to clear it. *"No!"*

Red velvet robes. The *Signoria,* advisors to the Doge himself.

The great procession moved in stately file across the Piazza San Marco, followed by the forty-man *Quarantia.* Then came the leaders of the Church—bishops, priests, monks. Then the gold-leafed, canopied reliquary, borne aloft by four priests.

And everywhere, the torches and torchbearers.

The Feast of Saint Mark. The city in all its splendor.

She walked with solemn pace, far back in the procession. A great honor to be seen in public on such a night as this, with most women hidden at home, or at the far edges of the large watching crowd. Her hair piled high, a cap of gold filigree on her head. Necklace of pearl and amethyst. She walked with eyes held low, measuring her steps, as flickering torchlight fell across the stones beneath her feet.

"Contessa." A whisper.

The back of her neck grew tight. She shifted her eyes left, from where the sound had come. Nothing but shadows, onlookers standing in respectful reverence, and in the distance more torches, always more torches.

"Contessa!" Louder this time, insistent.

She looked up. Startled murmurs from the onlookers. A shifting of the crowd, jostling, then a parting of bodies.

"Contessa, your mercy!"

She raised a hand to her breast, heart pounding.

Ludovico Contarini, far ahead in the procession, turned his great silver head and looked back at her and the movement in the crowd, his heavy profile outlined by torchlight.

A break in the crowd. He stumbled forward. Her lover, Marcangelo. Hands and forearms streaked with blood. Blood smeared across his tunic, drops matting his dark beard, dripping down onto the stones of the Piazza. The blood of others.

Murmurs rose from the crowd.

"Your mercy!" he gasped. "I beg your mercy!"

She drew back in horror, aware that Ludovico Contarini stood farther ahead in the procession, watching them both.

Marcangelo raised a bloody hand toward her.

"Contessa, please, your mercy!"

"Assassino!" The cry pierced the crowd, sending ripples through its close-packed ranks. *"Assassino!"*

He glanced toward the harsh cries, then turned back to her, terror in his dark eyes.

"Help me!" he pleaded. "I beg of you!"

He grabbed at her wrist with a bloody hand. She screamed,

and tried to pull away. Up ahead, Contarini rumbled a deep-voiced command. Guards emerged from the shadows, and laid hands upon her lover. More figures broke through the agitated crowd. The *Signori di Notte,* the Lords of the Night.

The leader of the *Signori* approached with sword drawn.

"This man," he said, pointing to Marcangelo, "is under arrest in the name of the Doge and the Republic for murder!"

A gasp swept through the crowd. Marcangelo twisted in the grip of the men who held him, but could not break free.

He looked at her directly, dark eyes pleading.

"Mercy!" he cried. "In the name of God, Contess—"

A blow to the face silenced him. His head hung down. More blood, his own blood now, dripped down onto the stones.

The leader of the *Signori* stared at him with contempt.

"You dare address your betters, and beg for their help? And blaspheme God's Holy Name with a murderer's plea?"

He spit upon Marcangelo's lowered head. *"Assassino!"*

Then the leader of the *Signori* turned to his men.

"Take him away. Cast him into darkness."

She saw the torchlights flickering before her eyes, and felt the blood rushing from her head. She looked away from the spectacle of her lover, Marcangelo, covered with blood, the Lords of the Night dragging him off to the Doge's dungeons.

Then she found herself staring into the cold face of her husband, the Count Ludovico Contarini.

He stared back at her, and said nothing.

She raised a hand to her throat, feeling the dampness on her wrist as she did so. She looked down to see her wrist wet with the blood of her lover's victim.

A great roaring came down upon the Piazza then, like the cry of a maddened beast. It fell upon the halted procession, shuddering through the night with the fury of a wind from Hell.

The car shot by her, close enough to take off paint.

Connie cried out, blinking at the headlights sweeping past

her on Laurel Canyon Boulevard. She felt as if all the air had been sucked out of the car. She could not breathe. She had to get air.

She pushed open the door and staggered out onto the shoulder, gripping the side of the car for support. Passing cars whined in the night air as they shot by.

Leaning against the car's hood with both hands, she drew in the cool night air, wanting to close her eyes, but afraid to, for fear of seeing once again the torches, the red robes of the *Signoria,* the red blood on the stones of the Piazza—

Stop it! she ordered herself. *Stop it now!*

Her breathing returned to normal. She swallowed hard, and looked down at her hands resting flat on the car's hood.

She lifted her right wrist, staring at it with horror.

"No!"

The wrist Marcangelo had grabbed hold of, pleading for his life, the same wrist Tod Jarrow had seized at the violent end of their first interview—she held it out in front of her now, wet with blood, as the traffic roared past on Laurel Canyon Boulevard.

19

The Empty House

Connie sat in her driveway, listening to the pings and clicks of the Acura's cooling engine.

The house was dark, its windows unlighted. Ken and the kids should have been home by now. But that was a minor concern, almost an afterthought, compared to her terror of the blood.

Blood on her wrist that had come from a dream.

She had wiped it off with a tissue, gagging as she did so. Then she had thrown the tissue into the darkness, off to one side of Laurel Canyon Boulevard.

That blood could not have come from a dream.

There were several possibilities. She might have cut herself while opening the car door earlier.

But Connie was a medical doctor. She knew, examining her wrist now in the dim orange half-light of a sodium-vapor street lamp, that she had not cut or injured it in any way.

She might have imagined the blood on her wrist.

If I can imagine Venice and think it's real, why not blood?

But she had wiped this blood off her wrist and thrown away the tissue herself, and it had been very real blood. She could still see the stains it had made on the tissue, and smell the faint, coppery scent of fresh blood.

And she had not just imagined Venice, no matter what Jake Mauder said. She had not simply dreamed about it in some kind of fitful half-sleep. She had *been* there. She had *lived* it.

The torches. The procession. The Piazza. The blood.

She sat tensed, hands pressing down on the leather front seat, a faint sheen of perspiration beading her upper lip.

"Jake," she whispered, "if this isn't real, then why does it *feel* so goddamn real?"

Because now, she could hear him say, *things are starting to get a little more complicated.*

She got out of the car and walked toward the front door. Ken must have taken the kids out for something to eat. After the way he had yelled at her this morning, maybe he had taken them down to his parents' place in Newport Beach.

Maybe she would be hearing from his lawyer at some later date.

The prospect did not alarm her. She loved her husband and children. But the thought of losing them did not frighten her.

The blood was what frightened her.

And the dislocation, a sense of shifting back and forth between an unreal present, an impossible past.

She turned her key in the lock and opened the front door.

The entryway stood dark and empty. Out the living-room

window, she could see the distant lights of Los Angeles, and farther off, the ghostly silver curve of Santa Monica Bay.

"Anybody home?" she called softly, not expecting an answer.

"HEEEEEEEEEEEYYYYYYYYY, MOM!"

"Mommy! Mommy!"

Bright light burst from the entryway overhead. A huge vase of red roses on a side table seemed to leap out of the darkness. Connie stepped back and dropped her purse. She stared at the riot of red roses, spilling out of a bucket-sized crystal vase like some grand larceny from the Rose Parade. For a moment she almost expected to see Marcangelo stagger out into the entryway, leaving bloody footprints behind him.

Instead, Stevie came flying out of the kitchen like a bullet, grabbing her in an around-the-knees tackle, laughing deep in her throat, blue eyes snapping with delight. Trent came toddling after, holding out his arms to be picked up.

"Welcome home," Ken said, kissing her on the cheek. "Thought we'd surprise you."

"You sure did." She kissed him hard on the mouth, then closed her eyes so no one could see the tears.

"Mom," Stevie demanded sharply, "why're you crying?"

"I'm not." Connie smiled, tears glistening on her cheeks. "I'm just tired, honey. I need to get to bed."

"Grandma 'n' Grandpa're on the phone!"

Connie wiped at her tears. "Ken, I can't talk to them now."

"I think Mom just wants to ask you about something."

Connie stood in the entryway, feeling safe now, like someone rescued from a nightmare, and dropped into the heart of light.

Ken handed her the cordless phone.

"Connie? Heard they cooked up a little surprise for you."

"A wonderful surprise, Babs. Bryce on the line?"

"Right here, babe. Holdin' steady."

"The reason we called," Babs said, "is because a very special young lady has a very special day coming up—"

"Oh my God!" Connie cried. "I almost forgot!"

"Forgot *what?*" Stevie asked.

"It's not every year she turns seven. Bryce and I want to make it super special for her. You know that little beach down near Laguna, the one we love? We want to have a beach party there for her, Connie. You know, music, entertainers, fireworks, the whole show. Think she'll like that?"

"You know she will."

"Don't worry about a thing, Connie. I've got it all taken care of. You just make sure you find time to relax a little. Maybe get that husband of yours out on a boat." Babs's voice took on a mysterious note. "In fact, I think he just might have another little surprise cooked up for tonight."

"Sailing?" Connie asked, dreading the very thought of it just then, feeling already the seasick swell of waves beneath her feet.

"All our love to the four of you," Babs said, signing off.

Connie looked up with a troubled frown.

"Ken, are we going *sailing* tonight?"

"Not a bad idea. But I've got something you'll like better."

"Ken, we hardly got any sleep last night—"

"—and we're too tired to make dinner." Ken took Trent from her and set him down. "So that's why I made reservations for two instead, at Hot Thai on Melrose."

"For tonight? But what about the kids?"

"*I* will take care of them," Galina Marenkov said, stepping out of the kitchen, dish towel in one hand.

"Galina! You shouldn't be here this late!"

"I too am part of the big surprise, Connie."

"So," Ken asked, "have we got a date, or what?"

"Yes," she nodded, feeling that her world was back where it should be, locked into focus once again.

"Yes. I love you. I love all of you."

She started to cry again.

20
Premonitions

"**In**side!"

As they shoved him into the cell, he lost his footing, stumbled, and fell to his knees, banging both kneecaps hard on the concrete floor.

"Your new home-sweet-home, motherfucker."

One of the prison guards, Wexler, pudgy-faced, with greased hair, came over and unlocked Jarrow's handcuffs. As the cuffs fell off with a sharp clink, another guard, Sokowski, bleached-blond and hard-muscled, came in from behind and grabbed Jarrow's hair with a grip that almost yanked it out of his head. Jarrow clutched at his hair with both hands, mouth falling open from the intense pain.

"You try any fancy shit on us, motherfucker," Sokowski hissed in his ear, "and we pop your fuckin' eyeballs out, then make you *eat* 'em. Got it?"

Jarrow said nothing.

"*Got* it?" Sokowski yanked back until Jarrow was staring straight up at the ceiling.

"Got it," Jarrow said.

Sokowski released his grip, throwing Jarrow's head forward with a contemptuous fuck-you shove. Jarrow remained on his knees.

"Meet your new cellmate," Wexler said. "Name's Dethrush. A real made dude."

"That's D-e-t-h-r-u-s-h"—Sokowski spelled it out for him—"without the *a,* which stands for *asshole,* because he got that fucked out of him a *long* time ago. Say what, Deth babes?"

The cell's other occupant, a thin, wraithlike man with bony head and buck teeth, stared passively at Tod Jarrow and the two guards, only a nervous glitter in his tiny eyes and an occasional twitching of the cigarette in his spindly fingers giving off any signs of life.

"You learn from Deth," Wexler said. "You keep your own asshole tight and dry. And don't turn your back on *nobody*."

"And no fuckin' noise, shithead." Sokowski pointed a blunt finger from a heavily veined, thick-wristed hand. "Or we tear your fuckin' face again, and make sure this time it *stays* tore."

The cell door slammed shut. The guards' harsh laughter echoed down the cell-block corridor. Jarrow got up off his knees and went over to a rusted, mold-dark sink. He ran some cold water and applied it to the side of his face where the nightstick had hit him at the Hollywood Station. A large flap of skin had been sewn back clumsily into place, thanks to some patchwork plastic surgery.

But still, she'll come to me.

Dethrush crushed out his cigarette. He got up from the lower bunk where he had been sitting and came over to Jarrow with a nervous, skittering sideways movement, like a rat on crack.

"Hey, bad boy," he said, buck teeth pushing forward, "what they put you in here for?"

Jarrow turned off the water.

"Murder one, huh?" Dethrush skittered closer. "Huh? Huh?"

Jarrow looked at him. "Kidnapped a bunch of kindergartners. Cooked 'em. Ate 'em."

"Right!" Dethrush grinned, showing more gum than teeth. "Right, right, right, right, right—"

Jarrow ignored him. The little weirdfuck could be taken care of when the time came. But this was not the time.

He looked at Dethrush bobbing up and down in front of him.

"How's this place work visitors?"

"What you want with visitors, huh? Huh? Huh?" He circled around him. "Got yourself a twist, huh? Or maybe a little *boy*friend, huh? Yeah, that's it! You packin' in the shit, huh? Huh? Huh?"

"Fuck you," Jarrow said wearily.

"Hey!" Dethrush turned all business, his honor at stake now. "Don't fuck with me, man! Don't you fuck with *me*, uh, uh! 'Cause I'm Dethrush." He held up his hands, palms out, *Deth* tattooed on the lower finger joints of one, *Rush* on those of the other, except the tatoo artist had got the *s* backward. *"Deth! Rush!* You dig?"

"Okay," Jarrow said. "I'm scared."

"Just you remember." Dethrush lowered his hands and walked over to the cell's small barred and wire-screened window. "What you need with visitors, huh? You want smelly pussy, you just look out here."

Jarrow glanced out the window, which looked down onto a bleak extraterrestrial landscape lit by the eerie orange glow of sodium-vapor lamps.

"There's one now!" Dethrush called, pressing his face up against the window bars. "Hey, *pussy! PUUUUUSSSSEEEEEEE! EEEEEEEEEEEEEEEEEEEEEEEEEOOOOOOOOOOWWWW!"*

Dethrush rattled and howled at the window, trying to attract the attention of a young woman as she walked to her car beneath the orange lights.

Jarrow turned at the sound of running feet in the cell-block corridor. Sokowski stopped outside the cell door, chest heaving with exertion, joined by Wexler several seconds later, both of them carrying heavy clubs tipped with hard rubber.

"You in *deep* shit now, mamma," Dethrush muttered in his ear, then skittered over toward the bunk.

Opening the cell door, Sokowski shouted, "What the fuck I tell you about *noise,* asshole?"

Jarrow nodded to Dethrush. "Tell the noisemaker."

Dethrush shook his head and pointed a finger at Jarrow.

Jarrow turned on him. "You little shit—"

Sokowski stopped him, and threw him back hard against a cement wall, knocking the wind out of him.

"We know what he's full of." Sokowski raised the club. "Let's see what you got."

Jarrow lifted his hands to protect his face.

* * *

Farther north, in Westwood, not far from the UCLA campus, Jake Mauder put down his napkin.

Esther Mauder looked up from her own plate. *"Nu,* full already? Or maybe you just don't like my pot roast?"

"Maybe I just don't like your pot roast." Jake smiled at her. "Also, maybe I'm worried about my good student."

"So?" She started clearing the table. "What's to worry?"

Jake shrugged. "If I knew, would I worry?"

"She's a grown-up good student," Esther said, "with a good job, a good husband, and two good kids. She doesn't need an old *yenta* like you to worry about her."

Jake folded his hands and propped his chin on them.

"I don't like it, Esther."

"You've said that before."

"So, I'm repeating myself. These flashbacks she's been having, they're not like her. Maybe for someone with bad nerves. But Connie's got nerves of steel. She shouldn't be experiencing random fugues like this."

"Maybe she's tired," Esther suggested. "We all get tired sometimes, Jake."

He shook his head. "It's more than that. She's not tired. She's frightened. Very badly frightened."

"Of what?"

"If I knew, would I be sitting here worrying about it, wasting my dinner?"

"Once in a while," Esther said, "you can afford to waste one."

21
Assassin's Banquet

At Hot Thai on Melrose, they tasted the wine in silence.

"I went to see Jake this afternoon," Connie said. "About the Jarrow business. That's why I was so late getting home."

Ken's face showed no reaction. "What did Jake say?"

"A lot of things. Mainly, that I should drop it."

"What did you say?"

"What I believe. That Jarrow can still be helped." She saw Ken's face start to tighten. "But maybe Jake's right. Maybe I should hand it over to someone else."

"Whatever you decide to do, it can wait till tomorrow." He raised his glass. "Tonight belongs to us. To hell with work."

"To hell with work." Connie clinked wineglasses with him, glancing around at the beautiful flowers, the handsome waiters, the clean lines of eclectic California interior design, white with accents of gold—

Golden goblets, raised high before rich-robed dinner guests around the long table, candle smoke wafting up toward the frescoed, gilt-edged ceiling, musicians strumming *liuto* and *tiorba,* and echoing above it all—goblets, candle smoke, soft-stringed music—the many-voiced cry of *"Salute!"*

Connie jumped in her chair, almost dropping the wine glass.

Ken frowned at her. "What's wrong?"

She tried to smile.

Please don't let this get started again, she thought, *not now.*

She shook her head, finally managing to smile.

"I just—You know, I think that's Goldie Hawn over there?"

Ken turned. "Where?"

"There."

"Not unless she's in disguise. Here. Have some more wine."

She smiled, bracing herself for another sudden shift into that alien, hateful world. But the seconds passed, and nothing happened. She took a cautious sip of wine, closed her eyes, then opened them again, fully expecting to see the images of gold and candlelight, dark water and death.

You will catch your death, my lady.

Instead, she saw Ken talking to her across an open menu.

Drifting . . . down the dark river.

"I'm sorry." She shook her head, taking up her menu. "What were you saying?"

She sat tensed, waiting for the shift to come again.

"I said, I hope you approve of Mom's plans for Stevie's birthday party at the beach."

"Approve? I love it! Your mom is such a sweetheart."

"I know you're not crazy about beach parties."

"Stevie is. That's what counts."

Ken flicked the side of his wineglass, making it ring.

"I know you're not too crazy about sailing, either."

"Maybe not as crazy as you."

She took a sip of the Chardonnay, savoring its dry taste.

"I think we ought to go sailing again," he said. "Soon."

The Chardonnay went flat in her mouth.

"But, Ken! Stevie's birthday party—"

"We'll go after the party, and take the kids with us."

She looked away, watching a waiter make his way smoothly across the room, a large tray of food balanced on his shoulder.

Servants in livery, bearing silver platters. Other servants, pouring wine into golden goblets. A young boy singing to the accompaniment of a strummed *liuto*. Smoky candlelight throwing shadows on the frescoed walls of the great Contarini dining hall.

Connie uttered a soft cry.

And found herself staring into Ken's concerned eyes.

"Sorry," she said quickly. "Not enough sleep, I guess."

"You looked like you were drifting away there for a second."

Drifting . . .

"Connie?" He leaned forward. "You want to go home?"

She shook her head. "I'm fine."

He looked at her for several seconds. "Anyway, I've already called Stevie's teacher about makeup work—"

He went on, but she wasn't listening. She forced herself to concentrate on the physical details in front of her. The weight of the wineglass in her hand. Light glinting off silverware. Red roses in a crystal vase. Conversations drifting over from nearby tables. The distant clatter and bang of the kitchen. She made herself fixate on the real world, its shapes, sounds, colors, movements. She turned it into a mental alertness exercise, a tightening of her precarious hold on the here and now.

"But what do *you* think?" Ken asked.

She smiled uncertainly. "Sounds good, I guess."

He reached out and took her hand. "It'll be just us. Our family. Nobody else. Just us and the big blue ocean. You'll love it. Wait and see."

"If you say so." She smiled again, raising the wineglass to her lips with the other hand.

The sound of voices made her look up.

She saw Ludovico Contarini sitting at a nearby table, draped in his heavy red robe, a cruel smile twisting his thick lips.

She dropped the wineglass. It bounced but did not shatter. Wine spread rapidly across the tabletop.

A waiter rushed over with a towel.

She sat back and raised a trembling hand to her mouth.

"Connie, what's wrong?"

She shook her head, but did not speak.

Ken asked the waiter, "Ladies' room?"

"Out past the bar, then to your right, sir."

She shook her head again. "Ken, I'm okay."

"Come on." He helped her to her feet.

A large potted plant sat beside the dark wooden door to the ladies' room. Laughter floated over from the bar.

"You go in there for a minute while I get the car."

"Ken, it's nothing. Just—"

Just a fugue. Just a temporary mental lapse.

But these temporary lapses keep coming back, don't they?

Inside the rest room, Connie sat down on a pink plastic couch and watched two young women fixing their makeup in a long mirror above a row of sinks. Maybe if she went over and rinsed her face she would feel better. Her heart seemed to flutter as if she had an arrhythmia. But she knew what it was. Nerves. Fear. Terror.

So what happens when they keep coming back, Jake?

Just how complicated do things get then?

She tried to make herself go rinse her face. But her legs felt weak, her stomach upset. She leaned back on the pink couch, being careful to keep her eyes open, listening to the flush of toilets, the running of water.

"Grazie tanto, mia contessa!"

—ssssaaaaaa

Another bowed before her, kissed her hand with formal Venetian elegance. Dinner guests thanked her for the banquet. Servants cleared away plates and forks and knives. Musicians withdrew with their instruments. Most of the guests prepared to take their leave, moving through the huge marble foyer and down the outside steps to where their private gondolas awaited them. Seated at the far end of the long dining table, Ludovico Contarini nodded his great silver-maned head to her, as if to say that the few guests who remained would be talking with him now in absolute privacy.

She nodded, then withdrew from the great dining hall, speaking only in response to servants' questions of where to put this and what to do about that. Inside the kitchen, cleanup operations moved forward under the direction of the little hunchbacked, gray-haired cook, Giuletta. A serving girl threw leftover meat to the dogs. Other girls poured garbage and slops into wooden tubs to be carried outside later and dumped into the Grand Canal. Still others gathered linen towels and napkins to be washed and ironed.

The scullery maid Tulia looked up from where she scraped food scraps into a garbage tub. The ragged holes of her cutoff nose flared as she glanced across the kitchen at her lady mistress, the Countess. Tulia smiled, and the holes flared wider.

The Countess Alessandra Contarini looked away.

"Will there be more food or drink for my lord Count and the guests that still attend him, my lady?" the cook Giuletta asked.

"No." She shook her head, reaching for the heavy length of her dark reddish-brown hair and finding it coiled in a braid atop her head. "No, they are talking privately. My husband does not wish them to be disturbed."

"Ah." Giuletta's watery gray eyes glinted. "Politics, then. Or money. When men talk in private, it is always one or the other. Or both."

The Countess smiled, and turned to leave the kitchen.

"Perhaps," Giuletta added, lowering her voice, "what they speak of has to do with the silent guest."

The Countess stopped, and turned back around.

"None of my husband's guests are silent. What do you mean?"

Giuletta glanced about the kitchen. "The young bearded stranger, the one who came after the other guests had already arrived. He entered by the back door, through the kitchen. His boots and cloak were muddy, as if he had walked through the *calli* instead of riding in a gondola."

"I know nothing of this."

Giuletta nodded. "Begging my lady's pardon, you were not meant to know. Our master ordered me to greet the bearded stranger and lead him to one of the back rooms, there to stay hidden until the banquet was over and the other guests gone."

"Is he there now?"

"No, my lady. When you and the other guests had left the great hall, I brought him from the back room and took him there."

"He is still there?"

Giuletta nodded. "Yes, my lady."

"He said nothing to you, this bearded stranger?"

"He is a silent guest, my lady."

Alessandra turned and left the kitchen, lifting the hem of her long gown so that it whispered across the tiles as she walked quickly out into the grand hallway and down toward the great hall. Giuletta appeared in the hallway, scrambling after her like a crippled insect.

"My lady!" She reached out a hand.

The Countess Alessandra Contarini turned and stared at the servant who dared to touch her.

Giuletta withdrew the hand as if burned. "My lady—don't go in there. Whatever they speak of does not concern us."

She added, in a whisper, "It is not safe."

The Countess stared down at her. "Leave me. Return to your duties, Giuletta."

The cook nodded, hunched back rising above her shoulders.

"As my lady wishes."

Alessandra came to the large wooden doors of the great hall and stopped. The doors were pulled shut, casting that part of the grand hallway into shadow and half-light. She stepped back into darkness and stared at the closed doors, her bosom rising and falling with anticipation, and dread.

The elaborately carved doors had been in the Contarini family for hundreds of years. The upper panels depicted blessed souls entering Paradise among angels and trumpets. The lower panels showed in graphic detail the torments of the damned, all raging fires and howling demons.

Between the two doors, barely visible, gleamed a thin shaft of light where they had not been pulled quite shut.

Carefully, she stepped up and put one eye to the narrow crack, blinking as she peered into the great hall. The remaining guests sat at the far end of the table, gathered close to her husband's chair. One of the guests, like her husband, was a member of the mighty *Signoria,* the Doge's private council. Another was a powerful merchant, with ten new galleys being built for him at the Arsenal. Another was a Papal Emissary from Rome. The fat one with the hooded eyes was a retainer from the Duke of Milan. All their eyes were fixed on the bearded man standing near the table, like a witness at an inquisition.

The silent guest. Marcangelo.

She stifled a gasp. Her hand rose to touch the gold crucifix that hung between her breasts.

The Papal Emissary began to speak, and the other guests shifted their attention from Marcangelo to the man with thin, arthritic fingers and shifting eyes.

"Rome has little interest," he said, "in who rules Venice. So long as the new Doge remembers his obedience to the Vatican."

"The Vatican," said the tall, hawk-nosed member of the *Signoria,* "rules Rome, but not Venice."

"The Vatican," replied the Papal Emissary, smiling, "rules all Christendom, as Our Holy Father Julius taught you Venetians to your everlasting cost."

"Damn Pope Julius for a scoundrel and a traitor to Venice!" cried the merchant, slamming his fist down on the table. "Thank God and Saint Mark he is now dead, and in Hell where he belongs!"

"Enough!" commanded Ludovico Contarini, and the merchant fell silent. "We are honored to have Rome's support in this our undertaking," Contarini said to the Papal Emissary, then turned to the retainer from Milan. "But do we have Milan's support as well?"

The fat retainer blinked his hooded eyes. "Milan, like Rome, is indifferent to the present Doge, provided the new one respects Milan's interests."

Contarini nodded. "Then we have your word Milan will not take the assassination of the Doge as an excuse to attack Venice?"

A smile came over the fat retainer's face.

"We will wait and see," he said, "if you are able to effect your assassination"—glancing scornfully at Marcangelo—"with such an *assassino* in your pay."

"Do you insult my hired murderer?" Contarini asked slowly. "Or myself?"

"There's truth to what the Milanese lapdog says," the merchant grumbled. "This hired murderer of yours is nothing but a common cutthroat. A killer of whores and tavern wenches. How do we know he has the *colleoni* to kill a Doge?"

"And even if he succeeds," the hawk-nosed member of the

Signoria put in, "how do we know the plan itself will succeed? And that you will in truth become the new Doge?"

"Trust me," Contarini assured him. "It will succeed."

The hawk-nosed man said, "Our Most Serene Republic is very difficult to overthrow. Remember the fate of Marin Falier."

The men grew silent at the name of the Doge who had led a rebellion against the Republic more than two hundred years ago.

"He was beheaded for his crimes," the merchant said, his voice dropping low, almost to a whisper. *"Decapitati pro criminibus."*

"We play a dangerous game," said the retainer from Milan, "with death the penalty for each of us—if we are discovered."

"Or," added the *Signoria* member, "if we fail."

"This meeting has lasted long enough," the merchant announced, rising to his feet and glancing nervously around the room. "Who knows what servant might be listening at the closed doors, even now as we speak?"

Alessandra drew back in horror, heart pounding. She heard chairs sliding back from the banquet table, sheathed swords clanking. She looked about for someplace to hide. Even with her husband's powerful protection, it would be death to be found outside the doors to the great hall when they opened.

The sound of men's voices drew nearer to the double doors.

Close to despair, she saw it. A small room, little more than a nook in the wall with a narrow door. Hundreds of years ago, when the Contarinis' wealth had surpassed even the abundance of today, the room had been a servant's chamber. Now it was a storage closet, dark, crowded, most likely full of rats and spiders. She did not hesitate, but squeezed herself in among the foul-smelling rags, moldy mops, broken buckets.

Just then the carved double doors to the great hall swung open, and the conspirators came out into the grand hallway.

They drew their cloaks about them, hurrying across the

open marble foyer and down the outside steps to where their gondolas bobbed silently at striped mooring poles. Inside the grand hallway, Count Ludovico Contarini put a hand on the shoulder of his hired murderer, Marcangelo, and drew him close enough so that they could speak in whispers.

Whispers that could be heard in the narrow closet only a few steps away from them, where Alessandra tried to steady her breathing and ignore the scrabble of clawed feet in the darkness.

"My doubts of you increase, *assassino,*" Contarini hissed, his voice deep and powerful, even in a whisper.

"You too think I lack the *colleoni* to kill a Doge?" Marcangelo asked. "You shall see, my lord, when the time comes."

"I do not doubt your taste for blood," Contarini said. "You spill too much of that. I cannot deliver you from the Lords of the Night time and again. One day they will keep you in the Doge's dungeons, and kill you there."

"I do what I must," said the murderer.

"What *he* would have you do. The Dark Sorcerer."

Il stregóne morello.

Inside her darkened closet, Alessandra shuddered.

"A demon in human form," Contarini whispered. "He will be caught one day, and he will burn alive, tied to Saint Mark's Column. And you will burn with him. I do not want you in his service any longer. From this day forward you serve me, and no one else."

"I—" Marcangelo hesitated. "I am bound to him. His magic is deep and dark. What he wills, I must do."

"Leave him to me," Contarini whispered. "My power is greater than that of any senile sorcerer."

"But I am bound—"

"Go," Contarini ordered him, "quickly. Before some servant—"

"There she is!"

Alessandra drew back in the darkness of her narrow closet. Clawed feet scrabbled everywhere around her. Something crawled over her shoe. But the terror of the darkness was nothing to the terror of being discovered.

And indeed, she had been discovered.

"There she is!"

Connie came back with a jolt, gasping for breath.

An older Thai woman pointed a finger at her. "Right there!"

Connie ran a hand through her damp hair.

"Ever'thing okay," the older woman called to someone outside the rest-room door. "We find her now."

Connie got up slowly from the pink couch. She started to lift the hem of her long gown. But she wasn't wearing one— just the same silk dress she had come to the restaurant in.

She felt the fear dig its claws into her.

Outside the rest room, Ken came up to her.

"Connie, where *were* you?"

She swallowed. "In there. I think I passed out, sort of."

"Bullshit! We turned this place upside down."

"I was right there. Asleep. Or something."

Ken stared at her.

The other diners looked in their direction, the whole restaurant suddenly, unnaturally quiet.

22

Diagnosis

When Becky Martinez returned from her break, she saw a light flashing on the reception-room switchboard.

She got it. "Good afternoon. Dr. Stallman's office."

"Becky?" Ken's voice, but he sounded strange. "I've been calling for fifteen minutes. No one answers. Where's Connie?"

"I don't know, Ken. I just got back from my break."

"Is she there?"

"She was when I left. Let me go see if she's in her office. Hold on, Ken, okay?"

She pressed the hold button, wondering what was wrong

with Ken. He sounded jumpy, frightened, not at all like himself.

She glanced at the appointment book on the reception desk. All appointments for today had been canceled. Was Connie sick? But Ken thought she was still here. Frowning, Becky closed the appointment book. This wasn't like Connie.

The door to her office was open. Becky walked in, expecting to find a note on the desk, a message on the answering machine.

Instead she found Connie, standing near her desk, reading a book. It was the way she read under a deadline, trying to find a piece of information quickly, in too much of a hurry to sit down and read like a normal person.

Becky cleared her throat. "Connie?"

She looked up and cried out, snapping the book shut.

"Didn't mean to scare you. That must be some book."

Becky leaned forward to read the title.

Life Before Birth: The Case for Reincarnation.

"That's the one by Richmond Bregler, isn't it?" Becky asked. "The guy who lost his license and got kicked out of the AMA?"

"I was just checking a reference. What do you want?"

"Ken's holding for you."

"Tell him I'm with a patient."

Becky started to say something, then stopped.

Connie looked at her. "Please?"

"Sure, Connie. But what if he says it's an emergency?"

"Tell him the patient's an emergency, and I'll call back."

Becky nodded. "Sure." She glanced at a thick book lying in the middle of the desk, *The Story of Venice.* "A whole book on Venice, California?"

"Venice, Italy."

"Oh, I see. You ever been there?"

"No." She hesitated. "No, I've never been to Venice."

"I'll go tell Ken you'll call him," Becky said.

Connie leaned back against her desk and let out a long sigh.

Then she opened the Bregler book again, found her place, and went on reading. She shifted back and forth as she read, moving with the urgency of fear. After a while, she sat down at her desk, but continued to shift impatiently in the chair.

At one point she muttered to herself, "No wonder they threw this jerk out of the AMA! He doesn't know *any*thing!"

"But that's not why they threw him out."

She gave a startled cry and tried to close the book, knocking it off the edge of her desk instead, where it fell into the wastebasket with a heavy thud.

"Good place for it," Jake Mauder said, taking off his suit jacket and hanging it over the back of a chair.

Connie bent down to dig the book out of the wastebasket. "Ever hear of knocking first, Jake?"

"The door was open."

"I forgot to close it."

"If it's a bad time, I'll leave." He started to get up.

"Jake, no! It's just—You surprised me. That's all."

He glanced at the other book on her desk, *The Story of Venice*.

"Richmond Bregler and Venetian history," he said. "Such a combination. I take it the dreams have come back?"

She nodded, and felt the fear cut deep inside her.

"Is that what you were doing at that restaurant last night?" he asked quietly. "Dreaming of Venice again?"

"Who told you about that? Mr. Bigmouth Stallman? Ken called and told you everything, didn't he?"

"Maybe not everything. He told me a lot."

"He's an overprotective mother hen. He ought to mind his own goddamn business."

"Not in this case." Jake took off his black-frame glasses and squinted through the lenses, then, glasses still off, stared at Connie with his myopic brown eyes. "In this case, definitely not."

"You weren't there. You don't know what happened."

"So tell me what happened. But before you start, do you have a Kleenex or some— Ah, thank you. I don't know whether it's the smog or the sea gulls," Jake said, polishing his lenses, "but my glasses seem to be collecting more crap than usual this time of year. *Nu,* what happened at this restaurant?"

After she finished, she looked to him for a response, but Jake just sat there, and continued to polish his glasses.

"Ken says you disappeared from the ladies' room for a while. Fifteen, twenty minutes. Something like that." Jake put his glasses back on. "Where were you?"

"Venice."

"In other words, you have no memory of leaving the rest room? Or returning to it later?"

She shook her head.

Jake folded his hands in his lap.

"Well?" she asked.

He took out a small piece of paper and handed it to her. She could barely make out Jake's illegible scrawl. But she recognized the prescription for a new benzodiazepine derivative, the same one she had prescribed for Jennie Hodges.

"What the hell is this supposed to be?"

"You shouldn't prescribe for yourself. And I knew you'd never ask. So I took the liberty."

"Amnesia," she said slowly. "You think I'm suffering from amnesic fugue states, don't you? The kind where I wander around and do things, and then don't remember them?"

"There are several possibilities. That's one."

She balled up the paper and threw it into the wastebasket.

"I don't need any tranquilizers, thank you. I am not suffering from amnesia. I remember everything!"

Jake looked at her. "Do you remember where you were when you disappeared from the ladies' room in a busy restaurant with several people looking for you?"

"I told you already."

"Slipping off into another dimension? Time-traveling back to sixteenth-century Venice? With Richmond Bregler as your personal tour guide, no doubt."

"Okay, Mr. Confirmed Skeptic. Where do *you* think I was?"

"I'm at something of a disadvantage, because you haven't told me all the details of these dreams."

"Hallucinations," she corrected him. "If we're talking amnesic fugue states, we might as well get our terms straight."

"Whatever. Based on what you've told me so far, two things. One, you're in a restaurant and you start having hallucinations of a banquet. Obvious visual-stimuli associations. Food, dining. Restaurant, banquet. Simple connection. Right?"

She nodded, unconvinced, but she saw his point.

"Two, you have a hallucination of yourself hiding in a closet, where the rat crawls over your shoe. I don't know where you went when you left the rest room. But wherever it was, you hid. You didn't want to be found. Maybe somewhere back in the kitchen. Maybe under an empty table."

"They looked for me, Jake."

"Sure. Hot Thai's like any Hollywood restaurant, dark and crowded. Easy to miss someone, even if she's sitting at a table. And remember the people looking for you are distracted, upset."

"Okay, Jake. But why am I fugueing out like this? What deep-seated anxiety am I trying to repress?"

"It may not be all psychological, Connie. I think you should make arrangements to have a cranial MR scan, as soon as possible."

Her mouth dropped open. "Fuck you," she said.

She fell silent, overcome by the cold, paralyzing fear of a tumor lodged somewhere in her brain, like a malignant alien entity, making her see crazy things and do crazy things, and not remember them. Tears came to her eyes.

Jake reached out across the desk and took her hand.

"Everybody gets sick, Connie. Even doctors. But we don't take it so good. We're used to being objective about sickness, seeing it as something that happens to other people. Because that's how we have to see it to do our job." He squeezed her hand. "When it happens to us, we want to look at it like doctors still. But we can't. Because then we become patients."

She pulled her hand away. "There's nothing wrong with me. I'm not getting an MR scan."

He sat back in his chair. "That's up to you. But I think you're acting foolish not to consider all the possibilities. And I'm sorry to say, this is one of them."

She wiped at a tear.

"Also," Jake continued, "until we know more about this, you shouldn't be driving anywhere. It's not smart. Or safe."

"What am I supposed to do? Walk home?"

"You and Ken can work something out, I'm sure."

"This is bullshit, Jake."

"No, it's not, Connie. You trying to tell me you haven't already had flashes while driving somewhere?"

She remembered the nightmare on Laurel Canyon.

"No. Of course not."

"Avoid a life of crime, *bubeleh*. You're a lousy liar."

"Stop it," she said. *"Stop telling me what to do!"*

"Everything I'm telling you, I'd tell my own daughter. But don't you see? You *are* my daughter. The only one I'll ever have."

Moisture glinted in Jake's eyes, behind the thick lenses.

"Goddamn it, Connie. Don't drive."

23
Alibi

The drive from Hollywood to Long Beach was bumper-to-bumper most of the way, a slow-moving stream of idling metal, overheating in the late-afternoon sun.

Connie drove it with the air-conditioning on high, classical music on the sound system, sitting straight but relaxed, both hands on the wheel, senses sharpened by several amphetamine capsules she had taken before leaving the office.

So far, so good. No flashbacks, no hallucinations.

No momentary glimpses of Venice, of her life in Venice.

No coming attractions for the main show.

Near the end of the southbound 710, several miles before the downtown Long Beach exits, the traffic began to thin out. Connie reacted like any Southern California driver to sudden freeway open space. She floored the accelerator and let the engine run flat out, flexing her shoulders to work out the traffic-jam tension.

She glanced over at the Port of Long Beach, lying grayish blue and smogbound in the distance.

Sails of great galleys flying in the sun, oars dipping rhythmically into the turquoise blue waters of the Venetian lagoon. Ships from all over the Mediterranean, bearing their cargoes to Venice. Past the Lido and into the lagoon. Toward the golden domes and towers of the imperial city itself. Ships of all kinds. Galleys. Galleons. Barges. Gondolas.

The loud blast of an air horn from a tractor-trailer rig behind her punched through the Acura's air-conditioning. Connie snapped back into present reality, heart thumping inside her chest. She looked at the speedometer. Forty-five mph, and dropping. She accelerated to a safer speed, then pulled over into the next lane, away from the tractor-trailer rig. She must have eased up on the gas when she flashed back. She must—

Goddamn it, Connie. Don't drive.

The sun hung low in the sky as she rang the doorbell to Alice MacKendrick's apartment in Long Beach. She heard a fumbling at the door. It opened slowly to reveal Alice, trying to manage the wheelchair and door at the same time, all with her one good hand.

"Mom, where's Emilia?"

"Asleep," Alice said, the word slurred by her paralyzed facial muscles and the cigarette dangling from her lip.

"I didn't know she got paid to sleep on the job."

"Everybody has to take a nap once in a while, Connie. Even overachievers like you."

Connie tugged at the screen door, but it stayed shut.

Alice reached up and undid the lock with a shaking hand.

"Emilia went to one of those Mexican coming-of-age parties for her fifteen-year-old niece," Alice said, wheeling into the center of the living room. *"Quinceañera,* that's what they call it."

"Who took care of you while she was at the whatever?"

"Her older cousin, Guadalupe. Usual arrangement." Alice stubbed out her cigarette in the ashtray attached to the wheelchair arm. "So, what brings you down here?"

"Nothing special." She leaned over and kissed her mother on her slack left cheek. "I just felt like coming to see you."

Alice nodded. "Glad you could make it, of course. But weren't you just here a few days ago for your weekly visit?"

Connie stepped back from the wheelchair. "What kind of attitude is that? You act like you're not even glad to see me!"

"You know you're always welcome, et cetera." Alice took out a cigarette. "Come on, Connie. We both live in the real world."

Alice squinted at her through fresh cigarette smoke.

"You want to tell me what's going on? Or do I have to guess?"

Connie looked at her mother, fearful that she didn't have to guess, because somehow she already knew. It had always been like that, ever since she was a little girl. Sometimes she had tried to hide things from her mother, the way children will, but it never worked. Her mother always seemed to know what she was thinking, as if she could read her mind, or see inside her head, somehow.

"Mom, has Ken called here?"

"I can't see what that has to do with the price of butter in Japan. Or my question. But yes, he called." Alice took the cigarette from her mouth. "He's worried about you."

"He's always worried." Connie sat down on Alice's worn sofa. "He'll never stop worrying until he can put me in an old mayonnaise jar with holes punched in the lid. Like the ones I used to collect bugs in when I was a kid?"

"Traffic's usually pretty shitty on the 710 this time of day. Glad to see it hasn't ruined your disposition."

"What did he tell you? Everything?"

"He told me what happened at the restaurant." Alice flicked her cigarette at the ashtray. "He said he left messages for you all day today, but you never called back."

"I was busy. Jake came by to see me."

"Ken talked with Jake, too."

"I know. Ken called him this morning."

"He called him again later, before he called me."

Connie's head snapped up.

"Ken said he had to pry it out of Jake with a crowbar."

Connie sat on the sofa, lips pursed in silent fury.

Alice looked at her. "I don't know if Jake's right about this. But if he is, you sound like one sick kid."

"I am *not* sick! *I wish you'd quit saying that!*"

She stopped. "Sorry. Didn't mean to wake up Emilia."

"A nuclear blast wouldn't wake Emilia right now."

Connie looked down at the threadbare living-room carpet. When she looked up, she saw an uncommon sight.

Alice MacKendrick in tears.

"Mom—" Connie's own face began to tremble as she rushed over to the wheelchair, knelt down beside it, and took hold of her mother's one good hand, empty now, the cigarette crushed and smoldering in the ashtray. "Mom! What's wrong?"

Alice shook her head. "You can take it when you get sick. You expect that. What you don't expect is for your little girl to get sick. That's hard." She swallowed. "That's damn hard."

"Mom, please." Connie clutched her mother's right hand. "Please, don't." She bent her head forward, tears falling into her mother's lap.

She raised her head suddenly, and kissed Alice on the lips.

"Look." She got to her feet, wiping at the tears. "You've got to believe me, okay? I'm not sick. I'm not crazy, either. I do have a problem." She nodded, as if to acknowledge that. "A big problem. I don't know what to do about it just yet. But I can handle it." She took a deep breath. "I *will* handle it, okay?"

Alice looked up, the tears drying on her own face.

"It's about Tod Jarrow, isn't it?"

Connie stared at her.

"That's why you came down here today. To go and see him at Terminal Island."

They stared at each other, without speaking.

They were still staring when Emilia came in from the bedroom and said hello to Connie, and asked if she'd had a nice drive down from Hollywood.

24
Prisoner

Night had fallen by the time she left for Terminal Island.

The streets of downtown Long Beach were dark with despair. She could feel it in the stares of the poorly dressed people who watched her from sidewalks as she drove by. Signal lights changed colors at empty intersections.

She drove through the haunted industrial landscape of Terminal Island, past warehouses and storage yards, past massive metal containers stacked atop one another like used bricks, past lots filled with Japanese imports, past loading cranes looming vast and silent overhead—everything lit dull orange by the eerie glow of sodium-vapor lamps, pale fires burning against a dark night sky.

A tall concrete tower topped with bulletproof glass and machine-gun mounts marked the entrance to the prison itself. Heavy diesel fumes filtered through the damp, dead-fish smell of the sea.

An assistant from the warden's office, along with the guards Sokowski and Wexler, led her down a long corridor to the room selected for the interview. The room looked like the back end of a prison laundry. Large and small pipes crisscrossed overhead. The air felt damp and hot. Tod Jarrow sat in a chair backed up against a thick metal pole that extended from concrete floor to ceiling. They had cuffed his hands behind him, around the pole, and lashed both legs to the chair with reinforced packing tape.

Sokowski brought a chair for her, so she could sit facing him.

She looked at Jarrow, and took a deep breath. Sokowski and Wexler had used him badly. New deep cuts disfigured his face. The stitches holding them together made the old LAPD work look like Beverly Hills plastic surgery. His lips were split and puffed. His nose looked as if it had been broken, then awkwardly reset. One eye had swelled almost shut, the sclera blood red.

But the other eye, the good one, looked straight at her, still mesmerizing in its dark, intense power.

She felt the strong physical pull toward him again—felt it even as she tried to fight it, tried to deny that she was feeling it. She saw their naked bodies again, writhing on a gold-damasked quilt, felt him inside her, heard the rain against the windowpanes, falling down from a gray Venetian sky.

He stared at her with his one dark eye.

She thought he might keep staring at her like that, saying nothing, until the fifteen minutes they had allotted her were up.

Or maybe he might start calling her a whore, like he did the last time, in English or Italian, or both.

Instead he asked, "What the fuck are you doing here?"

"I came to talk with you."

"Get fucked." He sounded more tired than angry, the words slurred by his damaged lips. "Every time I talk to you, they beat the shit out of me. Go shrink somebody else's head."

She leaned in close to him, lowering her voice until she knew that he could hear her but Sokowski and Wexler could not.

"I'm not here on business. I came to talk, about Venice."

The one good eye stared at her, but he said nothing.

"What's going on, Tod? What do you have to do with it?"

"You know the answer to that."

"No, I don't. If I did, I wouldn't be here."

His puffed lip curled in an ugly sneer. "So go ask a shrink."

"God*damn* you," she said, her voice still low. "I'm not

here as a doctor! I'm here to find out what's *happening* to me."

"You think I give a shit about that?"

"I think you're part of it. I don't know how, exactly. All I know is that from the moment I first saw you, I've been having flashbacks to Venice. Venice hundreds of years ago. They're like dreams. But they're more than that. They're like episodes from another *life.*" The word lodged in her throat.

"Whatever it is, you're part of it, Tod. In some way I can't explain or even understand, your life is part of mine."

Wed to one eternity, Contessa.

She drew back from him, hearing it again, inside her head, the language she knew and did not know, hearing it as clearly as if he had spoken the words, but he had not.

She shook her head. "Who are you? What do you want with me?"

He sat there with his puffed lips closed.

You know me, yes, Contessa, you know me well.

"Who *are* you?" she asked him.

He looked down.

She reached out, grabbed his battered face, turning it up slowly until his one dark eye met hers.

"Who the hell are you?"

" 'Scuse me, Doc," Sokowski called out across the room. "Hands to yourself, please. No groping the inmate."

She dropped her hand from Jarrow's face.

"I'm the same person, then and now, Contessa, just like you."

The shock of hearing him actually say that word aloud hit her like a jolt of electricity. She saw the bearded face of her Venetian lover as he looked up at her with blood on his hands and begged for mercy, calling upon her by that title, his voice ringing out over the great open square of the Piazza San Marco.

The room they sat in seemed to grow smaller, closing in on her, pipes dropping down slowly from the ceiling, steam hissing through them.

"Marcangelo," she whispered.

"Alessandra," he said, the name catching in his throat.

They stared at each other, until she looked away, putting a hand to her head.

"It can't be real," she murmured. "Psychotic dream states—"

"It's no dream," Jarrow said, his voice taking on a sudden urgency. "It's real. You know that."

She looked up at him. "What *is* it?"

"Other lives. Other places."

"But it's happening *now!*" She leaned in close to him, so close their noses almost touched. "All of a sudden, without any warning, I'm in Venice. But Venice hundreds of—"

"Four hundred years ago."

She shook her head. "Impossible. Whatever happened that long ago—It's over. It can't keep happening again and again, like something on tape."

"It happens at the same time, then and now," Jarrow said tonelessly, as if reciting a speech from memory. "Planes of existence coincide. The cycles revolve in constant opposition, but the time lines themselves converge at the same point."

"Don't talk bullshit to me!"

He looked at her. "I'm not sure just how it works. The two time lines run on different cycles, then and now. But they overlap, somehow. They interact. When the lines approach the point of final intersection, one life eclipses the other."

She leaned close to him, feeling his breath on her face.

"Why did you drag me into all this?" she asked.

"I didn't. You were always part of it, Connie. Always."

"It didn't start until the first time I saw you!"

"In this life, Contessa. Only in this life."

She thought of the images from the other life—their bodies moving together, their lives intertwined, their destinies one.

"Let me out of it." She spoke calmly, her voice low. "I'll— I'll do what I can to help you."

Jarrow smiled at her, the stitches twisting his battered face.

"You think I care what happens to me? Here?"

"I want out of this!"

"I don't control what happens."

"Who does?"

"Nobody," he said. "It just happens."

But the sound of fear in his voice said otherwise.

"Who controls what happens, Tod?"

He started to say something, then stopped, and fell silent.

"Who controls it, Tod?"

He whispered something, barely audible.

"*Il stregóne morello.*"

But she heard it clearly, and she understood. The Dark Sorcerer. Yellow cat's eyes, glowing like witches' fire in the fog. Skin like wrinkled parchment. Hands like spider's claws. The Dark Man.

"Who is he?" she demanded. "What's his real name?"

Tod Jarrow turned pale beneath his bruises.

"Go back and ask him yourself."

"Why won't you tell me his real name? Are you afraid?"

"Fuck you, Contessa. I'm not afraid of anything, okay?"

"But you're afraid of him."

He lowered his head.

"Look, Tod, I just want out of this. I'll pay him whatever he wants. I'll do whatever—"

Jarrow's head snapped up, dark eyes tight with fear.

"Don't ever say that!" he whispered. "I *know* what he demands in payment. You don't."

A chill came over her then, despite the closeness of the room, and the steam hissing through the pipes overhead.

"Whatever it takes, Tod, I want out. You got me into this. You can help get me out of it."

He looked at her, as if seeing her clearly for the first time.

"You're wrong about that, Connie. You've been wrong from the start. Remember our first meeting? In this life? When you said that whatever I did was all my own choice? And I got—" He hesitated. "I got pissed off about it."

She remembered, and remembering, drew back from him.

He smiled his stitch-twisting smile. "Don't worry. I can't get loose. And even if I could, I wouldn't hurt you. I'm over that now. Only reason I got so angry that day was hearing you sit there and say I had a choice about what happened to me. When you knew better." His voice took a sudden lurch. *"When I knew that you knew better!"*

She saw the fury in his dark eyes.

"Now you really do know, Connie. Because now you're part of it, in this life and the other, just like I am. I don't have any control over what happens. But *neither do you.*"

She sat there, trying to absorb the horror of it, trying to understand that her own life was out of her control, in the hands of another, a nameless creature from the darkness—of the darkness.

She felt the sexual pull toward Tod Jarrow again, dark and dangerous, the way it had been that night at the Hollywood Station. But now their passion together, in this life and the other, lay beneath the shadow of the ancient, nameless one, the Dark Sorcerer.

Her heart beat faster. Her mouth went dry.

She reached for his face, fully conscious of her movements, but unable to stop them.

"Hey!" Sokowski called out. "Hands off!"

She moved in close to him, crushing her lips against his. His tongue thrust inside her mouth. She sought it avidly, holding nothing back. Jarrow's body arched against the metal pole to which it was bound.

The guards rushed toward them, yelling as they ran.

Rough hands pulled her back from him, tearing them apart. She stood up awkwardly, knocking over the chair, hearing it crash down onto the concrete floor behind her. And with that, her sense of ordinary reality returned. The strong sexual attraction dissipated suddenly, and she saw Tod Jarrow as dangerous once more, a dark-eyed psychotic in the service of darkness. A murderer who had kissed her again.

But this time she had sought and welcomed his murderer's kiss.

The guards shouted things at her, but she did not hear them. She and Jarrow seemed to be the only two people in the room just then—the only two people in this world, or any other.

"I won't come here to see you again," she said, her voice trembling. "They'll put you away. Everything will stop then."

He smiled at her, blood trickling from his split lips.

"It doesn't matter what you do. Everything will stay the same. Then as now, Contessa. Always. Wed to one eternity."

"I never want to see you again!"

He looked at her with his dark eye and bloody lips.

"I'll get out of here, Connie, and I'll come for you."

His words followed her down the long corridor and outside to her car, where the dark night sky that hung over Terminal Island and its prison seemed nothing more than an extension of Tod Jarrow's dark eyes, and the greater darkness that awaited them both, in Venice, four hundred years ago.

III

*dreams
of
sorcery*

25
Deep Water

Connie stood back from the crowd as Stevie leaned over and prepared to blow out the candles on her birthday cake.

"Mom!" Stevie turned to her. "Watch! Okay?"

"I'm watching," Connie said, forcing a smile.

Stevie took a huge breath and blew. Four candles sputtered out at first hit. Two more went as she reached the end of her air supply. She took a cheater's breath, and blasted the last one.

Amid the applause and congratulations, Stevie ran over to where Connie stood, the child's happiness humming like a generator as waves crashed onto the shore behind them.

I should be happy too, Connie thought, *because this is what happiness is all about.*

But for her it was a borrowed happiness, fragile as the first light of dawn. Knowing this, she leaned down and hugged Stevie close to her, trying to hold on to happiness the way it used to be.

Before Tod Jarrow came into her life.

And the Dark Sorcerer.

"You havin' a good time, Mom?"

"The best. How about you?"

Stevie nodded. "I love my party. I love the band and I love my cake and I love my presents. Especially my new BMX with the pink seat and the pink handlebars. And my new *Videogirl!* game. But I gotta go see Majesto now, okay?"

Connie watched as Stevie ran back to where Majesto the

Clown, a.k.a. Margo Klein of West L.A., was busy making balloons and pigeons appear from out of nowhere, to the delight of the children crowding in around him on the bright sand beach—so different from the darkness and despair of Terminal Island.

I'll get out of here, Connie, and I'll come for you.

She looked out to sea, beyond Majesto and his balloons, out to the breakers foaming white in the distance, gulls screaming and circling in the blue sky.

"Connie?" Ken asked, coming up to her. "You okay?"

She turned toward him, slowly. "Sure."

"You don't act like you're into the party spirit."

"I'm fine, Ken."

"Pickin' on her again, big brudder?"

A hard-edged blond with neon-colored sunglasses raised her shades and winked at him.

"Just having a private conversation, Lisa."

"Ain't nothin' private from family, bro'." Lisa licked icing off a bright pink fingernail, then asked Connie, "So, how are you?"

"I'm fine, Lisa. Thanks."

"Don't bullshit me, Connie. You know what I'm talking about. How *are* you? Really?"

"Lisa—" Ken began.

She turned to him. "If you don't want to hear this, big brudder, just go over there and stick your fingers in your ears." Then back to Connie. "I mean, there is no reason to go all remote and mysterious about it. A brain tumor's not always a death sentence, you know. Like, half of them aren't even malignant if you get to them in time."

"She *is* a medical doctor, Lisa," Ken said.

"So? Doctors always make the worst patients. Right, Connie?"

"That's what they say."

"Anyway." Lisa took a bite of cake and ice cream. "The thing is to get it looked at right away. Have you done that, Connie?"

"Not yet."

"See?" Lisa pointed her plastic spoon at Ken. "You've got to have it looked at, Connie. They have this new test thing. RMI—"

"MRI," Connie corrected her. "Magnetic Resonance Imaging."

Lisa nodded. "Whatever. It's where they can take pictures practically right inside your brain. A whole lot more effective than a CAT scan. Then, if there's something there, they just cut it out. Snip. Snip." Lisa traced the motions with her plastic spoon. "Then they sew you back up and send you home, good as new. Nothing to it."

Connie knew there was a lot more to it, but kept quiet.

"I mean, I hope it's *not* a brain tumor," Lisa said, finishing off the last of her cake and ice cream. "But if it is, I'll come up and take care of the kids while you're in the hospital, okay?"

"Thanks, Lisa," Connie said. "But what about Corey? You can't just walk away from your husband like that."

"Him?" Lisa shrugged. "Pack him off to Cozumel to go skin diving for two weeks. He'll love it."

Lisa Tate did not inspire affection in many people.

But Connie hugged her.

"You're a good sister, Lisa."

"Hey, look, us girls got to stick together. I mean, men are such assholes." She glanced at Ken. "Sorry if your ears are burning, big brudder. But you guys all know it's true."

Lisa squinted at Majesto and his show, and at two Mylar helium balloons that had escaped from their young owners and now drifted high across an azure California sky.

"There ought to be a law against those goddamn things," Lisa said. "They get tangled up in some high wires, then somebody's power goes down. Probably mine." She turned back to Connie. "So when are you guys moving down here to South Orange County?"

"We like it in the Hollywood Hills," Connie said.

"Why don't you talk her into it, Kenneth?"

He shrugged. "You know us men. Just a bunch of ass-holes."

"Touchy, touchy. Anyway, you guys think about it." She poked Connie in the arm. "And *you* go do what has to be done, girl. And let me know what they find out. Promise?"

Connie said she would and Lisa went off to break up a fight between two of her young nephews over one of Majesto's balloons.

"Lisa ought to have some kids of her own," Ken said, watching his sister walk away. "Then she wouldn't have the time or energy to run other people's lives."

"She means well. Besides, if you don't want to listen to her, just say so. Lisa's feelings don't get hurt very easily."

"That, by God, is true. Are you going to take her advice?"

"No."

"Why not?"

"Because I don't have a brain tumor."

"Jake thinks it's a possibility."

"Jake's not a neurosurgeon, any more than I am."

"He cares about you."

"Of course he does. But do I act like I'm sick? Do I have trouble with my balance, my peripheral vision? Do I smell rotten fruit, burning leaves? Do I suffer from double vision?"

Double lives, Contessa, not double vision.

She ignored that, and put a hand on his shoulder.

"I know what the signs are, Ken. I don't have them. If I did I wouldn't ignore them. But I don't, okay?"

"What happened at the restaurant the other night?"

"Nerves. Overwork. I need to relax. That's all."

"You'll relax when we take our voyage to Catalina. I've had the *Constance Merriam* all checked out. She's ready to go."

In the distance, Majesto's show was drawing to a close, with colored smoke, hoops, scarves, balloons, dozens of bal-loons—

The crowd gathered around the mountebank on his raised platform near the Grand Canal. In the background the golden domes of the Piazza San Marco shimmered above the turquoise blue waters of the lagoon. The mountebank, a Jew from the Ghetto, in tall peaked hat and colored robes, was selling vials of the famous Venetian *teriaca*—a mixture of molasses, frankincense, gum arabic, amber, opium, fennel, pepper, cinnamon, rose petals, and Cretan wine, guaranteed as an antidote to any poison, a cure for all ills. The mountebank held up the vial, proclaiming its virtues to one and all. The crowd moved in for a closer look. Farther down the Grand Canal, groups of singers, dancers, actors, and acrobats performed.

Connie blinked, took a breath, blinked again, and looked away.

Ken turned her around, so that she faced him.

"Look at me. What's wrong with you?"

Her cheeks were flushed, her eyes slightly out of focus.

"Nothing. I was—thinking about Mom. That's all."

"We need to get you off in that boat. The sooner the better."

"I don't know if I can spare the time right now."

"We talked about that already."

"I do have a job, Ken, and patients to take care of."

"Like Tod Jarrow?"

Sea gulls screamed overhead. Waves broke in the distance.

"I saw him again yesterday, but that was the last interview. The very last one. There's nothing more to learn about him."

Not in this life, anyway.

"What did you do at Terminal Island?"

"Come on, Ken." She sounded tired. "Let's not go through it right now. Not at Stevie's birthday party, okay?"

"What did you do at Terminal Island last night? What was important enough to risk your life that way, driving on the freeway, in your condition?"

"What do you think I did? Screw him in his cell?"

He caught her by the right forearm, the same one Tod Jarrow had grabbed that first day at the Hollywood Station.

"Don't do this to me, Connie. *Don't shut me out like this!*"

She looked away, and saw that all his family members were standing frozen in place, staring at them.

Later, when the kids went swimming, Ken kept Trent on the beach while Connie took Stevie a short distance into the surf.

Stevie gritted her teeth. "Mom, it's *cold!*"

"Come on! It's not so bad once you get all the way in."

Connie waded farther out, until she stood waist-deep. "See?"

A wave came in then, a big one, slapping them both hard. Connie kept her footing. But Stevie got knocked over backward.

She sat up, blowing salt water out her nose.

"Mom!" she yelled. "I don't *like* this!"

"Then go back on the beach and dry off."

"You comin' out, too?"

"In a minute."

Connie turned away from the shore. Then, timing it carefully, she dove under the next incoming wave, shooting through the frothy water like a seal, and surfacing on the other side.

She shook her head and shivered. The water was cold, the way it always is off Southern California, even in high summer. She took a deep breath and struck out from shore, using a slow, easy stroke. She stopped just past the surf line and started to tread water, bobbing up and down with the deep swells of the open ocean. She was not far from shore. She could see Ken and Trent sitting on the beach, and Stevie off by herself, huddled under a bright orange blanket, looking cold and unhappy. The waves rolled in toward the shore, breaking pale greenish gray against the sand. But out at this distance, where the surfers and strong swimmers were, the water had turned a deep, mysterious indigo blue.

She saw the ship then.

Oars flashed bright in the sunlight. A red and gold standard unfurled from the mast. Sails billowed full before the wind, hull and prow carved and inlaid with gold, glittering in the sunlight. The prow itself was an elaborate work of art, scrolled and gilded like the throne of a pope or an emperor. Red-robed members of the *Signoria* stood forward on the upper deck, black-robed senators of the Great Council behind them.

An imperial Venetian galley under full sail and oar. But not just any galley. *Bucintoro*. State vessel of the Doge himself.

Connie felt the pull toward the deck of that golden ship, like a magnet drawing her home—all its pomp and glory a symbol of the mighty Republic to which it, and she, belonged.

A wave broke over her and she went under, swallowing water.

She struggled to the surface, coughing and gasping for air.

She had stopped treading water while staring at the golden ship, frozen by its beauty and majesty. She looked around now for the *Bucintoro*. A two-masted sloop cut fast across the distant horizon. Closer in, a large cruiser with twin engines floated high in the water, a party of some kind in progress on its upper deck.

But the golden ship was gone.

She turned and looked back at the shore, much farther away now. She could just make out Ken standing in the water, waving his arms above his head to catch her attention, alarmed at seeing her so far from shore.

It would have been easy for her to raise a hand and wave back, to let him know that she was okay. But she did not.

Nothing was clear, not just then. She knew only that she was floating now between two worlds—the familiar world of the party on the beach, the strange world of the vanished golden galley.

Floating. Far from shore, in deep water, alone.

26
Horror Show

That night, exhausted, she fell asleep and dreamed.

She did not go back in her dreams, drifting backward down the dark river, into the dark waters of the canals of Venice.

Not at first.

She was driving fast and recklessly down the washboard roads of Terminal Island. Then she was walking, looking around. It was night, everything lit muddy orange by the sodium-vapor lights. The huge industrial machines were all in motion, no operators in sight. Giant cranes lumbered aimlessly like grazing dinosaurs. One leaned down toward her, steel jaws gaping wide. She started running, and stripping off her clothes. The more clothing she removed, the faster she ran, until she raced naked across the dark orange landscape, bare feet slapping asphalt, bare breasts jiggling with every step.

Then she was flying, soaring high above the lumbering machines and the orange lights, the fainter lights of Long Beach and the L.A. Harbor visible in the distance. She flew above the glass-topped guard tower with its machine-gun mounts, circling over it like a supersonic gull. Then she was inside the prison itself, still naked, moving down a long, dark cell-block corridor, the only light coming from inside the cells, falling in barred shadows across her naked flesh. The prisoners were all naked, many of them fully erect, some of them ejaculating at her through the bars, others reaching out to grab her, or hanging on to the bars and screaming obscenities at her, trying to squeeze their faces through the narrow openings.

Tod Jarrow was naked too, alone in his cell, face to the wall, arms raised above him. She saw his naked back and legs, the muscles large and well defined, and she felt the wetness between her own legs, the heat of her desire. She leaned against the barred cell door. It slid back soundlessly. She stepped inside the cell. The screams of the other prisoners had vanished now, the only sound a slow and steady pounding, enormously amplified, like the beating of a gigantic human heart.

He turned from the wall, huge penis erect, jutting out from his dark pubic hair like an angry red shaft. Feverish with the heat of her own desire, she bent down to take him in her mouth. He threw her back against the wall, pinning her hands above her head. Handcuffs clamped shut around her wrists. He put his hands to her breasts, pulling on her large, dark nipples until they stretched out long and hard, pointing up at him. He put his teeth to them, biting down hard. She threw her head back, mouth open, gasping for air. Her naked body jerked against the rough cement wall. He thrust into her then, filling her up with the great length and thickness of his passion, and his rage, her own wetness running down both their legs and onto the stained floor of the cell.

Sokowski and Wexler entered the cell. They were naked except for leather belts and shoulder straps. Sokowski carried a chain saw. Wexler pulled Jarrow off her, ripping him out of her. Jarrow started to ejaculate as he withdrew, and kept pulsing as Wexler dragged him backward, semen falling in stringy splotches across the cement floor. Wexler locked Jarrow's arms behind his back. Sokowski fired up the chain saw, yanking hard on the pull cord. An ear-splitting whine filled the cell. Sokowski laughed, his mouth hanging open, and drew the whirring chain-saw blade across the bars of the cell door. Metal squealed, grinding against metal. Hot blue sparks flew out across the cell like spray from an arc-welding gun. Sokowski, still laughing, turned and brought the chain saw down, chopping off Jarrow's erect penis at the root. Jarrow's mouth opened in a soundless scream. Blood burst from his groin, spattering her naked body and the cement wall behind her. Wexler laughed. Sokowski, laughing, turned toward her with the chain saw.

The cell went dark.

Darkness, then drift.

. . . d . . . r . . . i . . . f . . . t . . .

She was walking again, fully clothed now in a long maroon velvet gown with flared patterns of gold brocade, the neck cut so low her breasts almost fell out of it, the tops of her dark nipples peeking above the bodice line. She had trouble walking because of her *zoccoli,* the stiltlike high-heeled slippers worn by Venetian noblewomen. Her wooden heels clattered awkwardly over cobblestones as she walked down the dark, narrow *calle,* deserted at this hour except for rats and occasional young boys with torches, linkboys, hired to light the way for late-night revelers.

A drunken man staggered down the *calle* toward her, led by a crippled linkboy with one shoulder higher than the other. The man wore a grotesque, long-nosed mask. Masks were common enough in Venice, not only at Carnival but throughout the year. She raised a hand to feel her own mask, a small domino beneath a black veil. She stepped to one side to let the man and his linkboy pass by. He stopped instead and raised his mask. Most of his face had been eaten away by syphilis, leaving strips of raw meat, exposed bone, quivering muscle. One swollen eye bulged out at her. Lipless teeth grinned. Pieces of corroded flesh dropped off from his face as he stood there, mask raised. One piece fell onto the crippled linkboy's torch, hissing and smoking like fat in a fire. Another piece of decayed flesh plopped down between her half-naked breasts.

She screamed, and ran, hobbling down the narrow *calle* in her high-heeled *zoccoli.* Behind her she could hear the hunchbacked linkboy calling out to her.

Contessssssssaaaa—

Looking back, she saw the linkboy scuttling after her, his raised torch casting light back onto the mutilated death's-head that hovered behind him. She tripped on a broken cobblestone and fell forward, catching herself on her hands. Rats swarmed out from every corner of the dark alley. She got to her feet, hands scraped and bleeding, kicked off her *zoccoli,* and ran. A large rat slithered beneath her foot. She stepped down and crushed it like a slug. Blood and intestines squirted out on all sides, spattering her white silk stockings. She ran to the end of the *calle,* and into another.

She found herself in the Piazza San Marco at night, lit by torches and lanterns, filled with people of all kinds—rich and poor, mountebanks hawking *teriaca,* jugglers juggling, acrobats performing, beggars lifting their filthy rags to reveal running sores. Her breasts were bare now. Strange hands reached out to touch them. She moved through the gauntlet of groping hands, as she walked across the stones of the piazza without any shoes, her white silk stockings torn and soiled.

She passed by the great porphyry stone outside the Doge's Palace, where the heads of traitors to the Republic were displayed. Yellowish fluid leaked from the rotting severed heads, forming puddles on the crystal-flecked, dark purple stone. She recognized one of the severed heads as that of her husband, Count Ludovico Contarini. His gelatinous eyeballs turned down in their sockets and stared at her. His sagging mouth twisted up into a grin, sending cracks across his face. Black bile spilled from his mouth.

She was running again, up the *Scala dei Giganti,* the Giant's Staircase in the courtyard of the Doge's Palace, flanked by immense nude statues of the gods Mars and Neptune, their great stone phalluses erect and thrusting out at her. Two aged senators, gray-haired and bent-backed, stared at her soiled white stockings, then at her naked breasts, jiggling as she ran up the wide marble stairs, nipples large and aroused.

She moved through the deserted corridors of the Doge's Palace, dark except for a dim light coming from somewhere up ahead. She tore off her mask and veil, the better to see in the darkness, and moved toward the distant light. It led to an open doorway, and a narrow flight of stairs, twisting down into more darkness.

The light grew erratic as she descended the stairs, flaring up, fading back. The walls of the stairwell drew closer together. The heat increased. A sheen of perspiration glistened on her breasts. Her heart beat faster. The stairs continued downward, beneath the main floor of the Doge's Palace.

Into the dungeons.

She moved along an uneven stone corridor, trying not to step in pools of stagnant water that flooded the stone floor. Thick torches burned from tarnished brass sconces along the crooked stone walls. She came to a heavy oak door, its narrow window covered by a wrought-iron grille, too high for her to look into. Agonized screams pierced the grille, hoarse shrieks of desperation, as if the torturers were destroying the victim's soul along with his body. She raised a fist and hammered on the oak door. It made no sound. The screams from inside rose to a higher, more frenzied pitch. She pounded on the door, hammering at it until her wrist began to ache. Still, the knocking made no sound. The only sounds came from the torture victim, screams tearing through the wrought-iron grille.

The door opened, swinging back slowly, noiselessly. She stepped inside, wading through standing pools of congealing liquid.

Marcangelo lay stretched upon the rack. Blood and foam flecked his dark beard. His dark eyes bulged wide and sightless. Screams burst from his open mouth. His sweat-slick chest heaved like a bellows. One of the torturers, naked to the waist, gave another turn to the wheel on the rack, muscles standing out on his thick arms. Marcangelo's arms stretched another several inches above his head, straining in their sockets. His screams intensified. The torturer, groaning with effort, gave the wheel another turn. Marcangelo's right arm pulled loose from its socket, followed by his left. The tendons stretched taut as rubber bands, then snapped, popping loose from the bone. Marcangelo screamed, bloody slobber running down into his dark beard. Blood pulsed out from the two holes where his arms had been, spattering the stone walls and the naked flesh of the torturers.

She drew back in horror, into the sinewy, blood-soaked arms of a torturer. She twisted in his slippery grasp, turning around to see the laughing face of Sokowski, blond head running with sweat and blood. He shoved her back up against a stone wall, his hard chest pushing into her face, smothering her.

She found herself outside once again, in the piazetta, near the Doge's Palace. A large crowd shifted and surged around her. Hands grabbed at her naked breasts and long hair. Thick smoke, black and greasy, rose from the base of a tall granite pillar topped with the winged Lion of St. Mark, symbol of the city and the Republic. She made her way through the crowd, toward the pillar and the smoke, ignoring the hands that reached for her. As she drew nearer, she could see a naked man tied with heavy ropes to the base of the pillar. A pile of kindling had been packed tight around his legs and set on fire.

Marcangelo, burning alive.

His hair and beard blazed like a linkboy's torch. His face had turned black, puffed up with oozing juices. Part of his stomach fell out into the fire, along with poached intestines.

She screamed. It could not be heard above the excited cries of the crowd. She screamed again, her voice rising with the rancid smoke that curled up the sides of St. Mark's Column.

She sat up in bed, still screaming. A silk nightgown clung to her sweat-soaked body. The comfortable feather bed she sat on was rich with fine linens, silk sheets, gold-brocaded quilts. She got out of bed, trembling, and made her way in the darkness toward the locked and shuttered window. Cries of alarm sounded from the hallway outside her door.

She drew back the heavy metal bar and opened the shutters.

The moon was down, the world outside dark and forbidding.

Night covered Venice like an assassin's cloak. Distant torchlight glimmered fitfully from a lone gondola on the Grand Canal. A cold wind blew in from the open sea, chilling her damp body, lifting her unbound hair and scattering it behind her.

The door to her bedroom opened. A serving girl rushed over to her, shielding a candle with a cupped hand.

"My lady—" The girl's eyes grew wide. "We heard screams."

She turned and looked at the serving girl. "I was dreaming."

The girl shook her head in confusion. "Of what, my lady?"

She turned back to the open window.

"I was dreaming," she said, "of the sea."

27

Voyage

The *Constance Merriam* cut through offshore swells three miles out from its slip at Marina Del Rey.

The sun burned bright in a cloudless sky. Sea winds held back the smog. The channel between Santa Catalina Island and the mainland could grow rough at times, but the swells today were no worse than usual, and the boat was large enough to ride them.

But Connie hated boats, no matter how well they handled. When the *Constance Merriam* hit the open ocean with its heavy swells, she felt sick to her stomach, even though she had eaten lightly before departure, and put a Dramamine patch behind one ear. Now she sat on the bridge with Ken at the controls, Trent in her lap, Stevie leaning out over the rail, blond hair blown back, everyone wearing bright orange life jackets, the sea air crisp and invigorating.

Nothing helped. The sickness persisted, and grew worse.

Adding to it was the immensity of the ocean itself. Ken was a good and cautious skipper. The *Constance Merriam* moved along at a steady twelve knots. But still, Connie felt a terror of the sea. She held Trent close in her lap, and hung on tight to Stevie's hand, pulling her back when she leaned too far out over the rail.

"Feeling better?" Ken asked.

"A little."

"You'll get used to it."

He always said that, but it never happened.

"You didn't sleep too well last night. More bad dreams?"

She hugged Trent closer to her. "I can't remember," she lied. "I think I tossed and turned some."

She remembered how she had gone to sleep in this life, and awakened screaming in the other.

She gripped Stevie's hand.

"Mom! You're *hurting* me."

Connie relaxed her grip.

"You had me worried last night," Ken said. "You had us all worried yesterday, when you went for that long-distance swim."

"I didn't go out that far."

Stevie turned from the rail. "You did! You went *way* out!"

"Sure," Connie said.

Ken waited until Stevie had turned back to the rail before he lowered his voice. "She's right. You went out so far we even lost sight of you for a while."

She thought of the golden-prowed galley, *Bucintoro*, oars flashing in the sun, the Doge's ship of state, a vision from her other life floating serenely across the waters of the present.

Ken put a hand on her knee. "I don't like losing you."

"You won't," she said.

Not in this life, anyway.

Ken turned back to the controls and began making adjustments for a three-sailed cutter that had come up on them suddenly. He made a hard right turn, pulling around behind the sailboat rather than cutting across its bow. The *Constance Merriam* leaned sharply to one side. Connie tightened her grip on Trent and grabbed hold of the waistband to Stevie's shorts.

Ken increased the power and the *Constance Merriam* listed even farther to the right. Connie gritted her teeth.

"Sorry," he said.

"I hate it when it tips like that!"

"We don't have a choice. Sail has right-of-way over power."

"I hate to think what this would be like in a storm."

"Don't worry. I checked the Coast Guard reports. We're not supposed to hit any bad weather."

The *Constance Merriam* completed the turn, righting itself. Ken eased up on the power, and the boat settled back into its comfortable twelve knots per hour.

"Mom!" Stevie turned to her. "Can we go down to the front—"

"The *bow*," Ken corrected her.

"Can we go down and watch for dolphins, Mom? Please?"

"No. It's too rough right now."

"Mom!"

Connie looked at Ken, who said, "Of course everyone is wearing life jackets, and that's what the observation platform's down there for. I could cut back on our speed some, if that would make you—"

"Okay, okay."

No dolphins were in sight when they got down to the bow, but Stevie and Trent did not seem to mind. They just stood there, pointing out sea gulls circling overhead, staring at the waves. Connie stood next to them, holding tight to each child, feeling the dip and lurch of every wave.

Ken cut back the engines.

That seemed to attract dolphins—one dolphin, at first, several yards off the bow, leaping in and out of the water in graceful arches, keeping up with the *Constance Merriam*.

Stevie's eyes grew wide. "Mom! *Look!"*

"Fissie!" Trent squealed.

Another dolphin joined the first. Then a third appeared on the scene. All three jumped in and out of the waves together with perfect timing, like a synchronized chorus line.

"Mom," Stevie said, "isn't that totally *awesome?"*

Connie nodded, her seasickness forgotten.

"Fissie," Trent said again, in a hushed voice, not quite sure whether this was real or just something on television.

Connie put her arm around Stevie and kept her grip on Trent, the three of them watching the three dolphins, and vice versa, in some kind of mysterious natural counterpoint.

"Dad!" Stevie yelled up at him. "Stop the boat!"

Ken waved back to her and cut the engines to idle. As he came forward, making his way down to the bow, he carried a small cooler.

"What's that?" Connie asked.

Ken opened the lid, and nodded at the dolphins as they frolicked in the water. "It's for them."

The stench of close-packed baitfish wafted up from the cooler.

"Oh, gross!" Stevie held her nose. "El stinkorama!"

"Well, they seem to like it." Ken took up a handful of the smelly fish. "They might even do some tricks for it."

He leaned over the rail and held out the fish. The dolphins caught the scent right away. The nearest one came over, shimmied up out of the water and stayed there, beaked mouth open wide, squawking noisily. Ken tossed the fish. The dolphin caught it expertly, did a back flip, and disappeared beneath the waves.

"Wow!" Stevie said. "Just like at Sea World!"

She scooped up a dripping handful of fish and rushed over to the rail. All three dolphins had got into the act by now, dancing on their tails and squawking like seals.

Most of Stevie's baitfish fell into the water. But the dolphins retrieved them as expertly underwater as they had in the air. Soon the whole Stallman family was feeding the dolphins. When one leaped at Trent, the little boy burst into tears. But those tears turned quickly to squeals of delight.

After the baitfish ran out, the dolphins stayed for a while, cutting capers in the rolling waves. Then they took off in search of new prospects, sleek dorsal fins slicing the water like knives.

The Stallmans stood at the guardrail, watching them go, arms around each other, hands stinking of baitfish as they pointed to the dolphins swimming in the distance.

Connie realized that she had never been happier in her life, out in the middle of the great ocean, bound to her family by a love that seemed more real than the water or the sky, or the round horizon of the earth itself.

She let go of Venice, Tod Jarrow, and last night's dreams. For a while.

The *Constance Merriam* cruised on automatic pilot, following a computer-set course, as it approached the halfway point between Catalina and the mainland. Everyone was out on deck. Stevie sat drinking a strawberry soda and counting whitecaps. Ken had a line over the side, pretending to fish. Trent was asleep in a chair. Connie lay stretched out in the sun, working on her tan.

"Mom!" Stevie turned to her. "There's too many white-caps!"

The *Constance Merriam* gave a sudden lurch just then, as a big swell rolled underneath it. Trent rocked from side to side in his chair, but kept on sleeping. Strawberry soda sloshed from the can, spotting Stevie's T-shirt and shorts.

"Bummer!" she cried.

Connie sat up and squinted at the whitecaps in the distance.

"It *is* getting rougher out there," she said to Ken.

"Wind's picking up a little. That's all."

It continued to pick up. Ken began to secure all loose items on deck. Connie put the life jackets back on herself and Stevie, and Trent, who had awakened by now, hungry and cranky.

She went over to where Ken was lashing down some deck chairs.

"Think we should turn back?" she shouted above the wind.

He shook his head, not looking up. "We're past the point of no return now. Safer to go on into Catalina."

The whitecaps increased in size and number. Storm clouds

piled up on the horizon. The *Constance Merriam*'s rolling and pitching grew worse. Stevie and Trent sat outside, playing with the new *Videogirl!* Ken was back at his controls on the bridge.

Connie stood on the deck, looking out at the dark, angry sea.

And the golden ship.

Bucintoro, oars driving it forward across the calm waters of the lagoon, red and gold standard flying from its mast.

The change was far more dramatic this time than it had been the day before. The whitecapped waves of the stormy Pacific gave way to the placid, turquoise blue waters of the Venetian lagoon. The two images alternated, like pictures on a screen. First one, then the other. Flashing back and forth.

Connie's hands gripped the guardrail until her knuckles turned white. But she did not look away. She stared into the wind.

The golden galley was lined with dignitaries on its upper and lower decks. Red-robed members of the *Signoria* stood forward, her husband among them, Count Ludovico Contarini, followed by the dark-robed senators of the *Maggior Consiglio,* the Great Council. On a golden throne sat the Doge himself, Pasquale Cicogna, rebuilder of the Rialto Bridge, ruler of the Venetian Empire.

Ken Stallman sat at his controls on the bridge, trying to ride out the rough water as smoothly as possible.

"Dad!"

He saw Stevie clambering up the stairs to the bridge.

"Where's your brother?" he asked.

"Dad, Mom's gone!" Stevie's nose was running. Tears welled in her eyes. "I asked her somethin', and she didn't answer, so I turned around to look for her—And she was *gone!"*

Stevie started to cry.

Ken put his hands on his daughter's trembling shoulders.

"Honey, even if she fell overboard, she's got a life jacket—"

Stevie shook her head, tears running down her face.

"I *looked*, Dad! I looked in the water. She's not *there!*"

Ken nodded, and cut the engines to idle, his mind moving forward on several tracks at once. "Your brother okay?"

Stevie nodded. "He's down there."

Ken got to his feet, scanning the dark, whitecapped waters for any sign of an orange life jacket. "You go down and take care of him. He's your responsibility now."

"But—"

"No buts. Get down there and do your job."

Ken checked all the interior cabin space, looking under bunks, inside closets, opening head doors—anyplace she might be.

Outside, he checked the sides of the hull, the stern. He made his way to the bow, gripping the guardrail, looking at every exposed surface of the pitching, tossing boat.

He found nothing. As he clung to the bow rail, a large wave broke over the top, soaking him, threatening to sweep him off the boat and out into the angry, rolling sea.

He moved back to the main deck, looking out over the dark water, panic starting to set in now.

"Connie!" he yelled into the roaring wind. *"Connie!"*

Back on the bridge, he radioed an emergency report to the Coast Guard. After it was acknowledged, he hung up the microphone and looked out again at the turbulent waves beneath him, searching hard for a flicker of orange in the distance, staring at the emptiness until his eyes ached.

But he knew the truth now.

She was gone.

28
Lost

She left her seasickness far behind.

Oars slapped the water, driving the *Bucintoro* forward, giving it an awkward, rocking motion. But she suffered no queasiness, not even on the cramped rear deck, wedged back in among the few other noblewomen permitted aboard the Doge's ship of state on so solemn an occasion. She was a Venetian, born and bred to the water. The motion of a ship was to her no more than the movement of a carriage to some landlocked countess from Florence or Milan.

Ascension Day. *Festa della Sensa.*

Sposalizio del Mar. The Marriage of the Sea.

It was perhaps the most important ceremony in a city famous for its love of pomp and splendor. It celebrated Venice's centuries-old dominion over the Adriatic and the entire Mediterranean. Even now, after the Spanish had followed the Portuguese lead around the Cape of Good Hope and established a new sea route to the Indies and far Cathay, even now Venice ruled the spice trade of the East, and would do so always. She was a city built upon the sea, secure forever in her watery domain, unless the sea itself should rise up to take her back.

The *Bucintoro's* way was strewn with flowers. Thousands of cut blossoms lay floating on the waters of the lagoon. The Countess Alessandra Contarini saw their brilliant colors spread out like a rainbow carpet before the Doge's golden ship.

But she saw this through a long black veil, reaching almost to her feet, like those worn by the other noblewomen crowded to the back of the rear deck along with her. They stood off in a tight group by themselves, away from the dignitaries, isolated as women, cut off by their black robes and veils. All Venice's citizens took part in the general celebration of Ascension Day. But to be aboard the *Bucintoro* itself was a rare honor for any woman, and those present knew it. They stood as honored wives of *Signoria* and Great Council members, part of a grand and solemn ceremony.

Among themselves, they spoke of children and servants, as women will. But these were powerful women, married to powerful men. Their talk turned, as it often did, to politics.

"Such a holy man," said the Countess Antenori, in a voice low enough not to be overheard. "But Venice is hard on holy men."

Countess Laura Antenori, a tall woman with a long face and yellow teeth, came from one of the oldest families in Venice.

"He is Doge by God's election," whispered the Countess Maria Frascati. "Once when he was attending Mass at Corfu, the breath of the Holy Spirit blew the Host out of the hands of the priest and into the outstretched hands of Pasquale Cicogna. This happened years before he was elected Doge. But it showed that even then the Hand of God was upon him."

"Holy Spirit indeed," replied the Countess Antenori. "More likely an altar boy's fart."

"Blasphemy!" gasped Countess Frascati.

Countess Antenori smiled beneath her black veil, revealing long yellow teeth. "If Pasquale Cicogna is God's elect, then God is a poor judge of men."

Countess Frascati ignored this new outrage. "There have been other signs as well," she said. "Seven years ago, when the former Doge, Nicolò da Ponte, fell asleep at a reception in the Senate, his crown dropped off his head and rolled across the floor, until it stopped at the feet of Pasquale Cicogna." Countess Frascati lifted her chin. "Is that not a sign from God?"

"Yes," Countess Antenori said, "a sign that Nicolò da Ponte was a senile, stroke-ridden fool. Venice is well rid of him."

Countess Alessandra Contarini tensed her shoulders, aware that the subject of this bitter argument, Pasquale Cicogna, a mild-mannered man with a distracted aristocratic bearing, sat not far away on his shipboard throne, wearing his golden doge's robes and crown. She wished the two women would lower their voices, especially Countess Antenori. It made her uncomfortable to hear the Doge attacked like that within earshot of the man himself, and on Ascension Day, of all days.

It also reminded her of the plot against the Doge's life, set in motion by her own husband.

As if in response to some kind of telepathy, Count Ludovico Contarini, looming large in his red robe, turned his great silver-maned head back toward the rear deck where his wife stood among the women. She knew he could not see her face at that distance beneath her black veil, but she trembled all the same as she felt his dark predator's eyes pierce the veil, and look inside her soul.

Can he know that I listened at the doors of the dining hall that night? she asked herself. *God help me if he knows!*

"Furthermore," continued Countess Antenori, her voice low, "Pasquale Cicogna is mean and miserly. At his coronation, when he was carried around the Piazza, did he follow tradition and scatter gold *ducati* to the crowd? No. He threw cheap silver coins at them, worth no more than five *soldi* each!"

"He is frugal," Countess Frascati said. "There is nothing wrong with frugality."

Alessandra Contarini smiled despite her fears. Countess Frascati was notorious for her own stinginess.

"Wait and see," Countess Antenori said, her voice lowered almost to a whisper. "One day, if he is not very careful, and very lucky, someone will cut his miser's throat."

A blast of trumpets sounded across the water. Hundreds of boats of every description—galleys, gondolas, barges—followed the *Bucintoro* in its stately procession to the open sea. Among them was a boat carrying musicians and two large antiphonal choirs. They sang and played a motet by the great Giovanni Gabrieli, a setting of the Fifty-first Psalm.

Asperges me byssopo, et mundabor.

Lavabis me, et super nivem dealbabor.

Alessandra heard the familiar Latin lines echoing out over the water, sung by the great double choirs in glorious antiphony.

Purge me with hyssop, and I shall be clean.

Wash me, and I shall be whiter than snow.

A prayer for redemption and forgiveness, a washing away of crimes and evil. She heard the music and the voices raised in song, and shuddered.

"It is not so easy as you might think to kill a Doge," whispered Countess Frascati, her words cutting through the trumpets and the singing voices.

"Only a fool does it with his own hands," Countess Antenori said. "A man of power and prudence hires an *assassino.*"

"And then loses his head to the porphyry stone," Countess Frascati replied, "or burns alive at St. Mark's Column, because the *assassino* breaks under the tortures of the Ten, and confesses all."

Alessandra saw the dungeons from her dream—Marcangelo stretched out on the rack, his arms torn loose from their sockets.

She raised a hand to her black veil.

"Are you ill, my dear?" asked Countess Antenori. "It wouldn't do to be ill, not on Ascension Day."

"Not," added Countess Frascati, "aboard the *Bucintoro.*"

"I was overcome," Alessandra said, "by the music."

"Hmmm." Countess Antenori turned her veiled face toward the boat with the musicians and the double choirs, as if noticing them for the first time. "Pretty, if you like that sort of thing."

"It's not so easy to hire an *assassino* who won't break under torture," Countess Frascati said, getting back to the point.

Countess Antenori shrugged. "Like everything else, it's a matter of money. Pay him enough gold *ducati,* and your *assassino* will keep his mouth shut."

"Laura, my dear—" Here Countess Frascati's voice dropped so low as to be almost inaudible. "You forget the power of the Ten. Their spies are everywhere."

"I don't forget them. Nor do I overrate them. The members of the Council of Ten are very powerful and efficient men." Countess Antenori's own husband was a member of Venice's dreaded secret council. "But they are still men, not gods. They cannot be everywhere, at all times. They cannot see into the heart of every Venetian, no matter what the common people think."

"All the Ten would have to do," Countess Frascati said, "is get to your *assassino.*"

"In that case, Maria dear, you betray the *assassino* before he betrays you." Countess Antenori smiled beneath her black veil. "Use him to do the job. Then, once the work is finished, throw him away, like a damaged tool."

Countess Frascati sighed, conceding the point.

"Obviously, Laura, you've given this some thought. But I still believe it would be hard to find someone bold enough for the job, no matter how much you paid him."

Countess Veronica Bragadin spoke up then in her high, childlike voice. "Some *assassini* are very brave. And some, they say, are wonderful lovers."

The other three veiled faces turned in her direction.

Veronica Bragadin was almost as young as she sounded, not yet out of her teens. But she already had a reputation for taking lovers, male and female, from all parts of Venice, including the monasteries and the convents.

"Who in her right mind," asked Countess Frascati, "would want to go to bed with a hired murderer?"

Alessandra felt her face flush and was thankful for the veil.

"Just think of the danger!"

Veronica Bragadin laughed softly behind her black veil. "But think also of the excitement!"

Alessandra felt herself becoming aroused, beneath her black veil and gown, aboard the *Bucintoro,* amid the solemn splendor of Ascension Day. She thought of how the danger in Marcangelo's life had drawn her to him in the first place, and drew her still—despite the risk, and the certain knowledge of what would happen if her husband, Count Ludovico Contarini, should ever come to learn of her infidelity.

You will catch your death, my lady.

"Go to bed with a common murderer!" Countess Frascati sniffed. "Might as well go to bed with a—sorcerer."

"There are those who have done it," Countess Antenori said.

Veronica Bragadin leaned forward. "Really?"

"Can you imagine?" Countess Frascati shuddered with elegant disgust. "Going to bed with some wrinkled old man who might turn himself into a horned demon halfway through?"

"There are sorcerers in this city," Countess Antenori said quietly, "who have far greater power."

"Personal friends of yours, Laura?" Countess Frascati asked.

Countess Antenori spoke softly behind her black veil. "You have heard of the one they call *il stregóne morello?*"

Alessandra saw the withered skin, the yellow cat's eyes, calling to herself and Marcangelo, drawing them into a dark river of death—realms of blood, fire, pain, the destruction of Venice, and the world they knew.

"The Dark Sorcerer?" Countess Frascati mused over it. "What a strange thing to call yourself! What's his real name, Laura?"

"That *is* his name."

"Nonsense! An actor, no doubt. Worse yet, a Jew! A common mountebank from the Ghetto."

"He is no mountebank. There is power to his potions."

"Really? You must tell us, Laura dear, *every*thing you know about this sinister magician."

"Yes, Laura!" Veronica Bragadin said. "Tell us, please!"

Alessandra Contarini, obsessed by her own fears, the dreams of blood and death, the things she had heard at the doors of the dining hall, became interested now in the conversation of the other women. She looked away from the ships and flowers floating on the water, the choirs and musicians, all the marvels of Ascension Day, and turned her attention to Countess Laura Antenori, inscrutable behind her black veil.

"They say," she began slowly, "that he gave the Duchess of Milan the fearful potion she used to kill her last lover."

"Oh!" Countess Frascati whispered, shocked. "Her last lover was the son of one of the Pope's mistresses. The poison made him go mad and cut off his, you know, and then disembowel himself. This Dark Sorcerer of yours *is* a bad one, isn't he, Laura?"

"They say," Countess Antenori continued, "that he first came to Venice along with the first outbreak of the Black Death, the Great Plague. In fact, they say he was on board the trading ship from the Black Sea that first brought the Plague to Venice, and then to the whole world."

The other women fell silent against a background of trumpets and double choirs. They all knew that the Plague had first come to Venice almost two hundred and fifty years ago.

"How—" Countess Frascati stopped, and cleared her throat. "How old did you say this sorcerer of yours was, Laura?"

"No one knows. But some call him the Ancient One."

Cold fear came over Alessandra Contarini. The trumpets sounded harsh and discordant to her ears now. The double choirs sang with demonic voices.

"They say that all the rats of all the *calli* in the city are his servants and spies. They say he can command the winds and the waves." Countess Antenori's voice took on a strange, uncertain edge. "They say that he knows the great secrets of life and death, and the far greater secret of transmigration. The passage of the soul from body to body, rebirth after rebirth, throughout the ages, until the end of time, and beyond."

Wed to one eternity.

Alessandra's face was damp beneath her black veil.

Countess Frascati sniffed in disbelief. "Surely you don't believe that transmigration nonsense, Laura? Where you come back after your death as a monkey or a cat, or a common field mouse? It's not only blasphemous. It's impossible!"

"For a sorcerer with such powers, nothing is impossible."

"Where did he learn his magic, Laura? In a tavern in Genoa?"

"They say that in the beginning he came from somewhere east of Samarkand, in the great mountains that bar the way to far Cathay. They say also that he was not born of woman, but took his present form in an empty tomb, when the first men walked the earth."

Countess Antenori smiled strangely. "But these are stories. Who knows the truth about sorcerers?"

The *Bucintoro* came to a lurching stop at the edge of the open sea. Hundreds of boats stretched out behind it in a long line extending back to the Grand Canal. They carried minor nobility and clergy, prosperous merchants, naval officers, sailors, artisans, fishermen, gondoliers. Crowds filled the Piazza San Marco and lined the banks of the Grand Canal. The bells of all the churches in the city rang out over the water. Sea birds circled overhead, their cries drowned out by the ringing of the bells.

The Doge stepped forward, resplendent in his golden robes and crown. In his hand he bore a golden ring, a symbol of the one given to Doge Sebastiano Ziani by Pope Alexander III in 1177 to honor Venice's dominion over the sea. The present Doge, Pasquale Cicogna, lifted his hand and raised the golden ring above the turquoise blue waters of the Adriatic. Then he spoke the traditional words, over four hundred years old, that celebrated the Marriage of the Sea.

"Ti sposiamo, O mare, in segno di nostro vero e perpetuo dominio."

"We wed thee, O Sea, as a sign of our true and perpetual dominion."

Cannons thundered on the mainland. Church bells rang out across the city and the sea. Trumpets sounded and double choirs sang. Cheers rose from the crowds massed in the piazza and along the Grand Canal, and from all the observers in all the boats stretched out behind the *Bucintoro*.

The distinguished members aboard the Doge's golden ship added their own voices to the cheering crowds.

All except the Countess Alessandra Contarini.

The magnificent ceremony of the Marriage of the Sea held a different meaning for her today.

Wed to one eternity.

Marcangelo. The Dark Sorcerer. Her own husband, Ludovico Contarini, plotting against the life of the Doge.

Darkness. Corruption. Sorcery. Death.

A wind off the water rustled the golden robes of the Doge. The wind blew harder. The church bells continued to ring. The cannons thundered. The crowds cheered. But the wind built suddenly to a terrifying intensity, threatening to blow away the *Bucintoro,* the attendant boats, the crowds in the piazza, the Imperial City of Venice itself.

The wind ripped the veil from Alessandra's face. Her black gown billowed about her. She reached for something to hold on to. But the wind picked her up off the deck of the *Bucintoro* and hurled her headfirst into the water. She clawed her way to the surface, gasping for air, the long black gown dragging her under.

The water changed. Turquoise blue to dark gray.

She looked around for the *Bucintoro,* for one of the attendant boats, for someone to pull her out before she was dragged under again and drowned. But no boats were in sight—only rolling dark waves, and a dark sky filled with storm clouds and rain.

A huge wave crashed into her, pulling her under.

The whole world became water.

"Daddy! There she *is!"*

Ken Stallman sat bent over the radio on the bridge and did not hear his daughter. The Coast Guard rescue cutter he was in communication with lay hard by the *Constance Merriam.* But because of the storm's fierceness, its driving wind and rain, they were forced to rely on the radio.

"—will not endanger the lives of my crew," crackled the voice of the Coast Guard captain, "or the lives of your passengers any longer by letting you continue the search under these conditions. Do you read me, *Constance Merriam?* Over."

"Dad!"

"I read you. Over." Tense with anger and despair, Ken turned to his daughter. "What is it?" he snapped at her.

"I *saw* her! I saw *Mom!*"

She pointed to the storm-tossed waters.

He saw it then.

A flash of bright orange, riding the crest of a dark wave.

"—to turn and head for shore at once," the Coast Guard captain continued, "or we will be forced to board you without permission and place you under arrest. Do you read me? Over."

On the bridge of the Coast Guard rescue cutter, static and howling wind were the only sounds that came back on the receiver.

"Do you read me?" the Coast Guard captain repeated. "Over."

But the bridge of the *Constance Merriam* was empty now.

If the storm had been less fierce, Ken might have tried to bring the boat closer to Connie. But he could not steer with any accuracy in waves of this size, and if she got sucked under the hull, she could be caught in one of the twin propellers. She was close enough now to be brought on board.

Ken leaned over the starboard rail, waving to Connie and calling out to her, a life ring under his arm with a line attached to the main deck. Stevie stood beside him, hanging on to the rail with both hands.

Ken turned to her. "Go keep an eye on your brother."

"He's strapped in his car seat. I want to *watch!*"

"Stevie!"

"I was the one who *saw* her, Dad!"

"All right. But don't let go. I'm not doing this twice."

He looked out at the dark rolling waves, and panicked when he saw no sign of Connie. A huge wave shifted, and he spotted her again, a fleck of bright orange bobbing in the wave's deep trough.

He climbed up onto the railing, steadying himself with one hand, holding the life ring in the other. Then he jumped.

The cold slammed into him like a fist. Powerful waves hurled him about, sweeping him away from the *Constance Merriam,* and away from where he had last seen Connie. He struck out blindly, battling the angry swells. Sea spray blew into his face. Rain hammered down from above. The storm winds howled like demonic things, hunting for prey. All the world turned dark, brutal, desolate. His arms began to ache. His lungs burned.

He saw her then, through the blinding spray and rain—one wave over, perched on the edge now, then slipping down into the trough, and disappearing beneath the dark water. Fear gave him strength. He drove through the water, kicking and pulling.

"Connie!" he cried, his voice drowned out by the howling fury of the storm. *"Connie!"*

A large wave rose and fell before him.

He saw no sign of the orange life jacket.

Then, several yards in front of him, a hand emerged.

"Connie!" he shouted, and threw her the life ring.

She reached for it, and managed to hook one arm around it.

"Ken!" she cried, her mouth full of water.

He grabbed hold of her, squeezing too hard in his joy at finding her alive. He saw her wince, and released the pressure.

"Just hang on to this thing, and don't let go, okay?"

She nodded, eyes dazed, uncertain.

"I thought we lost you," he said. "I—"

The line attached to the life ring grew taut and jerked forward, dragging Connie through the water. Ken had to grab onto the ring himself to keep from being left behind. As they moved forward, Ken looked up through the wind and the driving rain, and saw men from the Coast Guard rescue cutter on board the *Constance Merriam,* hauling in the lifeline hand-over-hand, drawing them back to the boat, and out of the storm.

29
Recovery Room

Ken sat in the room with her, waiting for the test results.

It was not bad, as hospital rooms went—private, pleasant, with a window that looked out on green trees and blue sky.

The tests were unnecessary, but she hadn't argued with Ken about that. She knew why he wanted her to have them done.

"This room must be costing us a fortune," she said to him.

"Just pretend it's a luxury hotel suite."

He tried to smile, but it came out wrong.

She picked up his hand and squeezed it gently.

"Come on, Ken. I don't have a brain tumor."

He nodded. "Whatever it is, we'll know soon enough. We won't be in the dark anymore."

She thought of darkness, and remembered Venice.

Darkness. Corruption. Sorcery. Death.

She would have to tell him the truth. Soon. But not now, not here. Not in an antiseptically lifeless hospital room.

She needed to scratch an itch on the lobe of her right ear, but Ken would not let go of her right hand. She reached over awkwardly with her left and scratched the earlobe.

Ken looked down at her hand. "I don't think I've ever really told you what you mean to me. Maybe this isn't—"

He looked up at her, his eyes watering.

"Ken." She reached out and hugged him, her own eyes tearing up. "Please. I promise you, my life is *not* in danger, okay?"

Not this life, anyway.

"It's nice to see everyone so close."

They broke apart at the intrusion of a new voice.

It belonged to a stunning Japanese-American woman who looked more like a fashion model than a doctor, even with her white hospital coat, clipboard, and computer printouts. Despite her youthful appearance, Cheryl Kitahara, at forty-two, was seven years older than Connie, and one of the top neurosurgeons in Los Angeles. When Connie realized that Ken was determined to put her through a full brain-tumor checkup, she decided that she might as well get the best, and had asked for Cheryl Kitahara.

"This shouldn't take too long," Dr. Kitahara said, paging through her printout sheets.

Ken went to get her a chair.

"No, thank you, Mr. Stallman. That won't be necessary." She said to Connie, "I could probably just let you look at these yourself, Dr. Stallman. But since this isn't your specialty, it might save time if I explain."

She glanced up from her printouts and saw Ken sitting on the hospital bed again, holding Connie's hand, with the look of someone bracing himself for the worst.

Dr. Kitahara smiled at him. "First, the good news. The MR scans show no abnormal growths or formations of any kind."

Ken stared at her. "What about the brain tumor?"

"There *is* no brain tumor, Mr. Stallman."

He shook his head. "I'm sorry. I don't understand."

"Your wife does not have a brain tumor."

The muscles in his face went slack. He took a deep breath and let it out slowly.

"I don't mean to sound stupid," he said at last. "But are you sure about that?"

"Absolutely." Dr. Kitahara paused, a cautious professional. "No one can predict possible future complications, of course. But for right now, there is no indication of a brain tumor."

Connie had expected this. But she frowned, remembering something Dr. Kitahara had said earlier.

"What about the bad news?" she asked.

Dr. Kitahara glanced at her. "Did I say anything about that?"

"You said, 'First, the good news.' That usually means there's some bad news to follow."

"Sorry. I didn't mean to give that impression. It's not what you'd call bad news, exactly." Dr. Kitahara tilted her head so that sunlight from the window caught her shining black hair.

"More like strange news." She held up one of the computer printouts and handed it to Connie. "This is an EEG we ran on you."

"I don't remember that."

"You were asleep. Fast asleep. Probably exhausted from the sailing accident. I didn't want to wake you to do the MR scans just then. But I did want a preliminary report. So I ran an EEG."

Connie studied the printout, as Dr. Kitahara continued. "The brain-wave patterns are atypical, to say the least. The delta rhythms, the ones you're looking at now, are pretty much what we'd expect from someone in the deep-sleep stage. But this—"

She handed Connie another printout.

"Those are the alpha rhythms, the so-called dream rhythms. Notice the extreme variations. And I'm just showing you part of the readout. At one point the EEG recording monitor went crazy. We thought we might have to stop the test."

Connie looked up from the printout, then handed it back to her without saying anything.

"What do they mean?" Ken asked.

Dr. Kitahara turned to him. "We're not sure, Mr. Stallman. We don't know very much about alpha rhythms, or the dreaming state of human consciousness."

She turned back to Connie. "But we do know this much. The dreams that you've been experiencing lately, the ones that have alarmed both you and your husband, must be very strange dreams to produce"—touching the printouts—"something like this."

After discussing follow-up procedures for a few more minutes, Dr. Kitahara shook hands with both of them, then left the room.

Ken came over and sat down on the bed again, his shoulders slumping forward. He looked tired, and worried.

Connie reached up and hugged him.

"I won't say I told you so," she said, "but I did."

When she pulled away, he still had the same worried look on his face, more intense now than ever.

"What's wrong?" she asked. "Don't you believe her?"

"Why did you jump overboard? And risk your life, and ours?"

She knew it was coming. She was surprised he hadn't asked her sooner. But this was not the right time or place.

"Can't it wait, Ken?" She gave him her best smile.

"No, it can't! I've waited long enough. I want an answer!"

The violence in his voice shocked her.

He thinks I tried to commit suicide, in front of the kids.

She cleared her throat. "I didn't do that, Ken."

"Didn't do what? Risk all our lives?" He leaned closer to her. "You bet you did! We could have all gone down in that storm, while we stayed out there looking for you. The god-damn Coast Guard cutter could have gone down! Not to mention the effect it had on Stevie. But I won't even get into that!"

She waited until he was finished before she said, "I didn't mean that. What I meant is, I didn't jump overboard."

His eyes turned colder than she had ever seen them before.

"We've always been honest with each other, Connie. Don't start playing games now. I've got everything in the world that matters to me on the line right now. *Everything!*"

"I'm not playing games."

She braced herself for an explosion of some kind.

He leaned back and looked at her. "If you didn't jump overboard, then where the hell were you for almost two hours?"

She winced. "Was it *that* long?"

"It seemed even longer. It seemed like the rest of my life."

She felt her heart ache for the pain she had caused him, and Stevie, and even Trent, too young to know what was going on, but old enough to sense the panic around him.

She blinked back her tears. "Are you sure you want to know?"

"If it's the truth, yes."

She swallowed. "It's the truth." She looked up at the door to the hospital room. "Would you mind closing that?"

The room seemed smaller with the door closed, like a confessional.

He sat down on the bed again. "Just promise me one thing."

"What?"

"That you won't say you fell asleep. Or can't remember. Or some other bullshit like that."

She shook her head. "I said it's the truth. It is."

She told him. Everything.

During the whole story, he listened without asking questions.

After she finished, she waited for him to speak.

He got to his feet, slowly, as if he had bones made of glass, and too quick a movement, too sudden a turn, might shatter them to fine powder. He looked out the window, his back to her.

He stood there for a long time, staring out the window.

She wanted to shout something at him—anything to break the endless, hanging silence.

When he finally turned around, she saw the tears on his face.

"Ken!" Her own voice broke. "What's wrong?"

He shook his head, unable to answer that question.

"You've got to go see Jake," was all he could say.

30
Black Magic

The screaming echoed down the dark cell-block corridor.

Frenzied. Mind-shattering. Insane.

Sokowski ran toward the sound, clutching a two-foot rubber-tipped club in his right hand, muttering to himself.

"Goddamn motherfuckin' asshole son of a *bitch!*"

He stopped to flick on a bank of low lights, glancing at his watch as he hit the switch. 11:47 P.M. Thirteen minutes to the end of his shift, and Jarrow throws a screaming fit.

He ran the rest of the way down the long, low-lighted corridor toward Jarrow's cell, ignoring the screams and yells coming now from the other cells he passed along the way.

He would make Jarrow pay for this, on his hands and knees.

He stopped in front of Jarrow's cell, large-muscled chest heaving, sweat streaking his face, murder in his pale gray eyes.

"Wexler!" he screamed. "Where the fuck are you?"

No answer came from the other end of the corridor.

Sokowski turned to the cell, and looked at the mess inside.

Jarrow lay doubled up on the cement floor, both arms crossed over his stomach, eyes shut, mouth open, screaming as if his guts were being ripped out, one yard at a time. Dethrush lay on his belly, face to the floor, a lazy stream of blood and puke oozing out his mouth, making abstract patterns on the cement.

Sokowski glanced down the corridor once more, looking for Wexler. He should wait for him, according to the rules. But fuck the rules. Old Deth looked dead already, and Jarrow was getting his guts chewed up by something—bad drugs, probably.

Sokowski activated the lock. The cell door slid back. He stepped inside, the door closing automatically behind him. He raised the club, tensing his muscles, just in case this turned out to be some kind of trap. But nothing changed. Dethrush remained flat on his face, blood and puke drizzling out his mouth. Jarrow twisted around on the floor, screaming.

Sokowski went over to Dethrush and kicked him in the ribs. Dethrush gave out a low groan, the kind a dying horse might make. More blood and puke bubbled up from his mouth. Old Deth was still alive after all. But he wouldn't be any trouble tonight, except for the medics at the infirmary.

Sokowski moved over to Jarrow. "Keep it down, motherfucker."

Jarrow screamed even louder, writhing on the floor.

Sokowski kicked him in the kidneys. "I said keep it *down!*"

Jarrow's screams turned to whimpering moans. He gritted his teeth and twisted on the cement floor, drawing his arms and legs up into a ball.

"Over on your face, just like your old buddy Deth. *That's* right, motherfucker. Now, hands behind your back."

Jarrow gasped, struggling to speak.

Sokowski bent down close to him. "I'm gonna cuff you now, motherfucker. You try and pull any shit on me, I'm shovin' *this*"—raising the rubber-tipped club—"all the way up your fuckin' asshole. Sideways. Got it?"

Jarrow moaned something that might have been a yes.

After he locked the handcuffs in place, Sokowski squatted down beside him and asked, "Whatsa matter? Tummy ache?"

"Stoma—" Jarrow gasped. *"Hurts!"*

Sokowski sighed. "Guess we gotta drag you down to the infirmary and get the shit pumped outta your guts." He glanced at Dethrush. "And see if they can get old Deth fixed up, too."

Sokowski suddenly felt tired, and bored. The excitement was all gone now. He had wanted to bust Jarrow up into a thousand pieces tonight. He had been looking forward to it. But there was no point to that now. Whatever was doing a number on his gut had hold of him good and tight. Maybe it was even gut cancer. Fuck it. Let the medics figure it out.

"What's up, Luke?"

Wexler stood outside the cell, fat face red and sweaty.

"Quit standin' there like it's some kinda fuckin' zoo. Get your fat butt inside here and help."

"Fuck you. I came quick as I could."

"Yeah, I bet you came quick. Then it took you a whole twenty minutes to find enough Kleenex to wipe off your drippin' pud."

"Fuck you," Wexler wheezed, stepping inside the cell and going over to Dethrush.

At the infirmary, the male nurse on graveyard shift prepared a hypodermic needle and syringe for sedating Tod Jarrow, who kept moaning softly now, like a sick child.

The doctor examining Dethrush looked up suddenly and said to the nurse, "Wilson, we have a problem here."

Wilson glanced at him.

"Someone has torn this man's tongue out of his head."

Wilson stood there, holding the hypodermic needle, Wexler and Sokowski several steps away, no sound in the room except for the buzzing of fluorescent lights and Jarrow's soft, childlike moans.

Sokowski was the first to figure it out. But by the time he had the pieces in place, it was already too late.

Jarrow sat up on the examining table and grabbed the syringe from Wilson's hand. Sokowski moved in on him, club raised for striking, just as Jarrow had expected. Instead of trying to run or duck, Jarrow threw himself straight at Sokowski, ramming the hypodermic needle into the guard's crotch. Sokowski screamed and bent over, grabbing at his crotch. Wexler came in behind him, swinging blindly. Jarrow turned Sokowski around, using him as a shield. Wexler's first blow landed on the hard part of Sokowski's skull, bouncing off it with a hollow sound.

"Fuckin' *shit!*" Sokowski screamed.

As Wexler raised his club to strike again, Jarrow unsnapped Sokowski's holster, drawing his .38 Smith & Wesson service revolver. When he realized what was happening, Sokowski tried to stop it. But his reflexes had been slowed by pain and fear, and when he reached for his holster, it was empty.

Jarrow did not even shout a warning. He simply gut-shot Wexler at point-blank range. The .38 roared, punching Wexler below the belt, tearing through his lower intestines. Wexler's legs gave out under him and he sat down hard, crashing into a medical-supply cart, sending bottles, tools, and bandages flying. He let out a loud, honking fart. Then, when the pain began to register in his torn intestines, he started to scream.

Jarrow turned and fired at the doctor on the other side of

the room, where he was punching the buttons of a desk phone, trying to get help. The bullet missed the doctor but hit the phone, blowing it off the desk and back against the wall. The doctor stood there, receiver still in his hand, unattached cord swinging free.

He dropped the receiver and put up his hands.

"Okay," he said, his voice skipping up a few steps. *"Okay!"*

"Down on the floor, Doc," Jarrow called to him, glancing at Wilson, who was already down. "Hands behind your head."

The doctor dropped to the floor.

Jarrow turned to Sokowski, who was still bent over, working on his crotch. The hypodermic needle had pierced his penis and right testicle, lodging solidly in thigh muscle. Every time Sokowski tried to pull it loose, the pain made him stop and grit his teeth.

Jarrow stuck the muzzle of the .38 in Sokowski's right ear.

"One wrong move," he said softly, "and the fat boy"—nodding at Wexler, still screaming on the floor—"will be combing your brains out of his greasy hair. Got it, pal? Don't nod or talk. Just blink. Once for yes. Twice for fuck you."

Sokowski blinked, once, very carefully.

Keeping the muzzle in Sokowski's ear, Jarrow turned to Wilson.

"Come on, fruitcake. Get up. You're part of this, too."

Wilson rose slowly to his feet, eyes on Jarrow.

"You both know how this goes," Jarrow said to them. "You're my passports. You follow my directions, you might still be alive after I'm out of here."

Wilson nodded slowly. "Whatever you say."

Anger sparked in Jarrow's dark eyes. "Listen, faggot! Get this much straight. I am *not* crazy! So don't fuckin' baby me along like I am, okay?"

Wilson said nothing, just looked at Jarrow with what he hoped was a neutral but sympathetic expression.

"Put your arm through mine," Jarrow ordered Wilson, "just like we're boyfriends, sweetie pie. And keep it there. Now, we go on outside. Together. Just like the three fuckin' musketeers, okay?" He nudged Sokowski with the .38. "Come on, Blondie. *Move* it!"

"I-can't-walk,"Sokowskiwhispered,"with-this-thing-stuck-through-my-cock."

"Sure you can." Jarrow grinned at him. "It's good for you."

"Shot!" Wexler screamed at Sokowski as they moved past him, tears and snot running down his face, hands trying to hold in his guts, blood spilling out from them. *"Help* me, Luke! I'm *shot!"*

They were near the infirmary door when it burst open.

Guards rushed in, shotguns raised for firing.

"Freeze, asshole!" ordered the first one in.

Jarrow pulled the trigger of the .38. Sokowski's blood and brains blew across the room, spattering the guards and the door.

Jarrow shoved the .38 against Wilson's throat, Sokowski's blood flecking the barrel.

"Don't!" Wilson gasped. "Don't let him kill me. Please!"

"Get out," Jarrow said to the guards, his voice low and steady. "All the way out. Close the fucking door behind you."

The guards hesitated for almost a full minute, shotguns aimed at Jarrow, who held Wilson in front of him as a shield. Wilson was weeping now, his sobs the loudest sound in the room.

The first guard in nodded to the others. They all withdrew. Jarrow knew they would cooperate. They had no choice.

But he was not concerned with them any longer.

He was thinking of what he had to do next.

And for the first time that night, his courage wavered.

Could he do it? Now that he had to, could he still do it?

Now that he wanted to summon him, would he still appear?

Il stregóne morello.

"I've killed one!" he cried. "The other will die soon."

He glanced at Wexler, moaning now, holding his stomach.

"Do you demand more sacrifices?"

Jarrow's voice rang out across the infirmary.

But he spoke in Italian now, not English.

"Must I kill this one, too?" He pushed the .38 muzzle into Wilson's throat, right up underneath the jawbone.

Wilson groaned in terror.

The fluorescent lights overhead blinked once, twice.

He saw them then, as if in a vision. The yellow cat's eyes. The withered skin. The long-nailed spider's claws.

He had summoned him. And he had appeared.

Il stregóne morello.

A violent tremor seized Tod Jarrow.

He took the gun from Wilson's throat and raised an empty hand before his own face, turning away from what he had called forth.

The door to the infirmary opened, and the guards rushed in again. This time they found Wilson standing there alone, blinking in the fluorescent light, tears still in his eyes. He stood to one side as armed guards poured into the room.

"Where's Jarrow?" asked an assistant warden.

Wilson shook his head. "Gone."

31

Breakdown

"Of course," Connie said, "Ken thinks I'm crazy."

Jake Mauder smiled at her. "He should know."

He stopped smiling. The jokes were over.

"I've told you everything," she said.

"Almost everything."

"What have I left out?"

"Just the truth."

"I don't follow you, Jake."

"Come on, Connie. You want *me* to be the first to say it?"

"You think I'm suffering from psychotic—"

She stopped, the words like ashes in her mouth.

Jake said nothing. Her eyes began to water. What else could he think? Before this happened to her, she would have arrived at the same diagnosis of a patient with similar symptoms.

Psychosis. Dementia. Breakdown.

She took a deep breath. "They're *not* hallucinations, Jake."

"Come on, Connie."

"These things that happened to me in Venice—"

"That you *think* happened."

"How can I experience things I know nothing about?"

"Information stored in long-term memory, then called up in random sequence. Nothing more to it than that."

She shook her head. "The information just isn't there, Jake. Before this started happening to me, I knew *nothing* about Venice. But I know all about it now."

Darkness. Corruption. Sorcery. Death.

"And these things I know, they're not part of me, Jake." *They're not part of this life at all.*

"Come on, Connie."

She stared at him. "You'd rather think I'm crazy, than admit that I'm having paranormal experiences. It's easier for you that way, isn't it, Jake?"

"What the hell do you know about easy?"

He got to his feet. "You think I'm *enjoying* this? You're not just the best doctor I ever trained, you're my *daughter*. And now, to have this happen—"

Tears formed in his eyes, behind the thick lenses.

"You don't have a Kleenex, do you?"

She nodded, and handed him one.

He blew his nose loudly.

She went over to his side of the desk and hugged him.

"I love you, Jake. But you're wrong this time, okay?"

"Don't kid yourself, Connie."

"What do you mean? I'm functioning. I'm thinking clearly."

"For now, yes."

"What do you think I should do?"

"You need intensive therapy. Right away. I'm not the one to provide it. I'm too emotionally involved. But I can recommend other doctors, other institutions—"

"Institutional therapy? Jake, I've got a practice to run."

"Not anymore you don't."

"You're telling me to quit working?"

"I can't tell you what to do, Connie. But I can tell you this. If you ignore what's happening, it will get worse, a lot worse. You could find yourself in a padded room one day soon, screaming, being eaten alive, in your mind, by rats coming out of the—whatever they call those goddamn little alleys in Venice."

"Calli," she said softly, remembering.

Jake nodded. "If you let things get that bad, the only solution then might be a surgical one."

"A prefrontal lobotomy?"

He looked at her, then turned away.

She went back to the chair in front of his desk and sat down.

Jake walked over to one of his bookcases and just stood there, head bowed, not even looking at the books.

After what seemed a long time, she said, "Jake?"

"What?" He did not look up.

"What if I'm right?"

"About this *meshugaas* in Venice?"

"What if my life in Venice, four hundred years ago, is real?"

"If I thought that, I'd do just what I'm telling you. Close down my practice, put myself in therapy—"

"But Jake, what if it's *real?*"

She heard papers rustle, and looked up to see him rummaging through a sprung drawer in one of his overloaded filing cabinets.

When he found what he was looking for, he walked over to her, slowly, staring at a business card in his hand.

He gave it to her.

ZENOBIA HOROWITZ
PSYCHIC SEER CABALIST
ASTRAL PROJECTION CHANNELING REINCARNATION
TAROT READINGS NUMEROLOGY
MISTRESS OF THE KABBALAH
ALL MAJOR CREDIT CARDS ACCEPTED

She looked up at him. "What's this? Some kind of joke?"

"You ask *me* to believe in reincarnation, then you talk jokes?"

"Zenobia," Connie said, reading from the card. "Sounds like a character from one of Stevie's video games."

"It's a strange name," Jake agreed. "She's a strange person."

He took a seat behind his desk again. "We went to college together. Brooklyn College. I was premed. She was, what? Philosophy, something like that. Her maiden name was Mandelbaum, so we used to see each other in line a lot at registration. Anyway, after her husband's death she moved out to L.A., set up shop somewhere on Fairfax. She has a big following, people who swear by her. She's an intelligent woman. Weird, but intelligent."

"How come when she believes in reincarnation, she's just weird? But when it happens to me, I'm psychotic?"

"Because Zena's not a trained psychiatrist. Trained by me. She doesn't have a practice and a family. And she— She's not my daughter, goddamn it."

Connie looked at the card again. "Thanks, Jake. I know you wouldn't do this for just anybody."

"I can't even believe I did it for you. Go see Zena if you have to. But you know what I think you should do."

"Quit my job, and put myself in therapy?"

"At least take a leave of absence, *bubeleh.*"

"Jake, I'm not endangering the lives of my patients."

"How do you know? If you were a surgeon, would you keep operating under these conditions? Never knowing when you might slip into a fugue state, right in the middle of an operation?"

"It's not the same, Jake."

"Isn't it? This business of ours, psychiatry. Such an easy job. But we can kill patients too, as surely as a surgeon can. The surgeon uses a knife. We use the power of the mind itself, a far more dangerous instrument."

"I'm not going to kill anyone, Jake. Or quit my practice."

"It's up to you. But don't wait too long."

"What?"

"Don't wait until something terrible happens."

Jake's voice dropped almost to a whisper.

"Don't wait until someone dies, Connie."

32
Psychic

That evening, after the slow, deliberate rhythm of the night world began to pulse through the city like thick blood, down in Long Beach, on the second floor of a faded pink stucco apartment building, Alice MacKendrick sat in her wheelchair, awake and alone.

Emilia had gone to bed hours ago. The night lay quiet through an open window, except for the rumble of a passing car.

Alice often sat up late, smoking and drinking, living in a frozen past, killing time in the present, not thinking about the future. Tonight, she thought about all three.

Especially the past.

Rural Pennsylvania, over sixty years ago.

Venice, four hundred years ago.

Alice had always had The Gift, as her people called it, ever since she was a little girl. Her people were immigrants who had escaped the coal mines of Wales and come to the farming country of Pennsylvania. She was six when they first knew she had The Gift. Her grandmother, Morgan Lloyd, had been telling her about the horrors of life in the Welsh mines. Suddenly, young Alice Jones went into a trance, body rigid, eyes staring. She began to speak of the Great Disaster of 1873, a cave-in that took the lives of sixty-eight miners. She spoke in the voices of the trapped miners themselves, describing the Disaster through their dying eyes.

Gwyneth Jones, Alice's mother, said the child had a fever that made her babble nonsense. Morgan Lloyd, who had possessed The Gift herself as a girl, declared young Alice a visionary, a witch. But she did not use those words. She used an ancient Celtic word, older than the Welsh language itself, going back to the time when all Celts spoke the same language and practiced the same religion.

Druida. Prophetess. Sorceress.

Throughout Alice's childhood and adolescence, the visions continued. The Gift grew in power and complexity. Sometimes the visions were glimpses of the future. More often, they were of the past—sometimes, the very distant past. Once she had a terrifying vision of a Fire Festival held by ancient Druids in the wild mountains of North Wales. She beheld an enormous figure of a man, almost fifty feet high, made of wicker. Inside the wicker man, like rats in a trap, the sacrificial victims waited to be burned alive when the wicker man was set on fire at the end of the festival. Alice experienced all this through the eyes of a young Druid priestess, condemned to death by her father's enemies. She saw the flames and smoke rising from the burning base of the wicker man. She felt the fire eating into her own flesh.

The visions became less frequent, less intense, after she moved to California, away from her family. But her fear of The Gift was so great that it kept her from marrying for many years. She did not want to pass such an evil thing on to her own children.

Before accepting Andrew MacKendrick's marriage proposal, she had first traveled back to rural Pennsylvania where her grandmother, Morgan Lloyd, very old and almost blind, lay dying.

"If I have children," she asked her, "will they inherit it?"

Morgan Lloyd, her chest heavy with congestion, turned her faded eyes to her granddaughter. "The Gift chooses the person and the time. It may skip one generation, or one hundred. In our family, The Gift, when it comes, comes only to women."

Alice MacKendrick sat in her wheelchair now, remembering.

She had never told Connie about The Gift. There had been no need. After passing the anxious years of Connie's early childhood, always waiting for some manifestation—a sign, a vision—Alice at last decided, after Andrew MacKendrick's death, that her child had been spared. The Gift had skipped over Connie's generation. And for that, Alice MacKendrick was thankful.

Now, things had changed. When Ken called to tell her about the boating accident and Connie's hospital-room confession, she knew what had really happened. The Gift had not skipped Connie after all. It had merely chosen its own time.

This was the Third Great Trial.

First, Andy's death. Then, her own illness. And now, this.

Alice automatically reached for a cigarette with her good right hand, then stopped. She wanted a cigarette, and a drink, something heavy and potent. Something that would go straight from mouth to brain, easing the burden of consciousness, keeping The Gift pushed back into the dark side of her mind, where it belonged.

But not tonight. No drugs tonight. She wanted The Gift to come forth. She hated it and feared it. But tonight, she wanted it. She needed it. Connie was in trouble.

She thought of calling Connie, and telling her what she was up against. But what good would that do? Just scare her to death, make her more confused and frightened than she already was.

Besides, if she did it right, Connie might never have to know.

That would be best. Resolve this crisis for her. Get her out of trouble. Then let her go on leading a normal life, never having to find out about The Gift.

"Fool!" cried a ravaged voice. "How can she lead a *normal* life? She has The Gift!"

Alice looked up, heart beating faster.

Morgan Lloyd stood before her, rotted flesh falling from her face, grave worms feasting on what remained. Her blind eyes, milk white with cataracts, swiveled in sockets of bone.

"Druida!" screamed the face. "The Gift!"

Beads of sweat stood out on Alice's own face. The vision was horrifying, and full-sensory, as always. She could smell the stench of her grandmother's decaying flesh. But she was glad to see this horror. It meant The Gift was working, emerging from the cellar of her mind, where she had kept it hidden all these years.

A new vision began to form. The decaying corpse of Morgan Lloyd faded slowly into fitfully lighted darkness. Not the darkness of night in an open field, but something far more deadly. She saw a close, low-ceilinged room, and smelled dank water, heavy with the stench of raw sewage in the night air.

She saw two shadows in the darkness—one young and strong, but trembling with fear, the other old and evil, and in control. Pools of light shimmered in the darkness. Gleams of gold, revealing ancient books and manuscripts, and flickering, half-melted candles, and eyes in the darkness, yellow and malignant.

"Once again," hissed the old one's voice, "you have come to me of your own free will."

"I had no choice!" This was the young man speaking, his voice bitter with fear and hatred. "They had me locked in a cage. They kept me from her! I had to escape! *I cannot live without her!"*

Alice moved into his mind to see the one he spoke of. And despite the long, dark reddish-brown hair, the elegant Venetian clothing, she recognized her own daughter.

"You shall have her," the old one said, his voice dripping venom. "In both lives, now and then. All in good time."

"I will have her *now!*" cried the young man.

"You." The old one pointed a finger at him, hooked and spindly like a spider's claw. "You do not control the cycles of the lives and the ages. *I* do. The time for you to have her will come when I decide, not when you wish."

The evil emanating from the old one was so strong and terrible that Alice could actually feel it clutching her heart, making her more afraid than she had ever been before.

"However," the old one said, malicious laughter caressing the word, "because I am by nature generous, and because you have served me faithfully and well, you shall go back to her, in the other life. But there are things I want from *her.*"

The last word struck a chill into Alice's heart.

"Of course, Master."

"I want her brought back here, with you. All in good time."

"Yes, Master."

"I also want—"

He paused then, producing a silence so intense that the only sound Alice could hear was the steady beating of her own heart, crashing like thunder into the void.

"I also need," he said, "her children."

"No!" Alice cried.

The old one looked up. The darkness receded. She saw his face, and drew back into the wheelchair, fear gripping her paralyzed limbs. Once, in a vision when she was younger, she had seen the face of an evil man, a Druid priest who drank the blood of virgins in the name of his dark god. Men had breathed his name in frightened whispers. The Hand of Death. The face of this man had been horrible to look upon, the visage of evil incarnate.

But it was nothing to the face she saw now.

Staring deep into her own eyes.

The Dark Sorcerer. *Il stregóne morello.*

Who are you? she heard the voice ask inside her head. *And how did you come to me?*

"No!" Alice whispered, twisting in her iron chair, trying to turn away from the face.

Why did you come to me? asked the voice. *What sacrifice do you bring for me?*

She fought against the vision, and the power that was trying to pull her into the darkness. The Dark Sorcerer reached out a spider's claw toward her. She screamed. The vision wavered, and began to fade. She felt it rushing back from her, falling into endless darkness. She threw back her head, mouth open, gasping for breath, her one good hand gripping the arm of the wheelchair until it seemed to tremble in her grasp.

Water, now. Dank water, stinking of corruption. Then clear water, fresh and clean, smelling not of the sea, but of something else—medicinal, chemical. Alice let out a shuddering breath.

Connie broke the surface of the water, gulping down air.

She turned, and started to swim another length of the pool, back toward the shallow end, on top of the water this time.

The pool lights made the water soft aquamarine, shimmering like a magic spring beneath the night sky.

Ken swam up beside her. "You were under a long time."

"I was holding my breath the whole way."

"That's good to know."

"I like to swim underwater, Ken."

"I thought we both got enough swimming the other day."

"That was the ocean. This is the pool. It's different."

"Just be careful when you're in the water, okay?"

"Quit hovering over me, Ken! First, you waited for me to die from a brain tumor. Now, you're waiting for me to go crazy."

"I just don't want to lose you," he said.

He kissed her, hard. And there, for an instant, suspended in water, as if in time, she imagined herself in Tod Jarrow's arms again, their tongues inside each other's mouths, their hearts beating together with the rhythm of one heart.

Marcangelo.

Their arms around each other, she and Ken started to sink. They surfaced, spluttering and laughing.

Ken's laughter stopped suddenly.

"You were thinking of him again, weren't you?"

She felt violated, as if Ken had crawled inside her mind.

Turning from him, she swam toward the side of the pool, where she rested her arms on the concrete, breathing hard.

He came up beside her, moving through the water quietly.

"How romantic," she said, not even looking at him.

"I'm sorry. I just got that feeling. Was I wrong?"

"We better get to bed. I have to be up early tomorrow."

"You're going back to work?"

"It's about time. I've been away long enough. First the accident. Then the hospital tests. Then all day today with Jake."

"Does Jake think you should go back?"

"Of course not. Jake wants me to check myself into a psychiatric institution and get some therapy. I'm sure you agree."

"No reason to act nasty about it."

"Sorry. I'm tired of this. I want to get on with my life."

"There's life outside work. Stevie. Trent."

"Ken, you knew what kind of person I was when you married me. I worked hard to get through med school. I've been working hard ever since, because I *want* to. Work's what my life's about."

Water sloshed against the side of the pool.

"Is it safe for you to go back to work this soon?"

"I can see you've been talking to Jake."

"If Jake's concerned, there must be a reason for it."

"The reason is he has one simple answer for what's happening to me. I'm going crazy. But he's wrong, Ken."

He looked at her and said nothing.

"I'm not going to kill anyone, no matter what Jake Mauder thinks. I'm going to help people, just like I always have."

"People like Tod Jarrow?"

She shook her head. "I can't help him anymore. First thing

tomorrow, I'll hand the case over to someone else. Maybe Lou Pelham. Whatever, I'm finished with Tod Jarrow."

The phone rang at the poolside extension.

"Let me get it!" She lifted herself out of the pool.

"I've got it," he said, reaching for the receiver.

"Ken, I want to *answer* it!"

She shook off the excess water and picked up the phone.

"Hello? Yes. This is Dr. Stallman."

The muscles in her face went slack.

"What's wrong?" Ken asked.

"Yes. Of course, I understand. Yes, I'll be careful."

"Connie, what's wrong?"

"I see. Yes. Of course, I'll discuss this with my husband. Thank you for calling, Lieutenant."

She stared at the receiver a moment before replacing it.

"That was Dormer, at the Hollywood Station. Jarrow's escaped from Terminal Island." She looked at the pool, the yard, the house above them where Stevie and Trent lay sleeping. "He says we should hire professional twenty-four-hour security protection. He thinks I could be the first one that Jarrow—"

She remembered the promise then, made at Terminal Island.

I'll get out of here, Connie, and I'll come for you.

33

Jumper

Inside the elevator on the main floor of the California Pacific Savings and Loan Building in Hollywood, the young woman with the pinched face and oversize aviator glasses pushed the button for Tramonto, the restaurant on the top floor.

The man standing next to her said, "Doesn't open till eleven. They used to serve breakfast, but—"

"I work there," she said, in a tone meant to discourage further conversation.

She stood and watched the floor numbers flashing on the display as the elevator car ascended, her shoulders hunched over slightly, light polyester jacket unzipped.

The young man who had tried to strike up a conversation with her, a very junior member of a CPA firm on the twelfth floor, watched her out of the corner of his eye. She wasn't bad-looking. Not exactly dressed for Hollywood. Not enough slinky style, acrylic nails, and nerve-gas perfume to be an aspiring actress or a working hooker. Not enough purple hair and leather underwear to be part of the club scene. Still, she had possibilities. Dates were hard to find. And she didn't look like the kind of girl who would give you AIDS.

The elevator stopped at the twelfth floor.

"This is where I get off." He smiled at her. "Have a nice day. Maybe I'll see you at Tramonto sometime."

She looked at him and said nothing.

By the time the elevator reached the top floor, she was alone. The doors slid open. She walked out past a glass display case that advertised Tramonto's live jazz group of the week. At the bottom of the case sat plastic models of lobsters, crabs, and sushi rolls.

"Excuse me!" a voice called out. "We don't open till eleven."

She turned and saw her, jeans and T-shirt, cleaning rag in one hand, spray bottle in the other. A working member of management.

The woman with the aviator glasses said, "I'm Cindy's friend. Cindy Gill? Night shift at the bar? She left her sweater here. I came to get it for her."

The other woman pointed with the spray bottle. "Go see Tony at the register. If the cleaning guys found it, he's got it."

She nodded. "Okay if I use the rest room first?"

"Sure." She pointed with the bottle again. "Back there."

"Thanks," she said, but she knew where it was.

She walked up slowly to the rest room, looked back to make sure the other woman was not watching her, then walked on by. She could hear a male voice laughing in the distance, probably Tony at the register. She stopped at a closed side door that looked as if it might lead to the kitchen or a storeroom. She turned the handle. It was not locked.

The door opened into a narrow stairwell with cement walls and a metal handrail. She closed the door and started up the stairs, her running shoes scuffing on the metal steps, the sound echoing inside the cement stairwell. At the top of the stairs she found another closed door. She turned the handle, but this one did not open. Despair came over her, then rage.

She slammed her fist into the door. *"Shit!"*

Her voice rang off the metal steps and cement walls.

She took a deep breath, and tried the handle again.

This time, the door opened.

It led out onto the roof of the building. Blades revolved slowly inside large ventilator stacks. Traffic noise, deafening down below, seemed distant and muted up here. She walked across the rooftop, gravel scraping underfoot. At the side of the roof overlooking Sunset, she came to a low restraining wall. She got up on it, balancing herself. The top of the wall was no more than three feet wide. She moved over to the edge.

The wind was stronger up here. It whipped at her jacket and her plain brown hair. Standing on the edge, Jennie Hodges took a deep breath and looked down.

Twenty-five stories straight down to Sunset Boulevard.

Connie was in her office, reading the runaway shelter's report on Blair Renley, when the call came through.

"Dr. Stallman? Sergeant Dan McCallum. LAPD, Hollywood Division. I understand that Jennie Hodges is a patient of yours?"

"Yes, she is. What's wrong?"

"She managed to get herself up on the roof of the Cal Pacific Building on Sunset. That's where she is right now. Twenty-five stories up, threatening to jump."

"God, no," Connie breathed.

"She may be bluffing, but it doesn't look like it." McCallum paused. "An officer tried to make a grab for her when she was talking to one of our suicide-prevention specialists. She pulled back from him, almost fell over the edge."

Connie remembered Jennie's threat in her office that day.

I hope you're the one who has to come and identify me!

Then it was Jake's voice she heard inside her head.

Don't wait until someone dies, Connie.

"Still there, Dr. Stallman?"

"Yes."

"Like I say, we don't always notify the jumper's doctor, assuming they have one, right at the beginning of something like this. But Lieutenant Ed Dormer here at the Hollywood Station said he's had dealings with you before."

"Yes."

"Said you're the kind of doctor who gets involved with your patients, and that you'd want to be in on this."

"I'm just a few miles west on Sunset. I'm leaving now."

"We got Sunset roped off for a four-block area around the building. You'll want to take Fountain or some other side street. The officer on the cordon can let you through."

Don't wait until someone dies, Connie.

The intersection on Sunset below the Cal Pacific Building swarmed with spectators. Secretaries and clerks on lunch breaks. Lawyers and executives on their way to meetings. Unemployed actors and street people sitting on bus benches. All of them with their necks craned up toward the top of the building, right at the very edge, where Jennie Hodges stood poised like a circus high-wire performer, incredibly tiny at that distance, motionless, waiting.

No one yelled for her to jump, or shouted anything at the solitary figure standing on the edge. But they were thinking it, almost willing it. Connie could hear it in the unnatural silence that gripped the intersection.

Get it over with, she could hear them thinking. *Either jump or don't jump, but don't just stand there all day.*

An officer from the cordon led Connie through the crowd

and into the lobby of the Cal Pacific Building, where other officers guarded elevators and stairways.

"This is the jumper's doctor," he said to an officer near one of the elevators. "We need to take her up to the roof."

"Will do."

On their way up, Connie asked, "Where are the fire trucks?"

The officer looked at her. "Excuse me?"

"They'll need nets, won't they? In case—"

"If she jumps on us, ma'am, a net won't do much good. She's going to weigh a lot more by the time she hits the ground. It'd be like using a Kleenex to catch a bowling ball."

The rooftop was crowded with various groups of professionals, standing close to or back from the edge of the roof, depending on their importance to the operation. The media people clustered back near the door to the roof with their video cameras and microphones, shouting dispatches into mobile telephones.

"Don't let those clowns know who you are," the officer had cautioned her in the elevator, "or we'll never get by."

As they made their way through the media phalanx, a television reporter stuck a microphone in Connie's face.

"Miss, are you a relative?"

"She's with the department," the officer said. "We'll answer your questions later. Just give us a break and let us through, okay, guys?"

They passed by the officers in charge of the operation, and stopped just behind the members of the suicide-prevention unit, who stood at least ten feet back from where Jennie Hodges balanced on the narrow edge overlooking Sunset Boulevard.

Connie's heart clutched at the sight of Jennie standing there, shoulders hunched, facing sideways so that she could keep one eye on the crowds below and another on the officers behind her.

A tall officer came up to Connie. "Dr. Stallman? Sergeant

Dan McCallum. Glad you could make it. She hasn't done much talking. Hasn't even asked to see anyone. I'm afraid she's pretty serious about this."

He led Connie up to the boundary of the suicide-prevention line, where a young woman whispered instructions to her in a barely audible voice.

"Don't get too close, or make any sudden movements. If she turns away from you and looks down at the street, *shut up*. If she starts yelling at you, stay cool. If she looks like she's getting ready to jump, we'll take over. Okay?"

Leaning forward slightly, her throat dry, Connie called out in a low but clear voice, "Jennie?"

Jennie Hodges stood parallel to the edge, looking straight ahead, out toward the Pacific Ocean, hidden by layers of smog. She stood motionless, except for her plain brown hair, lifted and scattered by the wind.

"Jennie?" she called to her again. "It's me. Connie."

Jennie did not respond.

"I came as soon as I heard about it," Connie said.

Jennie turned her head, only her head, and stared at her with flat eyes behind the oversize aviator glasses.

"So this is what it takes for you to return a phone call."

Someone behind them stifled a laugh.

"I've been away, Jennie. I've been having—"

She stopped, wondering if it was the right time to be talking about this, in front of the police and the media.

But the girl's life was in danger.

"I've been having problems of my own, Jennie. Serious problems. I've been in the hospital."

"Is that supposed to make me feel sorry for you?"

"No. I'm just explaining why I haven't been there for you."

"You think that's why you're here now? Get real, Connie. You're here for yourself, just like all these other assholes."

Jennie looked away again, out toward the unseen ocean.

Connie could feel the tension ripple through the suicide-prevention officers around her.

Jennie turned back toward her suddenly.

"If you're really here for me like you say you are, Connie, tell me something. Okay? Tell me one good reason for going on living." She stared at her through the aviator glasses, wind scattering her plain brown hair. "Just give me *one good reason.*"

Connie wanted to tell her the best reason, that people loved her and wanted her to go on living, people like those gathered here around her today, trying to save her life.

But before Connie could speak, Jennie disappeared.

In her place, Connie saw a dark-robed figure standing atop a high, solitary column, rising out of nothing, silhouetted against a blinding white sun, like a stylitic saint in the desert.

The black-robed figure turned, stretched out an arm, and pointed it at her. The blinding sunlight dimmed to darkness. The figure on his column rushed up toward her, until she could see clearly the withered skin, the burning yellow eyes.

Connie's heart contracted.

Il stregóne morello. The Dark Sorcerer.

The creature laughed, the sound high and evil, like the whining of a black wind through the bones of the dead.

He vanished, and Jennie returned.

Connie shook her head, found her voice. "There's—lots of reasons, Jennie. All the reasons—"

"You don't care," Jennie said quietly, and blinked, one single tear trickling down her cheek like a tiny liquid pearl.

"Nobody cares."

Jennie looked away, down toward Sunset.

Silence locked onto the rooftop. Connie could hear her own breathing, and that of the officer next to her.

Jennie looked up at them, and gave a small sob.

Then she stepped off the edge.

Connie reached out her arm.

Jennie fell in silence. In the movies, there would have been a long, shattering scream, fading away slowly. But Jennie had not had time to fill her lungs before she jumped.

The whole rooftop listened to the silence.

A muted sound came up from the crowd below, like a

collective groan. Then the screams broke out, shouting, police officers on bullhorns telling the crowd to get back.

Connie stepped up to the edge and looked down.

He had killed her. She knew this. *He* had wanted her to die, had not wanted Connie or anyone else to save her.

And so, she had died.

Connie looked up and saw Lieutenant Ed Dormer.

He put a sympathetic hand on her shoulder. "No one wins them all, Dr. Stallman. You and your husband going to get that twenty-four-hour security protection we talked about?"

She shook her head. "We—haven't decided, exactly."

"I wouldn't wait too long. We found a young woman's body in an alley near Selma and Vine this morning. All over the alley. She was alive through most of the knife-work. Lab tests aren't in yet, so we're not sure it's Jarrow. But it's got his signature."

"I see."

"I'm not sure you see the whole thing. The greatest danger is to yourself, of course. But serial killers are very unpredictable animals. They don't always follow established patterns, not even their own. In Jarrow's case, given what we know about him, he may come after your husband first."

She looked up at him.

"Or your children."

The terror took hold of her then, as reporters shouted out their questions on the rooftop behind them, and down below, in the streets of Hollywood, onlookers and passersby wondered aloud at the spectacular public death of a lonely, unhappy woman.

34

Assignation

Connie sat alone in her office, late in the afternoon of the day Jennie Hodges died, going over everything once again.

How it had happened. How it might have been prevented.

What to do now with her own life and career.

Becky Martinez stepped into her office.

"Sure you want me to leave now, Connie?"

"Sure, Becky. Go ahead."

"I could stay and help answer the phones, at least."

"I can answer my own phone."

"Don't do this, Connie. You didn't kill Jennie. She did."

"Thanks, Becky."

Becky turned to leave, then stopped.

"I have this relative in Mexico, a great-aunt, and she's really into what they call *brujería* down there. You know, like witchcraft, sorcery? Anyway, my aunt says that whatever happens to you is caused by how you feel about yourself, deep down inside. I mean, she's crazy because she believes in that stuff, right? But still, maybe there's something to it."

After Becky left, Connie sat in her office, thinking.

About Jennie. Jarrow. Ken. Trent. Stevie. Her mother.

And what Becky had said.

So how do I feel about myself? What do I want to happen?

The phone rang out in the reception area.

She picked it up. "Beckford Clinic. Dr. Stallman speaking."

There was silence on the other end.

"Hello? Hel*lo?* If there's someone there, I can't hear you."

She reached out a hand to shut off the speakerphone.

"Don't hang up, Contessa."

She drew back from the phone, as if it had become alive.

"You're hard to get hold of. I called all morning. That girl you have answering the phone wanted me to leave my name and number." Tod Jarrow laughed. "But I couldn't do that, could I, Contessa? Information like that might get into the wrong hands. Get the wrong people all excited."

She sat staring at the phone, as Tod Jarrow's disembodied voice echoed from the speaker.

"So I kept calling. That girl you've got working the phones, she's some Latin babe, isn't she? At least she's polite about the name-and-number shit. Anyway, I decided to try you one more time, *just one more time,* here at the end of the day, and

what do you know? Finally, we make contact. All's well that—
Still there, Contessa? I'd hate to think you just left me here
shooting the shit by myself, while you're off in the next room,
calling the—"

"I'm *here!*"

"That's good. It's nice to know someone's listening. Because even if you're not quite as hot to fuck me right now as
you were that night in the Hollywood Station—"

She thought of that night again, and then of his latest victim, her body parts found in the alley near Selma and Vine.

"—you still want to remember that we share some important common interests, Contessa, you and me."

Wed to one eternity.

"You don't want to go snitching on me to the cops, Connie.
That would be really stupid. Because for one thing, it would
make me mad. And if I get mad, even though I adore—"

The word sounded obscene, spoken by Tod Jarrow's
disembodied voice, as if a rat had stood up on its hind legs and
said it.

"—I might want to do something to hurt you. Maybe do
something to that blond surfer dude you're married to. Or
even to those two cute little kids of yours."

Her heart seemed to stop.

"I saw them today, Connie. They really *are* cute. Made me
think about what our kids might look like, someday."

"What do you *want?*"

There was silence on the other end.

Don't hang up now, please. Don't come after Stevie and—

"I want you," he said. "I want to see you again."

She listened to the sound of her own breathing.

"You're the reason I broke out of that shit hole, Connie.
You're the reason for everything I've ever done."

She thought of his latest victim, of all his other victims.

"Everything. In this life, and the other. In all the lives." His
voice dropped to a bitter whisper. *"Everything."*

She turned away from the phone.

"Still there?" asked the disembodied voice.

"Yes," she said. *"Yes!"*

"You don't want to see me anymore, do you?"

She tried to speak, but could not.

Force yourself! It's either you, or Stevie and Trent.

"Yes," she managed. "Of course—I want to see you again."

"Now?"

"Yes."

"Here's where I am." He gave her an address off Franklin and La Cienega, not far from the Beckford Clinic.

"My God, you're right here in Hollywood!"

"Where did you think I was calling from? Venice?"

She closed her eyes.

"Listen up, Contessa. You're probably wearing one of those thousand-dollar suits, so we don't want to make this too obvious. There's covered parking here, but don't use it. Park on the street. Ring the intercom for 11B. When I ask who it is, you say—Alessandra. For old time's sake. I buzz you in, you come up to 11B, knock on the door. I'll be carrying when I open the door, but it's for unexpected visitors, not for you. Okay?"

"Yes."

"It shouldn't take you more than twenty-five minutes, even with traffic. If for some reason you don't show up after half an hour, I may get very nervous, because I'm a nervous sort of guy. I may just go pay a visit on my own."

Suddenly her terror turned to fury. "Don't *threaten* me! I'll do what you want! But don't threaten to hurt my children!"

"I'm not threatening you, my one and only true love. I would never do that. I'm just making sure you know the rules of this little game, so you don't break them by accident."

She sat there, staring at the phone.

"See you in twenty-five minutes, Contessa."

There was a click, followed by the buzzing of the dial tone.

The street in front of the green stucco apartment building was parked solid. She had to leave the Acura two blocks away.

She pressed the buzzer on a rusted wrought-iron gate.

"Yeah?" Jarrow answered through a bad connection.

"It's me—Alessandra."

The buzzer brayed at her, and she pushed open the gate.

A small pool took up the center of the courtyard. Dead bugs floated on the surface of the water.

She knocked on the faded wooden door to 11B.

When it opened a few inches, she saw the muzzle of an automatic revolver. That did not frighten her as much as the one dark, angry eye staring out at her from the crack in the door.

Jarrow opened the door a little wider. "Get in here."

As she stepped inside, he closed the door after her. She could not bring herself to turn and look at him just then, standing behind her with a gun in his hand, so she looked at the apartment instead. It was a cramped single, bathroom and kitchen nook off to one side, a frayed green sofa that probably made into a bed, a dark-brown carpet, stained, and smelling faintly of mildew. Like many cheap Hollywood apartments, it had a wood-burning fireplace. A fire burned there now, logs crackling in the unscreened grate.

"All the comforts of home," he said. "My home, not yours. Nothing like what you're used to, is it, Contessa?"

She turned and looked at him.

He had put the gun away somewhere and stood there dressed in stone-washed denims, running shoes, and a T-shirt. His face still bore the old bruises and stitches, with some new scars now, dark eyes overshadowing everything, full of pain and hatred.

They stared at each other in complete silence, a perverted innocence to it, as if they were on a first date, and this was that awkward moment after the movie and the food, with no one knowing quite what to say or do.

"I dreamed of this," he said, "inside. When they were beating me up, or shooting me full of shit. I dreamed of it like this, in this life."

She said nothing. Logs sparked in the fireplace.

"Before I saw you that day in jail, I wanted to die, in this life. I thought it was all over. Then you walked in. Everything was different. Hair, clothes, language. But it was still you."

He breathed softly, *"Alessandra, mia bellissima."*

"Then why did you try to kill me?"

The anger came back into his dark eyes. "I didn't try to kill you! I can do better than that when I try, Contessa. But I was mad at you. Because you didn't care whether I was alive or dead!"

His dark eyes filled with tears.

"You still don't care," he said.

She saw Jennie Hodges again, balanced on the fatal edge. *You don't care. Nobody cares.*

All her emotions, personal and professional, spilled over into a rush of sympathy. She stepped toward Tod Jarrow and put a tentative hand to his scarred face.

He grabbed for her, kissing her hard, desperately, like a thirsting man at the fountainhead.

It leaped the dark chasm of time then, like spectral fire, coming back to her with a blinding suddenness.

The passion. The desire. The physical hunger.

He started to pull at her clothes, moaning softly.

"Here." She pushed his hands away. "Let me do it."

What am I doing? she thought, as she took off her clothes, throwing them on the sofa. *My God, what am I doing?*

He threw her down onto the stained brown carpet and entered her with one groaning movement, the whole thick length of him pushing up into her, slamming against her insides.

"Sto—" she gasped. "You're hurt—"

Then she started screaming, voice hoarse, clawing at him, trying to pull him even deeper inside her, harder, as the madness took hold of her.

He clamped a hand over her mouth.

He's going to kill me, she thought, with a strange, detached calm, as if watching it happen to someone else.

"Not so loud, my love," he whispered, leaning over her,

sweat from his face dripping down onto hers. "We don't want the whole world to know about our happiness, do we?"

Then the thrusting and the wanting went on, more fierce than ever, as light from the burning fireplace flickered across their naked, sweating bodies, and Connie felt herself swept up within his power once again, in this life, and the other.

An orgasm rolled through her like thunder, tearing apart the firmament, shattering the foundations. Gasping for breath, mouth wide open, head thrown back, she turned toward the fireplace.

She screamed again—in terror, this time.

She saw two figures tied to St. Mark's Column. Herself and Jarrow. Alessandra and Marcangelo. Their bodies gleamed slick with sweat. Flames leaped up from the bonfire at their feet. Her long hair was on fire. They were both burning alive.

She turned away from the vision in the fireplace. Something was being done to her hands. She looked up in confusion. Jarrow pulled on the knot that tied her hands above her head to the leg of a chair behind her.

"What—" she asked, trying to get up. "What are you—"

He took hold of her dark nipples, erect and swollen now to almost twice their normal size. He squeezed them between thumb and forefinger. Gently at first. Then harder.

"*Stop* it!" she cried. "You're *hurting* me!"

"Relax," he murmured, a thin smile on his sweating face. "You'll get used to it. All women love pain. They fear it, but they want it."

He pinched her nipples hard. Then he took one in his mouth and bit down on it, making her cry out in pleasure and pain.

He started slamming into her again, body twisting and contorting, groaning like a man in the grip of a fatal seizure.

She twisted with him, the pain more intense than the pleasure now, the rope chafing at her wrists, muscles pulling in her arms. He started shuddering with his own orgasm, a tight squealing in his throat, like the cry of an animal under torture.

He withdrew from her abruptly, leaning on his hands and knees, breathing hard.

She closed her eyes, and felt something cold and metallic pressed against her throat. She opened them. Tod Jarrow lifted the knife from her throat. The blade was over a foot long, curved and one-sided, with a blood-groove running down its edge.

She tried to control her breathing, tried not to let him see how terrified she was.

He pressed the flat of the blade down against one hard nipple, bending it sideways. Then, the other. She gasped. Then he drew the long blade, flat edge against her naked flesh, slowly down the length of her body, across her rib cage, over her flat stomach, resting finally as a bridge across her dark pubic hair, handle on one thigh, razor-sharp point balanced lightly on the other.

She swallowed, dry and hard.

He raised the knife. She drew in her breath. He thrust forward, cutting the rope that tied her hands above her head.

She lowered her hands slowly, pieces of rope still twisted around them like bracelets. Pushing down on the dirty carpet with both hands, she sat up, and moved back until she leaned against the chair she had been tied to, her naked body running with sweat.

Jarrow was still on his knees, a naked suppliant, the large knife clutched in his right hand.

The fire crackled beside them in its grate.

35
Water Ritual

Ken was waiting for her when she pulled into the driveway.

"I called your office. Where were you?"

"I stopped by the Beverly Center on the way home, to find

something for the kids. I thought shopping might relax me, help me forget about Jennie."

She dropped her keys on the cement.

Ken bent over to pick them up.

"Thanks," she said. "It's been—a bad day."

"I'm glad you're home."

Stevie sat in the living room, playing a video game on the 70-inch Mitsubishi Big Screen. Trent was upstairs, fast asleep.

I saw them today, Connie. They really are *cute.*

"Stevie," Connie called to her, "I'm home!"

"Hi, Mom," she said, without looking up.

Connie knelt down beside her. "How's my girl?"

"Okay," Stevie said, eyes on the screen.

"I've been gone all day. Don't I even get a hug?"

Stevie turned to her, then made a face.

"Yuucch! You smell like cheap motel soap!"

Connie felt Ken watching her from the other side of the room.

She saw Jarrow's shower again, tile walls black with slime.

"That's not a very nice thing to say, Stevie. Mommy had to use the bathroom sink at work. She had a really bad day today."

"Your clothes look like you crumpled 'em up in a ball."

"Like I said, Mommy had a bad day."

After Stevie went to bed, Connie stood over the kitchen sink, wolfing down cold pizza.

Ken watched her. "I thought you weren't hungry."

"Just a snack."

"Don't you want to heat it up in the microwave?"

She shook her head, and took another bite.

Tomato sauce slopped onto her wrist, and she thought of the blood from Marcangelo's murder victim—Tod Jarrow's victim—staining her wrist that night on Laurel Canyon Boulevard.

She put down the pizza slice.

"Stevie was worried when you didn't come home tonight," Ken said. "That's why she acted the way she did."

"I understand, Ken."

"Still plan to keep regular office hours?"

"No! I've got too damn many things on my mind right now."

Like making sure Jarrow doesn't come after you and the kids.

"So you'll be taking some time off?"

"Yes, I will, starting tomorrow. Happy?"

"I don't want you to quit your job, Connie. I just think it's dangerous for you to keep doing it at this time."

She looked at him under the flat white light of the overhead fluorescents, knowing exactly how dangerous it was.

He came over and put his arms around her.

"You need to relax," he said.

She stiffened. "Not tonight, Ken."

"Okay. Then how does a midnight swim sound?"

"After this much pizza? I'd sink like a brick."

"How about the spa? A little hydro—What's it called?"

"Hydrotherapy."

"Yeah. Hydrotherapy. How about it, Doc?"

"Sure, Ken. If it'll make you happy, why not?"

She sat suspended in the spa like a fetus in the womb. The water was part of her and she was part of it, bubbling around her like warm amniotic fluid. Both she and Ken were nude.

She leaned back and stretched, lifting her breasts out of the water, dark nipples wet and glistening under the spa lights.

Looking at her naked body made her think of Jarrow again.

Why did I do it? When I've got Ken, why do I want Tod Jarrow?

Ken poured a fluted champagne glass of Dom Pérignon.

"Here." He handed it to her.

She rose up out of the spa, water dripping from her nipples like crystalline milk.

"You're trying to get me drunk, aren't you?"

"No, just a little more relaxed."

He came over and took one of her nipples in his mouth,

making it grow harder and larger as the water bubbled around them.

She stroked his hair. "What if the kids look out the window?"

"They should be asleep."

"What if a neighbor sees?"

"They should be asleep, too."

She felt Jarrow hurting her again, heard him telling her she would get used to the pain because she loved it.

She pushed Ken away from her.

"Not now, Ken."

He went back over to his own side of the spa.

She looked up at the house. "Maybe I should check on them."

"The kids? They're both asleep."

"I don't mean that. I mean check to make sure they're okay."

"You already checked the doors and windows twice. Is there something you're not telling me, Connie?"

She shook her head. "It's just—Jarrow."

"What about him?"

"I saw Ed Dormer today. At Jennie's suicide. He said he thinks we should put in that security system as soon as possible."

"Cops are very security-conscious. It's part of their job."

"He said they found a woman's body cut up in an alley near Selma and Vine. They think Jarrow was the one who did it."

"I can look into a security system for us."

"You act like he's not even dangerous! Believe me, he *is!*"

"I said I'll look into it."

She leaned back in the spa and closed her eyes.

Something tugged at her foot underwater. She shifted sleepily, balancing the champagne glass on her breast, knowing that what she felt was just a stray current, a random stream of bubbles.

But this current had fingers, long and bony, and what felt like claws, hooking into her left foot.

She opened her eyes and stared into the bubbling water.

Beneath the surface a dark shape, large as a full-size adult, crouched over her foot.

This is crazy, she thought, and tried to pull her foot free.

It straightened up then, rising out of the bubbling water, streams cascading from its body. It had Tod Jarrow's dark eyes. But it was flayed from head to foot, raw skin stripped of the epidermis, oozing blood. It reached out a hand toward her, all five fingers amputated at the second joints.

She cried out and threw her arms back, flinging the champagne glass over her shoulder, where it shattered against the cement.

Ken put down his own glass. "Connie?"

The thing changed shape, growing taller, darker, great wings sprouting from its hunched back, talons extending from its hands, dark eyes changing to a pale, viscous yellow. But they were not cat's eyes anymore. The thing standing over her in the spa was nothing like the Dark Sorcerer, *il stregóne morello.*

It was nothing human at all.

She screamed, and jumped out of the water, throwing herself onto the cement deck, not even noticing when a piece of broken glass cut into her knee, making it bleed. She backed up on her hands and knees, away from the thing in the spa, knocking over the Dom Pérignon bottle. Champagne bubbled out across the cement.

Ken grabbed hold of her. She struggled against him.

"Let me *go!*"

"You're okay, Connie."

"Let me—" Her breath started coming in spasmodic gasps.

"Just relax, okay?"

Her naked body began to tremble in his arms, shaking like a frightened animal. She shut her eyes tight. He brushed back some strands of damp hair clinging to her face.

"Is it—still there?" she asked, eyes closed.

"Is what still there, honey?"

"The thing in the water!"

"Nothing's in the water, except maybe some broken glass."

She opened her eyes.

The water in the spa bubbled clear and hot, and empty.

But something *had* been there, just moments before.

It had killed Jennie Hodges, and now it was coming after her.

36
Proof

Connie looked pale the next morning in her office.

"I want you to keep coming in," she told Becky Martinez, "to provide a sense of continuity for the patients. If they have any questions about me, tell them I've had to take some time off for personal reasons. If anyone wants to leave a message, just fax it to me at home, okay?"

"Sure, Connie."

"If an emergency comes up—an anxiety attack, something like that—refer the patient to Dr. Pelham. I've made arrangements with Lou to take my referrals."

"You planning on coming back?"

"Yes. I thought I made that clear."

"Are you sick and not telling us?"

"No, Becky, I'm not sick, just tired."

And scared. She thought of Jarrow, and the thing in the spa.

"Anything else?" Becky said.

"No, not that I— Oh, yes. Benjamin Simmons. Do *not* refer him—to Dr. Pelham, or to anyone else. Call me first."

"Sure, Connie. Is that it?"

"I guess so."

Becky hugged her. "Take care of yourself, Connie."

"Don't worry, Becky. I'll be okay."

After Becky left, Connie sat alone in her office, looking at the desk, the bookshelves, her diplomas framed on the wall—symbols of the career she had worked so long and hard to achieve.

"I'll be back," she said, as if talking to all her patients, past and present, assembled there in the office. "Wait and see."

Her phone rang.

She reached out a hand toward the speaker button, then stopped, remembering Jarrow's call from yesterday, his disembodied voice making threats against Stevie and Trent.

You won't make him go away by not answering.

She pressed the speaker button.

"Connie?" Becky said. "Some guy wants to talk to you, but he won't give his name. I think it's that same creep who kept calling all day yesterday. Want me to tell him to get lost?"

"I'll take it, Becky, and tell him myself."

There was a click. The call transferred over.

"Still feelin' good, Contessa?"

She tried to keep the disgust out of her voice. "I'm okay."

"*Okay?* I thought you'd be a lot better than that, the kind of session we had last night."

"Is there something you called about?" Anger edged her voice.

"Oh, I'm sure you have places to go, things to do. Busy, professional lady like yourself. I just thought maybe you might want to work me into your schedule sometime."

"Not today," she snapped, without thinking.

Then she told herself, *Easy. You don't want to upset him.*

"So that's the way it is," Jarrow said.

"That's the way it is today, yes."

"Maybe I'll just have to call you again tomorrow."

"I won't be in the office tomorrow."

"Then maybe I'll have to drop by your—"

She gave him her home phone number. She didn't want to.

But neither did she want him meeting the kids when they came home from school. He made her repeat the number while he wrote it down.

"We'll talk tomorrow, Contessa. Maybe I'll call while you're fucking your husband, and you can tell me how you feel then."

She punched the speaker button hard, cutting off his voice, wishing that she could cut him out of her life as easily.

The librarian at the UCLA Research Library, a thin young woman with large green eyes, handed Connie a copy of the floor plan.

"Here's the Continental Renaissance Collection." She outlined it with her mechanical pencil. "You take the stairs or the elevator to get there. You can access the computer catalogues at any one of these terminals." She checked them off. "All documents must be used in the reading room for that area. You're allowed no more than four documents on any given day."

"I just need something that goes into detail about the Contarini family in late sixteenth-century Venice, around 1594."

The librarian thought about it. "That shouldn't be too hard. They were a very distinguished family back then. Any member in particular that you're interested in?"

"The Countess—Alessandra Contarini."

Of the four books they brought to her in the reading room of the Continental Renaissance Collection, two were general histories that mentioned Giovanni Contarini, and his son Ludovico, only in passing as members of the *Signoria*. The third was a specialized volume on Venetian art that singled out Ludovico Contarini as a patron of musicians.

The fourth book was the one she wanted.

Names from the Golden Book. Published in London in 1863, it was old and brittle. Parts of the binding cracked and floated down onto the library table when she opened the book. The thin, faded pages crackled as she turned them. Its title referred to a far older book that once contained the names of all the noble families of Venice, the famous *Libra d'Oro,* the Golden Book, burned by Napoleon. *Names from the Golden Book* had biographical information on the Venetian nobility from the 1400's through the late 1500's.

Connie turned to the index, and ran her finger down the entries listed under *C.*

Cambrai, League of.

Cambrai, Treaty of.

She moved farther down the list.

Chioggia.

Chios.

Christian League.

Cicogna, Pasquale, Doge.

She thought of the Doge sitting in his golden robes aboard the *Bucintoro* on Ascension Day, of the plot to kill him set in motion by her husband, Ludovico Contarini, to be carried out by her lover Marcangelo, Tod Jarrow in this life, a murderer then and now.

The reading room seemed to grow cold.

Clement VIII, Pope.

Coducci, Mauro.

Cognac, Holy League of.

Too many C*'s,* she thought. She expected it would be even worse when she got to *Contarini.* In *The Story of Venice,* she had read that the Contarini family produced no less than five Doges during the seventeenth century alone.

Contarini, Alessandra Angelica Anna Maria, Countess.

She felt a shock of recognition course through her body, making her blood tingle. There it was, the proof. Alessandra Contarini was not some figment of a psychotic imagination.

She actually *had* existed.

Still exists, Connie thought, her heart beating faster.

She turned to the first page number, fingers trembling slightly as she flipped through the brittle pages.

Then she began to read.

Born 1570, died 1594, perhaps the most tragic and shameful member of this otherwise illustrious family—

She stopped reading. Died 1594? That was the year she kept flashing back to, the year when everything was happening—her love affair with Marcangelo, her husband Ludovico's plot to kill the Doge. A chill crawled up her spine. What did she die of?

What did I *die of?*

She read on.

Related to the famous Dandolo family on her mother's side, the Countess Alessandra Contarini was, according to accounts of the day, a great beauty. Young and fair, with long russet-coloured hair, she undoubtedly served as the voluptuous nude model for Tintoretto's masterpiece 'Venus in the Garden of Love' that now hangs in the private collection of a noble Russian family in St. Petersburg. Her husband, the Count Ludovico Contarini, a man of enormous social and political influence, was, by all accounts, a kind and loving husband to his bewitching young wife.

"Kind and loving!" Connie muttered to herself. "Bull*shit!*"

Several people in the reading room looked up.

Embarrassed, she returned to her book.

Alas, for the noble Count, his fair young wife turned out to be bewitching in deeds as well as looks. Conspiring with a local ruffian of despicable character, one Marcangelo Mosca, a so-called 'assassino,' or murderer for hire, the fair Alessandra plotted the cold-blooded murder of her lawfully wedded husband. The manner of execution chosen by the two illicit lovers, for so they appear to have been, was especially heinous and un-Christian, as it involved the use of black magic and the forbidden arts of sorcery.

Connie looked up from the book, frowning. What plot against Ludovico Contarini? And what about Ludovico's plot against the Doge? Why no mention of that? Wasn't it "especially heinous," too?

She looked at the title page of *Names from the Golden Book* to see who had written such a one-sided account.

The Hon. Sir Hugh Selwyn-Fitzmaurice, B. Litt., Oxon.

The old-boy network, she thought, turning back to the story.

Seeking out a reputed master of the black arts, a nameless mountebank known only as the Dark Sorcerer, the fair young Countess and her murderous lover secured the means of casting a dreadful and fatal spell upon the hapless, unwitting Count. Fortunately for the Count, and for the entire Contarini family, the dastardly plot was discovered and the adulterous malefactors apprehended.

Although the use of black magic and sorcery might well have brought the matter to trial at a court of the Inquisition, which flourished in those evil times, Venice refused to play the thrall to Papist domination and openly defied Rome. The treacherous couple were tried by the infamous Council of Ten and found guilty of sorcerous practices and attempted murder. Whereupon, they were both burned alive at St. Mark's Column on a Friday, the 23rd of July, the unfortunate young Countess not having yet attained her twenty-fourth birthday.

So that was how it ended. That was how she died.

How I died, she thought. *How I'll die again, back then.*

A dark terror from the distant past came crawling over her. It was all there, in the book. Ludovico. Marcangelo. The Dark Sorcerer. Death by fire, burning alive at St. Mark's Column, like Marcangelo in her nightmare. She looked again to see if there was anything more, any other clues to what had happened in the distant past that was now her present.

And her future.

The burning was attended by a large crowd, some of whom claimed to see the soul of the dying Alessandra rise from her charred body and fly away through the smoke, this being yet another instance of the credulous superstition of the common Italian peasantry, a lamentable condition that can still be observed in that backward region, even by the well-bred traveler of today.

She saw Alessandra's body, *her* body, writhing in unbearable agony, burning alive at the Column of St. Mark.

She slammed the book shut.

The sound rang out across the reading room of the Continental Renaissance Collection like the closing of a coffin lid.

37

Consecration

She studied her face in the bathroom mirror.

Who are you? she asked the pale, sad-looking face that stared back at her from the mirror. *Who are you, really?*

She was two people. But this was no schizophrenic fantasy.

She didn't *think* she was two different people. She *was*.

Constance Merriam MacKendrick Stallman, in this life.

In the other, Alessandra Angelica Anna Maria Contarini.

A television anchor's voice came through the closed bathroom door from their bedroom where Ken sat watching the late-night news.

Connie caught something about *another Jarrow victim*.

She opened the door.

"—recently escaped from Terminal Island, killing one prison guard in the process. Tod Jarrow is the prime suspect in a string of mutilation-torture killings involving at least twenty women in the greater Los Angeles area. But earlier this evening, he may have gone ahead and made it twenty-one. For more details, we go to Richard Briscoe in Hollywood. Rich?"

"Thank you, Leslie. Up here in the Hollywood Hills, home to movie stars like Jack Nicholson and Marlon Brando, residents usually feel protected from the mean streets down below. But that comfort zone was violated tonight at about six-thirty P.M., with the discovery of the nude body of a young woman by the side of a quiet residential road, not far from Mulholland Drive."

The video footage showed the body bag, uniformed police officers, harsh lights shining into dark undergrowth.

"The nude body, mutilated and dismembered, was discovered by two teenage boys who phoned it in to the police, thinking they had found the remains of an animal sacrifice by a local Satanic cult. Although body parts are still undergoing forensic examination by the LAPD, and identification of the victim is being withheld pending notification of relatives, the police are almost certain that this savage slaying is the latest work of escaped serial killer Tod Jarrow."

The tired-looking face of Lieutenant Ed Dormer appeared in closeup on the screen, an identifying caption below.

"Let's put it this way," Dormer said, "if it's not Jarrow, it's someone who's copying him. We think it's Jarrow."

The screen cut back to Richard Briscoe.

"Meanwhile, shock waves of fear are spreading through this wealthy, secluded community. Local security services report that requests for personal bodyguards are up eighty percent compared to this time a year ago. While the LAPD cautions against panic, they say there *are* steps that residents can take to protect themselves."

Ed Dormer's face popped up on screen again. "Obviously, young women should be very cautious about going out by themselves. They should report any suspicious persons they see."

A closeup of a prison mug shot of Tod Jarrow filled the screen, the stitches and scars highlighted by television's glaring, contrasty colors.

Connie looked away from the screen.

"And no one," Dormer continued, "under any circumstances, should be picking up hitchhikers, or stopping to help stranded motorists." He paused, creating expensive dead air. "We'll find him. We're concentrating on the Hollywood area right now, but we've got the nets spread wide. We'll find him."

Ken snapped off the set, putting down the remote. "I would have shut it off sooner, but I thought you wanted to hear it."

"Thanks." She shivered, rubbing her bare shoulders.

She came over and sat down on the bed, dressed only in

bra and panties. Ken was naked, covers pulled up to his waist.

He asked her, "Going to sleep like a lingerie model?"

She gave him a distant smile. "Not really." She unsnapped her bra and took off her panties, tossing them on the floor beside the bed, then pulled back the covers and snuggled inside.

Ken moved over toward her, his erect phallus poking its swollen head out from beneath the covers, throbbing slightly, like a questing animal.

She put a hand on his chest, stopping him. "You are going to really hate me for saying this. But I'm—Not tonight, please?"

He tried to mask his disappointment. "Okay, Connie."

"I really do love you, Ken. I just—"

"It's okay, Connie."

She looked at him, her eyes moist. "You going to go out and find some other woman now?"

Then she thought of her own encounter with Jarrow last night.

Ken waited for several seconds before answering.

"I'm not looking for reasons to get rid of you. How about you? Looking for a good reason to dump me?"

"No." She reached out and took him in her arms, kissing him, holding him close to her. "No. I love you. I really do."

They held each other tight, hearts beating together, their soft breathing the loudest sound in the room.

If only this was it, she thought, warm and safe in his arms. *If only the other things didn't exist—Jarrow, the other life.*

But they did, and the warm, safe feeling passed. She and Ken separated, moving to their own sides of the bed.

After several moments of silence, she asked, "Were you able to look into the—you know, the security thing?"

"I think I managed to come up with something."

She looked over at him. "What is it?"

"They'll be installing it tomorrow. You can find out then."

"Ken! I want to know *now!*"

"I wouldn't want to spoil the suspense for you."

She punched him playfully on the arm, then smiled at him.

"Thanks for taking care of it, darling. It makes me feel better about everything, even though Stevie's still in school—"

"Just one more day."

"What?"

"Tomorrow's the last day of school."

"My God, you're right! I completely forgot."

"Obviously you didn't check with Stevie, or she would've set you straight. She's been telling everyone about it."

"Not everyone. She doesn't think I'm worth talking to."

"She'll get over it. Just give her time."

"I know. But it's hard having her hate me this much. I thought she'd at least wait until she was a teenager."

"She doesn't hate you. She's just not sure she trusts you."

"It's the same thing, for a kid that age."

"No, it's not. If she didn't love you, it wouldn't matter whether or not she trusted you."

Connie looked at him. "Do you?"

"Do I what?"

"Trust me?"

"I want to. More than anything else in the world, I want to."

Then he asked, "How did it go at the UCLA Library today?"

"I found this old book about Venice written by some snobby old Victorian Englishman. But I learned something from it. I learned that the person I was—or am—actually existed. She really lived in Venice four hundred years ago."

And died there, burning alive on the Piazza San Marco.

A long silence followed before Ken asked, "Any problems?"

She frowned, at first in confusion, then in anger when she saw what he was getting at. "No, I did not freak out in the library. I did not crawl under the table and start screaming at the top of my lungs. Or throw rare books and manuscripts around the room."

"I don't think you're doing any of this on purpose, Connie. It's something you can't control. That's what worries me."

A chill came over her, under the covers, because he was

right. Not about what he thought was happening to her. But about the control part. It *was* out of her control.

For now, she thought, *but just give me some time.*

And some luck.

After the lights were out, she lay awake, staring into the darkness—watching as her eyes adjusted to the faint moonlight filtering in through drawn curtains, picking out familiar details that now loomed dark and strange. Dresser. Mirror. Chest of drawers. Thinking, as she lay there, of Tod Jarrow in this life, Marcangelo in the other. Of her own confused life, lives, in uncertain transit between the two worlds.

She drew in a deep breath, smelling the aromatic smoke of burning incense. Her muscles tensed. But it was too late. The shift had already begun.

Voices chanting inside the great Basilica. Priests and acolytes. Smoke from censers drifting up toward the glimmering mosaics on the church walls. God, saints, angels. The sound of trumpets, stringed instruments, flutes, recorders. Double choirs singing one of the *Sacrae symphoniae,* the Sacred Symphonies, text set to music by the great Gabrieli. Rich and elegant, echoing inside the Basilica with haunting solemnity.

She looked up from where she knelt at a pew, and through her black veil saw Marcangelo near the back of the church, trying to look like a worshiper, the lust they felt for each other blurring the notes of the glorious music, making the incense itself smell rank with earthly desire.

Outside, now. Hurrying through dark *calli,* smoke from distant torches replacing the smell of incense. Both of them wearing heavy wool cloaks and dominoes.

He grabbed her suddenly and turned her toward him, kissing her hard, their black masks rubbing against each other.

"No!" She turned away. "Not where other eyes can see us!"

"I don't care." He drew her to him. "I want you. Now."

She looked at him through her mask, the black veil discarded.

"Have you forgotten what you do for my husband? The

need for secrecy? Or—" She paused, taunting him. "Or has he chosen someone else to do his work?"

"He needs no one else. But no more talk of him. Tonight I wish him at the bottom of a canal, his mouth full of shit, the fish nibbling at his eyes." He put a hand to her reddish brown hair and pulled her head back, hard. "Tonight," he whispered, his breath hot on her throat, "all Venice belongs to no one but you and me."

Water. Slapping against the side of a canal, the hull of a gondola. The soft splash of the gondolier's pole thrust into the dark water, then the swirl as he leaned into it, pushing the sleek craft forward. From inside the *felze*—the small enclosed cabin for passengers of the gondola, black curtains drawn over its windows—came whispers, laughter, sudden cries of pleasure, and pain.

Half sitting, half lying on a red velvet seat inside the *felze,* still wearing their black masks, the front of her gown undone, her breasts bare, dark nipples large and glistening in the muted orange light of a single candle flickering in a brass holder shaped like a seahorse. His codpiece removed, phallus jutting up from his blue tights, the skirts of her gown lifted up over her pale white thighs. He took her large nipple in his mouth and bit down on it, teeth sinking into dark velvet flesh.

"Stop!" she cried. "The pain!"

He looked up at her, his dark eyes liquid in the candlelight.

"The pain makes the pleasure more intense. Sweetness and spice. Light and shadow. The balance of opposites." A smile flickered across his lips. "Your power and privilege have kept you from understanding this, Alessandra. The pleasure that comes from pain." He took her nipple gently between forefinger and thumb. "When I bite them, they grow large with excitement. *They* understand." He squeezed her nipple, hard.

She hissed between clenched teeth.

Then he started pushing his way inside her. She was wet and ready, but he was too large and it hurt. Hurt terribly, tearing into her like a blunt piece of iron, detached from his body. She threw her head back, eyes shut tight with pain, Marcangelo's steady, brutal ramming in dramatic counterpoint to the gentle rocking of the gondola.

She opened her eyes. And saw a mirror image of herself on the ceiling of the room. Naked white body spread out on fine linen sheets, hands tied behind her head to a bedpost, the large areolae of her dark nipples stretched oblong on her flattened breasts. Marcangelo sat astride her, moving in and out of her, his black mask exchanged for a grotesque Carnival mask with a long nose and red eyes. She still wore her own domino, nude body covered with cold sweat, groaning with pain now as he thrust into her and tried to make it hurt.

He pulled out, dribbling over her thighs and legs, then took off his Carnival mask, and put his face down there, using his tongue on her wetness, biting at the tender flesh, his dark beard scratching the inside of her thighs. Another face bent over hers. A dark-eyed serving girl with long black hair and deep copper skin. She was nude, her body heavy and sensual, breasts drooping, tipped with swollen nipples. She reached out her hands and began plucking lightly at Alessandra's large dark nipples, increasing their size and hardness. The girl smiled lewdly at her, full lips pulled back over small white teeth. Alessandra looked away, repelled. This was how the lascivious young Countess Veronica Bragadin took her pleasure, with a man and a woman in the same bed. But Alessandra did not share Veronica's debased tastes. Marcangelo had never done this to her before. Why was he now—

The serving girl pressed her full lips against Alessandra's, forcing her tongue deep inside her mouth. Alessandra tried to turn away, struggling against the ropes that restrained her as the girl explored the inside of her mouth and the pressure of her tongue, one hand lazily stroking an erect nipple at the same time.

Alessandra broke free from the unwelcome kiss, turning her face to one side. "Whore!" she gasped at the girl.

The dark-eyed serving girl laughed softly and licked the

side of Alessandra's throat, then whispered in her ear, "We are *all* whores, Contessa."

She looked down at Marcangelo, his dark beard damp and beaded with her wetness, smiling up at her from between her legs, savoring what he saw.

She glanced about the room. Mirrors on the walls and ceiling. Obscene ivory statuettes on side tables. Pornographic sketches by the debauched Pietro Aretino, tossed carelessly onto a gold-brocade-trimmed chair in one corner. Goblets and beakers of wine. Cheeses and oysters. The food of lechery. It was a room in a common bordello, not even the house of a registered courtesan. The dark-eyed serving girl kissing and caressing her was some whore from the shipyards of the Arsenal. Alessandra's body recoiled against the outrage. Why had he brought her here? *How* had he done so? By drugging her wine? Or pressing a handkerchief dipped in deadly nightshade against her face inside the *felze* of the gondola?

The dark-eyed serving girl put her mouth to one of Alessandra's large nipples and began to suck at it hungrily. Marcangelo pressed his beard, damp with her own wetness, against the other nipple, biting it hard. The serving girl reached down a hand between Alessandra's damp white thighs and fondled her wetness. The Countess arched back her head on the satin pillow, her breathing loud and erratic.

Marcangelo lifted his mouth suddenly from one swollen nipple, his teeth raking across her breast. He grabbed the serving girl by her long black hair and yanked back on it, jerking her up to her knees, full breasts wobbling, head pulled back. From a side table he took a curved Turkish dagger and drew its edge slowly across her exposed throat, severing the jugular vein. When she tried to scream, blood bubbles formed in her mouth. Blood sprayed in a fine mist over Alessandra's naked body, spotting her face and hair, and black mask.

"Marcangelo!" she screamed at him, twisting in the ropes as blood spattered her flesh.

The serving girl had stopped struggling. She hung limp in

his arms, head fallen forward, thick blood oozing down over her heavy naked breasts. Marcangelo, his dark eyes glazed, began to mutilate the body, cutting into the dark olive skin, chopping off the extruding parts, all the while oblivious to the screams and struggles of his lover beneath him.

"What are you *doing?*" she shrieked. "Have you gone *mad?*"

"He is preparing a sacrifice, for me," murmured the voice at her ear. "And for himself, a consecration, a dedication to the greater deeds to come."

The voice echoed like a whisper from the tomb, cold and evil, carried on the black winds of death. She turned her masked and bloodied face toward the voice.

She screamed in terror.

The Dark Sorcerer stood beside the bed, his wrinkled face wet and oozing, like something dredged up from beneath a black canal. The yellow eyes burned with a sick and feverish light. He stood in front of the mirror on the wall, but his black robes and bent body cast no image in the glass. He smiled at her, revealing even rows of sharp, pointed teeth.

Marcangelo continued to cut apart the serving girl's body, precisely and dispassionately as a butcher. Hot blood spilled down onto Alessandra's naked flesh and the fine white linen, turning the bed into a reeking slaughterhouse pallet.

She had stopped screaming now, her voice hoarse and aching. She stared at the atrocity taking place above her, senses numb with horror, unable to believe that any of this was happening, wanting to turn away from Marcangelo's blood ritual.

But she did not turn, fearful of seeing once again what stood beside the bed, casting no image in the mirrors of the room.

Marcangelo poured blood down on her from the serving girl's thigh, drizzling it over her breasts and onto her face. She shut her eyes, then her mouth, as the blood dripped into it. He raised both hands above his head, dark red to the elbows, naked chest streaked with blood.

"Powers of Darkness!" he cried. "Forces of Evil! This I do to consecrate the death of a Doge." He looked down at her. "And to consecrate our love for all eternity, yours and mine."

Wed to one eternity.

He took the Turkish dagger, wet with hot blood, and cut the ropes that bound her. Then he reached down and took her in his arms, her flesh slippery in his bloodstained grasp.

"Get awa—" she gasped, pushing against him. "A*way* from me!"

She struck at his chest and face with her bloody fists.

The Turkish dagger fell from his grasp, clattering to the tile floor. She struck at his eyes and mouth. He covered his face with blood-red hands. The Dark Sorcerer's piercing laughter rang in her ears as she struck at her lover, again and again.

She rolled out of the blood-soaked bed, wet feet sticking to the tiles. Marcangelo came after her, tried to grab her by the shoulders. She turned and pushed at him, shoving her hands flat against his chest, pushing him harder than she had ever pushed anyone or anything in her life. He stumbled backward, crashing into one of the mirrors. Glass shattered. The reflected image of the bedroom cracked and fell apart, dropping into fragments. The shrill laughter of the Dark Sorcerer carried across the room, a mocking, evil *obbligato*.

She turned, and saw his face, mere inches from her own— yellow eyes burning, mouth open, tongue long and narrow like a snake's, darting in and out between rows of pointed teeth.

She struck at the loathsome face, her fingers hooked into claws. The withered skin gave way like rotted mush, sticking to her fingers, dribbling down her wrists. She screamed, backing away from him, then turned and ran. Into a mirror. She pressed her naked body flat against the glass, screaming, hammering at the glass, as he touched her with a hand cold as death itself.

"Stop it!" But it was not her voice that cried out.

"Connie! *Stop* it!"

She found herself kneeling on the sill of their bedroom

window, curtains torn back, face and breasts pressed flat against the glass, arms spread wide, beating with her clenched fists on the windowpane, mouth open, gasping for breath, sweat running down her face and naked back.

Ken had hold of her shoulders, his own breathing ragged.

She swallowed hard. Her throat ached from the screaming.

They remained like that for several seconds, as their breathing slowly returned to normal.

She started to get down from the windowsill.

He stopped her. "Let me—help you."

She got down, leaning on him. Her legs felt wobbly. When she tried to walk unaided, she almost fell. He guided her over to the bed. She sat down on her side, the sheets damp and cold with sweat. Ken leaned against the windowsill, arms trembling.

At last he turned to her, and said, "Okay."

She waited for him to go on.

"Okay what?" she asked.

"That's it." He took a deep breath. "Did Jake give you any references? Any other doctors to see about this—problem?"

She nodded.

"Then you're going to one of them tomorrow. If you want, you can go by yourself. If you're not up to it, I'll drive you."

"I can drive myself."

"Mommy!" Stevie's frightened voice came from outside the bedroom door. *"Daddy!* What's *wrong?"*

They could hear her sobbing behind the closed door.

"It's okay, baby!" Connie called back to her.

But nothing was okay.

38
The Mysteries

Zenobia Horowitz had her office on Fairfax, near Beverly.

A narrow two-story building, wedged in between a kosher butcher's and a custom tailor's, with a bus-stop bench out front advertising the services of an Orthodox Jewish funeral home, it looked nothing like the authentic occult shop Connie had stepped into once as part of a bet with another medical student. It bore no flamboyant lettering outside, no suns, moons, stars, or sacred eyes, no Aubrey Beardsley-type drawings of ethereal young women with long, serpentine hair.

Inside, it looked like the office of a struggling tax preparer. A gray metal desk and filing cabinets complemented chrome waiting-room chairs with Naugahyde backs and armrests. A sickly potted plant stood in one corner of the room, a water cooler in the other, an unopened water bottle on the floor beside it.

The only unusual thing about the room was a tall, thin woman dressed in a black running suit, her iron gray hair, long and straight, drawn back from her face and tied behind her head with a leather thong. She had her eyes closed, fingers at her temples, mouth open slightly as she breathed with a deep, meditative rhythm.

Connie took a seat, quietly, watching her.

The woman's eyes opened.

"Are you Zenobia Horowitz?" Connie asked her.

The woman shook her head slowly. "I'm Rachel. And I'm stuck on the goddamn Thirty-second Path, the Ascent of Saturn to *Yesod,* and I'm fucking sick and tired of it. You know what I mean?"

She took a pack of Virginia Slims from her purse and lit one angrily, blowing smoke out her nose, then offered the pack to Connie, who shook her head.

"Patience, Rachel, my dear," called out a voice from the other room, flat and slightly nasal, almost like a feminine version of Jake's, but with a much heavier accent, half-German, half-British. "The Tree of Life is not mastered by an act of the conscious will. It is not something just to *do*. Like to drive a car or to make a *kreplach*. You know this by now."

From out of the open door behind the metal desk came a short, medium-sized woman with a flower-print dress, purple cardigan sweater, dangling earrings, athletic shoes, and short curly hair dyed eye-popping red.

"So," smiled Zenobia Horowitz, earrings jangling, "what's to get so sick and tired of?"

Rachel waved her cigarette in the air. "It's frustrating! It fucks up my head."

"Here." Zenobia handed her several sheets of paper. "I copy this for you. Memorize it. Everything. The God-name. The Archangel-name. The Magic Weapons. The Symbols. The four colors of *Atziluth, Briah, Yetzirah,* and *Assiah.* Also, the Tarot cards corresponding to this Sphere. *Then* you get to *Yesod* by the Thirty-second Path, Saturn or no Saturn. Wait and see."

Rachel sighed. "That's a lot of shit to remember, Zena."

"It plants the Tree inside your soul. Take it home with you. Memorize! Memorize!"

"Okay, Zena." Rachel folded the papers and put them in her purse. "How much do I owe you?"

"Two hundred and fifty dollars. Check, credit card, cash."

"Okay if I write you a check off my revolving line?"

"No problem. I get you a receipt, my dear."

Expensive, Connie thought. *Weird, but expensive.*

Rachel looked up from where she was writing the check.

"I keep too much cash in my main account, my fucking ex comes down on it like a dog in heat. You know what I mean?"

Connie nodded. "Sure."

"There." Zenobia handed Rachel her receipt. "You have the copies. You memorize them. I see you again next week, by which time you master the Thirty-second Path and the Sphere of *Yesod,* and you are one happy girl, no?"

"I hope so, Zena. *Ciao.*" Rachel glanced at Connie. "Good luck, okay?"

After seeing Rachel to the door, Zenobia came back and stood over Connie. "So, my dear. How can I help you? Usually, I never forget a face. But I must say, I don't remember yours."

"Connie Stallman. Jake Mauder sent me."

Zenobia clapped her hands together, rattling the collection of bracelets on each wrist. *"Ach,* of course! Connie! Jake's good student of psychoanalysis. How *are* you, my dear?" Zenobia shook Connie's hand with both of hers. "Jake said he gave you one of my cards. So you know who I am. Call me Zena."

She sat down in a Naugahyde chair next to Connie.

"So. Jake calls me. Tells me he is referring this good student of his. A doctor with her own practice, a psychiatrist at the Beckford Clinic in Hollywood. Right? Naturally, I am curious. Why does he send her to *me?* Jake, I love like a brother. A good man, and a wise one. But for the Mysteries—" Zenobia shrugged. "For the Mysteries, he has no *Sehnsucht,* no passion, no desire. You understand?"

Connie nodded. "I think so."

"So, you are his student. Why are you here?"

Connie told her, briefly.

Zenobia rested her chin in one hand and studied Connie.

"You've been traveling the Paths, my girl," she said quietly, "without anyone to guide you. A dangerous journey. Now, you are in trouble, so you come to me. Right?"

Connie nodded. "I'm in trouble."

Zenobia smiled, then reached out and squeezed her hand.

"Do not worry, my dear. You came to the right place." She sighed. "But so much work to do! And if already you're in trouble, so little time. Nevertheless, I must hear it all. *Every*-thing. Every-last-little-detail." Zenobia emphasized the words with her thumb and forefinger in a circle, as if pinching each word. "But, not here!"

She got to her feet, adjusting the purple cardigan. "This place—" She grimaced at the office. "A real pain in the ass, no? But I keep it that way for a reason! Cuts down on the crazies, the ones who are not serious. The ones who come looking for the frisson, the cheap thrill, instead of the *Sehnsucht*. You understand what I mean?"

Connie nodded.

"Come! We go upstairs now. To *my* place, where *I* live. You have a long story to tell me, and I want to hear it all. But I might as well be comfortable while I listen. And you too, no?"

Upstairs they entered a different world. Long tables lay covered with the paraphernalia of ceremonial magic. Candles, chalices, cups, amulets, pentagrams, wands. A large male cockatoo sat on an open perch. As Connie walked by him, staring, he opened his mouth and let out a shrill *c-a-a-a-a-aw*, the feathers of his crest arching up as he screamed. She backed away, almost stepping on a gray and black striped cat underfoot. The cat hissed at her, and twitched his tail.

"*Ach,* ignore him!" Zenobia said, shooing the cat away. "He has a most disagreeable temperament."

Connie looked at the cat, then at the great white bird with his yellow-feathered crest, then at the cat again, skulking behind the leg of a side table.

"Do they get along? A cat, and a bird without a cage?"

"Perfectly! The harshness of *Geburah*"—pointing to the cat, then the bird—"and the mercy of *Chesed,* two opposites balanced by the mediating beauty of *Tiphareth.* Like brothers they get along."

Connie's eye was caught by a large poster on the opposite wall. It seemed to be a type of diagram, with ten circles arranged in three rows and connected by lines, like spaces in a maze. Inside each circle was a pictographic symbol, and above it, a word in ancient Hebrew letters. Connie stared at it, fascinated. It seemed as if it *ought* to have a meaning. But she couldn't make heads or tails of it.

"What's *that?*" she asked Zenobia.

The older woman looked up from where she was pouring two cups of tea. "That, my dear, is the *Otz Chiim.*" She pronounced the *ch* with that throat-clearing sound Jake used when he said *chutzpa.* "The Tree of Life. The map of the world, the universe, and the human soul. The living heart of the Great Kabbalah. For now, too complicated. Later, we talk about it."

"But what does it *mean?*"

Zenobia smiled, amused by Connie's insistence. "A preview, then. What they call in the movies, a coming attractions. Right?"

She put down the teapot and walked over to the large poster, pointing to each of the circles in turn as she talked.

She started with the circle at the base of the diagram.

"The Sphere of *Malkuth.* The Earth. The place where we are now." Inside the circle, a young woman, wearing a crown, sat upon a throne. "The place that most people think is the only place."

Zenobia traced a straight line up to the next circle.

"This is the Thirty-second Path, the one our friend Rachel struggles with so. It leads to the Sphere of *Yesod.*" She pointed to a muscular naked man. "The Foundation. The first Sphere where we can work magic. But also, the Sphere of Illusion. A place where magic can be worked against us."

She moved on an inclined line to the right.

"The Sphere of *Netzach.*" A beautiful naked woman. "Victory. But this is the victory of love, under the influence of Venus."

She turned to the upper left of *Yesod.*

"The Sphere of *Hod.*" A hermaphrodite, the creature of both sexes. "Glory. The form of the astral consciousness. The three Spheres above *Malkuth—Hod, Yesod, Netzach—*form the Astral Triangle that affects our Physical Life."

She moved up the straight line from *Yesod* to the circle directly above it. "The Sphere of *Tiphareth.*" Connie saw three figures: a noble king, an innocent child, and a sacrificed god.

"The Sphere of Beauty, or Splendor. This is the harmonizing beauty that blends differences and balances opposites. Like the great friendship between my two strange pets." She nodded in their direction, where the cockatoo preened his feathers on the perch and the cat lay sleeping beneath it. *"Tiphareth* balances two mighty and opposing Spheres."

She moved to the upper left. "The Sphere of *Geburah*. Force. Power." A great warrior rode in his chariot. "The force that purifies, like the Wrath of God."

She pointed to the upper right. "The Sphere of *Chesed*. Mercy. Forgiveness." A noble king, wearing a crown, sat upon a throne. "These three Spheres—*Chesed* and *Geburah*, balanced by *Tiphareth*—form the Ethical Triangle that guides our Moral Life."

She pointed quickly to the three Spheres that comprised the top of the diagram. "On the right, the Sphere of *Chokmah*. Wisdom." A bearded man. "On the left, the Sphere of *Binah*. Understanding." A dignified, mature woman. "And above all, the Sphere of *Kether*. The Crown of the Tree." A bearded king on a lordly throne. "These three—*Chokmah, Binah, Kether*—form the Supernal Triangle, the one that creates our Spiritual Life."

Zenobia turned away from the diagram, folding her arms.

"So. That is the *Otz Chiim*, the Great Tree of Life. There is much more to it, of course. The three Spheres on the left form the Feminine Column of Severity. The three on the right, the Masculine Column of Mercy. The four in the middle, the Neutral Column of Mildness. Then, for every Sphere, there is the God-name, the Archangel, the Host of Angels, the Magic Weapons and Symbols, the four suits of the Tarot cards, the four corresponding colors in *Atziluth, Briah, Yetzirah,* and *Assiah*. But all that, later."

Connie stared at the diagram, her head swimming.

"But what does it *do?*" she asked.

Zenobia moved in on her until they were standing face-to-face.

"It gives you control of your own life, and of all the powers in the universe. Which are the same thing. Because, you see, the Tree *is* the universe, and the Tree is inside you. Do you understand what I am saying?"

"Yes. I think so."

"Now, we are going to hear about your experiences, my dear. And, while you talk and I listen, we will both drink tea."

Connie looked at the cockatoo on his perch and the cat beneath him. "Are those their names? *Geburah* and—whatever?"

"No, no. They have ordinary names. The cat, he is Paracelsus. The bird, Cornelius Agrippa." Seeing the look in Connie's eyes, she added, "Not that I think they are the reincarnated souls of those two great magicians. But they have all four crossed on the Paths at one time or another, I am sure."

Zenobia handed her a cup of tea with a rose-chintz design.

"You must forgive me. No one in America drinks tea."

"I drink herb tea," Connie said, "sometimes."

Zenobia waved a hand in dismissal. *"Ach!* Kool-Aid tea. I learned to drink tea from my mother, who was born in Palestine under British rule, before it became Israel. As a young woman, she moved to Berlin, where she met my father and where, eventually, I was born. We left there when I was still a young girl, in the late twenties, when things were starting to get not so happy, and we moved to Palestine." She stared into her teacup, as if seeing the past there. "I came to America to go to university and never left. My mother and father are dead now, of course. But I still get back to Israel occasionally, where things are not so happy there as they once were." She looked at Connie. "Real happiness is what we carry with us, inside. Don't you agree?"

Connie thought of her own mother in the wheelchair, with a love that was stronger than death, and she said, "Yes, I do."

"Here, my dear. Have a macaroon."

Connie thanked her and bit into it. "Ow!"

"Hard as iron, aren't they? They're easier to chew if you dip them in the tea first. I keep hoping for a client with really strong teeth, someone to finish off the damn things. Now. You must tell me all about yourself. Your own parents. Your husband. Your children. Your life—Your journey along the Paths."

Connie told her everything then. This was the third time she had gone through it. First with Ken, then with Jake. But this time she felt no constant undercurrent of shock, disbelief, or pity. Zenobia listened as carefully as Jake Mauder had, but with more intensity, as if she was going through it with Connie, detail by detail, step by step. She did not ask questions. She interrupted rarely, and then only to have something repeated.

They stopped for lunch. But they did not really stop. Zenobia seemed to have had everything prepared in advance. She brought out their lunches on TV trays, so that Connie could keep talking while they ate, and Zenobia could continue to listen.

By the time Connie finished, it was the very end of the day, the moment before the light dropped suddenly into darkness, the way it always did in Southern California, a land without twilight.

Zenobia sat silent in her chair, an empty teacup on the table beside her. Several lamps were turned on, multicolored Tiffany shades diffusing the light. An old grandfather clock ticked loudly in one corner of the room.

Connie looked over to where Cornelius Agrippa, the cockatoo, shifted position on his perch, grasping it firmly with his claws, crested head bent forward, the light from a nearby lamp casting his shadow, dark and exaggerated, against the far wall. Down below, Paracelsus paced back and forth with the sinuous movement of a night-stalking cat.

Zenobia looked up at her. "We will try something now. It is not entirely safe. But it is necessary, I think."

"What do you mean?"

"You and I, we, are going to meditate on the power of the Sphere of *Geburah*. Not like the crazies in their show-off way, with the *om*-noise and the lotus position. We meditate by concentrating on the image. By filling our minds with it."

Zenobia pointed to the diagram of the Tree of Life, and Connie followed the line of her finger to the middle circle on the left.

"*Geburah*. Harshness, but also Strength. We need this strength, as protection, for what we do next. But of that, later. Now, we concentrate upon the image of *Geburah*. The great warrior in his mighty chariot." Zenobia closed her eyes as she spoke.

"Visualize! See it before you!"

Connie closed her own eyes. She saw a vast, empty plain, stretching to the far horizon, the ground dry and cracked. Across that plain, his chariot drawn by four powerful horses, rode a warrior from legend, hair and beard whipping in the wind, armor gleaming. The wheels of his chariot struck sparks from the ground. The eyes of his horses gleamed wild and piercing, their nostrils flaring. Hoofs pounded the dry, cracked earth.

Connie, her eyes still closed, heard Zenobia speak.

"Now, with the protection of *Geburah* strong about you, like a cloak of courage, concentrate upon the Dark Sorcerer." Her voice dropped low, as if whispering a curse. *"Il stregóne morello."*

Connie gasped.

"Do not fear him," Zenobia said. "The power of *Geburah* will protect you. You must call forth his image in your mind, dreadful though that may be. But you *must* do this!" She took a deep breath. "Go, now. I will be with you."

Connie saw the dark shape again, standing before the mirror, casting no image. The withered skin. The spider's claws for hands. The pale yellow eyes. Burning, now, in the fog. Then, in darkness. The yellow eyes expanding, growing larger, until they seemed to swallow her up whole, drawing her deep within them, body and soul. Then the voice, behind the eyes.

Why do you call upon me? it hissed inside her head. *Contessssssssssssssssaaaaaaaaaaaaaa.*

She gripped the arms of her chair, heart pounding.

I will come for you, it hissed, *all in good time.*

"No," Connie whispered, then, shouting, *"No!"*

The voice broke into a high, evil laugh.

"By the power of the Archangel Khamael!" Zenobia cried. "By his Host of Seraphim. By all the Living Creatures, *Chaioth ha Kadesh!* We reject you. We *defy* you!"

The evil laughter turned to enraged snarling, like the roar of a great jungle cat.

Connie opened her eyes, and saw Paracelsus crouched on the floor before her, tail twitching.

"Geburah!" squawked Cornelius Agrippa, his crest arching.

Zenobia nodded, an approving look in her eye. "Not bad, my girl. For a first confrontation with such a one, not bad at all."

She raised a hand and smoothed her dyed red hair. Connie noticed that the hand trembled slightly.

"So," Zenobia said, "now we know, don't we?"

"What?"

"Have you never been tested, my dear?"

"For what?"

"Psychic abilities. Extrasensory perception. Paranormal sensitivity. Different names for the same thing. Have they never had you identify colors and geometrical shapes while blindfolded? Communicate with someone mentally in another room?"

"Never."

"Strange. Your ability is quite remarkable. I'm surprised no one has noticed it before."

"What do you mean?"

"What is happening to you, these journeys back to Venice, you have not brought about all by yourself. Another force is involved. This much I suspected from what you said. Now we have proved it here, today. But the intensity of your visions, their frequency—all this would not be possible without your psychic sensitivity." Then, under her breath, "And I am sure he knows that, oh yes."

"Excuse me?"

"You have the Power, my girl. You have gone back and forth in time, spanning years and dimensions. All this on your own, without any training or guidance. Properly instructed, you could no doubt elevate poor Cornelius Agrippa over there, and lift him up to the ceiling, screaming and flapping his wings in terror. All that, as easily as changing a television channel by remote control. Easier, in fact. No buttons to push. Except those inside your head."

Connie sat back in her chair.

"This does not run in your family?" Zenobia asked. "Neither parent had the Power? Grandparents? Distant relations?"

Connie shook her head to all the questions.

"Again, strange. This kind of thing almost always runs in families. But, who knows? This time, maybe not. It is strange. But it happens."

"Why did you have me do that?" Connie asked. "Why did you have me contact—*him?* He killed Jennie! He made *me* kill—"

The word caught in her throat.

In the silence that followed, the ticking of the grandfather clock became the loudest sound in the room.

"Beneath the Tree of Life," Zenobia said, "there is another tree, a Tree of Death. It is an inversion of the Tree of Life, its powers demonic forms of those that spring from the Great Tree."

"I don't understand—"

"This one you called forth, he is the root of that Dark Tree."

"But who *is* he? I've never heard him called anything except the Dark Sorcerer. He has to have a name!"

"Oh, yes," Zenobia said, and as she spoke a shadow seemed to fall across her face. "Of that you can be sure. He has a name."

"What is it?"

Zenobia shook her head. "Not tonight. There are things I must do first. I must consult my books. I must think. I must meditate. I must travel my own Paths. In the meantime, you go home to your husband, your children. Protect yourself and them from this Tod Jarrow, who is *his* creature, in this life and the other. Tomorrow, when you come to see me again, I promise you, I will tell you his name."

"But why can't—"

Zenobia raised a hand. "Don't be impatient, my dear. Believe me, when I tell you his name, you will be sorry you ever heard it."

39

Summons

As Connie pulled into the driveway that night, she reached for her remote-control garage-door opener.

Then she put it down, and turned off the engine. She didn't want to open the garage door and have Ken come running out to see how she was. If he asked her how things went today, and he would, she was going to lie to him. And if Jake called tonight, which he might, she would lie to him, too.

She thought of what Zenobia had said about all these lies as they walked to the door of her drab downstairs office.

"Lies? *Ach!* Think of them, my dear, as necessary fictions. Since today you talk so much of Venice, I quote for you a saying of Paolo Sarpi, the famous Venetian diplomat of the seventeenth century. In Italian it goes, *'Non dico mai buggie, ma la verità non a tutti.'* In English, 'I never tell lies, but the truth not to everyone.' Good, huh?"

Connie smiled to herself. At least that was one thing she wouldn't have to worry about. Even if Ken found out who Zenobia was, he'd never get anything out of her the way he always did with Jake Mauder. Zenobia, she was sure, could keep a secret.

She got out of her car and headed for the front door.

A bright light exploded in her eyes. A break-in siren began to wail. She raised a hand against the blinding light.

A tough female voice hammered at her from the darkness behind the light, amplified by a heavy-duty loudspeaker.

"Stop where you are! And identify your—"

Ken's voice broke in. "Okay, Lisa. Knock it off."

The blinding light winked out. The siren fell silent.

Connie blinked her eyes, still seeing bright spots.

The front door opened, silhouetting two figures in the doorway. One of them she recognized as her sister-in-law Lisa Tate, wearing khaki shorts and a pink *Cancún Cantina* sweatshirt.

Lisa came forward, hands in her pockets, a smug smile on her face. "Hey," she said to Connie, "is that one hell of a security system, or what?"

"Not bad, Lisa."

"Surprise you?"

"A little."

Ken said, "It wasn't supposed to be that much of a surprise. But my kid sister has this thing for practical jokes."

"Aahh! Connie's a good sport, aren't you, Con?"

Lisa gave her a quick, bone-crushing hug.

"What kind of light is it, Ken?"

"High-intensity flood, triggered by motion-sensors. I had it turned off because you were coming home. Lisa turned it back on."

"I thought you'd get a buzz out of it," Lisa said, and shivered in her pink sweatshirt. "Goddamn, it's *cold* up in these hills at night! Let's go inside."

As they walked toward the front door, Connie asked, "What else does this super system do? Shoot laser beams at intruders?"

"High-sensitivity microphones and compact video cameras are concealed around the outside of the house," Ken said, holding the front door for his wife and sister.

Lisa poked him in the stomach as she passed by. "You're getting fat, big brudder. You need to do more sit-ups."

"The way it's laid out," he continued, closing the front

door and double-locking it, "no one can come up to this place from any direction without setting off lots of bells and whistles."

"Where was Lisa when she was talking over that loud-speaker?"

"In here." Ken opened a closet door in the kitchen that led to a large, deep room running back underneath the stairs.

"My pantry! What did you do to it?"

"Improved it. You weren't using most of the available space anyway. Your stuff's over on that side now."

The rest of the pantry was taken up by a multi-screen video-monitor display, with a microphone and an operations console.

"This is how you work the loudspeaker. That's volume control. Believe it or not, Lisa didn't have it all the way up. You could blow out somebody's eardrums if you wanted to. These buttons here control the different hidden cameras. Zoom and track. Each camera has its own screen. These buttons over here give you additional floodlights. I can't show you now without waking up the neighbors, but you could light up this place like Dodger Stadium at night."

"I'm impressed," Connie said. "But why is it in my pantry?"

"It's not just a pantry anymore. It's a safe room. If the lights and siren ever go off, get yourself and the kids in here on the double and lock the door. That way you won't present a visible target to anyone outside. If the intruder isn't scared off by the light show and breaks into the house anyway, it's going to be hard for him to find you, and even harder for him to get to you."

He pointed to the pantry door. "This may look the same, but it's got a steel plate inside it now. Hard to break down or shoot through. The door has a constant marker light above it so that you can always find the safe room, even if it's the middle of the night and somebody's cut the power from outside."

Connie stepped out of the room to look at the marker light.

"Suppose somebody *does* cut the power, or it goes down all by itself. Will any of this stuff keep working?"

"Generator's got enough juice to run everything for seventy-two hours. But you won't need it that long. Because this"—tapping the microphone—"lets you talk directly to the police station."

"Do I have to dial 911?"

Ken shook his head. "When the alarms go off, the system automatically patches you into the police dispatcher."

"And if it's a false alarm?"

"You tell them it's a false alarm. No problem. But just make sure it *is* a false alarm."

"How much did all this cost?"

"A lot. But it could have been worse. Guy who did it's a friend of Dad's. We got it for way under market. Not that I put a price on my family's safety. This would have been worth whatever it cost. It's just what we need. Automated. Almost fail-safe."

Connie thought of the nameless evil she and Zenobia had confronted earlier, and how useless all this would be against something like that.

But she said, "Thanks, Ken, for taking such good care of us."

She put her arms around his neck and kissed him.

"Hey, big brudder!" Lisa called from the kitchen. "You haven't even told her about the best part yet!"

"Ken, what's that?"

"Me!" Lisa stuck her head into the pantry.

"Lisa's going to stay with us for a while. Keep an eye on the kids during the day while you're—away."

"Lisa, that's really sweet of you."

"Don't mention it!" Lisa slapped her on the shoulder. "It's no pro— *Whoa!* My popcorn!" She ran back to the kitchen.

Connie looked at Ken. "You don't think I'm capable—"

"It has nothing to do with that," he said. "Even though

you're off work for a while now, you won't always be home during the day. Like today, for example."

She launched into her lie. "I had to drive to Pasadena—"

Ken held up a hand. "Whatever. The thing is, you won't always be here. But the kids will. Stevie's out of school now."

"What about Galina?"

"We pay her for domestic work, not guard duty. Not that Tod Jarrow's likely to come by. But I'll feel better with Lisa here."

"Stevie likes to play outside. She'll want to ride her new bike around the neighborhood."

"She won't be riding until Jarrow's back where he belongs."

"Have you told her that?"

Ken nodded. "We had a long talk. She understands."

Connie sighed, realizing that Ken had a direct line to Stevie that was closed to her for now, maybe forever.

"Do you want to hear what happened to me in therapy today?"

"Not unless you want to tell me. It's going to take time, babe. I know that." He reached for her hand. "I'm just glad you're finally starting to get some help."

His eyes began to water. "I'm so damn glad, Connie."

She put her arms around him and held him close.

"Mom?" asked the voice behind her.

She looked up, wiping at a tear on her own cheek, and saw Stevie standing in the doorway to the pantry.

"Aunt Lisa bought me that new video game," Stevie said, her voice unusually quiet and subdued. *Zorena's New Galactic Adventures.* You know the one?"

Connie smiled, Zorena reminding her of Zenobia. "Sure."

"Well, since there's no school tomorrow—Could you play it with me, Mom?"

Connie tried to keep the tears back. "You bet!"

She and Stevie sat on the living-room floor, playing *Zorena's New Galactic Adventures,* while Lisa watched from the sofa.

"Hah! You just lost a whole starship squadron, Connie!"

"This is a lot harder than it looks, Lisa."

"Watch out for the meteor-sweepers, Mom!"

"Lisa, where's Ken?"

"Upstairs, trying to put Trent down for the night."

"Your brother's the greatest. You know that, Lisa?"

"He's okay, for a guy."

The phone rang.

Jake, Connie thought. "I'll get it!"

"You stay in the pilot's seat, Commander. *I'll* get it."

Connie rose to her feet as Lisa picked up the receiver.

Lisa put her hand over the mouthpiece. "Some guy says he's A Friend. You got any male friends calling this late at night?"

"Does it sound like Jake?"

"Who's Jake?"

"Never mind." Connie took the receiver from her. "Jake?"

"Hello, Contessa."

She realized that Lisa was watching her, and said, "Yes?"

"Yes?" Tod Jarrow mimicked her. "What's with this 'yes' shit? Your husband sitting there, trying to listen in?"

"Not right now, thank you."

"Who *is* it?" Lisa whispered.

Connie waved her hand in a way that said, don't worry, just some jerk. Lisa shrugged, and went back to the couch.

"Don't sweat it, Contessa. I'll do the talking. You just listen. Real close. Then say yes, one more time."

"What do you want?" Connie asked, in a voice low enough not to be overheard by Lisa or Stevie.

"I want to see you again. Tonight."

Connie gave a short, bitter laugh. "I'm sorry, but I'm not interested at the present time."

She stopped, afraid that she might have gone too far.

Then she remembered the security system, and the safe room.

Fuck you! she thought into the phone. *Just try and come up here after us, and see what happens.*

But Jarrow sounded reasonable, for him. "No way, huh? Well, I sort of thought you might say that. So I decided to give you an incentive. Got it with me right now. Say hello to Connie, Mom."

It took all her self-control not to start screaming.

It required everything she knew about mental discipline to fix her attention on one particular, physical thing—a lamp on the other side of the living room—and make that her reference point, her reality lifeline.

"Connie?" Alice MacKendrick's voice crackled across the distance from Long Beach to Hollywood.

"Yes?" she said, staring hard at the lamp.

"I'm okay," Alice said slowly. "Don't worry about me. But Emilia—" Her voice seemed to stick.

Connie gripped the receiver. As she stared at the lamp on the other side of the room, she could feel the darkness closing in.

"Don't tell Ken about this," Alice said. "Or the kids."

"No," Connie promised, her voice flat.

"Time's up, Mom." Jarrow came back on the line. "I know you girls could probably talk the night away, but we got to get down to business. Still there, Contessa?"

"Yes."

"I didn't want to think you lost your nerve and maybe signaled for your surfer-boy husband to call the cops on another phone."

"No."

"Because the minute I hear sirens downstairs, or see any flashing lights, I do to Mom what I had to do to that little Mexican bitch who tried to give me shit at the door. The assholes may get me, but they won't get Mom. You understand, Contessa?"

"Yes."

"Good. Now, I'm a little farther away this time, but of course you know right where I am. And it's such a lovely night for a drive. Not too much traffic. Clean freeways. You should be able to make it down here in—what? Forty-five minutes?"

"What if there's—"

"Problems? An overturned tanker truck, somewhere on the 710?"

"Please—"

"Okay, you got exactly one hour. But I don't have to tell you what happens if you break this date, do I, Contessa?"

There was a click, then the hollow buzzing of the dial tone. She started to hang up the receiver, and almost dropped it.

"You okay?" Lisa asked.

"I've got to go somewhere. A patient. It's an emergency."

"Want me to go with you?"

"No. Tell Ken I'll only be a few minutes, okay?"

"Mom?" Stevie called. "You coming back?"

Connie walked over and put her arms around her daughter.

"I'll come back. I promise."

IV

*dreams
of
death*

40
Reckoning

She knocked on the door to Alice MacKendrick's apartment in Long Beach at 10:33 P.M., three minutes after Jarrow's deadline.

She waited.

Nothing happened.

No sounds came from within.

Her head swam. Her knees felt as if they might give way.

"It's me!" she called through the closed door. "Connie!"

A scratching came from the other side of the door, then the sounds of a guard chain being drawn back, the deadbolt unlocking. The door opened partway, just enough for a person of average size to get through, sideways. The lights burned low inside. She could not see Jarrow, or his shadow. But she knew he was waiting for her behind that half-opened door, gun in hand.

She squeezed through, head and shoulders in first. Jarrow stood back and to one side, holding a Smith & Wesson .357 magnum.

"I'm alone," she said. "Can't you open this any—"

She looked down, and saw what was holding the door.

Emilia Santos lay sprawled across the floor, dead weight wedged tight against the door. Her soft brown eyes stared up into nothingness. She lay in a large pool of blood that was starting to congeal. The blood, almost two gallons of it, had come from the long knife slash that cut open her throat. Dark blood, thick and stringy, oozed up onto Connie's white Ree-boks.

She looked up at Jarrow. "What did she ever do to you?"

"Tried to slam the fucking door in my face." He motioned with the .357 magnum. "Now get in here and close it."

She squeezed the rest of the way in, trying not to look down at Emilia's butchered corpse. She glanced across the small living room, and saw her mother in the wheelchair, pale and shrunken.

"Mom?" she called to her. "You okay?"

"I said *close the fucking door!*"

"I am." She shut the door behind her and locked it, glancing down once more at Emilia's kind face, blank and uncomprehending in the grip of death.

"No time to give her a proper burial." Jarrow lowered the gun. "She's sort of a pain in the ass, lying there like that. But then, life's a bitch, right?"

He wore dark jeans and a black T-shirt, the knife he had threatened her with the night before strapped in a sheath to his thigh. He looked at her clothes, the stonewashed jeans and blue sweater she had changed into to play video games with Stevie.

"Nice to see you dressed casual for a change."

"Fuck you," she said, before she had time to think.

He laughed. "Hey, is that any way to talk to someone who loves you? Someone who goes to *this* much trouble"—pointing at Alice with the gun—"just to see you?"

"Do I get shot if I go talk to my mother?"

"Whatever you want. Your wish is my command."

He raised the .357. "Up to a point, Contessa."

Connie walked over to Alice's wheelchair, trying to keep herself under control. She reached down and put her arms around her mother, and kissed her. Then she started to sob.

"It's okay, honey." Alice patted Connie's face with her good right hand. "He hasn't done anything to me. Just—Emilia."

"Did she—"

Alice shook her head. "It was very quick. He slit her open like a fish." Then she added, in a voice so low Connie could barely hear her, "Dirty fucking no-good son of a bitch."

"Hey! Sorry to break up your girl talk. But this is kind of like a date, Mom. Me and Connie gotta jam!"

Connie turned to him. "How did you find out about her?"

Jarrow smiled his razor-edged smile. "My love, you're asking me to reveal trade secrets."

"Did you stop by my office—"

She thought of Becky Martinez lying on the floor like Emilia.

"You told me you wouldn't be in your office today. Remember? *I* do. Of course, maybe you weren't telling me the truth. Maybe you were there today." He shook his head in mock concern. "Just when I was beginning to think I could trust you, Contessa."

"I wasn't in my office today. Were you?"

"No." His good humor disappeared. "I said I'd call you and I tried to. At your house. You weren't there, either. But I didn't go by your fucking office! I *keep* my word, okay?"

The hatred in his dark eyes made her step back.

Lisa, she thought, realizing then how he had done it, calling the house, hanging up if Ken answered, flirting with Lisa in that phony sweetness-and-light voice of his, working on her patiently until she gave him what he wanted.

"Gotta get a move on, Contessa. Guess we could just go ahead and do it here on the floor. But that might offend Mom."

He flashed his razor-edged smile at Alice. "Sorry we can't stay for tea, Mom. Maybe next time." The smile vanished. "You saw me cut the phone wire, so don't try to plug it back in and call the cops. And don't try any other stupid shit, like screaming for help after we leave. Just sit tight till somebody comes by to check on you, tomorrow, or the next day. You may shit and piss yourself a little. But you'll make it."

"I don't have to call the police," Alice said calmly, looking up into his dark eyes. "They're already on their way."

Jarrow's head snapped up, the gun rising with it.

Connie wanted to slap her out of the wheelchair for that.

"What did you say?" he asked, moving forward.

"You heard me."

"Stupid fucking *cunt!*" He brought the gun up into her face. "What did you *do?* Set off a silent alarm?"

"Take that away from her!" Connie cried.

Jarrow glanced over at her. "Shut the fuck up!"

"Both of you shut up," Alice said, her voice flat, business-like. "I don't have any silent alarms around this place. You've been watching too many movies, Tod."

"Who said you could use my first name?"

"Don't be so formal, Tod. You can call me Alice. Anyone who sticks a gun in my face is practically family."

"Don't fuck with me, you old whore."

He thumbed back the hammer of the .357.

The air seemed to drain from Connie's lungs.

"Go ahead and pull the trigger, Tod," Alice said, her eyes on his, steady and unblinking. "That'll just bring *him* here even faster, won't it? *He* lives on blood and death, doesn't he, Tod? The bloodier the better. Blowing an old crippled woman out of her wheelchair might really turn him on."

For the first time Connie saw true terror in Jarrow's eyes.

"You're talking shit," he said, his voice suddenly hoarse.

"I think you know what I'm talking about, Tod. Your friend. Or should we say, your Master? The Dark dude? The one with the prune face and the yellow eyes?"

"Shut up!" Jarrow screamed, pointing the gun at her.

Connie threw her own body across her mother's.

"Get away from me!" Alice whispered. "I know what I'm doing!"

Connie looked up at her, shocked.

"I've seen the two of you, Tod," Alice said to him, "back there in Venice. He's not a pretty sight. Come to think of it, neither were you, all pale under that bushy beard of yours, almost ready to puke on your new blue tights."

Jarrow turned to Connie, the gun turning with him.

"You tell her about us, Contessa? About *him?*"

"No, she didn't, Tod. I found out all by myself. And I can bring him here, all by myself. I've done it before. Just a few days ago. Right in this room." She nodded at his feet. "Right where you're standing, in fact."

Jarrow stepped back, eyes dark with fear. *"Shut up!"*

"You won't scare him off that way, Tod." A sly smile crept over Alice's face. "Not even if you try it in Italian."

"You think I believe some shriveled-up old cunt like you?"

"Well, there's a bit more to me than that, Tod. It's not something I talk about much. In fact, I've never even told my own daughter about it."

Connie looked at her.

"I have this kind of talent," Alice said calmly, as if they were discussing a neutral topic, like stamp-collecting. "My grandma Lloyd used to call it The Gift. Other people call it other names. Second sight. ESP. Occult powers. I don't know what it is. I just know I have it. You have it too, Tod. Otherwise, Old Mr. Yellow Eyes couldn't use you like he does, could he?"

Jarrow flinched at the mention of the Dark Sorcerer.

"Grandma Lloyd on my mother's side had it when she was younger. Connie has it. I used to believe she didn't, but that was just wishful thinking." She turned to her. "Sorry about not telling you sooner. I guess it might have saved some trouble."

Connie stared at her, hearing Zenobia again inside her head.

This kind of thing almost always runs in families.

Alice said to Jarrow, "I don't get around much these days. But I can still move pretty fast, inside my head. All the way back to Venice, Tod, four hundred years ago. When I went back that one time and saw you, with *him*, he turned around and saw me. He wasn't happy about it. He doesn't like people crashing his party. He has my number now. You may know where I live, Tod." Alice gave him a chess-player's smile. "But so does he."

Jarrow raised the .357 magnum, hammer still cocked, only a light pull of the finger needed to fire it. "You're lying."

"Maybe I am, Tod. Maybe not. Hard to know for sure, isn't it?" She stared into his dark eyes, ignoring the gun pointed at her face. "One thing you *do* know. If you shoot me, the last thought in my mind when that bullet hits my face is going to be about *him*. Because I'm thinking about him right now."

A wave of sick fear flashed in Jarrow's eyes, followed by a look of the most intense hatred Connie had ever seen on a human face. The next few seconds seemed to stretch into eternity. She stood there, watching the standoff, unable to close her eyes or turn her head. She knew he was going to kill her mother.

"You're a tough, macho guy, Tod," Alice said at last. "Especially when it comes to cutting up a sweet little Mexican girl who didn't speak much English. But you're just a tiny bit afraid of Old Mr. Yellow Eyes, aren't you?" Alice's voice took on a strange, prophetic tone. "You're afraid that when he's finished with you one day, after you've killed enough people, he might decide to throw you away. Maybe take your soul and drop it into a smoked-glass bottle filled with scorpions, then put a cork in it."

Connie saw them first, outside the living-room window.

Red, blue, and amber lights, flashing off the jacaranda tree.

Jarrow saw her eyes move to the window, and turned in the same direction, the .357 turning with him. His finger twitched on the trigger. The gun bucked in his hand. Connie heard a loud, flat pop, then her ears stopped up. The walls of the room roared with sound. Glass blew out of the living-room window, tinkling onto the paved courtyard down below. Through her stopped ears, Connie could hear the crackle of police radios, the slamming of car doors.

"Shit—" Jarrow turned from the shattered window to Alice.

She was not even looking at him. She seemed to be looking past him, through him, beyond the walls of her apartment, to some distant place visible only to those with The Gift.

"He's coming, Tod," she said quietly, almost whispering. "He's seen me now, and you too, and he's coming for both of us."

Jarrow stumbled backward, groping for the front door-knob with one hand, pointing the gun at Alice with the other, but shaking now, as Alice might have shaken herself had she tried to hold the gun in her paralyzed left hand.

"Okay, Contessa," he said to Connie, his voice hoarse. "You win this one. But it's all over now, what we had between us. *I don't love you anymore!"*

He threw open the front door, eyes dark with hatred.

"I'll get you, your surfer-boy husband, your cute little kids. One by one. But I'll save you for last, okay?"

Then he was gone, footsteps echoing down the outside stairs.

It took several seconds for Connie to convince herself that he was really gone. She went over to the door and locked it.

"You might as well leave it open," Alice said. "Cops are going to be up here any minute now."

Connie looked at her mother, slumped down in her wheel-chair, drained of energy. She walked over to her, stepping around the dead body of Emilia Santos.

"How *did* you call them?"

"In my head." Alice gave a tired sigh. "It takes a lot out of you, and it's not as quick as a phone call. But it works."

"Did you really try to contact—"

She could not bring herself to name the Dark Sorcerer.

"No. I may be a crazy old woman, but I'm not *that* crazy."

"Then how could you be sure Jarrow—"

"I couldn't. But I thought he'd piss himself if I even mentioned Old Mr. Yellow Eyes. I was right." Alice gave a dry laugh. "At one point there, I think I even *smelled* piss."

Connie could hear the police officers now, footsteps climbing the outside stairs to Alice's apartment.

She said to her mother, "After they leave, I want to hear about The Gift. Everything. Okay?"

Alice nodded. "Would you get my cigarettes over there, please?" She pointed to the pack of Marlboros on a side table. "Little punk took them away from me."

"What if he hadn't been scared by your threat?"

Alice lit a cigarette. "He was."

"But what if he hadn't been?"

Alice looked up at her through the smoke. "It wouldn't have made much difference. Don't you see what's happening to him now, Connie? Can't you sense it?"

"What?"

"Him. Old Mr. Yellow Eyes. Whatever the hell his name is. There's no more Tod Jarrow. *He's* running him now, like a puppet on a string. Can't you see that?"

Connie stared at her mother.

A police officer knocked at the front door.

41
The Limit

She found a patrol car in the driveway when she got home.

The Long Beach Police must have notified the LAPD, who sent someone out to tell Ken.

Lisa opened the front door for her.

"I watched you come up on the video monitor. You okay?"

She nodded. "Where's Ken?"

"In there."

He was sitting in the living room with Lieutenant Ed Dormer.

They both got to their feet when they saw Connie.

She looked to Lisa for support. But Lisa was not her usual brash, assertive self.

"Want some coffee?" she asked.

Connie shook her head. "Thanks, anyway."

Lisa went into the kitchen, leaving Connie to face Ken and Dormer by herself.

Ken said, "I won't even ask why you didn't bother to call."

"I came back as soon as I could."

He walked over to the picture window and stood there, his back to her, hands in his pockets, staring at the darkness.

Dormer cleared his throat. "You're very lucky, Dr. Stallman. Three times in the ring with Jarrow. And each time you've walked away. But it was still a stupid thing to do."

"She's my mother, Lieutenant, not yours."

"It's smarter to let professionals handle this kind of thing."

"Professionals can make mistakes, too."

"We all make mistakes," Dormer said, pausing long enough for the Jennie Hodges reference to sink in. "But what you did tonight could have killed both you and your mother."

"I didn't think about that."

Ken turned from the window.

"Do you ever think about anyone except yourself?"

"Ken—"

"*Do* you?"

"Ken, I've had a bad night."

"What kind of night do you think we've been having here?"

Dormer saw his opportunity. "You two have a lot to talk about. I'd better get going before my wife calls the cops."

He turned to Connie. "Doctor, it's always a pleasure."

Then to Ken. "Tell your sister thanks for the coffee."

"I'll see you to the door," Ken said.

Connie heard their voices from the entryway, then the sound of Ken closing the front door and double-locking it. She walked over to the sofa and sat down. Her legs seemed to give way beneath her.

Ken came back into the living room, car keys in one hand. "Get your coat," he said. "We're going for a drive."

"This time of night?"

"Get your coat. You'll need it."

He drove fast over the rough back roads of the Hollywood Hills, accelerating into curves, grinding up inclines. Connie felt her back teeth rattle at every bump in the road.

"If you wouldn't mind slowing down just a little—"

He made a hard right, taking them off the road and onto a

narrow turnout. The tires squealed. The Cherokee Chief bounced over rocks and gravel. Connie was tossed from side to side. She smashed her shoulder up against the door.

"Ken! What are you *doing?*"

The Cherokee jolted to a stop, dust rising before it.

He got out, slamming the door behind him.

Connie sighed, and unbuckled her seat belt.

They were on a high ridge overlooking the lights of the city. Moonlight glimmered off a distant sea. Ken stood staring into the night. She came up beside him, shivering, head bent forward against the wind that whipped across the ridge top.

He turned to her. "I don't know how long you can take this—"

"Ken—"

"—but I have just reached the limit, okay?"

"What are you trying to say?"

"I won't let you keep putting us through shit like this!"

"You think I'm doing it because I want to?"

"You're doing whatever you want, whenever you want. And fuck the consequences. Fuck everything. Fuck me *and* the kids."

She thought of the things she could say to him, truths she had learned from Zenobia that day, and from her mother tonight.

But all she said was, "You're wrong."

"I've reached the limit, Connie. *My* limit. I love you. But I can't live with you anymore, if this is how it's going to be."

He looked at her, a single tear spilling down his cheek.

"I don't care how we work it out, Connie. You can stay. I can leave with the kids. Or the other way around. It doesn't matter. The money, the house—none of that matters now. The only thing that matters is, we can't go on this way."

She looked out to the lights in the distance, and beyond them to the ocean, pale and gleaming like a wash of stars.

"If that's what you have to do," she said, "then take the kids and leave. I love you as much as you love me. But I didn't choose this, Ken. Don't you think I'd stop it if I could?"

"I'd never leave just because you got sick, Connie. But you're not even trying to get well."

"I'm not *sick,* goddamn it! I've told you that before! But you don't believe me! You don't want to *see!*"

She grabbed him by his jacket collar. "Look, Ken, I'm fighting for my life! I'm fighting against a power that doesn't even have a name. But it's *real.* Very real. Tonight I stepped in the blood of someone it killed. The blood's still there." She pointed to her shoes. "It's *that* real!"

He tried to back up, unsettled by the intensity in her eyes.

But she would not let go of his jacket.

"It's real and it's deadly, and it's trying to kill us, Ken. You. Me. Stevie. Trent. It works through Tod Jarrow, but it's not him. If I thought it was just Jarrow, I would have tried to kill him myself tonight. But it's something else. Something that can't be stopped by your security system, or any security system in the world. Maybe it can be stopped by—my mother. Or by another little old lady you don't even know."

She paused, then whispered, "Maybe. Who knows?"

She dropped her hands from his collar and turned against the wind blowing inland from the sea. "I love you, and the kids. But I can go on without you, if I have to. I can face this by myself."

Ken looked at her, and said nothing.

Far below, barely audible at that height, a siren howled across the early-morning streets of Los Angeles.

42

The Forbidden Name

"**I**t is so much nicer out here, no?" Zenobia Horowitz smiled at her. "On such a day, who wants to be inside?"

They sat in the garden in back of Zenobia's office building, a small plot of greenery amid the urban congestion of Fairfax. Two royal palms grew near a white latticework gazebo. Water trickled soothingly from a stone fountain off to one side.

Bright red bougainvillea climbed a high stone wall. Connie and Zenobia sat in chairs beneath the gazebo, while Cornelius Agrippa the cockatoo preened his feathers on an open perch, and Paracelsus the gray-striped cat stalked smaller birds too quick for his aging reflexes.

Zenobia served tea on the redwood deck, and listened while Connie told her about the encounter with Tod Jarrow, and The Gift.

"That's all there is," Connie finished. "She's had it ever since she was a little girl, but she doesn't know where it comes from or how to use it."

"See? I was right!" Zenobia emphasized the words with her index finger. "These things *do* run in families!"

Connie stared at her teacup. "Yes."

She looked up at Zenobia. "So what's his name?"

Zenobia shaded her eyes, and looked at the garden.

"So lovely! The sun shines. The sky is blue. The birds sing, but poor Paracelsus cannot catch any, because he has grown old and fat. Meanwhile, here we sit—"

"Zenobia—"

"—and prepare to talk about the Angel of Death."

Connie drew back in her chair, as if a shadow had fallen between them. Sunlight leaked in through the gazebo like a malign, alien influence.

"It is good that the day is so bright," Zenobia said, "that we sit here surrounded by pleasant things. Because what we talk about now is dark and terrible. I must say the Forbidden Name."

Believe me, Connie remembered her warning from yesterday, *when I tell you his name, you will be sorry you ever heard it.*

"In Jewish and Islamic legend," Zenobia said, "there is an angel of darkness, an Angel of Death, who takes the soul from the body at the time of dying. As such, he is a Middle Eastern counterpart of Atropos, the Greek Fate who cuts the thread of life at the moment of death. But all this is legend. Myth. Stories that explain why things are the way they are."

Zenobia leaned forward. "We, however, talk of reality. Because, you see, the Angel of Death is no legend, no myth from the ancient days. He is real, all too real. He lives—no! That is the wrong word. He does not live. He *exists*. He *is,* like the dark reality of death itself. You understand?"

Connie nodded.

"His name," Zenobia said, "is the Forbidden Name."

She whispered it. "Azrael."

The name seemed to slither across the space between them, bringing with it a vision of yellow, hate-filled eyes and hands like spider's claws. Connie shut her own eyes against it.

Azrael. The Angel of Death.

"He is old," Zenobia said, "as old as life itself. When the first living creature drew its last breath, *he* was there to take it into the Dark Kingdom. When the first human tribes came together, he taught them fear and mistrust, and warfare. When the first cities were built, he walked their streets in darkness, bringing poverty, hunger, and plague."

Connie remembered the rumor, heard aboard the *Bucintoro,* that the Dark Sorcerer had come to Venice with the first outbreak of the Great Plague.

"He has his place," Zenobia admitted, "even in the Great Kabbalah. He is the root of the Tree of Death that underlies the glorious Tree of Life. He has his own part to play. But he *over*plays it! He hates life so, that he wishes to take the living even before their time. He is not a demon. He is an angel. But that makes him all the more dangerous. Like any angel of darkness, he has great and terrible powers. He can move at will along the Paths of the Tree, throughout all the Worlds of Time. And between those Worlds, he can control the transmigration of individual souls, moving the astral body from one reincarnate form to another, as easily as a child plays with one of those—what do you call them? Ah, yes! Video games."

Zenobia paused and took a sip of tea. "Bad news, huh?"

Connie could not speak.

"But—" Zenobia put down her teacup. "For all bad things,

no matter how evil, there are good things strong enough to work against them. That is one of the truths of the Great Kabbalah."

"But nothing can fight against death," Connie said. "Death always wins, in the end."

Zenobia nodded. "Or so it seems, in the Sphere of *Malkuth,* the Earth, the base of the Great Tree on which we live. But among the higher Spheres, there are those that can oppose even death itself. *Geburah,* the Sphere of Force and Power."

Connie saw again in her mind's eye the image of the mighty warrior, his chariot drawn by four powerful horses.

"And *Chesed,* the Sphere of Mercy and Forgiveness. These things can fight against death and be triumphant. Also—" Zenobia paused, as if reflecting. "Remember, he is *not* death itself. He is death's angel, death's emissary to this mortal world."

"But you said he hates life. All he wants is to destroy it."

"Well, yes. But perhaps it is the wrong word when I say he *hates* life. Maybe it is more like he loves life, with a dark and fatal love. He wants to possess it, to make it his own. To do this, of course, he must bring the living into the Kingdom of Death. So his is a confused and violent love, destructive of the very thing it loves. Like so much human love, no?"

Connie thought of Tod Jarrow, threatening to kill her family.

One by one, saving you for last.

"Is Tod Jarrow part of him?"

"They are not the same person. No, of course not. But the Angel of Death uses Jarrow, makes him do his dirty work for him, spreading death in the midst of life."

"How does he make him kill?"

"I'm afraid I'm not familiar with the terms of their original contract." Zenobia drained her teacup, then looked at Connie. "But I will tell you this. It involved something Jarrow wanted very much, more than anything else in the world. Something for which he was willing to sacrifice his happiness, and his life."

Connie thought of him in the Hollywood apartment that night.

You're the reason for everything I've ever done.

She looked at Zenobia. "But if he's being used by Azrael—"

"No, no, no!" Zenobia waved a warning finger. "We do not speak that name so lightly, as if he is our hairdresser or our stockbroker. It is the Forbidden Name. Do not forget that. Call him the Angel of Death. Or what they call him back in Venice, the Dark Sorcerer. That's fine, too. But do not use the Forbidden Name, unless you wish to bring him to you—"

Connie felt the back of her neck grow cold.

"—or until you confront him, in the Final Battle."

They sat in silence beneath the gazebo.

"Azrael!" screamed Cornelius Agrippa, crest arching out.

Connie gave a startled cry.

Zenobia got up and walked over to the cockatoo, wagging a finger in his face. "Stupid bird! Shut up!" She glanced at Connie. "Don't worry. It doesn't count when some animal says it."

Connie sat there, breathing deeply until her heartbeat returned to normal, thinking of her mother, alone in her wheelchair, ripe pickings for the Angel of Death.

"How could one person fight him, alone?"

Zenobia paused. "First of all, you do not do something like this for sport, like a gunslinger or a wrestler, to show how tough you are. You do it only to protect others, the ones you love."

"And if you do it for that reason, how is it done?"

Zenobia, for the first time since Connie met her, looked distressed. "This is not a good thing to talk about, even here, with the sun so bright, the sky so blue." She patted her dyed red hair nervously. "You do not go looking for a fight with the

Angel of Death, my dear. You don't even think of it that way. You take up the defensive position, always."

"How, Zenobia?"

"*Ach!* So many questions. Later, all right?"

She leaned forward and grabbed the older woman's hand.

"Zenobia, I have to know about this. My mother—" Connie paused. "My mother used her power, The Gift, to search for him back in Venice a few nights ago, to make some kind of contact—"

"*Ach, Gott!* Deliberately she did this thing? Why?"

"She did it for me. To try and help me, I think."

Zenobia sighed. "Well, what's done is done. But you are right. You must know about the defensive position now. *Ach,* so little time! But we do what we can. The defense against the Angel of Death involves the Paths of the Kabbalah, of course. Especially the two great Spheres, *Geburah* and *Chesed.* But to reach these Spheres, you must first ascend the Thirty-second Path to the Sphere of *Yesod,* the Foundation, and the two other Spheres of the Astral Triangle, *Hod,* Glory, and *Netzach,* Victory. You remember the images of *Netzach* and *Yesod?* The naked woman and the naked man?"

Connie nodded.

"That is part of the problem also. If we had more time, we could practice this. But for that, we must be naked, too."

"What?"

Zenobia held up a hand. "Please! Do not misunderstand me. I am not one of those sick people who write letters to *Penthouse* magazine. The Astral Triangle is the first level where we can work physical magic. But we can't do it effectively with our clothes on. The body has to be open to emanations from the Spheres, and able to emit its own emanations as well. Understand?"

"Sort of."

"But, as I say, there is no time. So, instead I must tell you about it. *Ach,* so many things to tell! Reincarnation. The Powers of Angels, Good and Bad. The Transitions from Path to

Path. All the things contained in the entire *Zohar,* the Book of Splendor, the Great Guide to the Kabbalah."

Zenobia shook her head. "What choice do we have? You need the defense. So, I must talk, fast. You must listen, carefully."

By the time Zenobia finished, late-afternoon sunlight was slanting in through the latticework of the gazebo. Connie leaned back in her chair, head swimming with details, images, visions.

Zenobia poured a cup of cold tea for herself and another for Connie. "This is what you call a crash course, no? I am sure I leave out many things. But you see what it demands? Why it is so dangerous? Why it must be done only as a last defense?"

Connie nodded, a hollowness inside her breast.

"Do you have a phone I could use?"

"Of course. One of those you carry around and talk into it like a microphone. No, stay there. I bring it to you."

Connie sat and stared at the garden in the late-afternoon light, thinking of Azrael, the Angel of Death, and her mother. She was still thinking about them when Zenobia came back and handed her a portable phone.

"Thanks. I know it's silly, but I want to call my mother."

"Don't apologize, my dear. We have talked of disturbing things this afternoon. You are disturbed. That is to be expected. Your mother, no doubt, is resting quietly at home, even as we speak. But call her. Set your mind at ease."

Connie smiled, listening to the connection click into place on the other end of the line. "The phone company was great about restoring her service this morning, right after—"

After Tod Jarrow cut her line with a knife last night.

A busy signal blipped incessantly in her ear. Connie frowned, and broke the connection, getting a dial tone.

"Busy?" Zenobia asked.

Connie nodded, dialing the number again. "That's funny."

Zenobia put down her teacup. "Today you tell me she has a new—nurse? No, that's not right. How do you call it?"

"Care provider," Connie said, remembering Emilia Santos, lying on the floor in a pool of blood, her throat slit open.

"Care provider," Zenobia repeated, filing it in her memory. "So. Maybe this new care provider is the one on the phone?"

"Maybe," Connie said, as another busy signal beeped at her.

But it was unlikely. She knew that her mother would not let a care provider tie up the phone like this.

Especially today, after what we talked about last night.

She hung up the phone and sat there with it in her lap, a worried frown on her face.

Zenobia said to her, "Don't allow yourself to become frightened. It's not useful. And it's not safe. The Angel of Death feeds on fear. He follows it home, like a shark tracking blood in the water."

Connie looked at her with eyes full of dread.

Out in the grass, Paracelsus pounced at a bird.

The phone rang in her lap. She jumped back in her chair, almost pitching the phone onto the gazebo floor. She caught it in time, then handed it to Zenobia, who picked up the receiver.

"Yes?" She frowned. "Yes, of course. Hold, please."

Not Jarrow! Connie thought. *Not him, please!*

Guess where I am now? she could hear him saying, then putting Stevie on the line, or maybe Trent.

Zenobia turned to her, hand over the mouthpiece. "It is for you, my dear. A Mrs. Amanda Baker."

Relief and confusion showed together in Connie's face as she took the receiver. "Mrs. Baker? Are you calling from my office?"

"Hell, no!" barked the voice on the other end. "I called your office and you wasn't there. They give me this number. I'm at home now. I need you to get the hell over here, fast as you can."

"Is something wrong with Benjamin?"

"Damn right somethin's wrong with the little freak! About

two this afternoon, he stands up and starts screamin' his damn-fool head off. Jabberin' on and on about—"

"Mrs. Baker," Connie interrupted. "Benjamin doesn't talk."

"He sure-God does *now!* Won't shut up. Keeps screamin' your name over and over, like some goddamn windup doll."

"My name?"

"Connie! Connie! Like that. Over and over. Enough to drive you friggin' crazy. Here. Listen. You can hear what I mean."

Connie heard Benjamin's rusted, unused voice calling out her name in the background, screaming it, again and again, like a repeating tape loop.

Mrs. Baker got back on the line. "If he don't shut up, or you don't get on over here and make him shut up, I'm kickin' the little freak out on his butt. Right now! The county can go ahead and just *keep* their goddamn money!"

"I'll be right over. Don't let him hurt himself, Mrs. Baker."

"He ain't hurtin' hisself none! But he's sure-God sendin' my blood pressure straight through the goddamn roof!"

"Just stay calm, Mrs. Baker. I'm on my way."

She hung up the phone. "Jesus!"

"A patient of yours, my dear?"

"A very special patient."

She told Zenobia about Benjamin Simmons and his catatonia, about the last time in her office when Benjamin suddenly spoke.

And named the Dark Man.

Zenobia nodded slowly, her expression grave. "Yes. This is possible. Quite rare, but still possible. The innocent child is an image from the Sphere of *Tiphareth,* Beauty or Splendor, the Sphere that balances opposites. And this child you describe, this Benjamin, is especially innocent. Innocent of human speech and all the deception that goes with it. And yet he called forth the Angel of Death. A very great power, for one so young and innocent."

Connie rose from her chair. "You mean Benjamin has something like The Gift?"

Zenobia looked at her. "You can be sure of it."

"Will *he* try to hurt him, because of that?"

"Perhaps. But the child's powerful innocence will protect him, even from the Angel of Death." Zenobia paused, then looked out at the garden, the cat in the grass, the bird on his perch.

"Be careful that he does not use this child against you." She paused again. "Because he will try."

43

One-on-One

The County of Los Angeles had been prompt about replacing Emilia Santos with a new care provider.

Not that anyone could take Emilia's place. Alice had made arrangements with the girl's family to attend her funeral in San Luis Potosí, in central Mexico. It would not be an easy trip for someone in Alice's condition, but she had been fond of Emilia.

She still could not believe the girl was gone.

The new care provider, Brenda Sue Harding, had recently moved to California from the rural Midwest. She had above-average size and strength, but none of Emilia's quiet kindness.

Late in the day following Emilia's death, Brenda Sue sat on the sofa, embroidering a sampler while she watched a television talk show about teenage mothers who lived at home.

Alice sat in her wheelchair and smoked, thinking about Connie, The Gift, Tod Jarrow.

And Jarrow's Master.

Who was he? *What* was he? What did he want?

What did he want with her daughter?

Sacrifice, she thought, not knowing how she knew this, trusting The Gift to give her the answer. *He wants a sacrifice.*

Alice was an untrained, intuitive psychic, with none of Zenobia Horowitz's profound knowledge of occult forces. But she had something more powerful at her command. When she opened her mind to The Gift, she became the psychic equivalent of a teenage computer hacker, cutting into labyrinthine systems by trial and error, winding her way through a complex maze to break suddenly into a world of hidden data banks, rich beyond her imagination.

Working this way now, she began to see what the creature with the claw-hands and the yellow eyes had planned for Connie.

And what she could do to stop him.

Brenda Sue snorted at a teenage mother on television.

"If she was *my* kid, I'd paddle her little butt till it was seven different shades of black and blue!"

She gave the sampler a smooth stitch, then glanced over at Alice, to make sure she hadn't set herself on fire with one of her stinky old cigarettes.

That was when she noticed him, the hunched-over little guy with ugly hands and a scrunched-up face, wearing what looked like a long black bathrobe, standing right there in the living room.

She put down her sampler, and got up from the sofa.

"Hey, buddy. You have a problem?"

The little old guy ignored her.

He stood in front of Alice's wheelchair, the two of them staring at one another, saying nothing, as if they were talking without moving their mouths.

Brenda Sue stepped up to him.

"I asked you a question, pal. You gone deaf, or what?"

He continued to ignore her, staring at Alice MacKendrick.

Brenda Sue boiled inside. She grabbed the rude little turkey.

And found herself holding nothing.

She blinked at her two big hands, clenched into fists.

Alice, coming out of a trance, noticed her for the first time. "Stay *out* of this!" she warned her.

Brenda Sue turned around, wondering how in the holy—

There he was. Ten feet or so behind her, but looking right at her this time, with ugly little yellow eyes that reminded her of an old alley cat she had picked up as a kid. His face was a wrinkled mess, the kind you saw on some of these crazy Californians, staying out in the sun too long, turning themselves into prunes.

"Martial arts stud, hey?" Her own eyes turned hard. "Well, you better use all the fancy footwork you got, mister. And hoof it on outta here pronto! Because when I get my hands on you, I am personally kickin' your bony butt right through that front door."

"Are you a woman?" The voice sounded hoarse and whispery. "Or a man who dresses to look like one? It is not easy to know, in this strange world."

"Okay, dirt bag! *That* is gonna cost you. I am now *breakin'* your butt before I drop-kick it out the window!"

She moved toward him.

He stood there, hunched over, watching her closely, yellow eyes filled with a deep, abiding hatred.

Then he began to—change. Stretch. Grow taller, somehow. His face changed, elongating, turning vaguely reptilian, or insectile. He was now very tall, even taller than Brenda Sue herself, who was unusually tall for a woman. She had to look up at him, becoming aware just then that something very strange was happening here, something that did not take place on a regular basis back in the Midwest.

The television screen exploded. Brenda Sue turned toward it with a startled cry. A strong wind began to blow. Tearing at window curtains. Overturning lamps. Knocking the telephone receiver off its hook. Alice MacKendrick sat in her wheelchair, gray hair blown back from her face, staring at the thing in her living room. Brenda Sue took a quick breath for courage, then doubled up her heavy fist and struck out at whatever it was.

The front door burst open, banging back against the wall. Glass exploded from the taped-over window. Razor-sharp fragments flew through the air. One sliced open Brenda Sue's right cheek. She gasped, and put a hand to her face. Blood welled up from the cut, oozing out between her fingers. A heavy red clay pot from the walkway outside flew in through the front door, smashing her face into a mask of blood. Brenda Sue screamed and grabbed at her face.

Metal balusters began snapping loose from the wrought-iron railing outside, flying in through the open door like deadly, black three-foot spikes. The first one punched into the center of Brenda Sue's chest, lifting her off her feet and throwing her back against the far wall behind Alice, impaling her there like a bug. Her screams turned into guttural howls. More balusters flew in through the front door, piercing her flesh, digging into the wall behind her. The howls gave way to short, grunting gasps as she hung there, impaled on the wall.

Then Brenda Sue fell as silent as the late Emilia Santos.

The terrible wind stopped abruptly. Objects dropped to the floor, or fluttered down into stillness.

Alice, trembling in her wheelchair, turned to look at the crucified body hanging on the wall behind her, blood running down the plaster and dripping onto the carpet.

"Look at me," said the hoarse, whispering voice.

She kept staring at Brenda Sue's mutilated body, thinking that this was the second person in less than twenty-four hours who had died trying to protect her. A sick rage shook her paralyzed limbs.

"*Look* at me."

An unseen hand grabbed hold of her face, squeezing her jaws until pain flashed through her eyes and up into her skull. The force turned her head around slowly, still squeezing hard, until she faced the yellow-eyed thing before her.

He had shrunk back to normal size, hunched over and wrinkled again, an old man with glittering yellow eyes and hands like spider's claws.

"Why did you call me here?" he asked. "What do you hope to accomplish by such madness?"

Alice stared at him, hearing the air wheeze inside her lungs.

"Your power is strong." He nodded his wizened head.

"Yes. But you cannot possibly use it against me. You must know this?"

The unseen hand released the pressure on her jaws enough to let her speak. But she said nothing.

He came closer to her suddenly, without any apparent movement, as if he had floated rather than walked. He stared at her, yellow eyes burning into her brain like searchlights.

"You want to save her, don't you?" The whispering voice carried a small note of surprise. "You want to save *la contessa?* The lovely young Countess Alessandra Contarini? *This* is why you have called me here? Yes?"

She felt her brain being eaten alive by the burning yellow eyes, their black pupils expanding into infinite nothingness.

"So touching! The mother offers herself as a sacrifice for the daughter. A worthless, crippled life in exchange for a young, vibrant one. It would wring pity from a heart of stone."

The laughter burst in her ears then, high-pitched, evil, a tearing sound to it, like the stripping of flesh from human bones.

"Don't let yourself get hard thinking about it," Alice said.

The laughter stopped.

"I've been sitting here," she said, "for the goddamn longest time, waiting for you, you yellow-eyed son of a bitch. And you know what? After all these years, I'm almost glad to see you."

He moved back from her. Instantly. One moment he was on top of her, staring into her eyes. The next moment, he stood back.

"So," he said softly, seductively, "you welcome me. You long for the comfort I bring. The release from a crippled, wasted body, put now, at last, to good use. The salvation of a beloved, only daughter. Comfort, indeed."

He raised a black-robed arm, gesturing with the spider's claw.

"Here. Come, little mother. Taste *my* comfort."

A galvanic force jerked Alice out of the wheelchair, and threw her down hard onto the carpet. Her body burned with agonizing intensity. She twisted on the carpet, writhing like a crushed insect, mouth wrenched open in a spasm of unendurable pain. Blood burst from her open mouth, her nose, her ears. Her body began to shake and twitch, as if in contact with a high-voltage current. Blood slopped out onto the carpet. Her eyeballs bulged, ready to explode inside their sockets.

Looking up through the blood, she could see him bending over her, yellow eyes burning, hoarse voice whispering to her.

"You wanted to die, *yesssssssssssssss,*" he hissed at her. "But tell me, little mother, did you want to die like *this?*"

Her whole world fell screaming into a chaos of blood and pain.

44
Visit

"**A**nd *st-r-r-r-e-t-c-h-h-h* . . . a-a-n-n-n-d *hold.*"

Lisa Tate gritted her teeth as she followed the bouncy blond up there on the Mitsubishi Big Screen, her own muscles straining inside a silver-blue leotard and black tights. She was not into this stuff as much as some people. It was Connie's tape, *Terelle's Aerobic World*. Lisa had assumed that Stevie would be monopolizing the Big Screen to play with her video game, *Zorena's New Galactic Adventures*. But Stevie had been strangely quiet today, probably because of last night, and that awful stuff with Connie and her mom, and that creep, whatever his name was.

Lisa hated to exercise, but she and Galina were planning to make ribs and home fries and corn on the cob for dinner tonight, a real down-home feed. There was no point in cooking a high-fat blowout like that if you couldn't eat it with a clear conscience.

"And *now*"—Terelle beamed from the Big Screen—"we raise the left leg *and* the right arm at the same time—"

Lisa shook her head, droplets of sweat beading her face. No way was she risking injury, not even for a rib dinner.

"Take five, Terelle," she said, snapping off the VCR.

She turned and looked at Stevie, who was working on a *Zorena* coloring book on the other side of the living room.

"Want to use the television now?" Lisa asked.

Stevie shook her head, without looking up. "Not really."

Lisa took a deep breath, glad to be finished with her exercises. Only the second day here and she was starting to feel right at home, almost. Lisa was a true-blue Orange County booster, with little love for L.A. But she had to admit that Daddy's guys had done a good job building this house. And Connie had made a really great lot selection, with a super view. And okay, maybe Ken had helped a little, too. Whatever, it was a nice place. And, of course, Stevie and Trent were wonderful kids.

When you looked at it the right way, things were going okay.

Lisa glanced at a wall clock, wondering when Galina would get back from the market. It was almost time to start dinner. She felt her stomach growl, and thought of that box of eclairs on the bottom shelf of the refrigerator. But no, she was not going to spoil her appetite for the rib dinner. Maybe she should call one of her sisters-in-law, Donna or Joann, down in South OC, except they'd probably be out right now. She couldn't call her husband, Corey, because he was diving in Cozumel, and besides—

The alarm went off with a stuttering wail.

Stevie looked up from her coloring book. Upstairs, Trent woke from his afternoon nap with a frightened cry. Lisa ran from the living room through the kitchen and into the pantry, its red safe-room marker flashing in time with the alarm. She sat down at the security console, pushing the buttons to activate SCAN OPTION for the hidden cameras. Lisa was good at this sort of thing. She glanced at the monitors for the different cameras, looking for the intruder whose approach had set off the alarm.

She found him, standing on the front porch.

A six-foot pink rabbit held a bouquet of red long-stemmed roses in one paw, and a letter in the other.

Lisa almost cracked up right there. Then she got serious and flipped the microphone to SEND, cranking up the volume.

"Attention!" she said in her best no-bullshit voice. "Step back from the house and identify yourself at once. You are under surveillance. This is *not* a recording."

She switched the microphone to RECEIVE.

The rabbit stepped back, stumbling off the porch, long-eared head cocked to one side, wincing from the loudspeaker's blast.

"Laff-O-Gram," he said, holding up the letter. "Ho! Ho! Ho!"

Lisa shook her head, a smile spreading over her face. Laff-O-Gram. Wouldn't you know it? She thought of the poor unemployed actor sweating inside that stupid rabbit suit. Probably farted when the alarms came on, then shit himself when the loudspeaker blasted him. She laughed out loud. She couldn't help it.

"Aunt Lisa?" Stevie looked in from the kitchen, concern in her blue eyes. "Is everything okay?"

Lisa got serious again. "I think so, babe. Let me check it out. Better safe than sorry."

She switched to SEND. "Who's it for? And who from?"

"Miss Connie—" The rabbit paused, trying to read from the letter. "—Starman."

"That's *Stall*man," she corrected him, "with two *l*'s."

"From Jake," concluded the rabbit, looking up into the video camera with his blank button eyes.

Jake—something. That guy Connie thought was calling last night, when it turned out to be Jarrow. Lisa learned from Ken this morning that Jake was some old guy, one of Connie's med-school professors, and a good friend. So the rabbit was for real.

The voice of a police dispatcher crackled from a separate speaker. "Trouble report on your system. Emergency dispatch or false alarm? Please verify. Over."

"Definitely a false alarm. Some guy from Laff-O-Gram with

a singing telegram. Can you believe it?" Then she added, "Over."

But the dispatcher had already signed off.

Lisa switched to SEND. "Stay right where you are. I'm coming to get the roses and the message. But I'm not standing there while you sing it to me, okay?"

The rabbit looked like he might have been trying to say something, but she pressed OFF instead of RECEIVE.

She got up from the console, and noticed Stevie still standing there in the kitchen, watching her. "Come here." She motioned to her. "Look what set off the alarm." She pointed at the monitor with the rabbit on it. "Big scary deal, huh?"

Stevie looked disappointed. "I thought it was a burglar."

"Nah." Lisa put her hand on Stevie's shoulder as they walked out of the pantry and into the kitchen. "Just a stupid pink rabbit with a singing telegram."

"Can I go to the door with you and look at him?" Stevie asked.

Lisa hesitated, her hand still on Stevie's shoulder. "No, but I'll tell you what. You wait here. When I come back with the roses, you can help me put them in a vase, okay?"

Lisa unlocked the two deadbolts, but left the guard chain on.

Then she opened the door, just wide enough to take the roses.

The pink rabbit was still standing there, the roses in his hand, flat button eyes staring at her.

"Okay," Lisa called to him, her face in the narrow opening. "Pass 'em through."

The rabbit reached out to her with the roses, then tilted them, the blossoms pointing at her, and shot her in the face.

The blast of the Smith and Wesson .357 magnum blew the rose petals loose from the gun barrel, scattering them over the front porch like confetti.

The high-velocity .357 shell smashed into Lisa's forehead, slightly above her left eye, and kept moving, digging a wound channel through the soft tissue of her brain, then exiting from the back of her head in a burst of blood and brains that spattered the walls of the entryway. She died almost instantly, the bullet's impact snapping her head back and breaking her neck.

Her body pitched back into the entryway, crashing down on the hardwood floor, one athletic shoe flying loose from her foot as the leg twitched aimlessly in a death reflex.

The rabbit hit the front door with his shoulder, snapping off the guard chain. Then he slammed the door behind him, leaning back against it, and pulled off his long-eared over-the-head mask. He saw the little blond girl staring at him from inside the entryway.

Stevie had been paralyzed by the sight of Aunt Lisa's head exploding, then her body flying backward and flopping down onto the floor. Her brain tried to put the pieces together. They would not fit. But when she saw Tod Jarrow's stitched, bruised face, like something from a horror movie, his dark eyes bright and crazy, everything clicked into place.

She turned and ran for the kitchen.

"Hey!" Jarrow yelled. "Come back here! You little *bitch!*"

He fired a shot, not trying to hit her, just hoping to scare the shit out of the little cunt and make her stop. But Stevie had already disappeared into the kitchen by then.

"Shit!" Jarrow muttered, and went after her.

Stevie ran into the pantry and started to shut the door behind her, pausing for an instant as she thought of Trent upstairs, just awakened from his nap, probably trying to squeeze past the stair gate right now and come down to see what all the noise was about. But she knew that she would never be able to help Trent if that guy with the messed-up face got hold of her.

She closed the pantry door just as Jarrow entered the kitchen.

"Come out of there!" he shouted, and rushed at the door.

Stevie turned the deadbolt seconds before Jarrow's shoulder hit the other side. The pantry door shuddered in its frame.

Stevie backed away from it, heart pounding.

A killing rage swept over Jarrow. He let it ride and pass, then willed himself to calm down, and breathe deeply.

"I'm going to start counting, okay? If you don't open by the time I reach five, then I start shooting. You hear me in there?"

From inside the pantry, silence.

He felt like an asshole, trying to scare a little kid with a countdown. But he needed this kid. She was part of his plan.

"One."

Stevie looked around the pantry for some place to hide.

"Two."

She knew bullets could go through doors and still kill you.

"Three."

But there was no place to go. The pantry was too small.

"Four."

She crouched down underneath the console and covered her ears.

"Five." Jarrow paused. *"Five!"*

He waited, watching the closed door.

"Dirty little fucker," he muttered, raising the gun, aiming high on the door, still trying for a scare shot rather than a hit.

He pulled the trigger. The bullet smashed through the wooden shell but ricocheted off the steel plate inside the door. It buzzed past Jarrow's ear and bounced off a ventilating hood before embedding itself in the opposite wall.

"Shit!"

Just a few inches over and it would have hit him in the face, right where he shot that other bitch.

"Open the door and come out of there, you little cunt!"

He started kicking the pantry door, teeth clenched in fury.

" 'Tevie?" asked the small voice behind him. "Aun'isa?"

Jarrow turned around, face twisted with rage, and saw Trent standing there in the kitchen, wearing his Teenage Mutant Ninja Turtles pajamas with long sleeves and feet. Trent, who had never seen anything quite like Tod Jarrow before, just stared at him, not sure whether he should be scared or laugh.

"Hey, there! How you doin'?" Jarrow bent over him, free hand extended, hiding the gun behind his right thigh.

Trent backed off, naturally shy, still not sure what to make of this strange man with the funny face.

"Come here!" Jarrow smiled at him. "I won't hurt you!"

That did it—the bruises, stitches, and dark crazy eyes, combined with a soul-chilling grin.

Trent howled and started to toddle across the kitchen.

"You little shit," Jarrow muttered, reaching out and grabbing him by the arm, then jerking him back toward the pantry door.

Trent howled, eyes squeezed shut, face turning bright red.

"Got your little baby brother here with me," Jarrow called to Stevie behind the closed door, knowing that she could hear Trent's screams. "If you don't open that fucking door and come out here right now, I'm shooting both his legs off, starting with the right one first. You hear me? It's your choice, sugar. You come out now, no one gets hurt. Otherwise, you'll be pushing him around in a wheelchair for the rest of his life."

There was the click of a deadbolt. Then the door opened.

Stevie stepped out of the pantry, cheeks wet with tears.

"Don't hurt him," she sobbed.

Jarrow stared at her as he held the gun raised in one hand, Trent squirming and squealing in the other. The little prick probably took after his old man, red-faced and ugly. But the little girl, even with her blond hair and blue eyes—the way she held her head, the way she moved—looked like Connie. Exactly. Jarrow felt a strange sense of biological eternity there in the Stallman kitchen, looks and personality and movement, passing from one generation to the next, marching straight down the gene track.

Stevie ran over to Trent and hugged him.

"Now that's real sweet," Jarrow said, to no one in particular.

From his jeans pocket he took out a roll of packing tape that he had lifted from a drugstore on Sunset earlier in the day.

"Okay, kiddies. I got to tie up your hands now. You try to run away from me, I'll tie your legs up, too." He smiled down at them. "So tell me. Do I have to do the legs, or not?"

Stevie looked up at him, fear in her blue eyes, but behind that, anger. "No," she said.

Jarrow pulled out a strip of tape with a sharp, ripping sound.

Stevie glanced at the kitchen clock. "Galina's gonna be back from the market soon."

Jarrow stopped, eyes narrowing. "Who's Galina?"

"The lady that takes care of us during the day," Stevie said. "She's out shoppin' because she and Aunt Li—"

She stopped, afraid that she might start crying again.

"Well." Jarrow tore off the length of tape. "If Galina is the world's luckiest bitch, right now she's stuck in some thirty-minute checkout lane—hands behind your back, honey, right, just like that—and she won't get home until after we're gone. So, that way, I won't have to do her like I did your auntie out there at the front door. Okay?"

Stevie nodded, feeling sick, the tears starting again.

Trent looked up at Jarrow, eyes wide with terror, fat cheeks streaked with tears, not sure what was happening now, or what was coming next.

"Meanwhile—" Jarrow wrapped the tape around Stevie's wrists. "The three of us are gonna take a nice little ride in that nice little van I have outside, and get to know each other a whole lot better. And that's *very* important, because—"

He stopped, and leaned down over Stevie, until he was close enough for her to see his battered face in all its graphic detail.

"Do you know who I am?" he asked her, leaning down even closer. "Do you know who I *really* am?"

Stevie shrank back, despite her anger. She knew his name now.

He was The Thing in the Closet, the monster that had scared her to death when she was only four. He was ugly and hateful, with dark, crazy eyes, and he was *real*, no matter what

Mom and Dad said, or how many times they checked the closet for her. He wanted to hurt people, hurt them bad, for no reason at all, laughing with his dark, crazy eyes as he hurt them.

But she was not going to tell him this.

Jarrow smiled at her, stretching his wounds and stitches.

"I'm your daddy," he said, grinning. "Your *real* daddy!"

45
Deathwatch

As Connie drove through rush-hour traffic from Zenobia's office on Fairfax to Mrs. Amanda Baker's residence in Culver City, she kept thinking of the busy signal on her mother's phone line.

Maybe she knocked it off the hook by accident.

But Alice didn't do things like that.

She was still worried by the time she reached Culver City.

The Baker residence was a faded yellow bungalow, with dying grass and one stubby palm tree. Spray-painted gang graffiti covered part of the sidewalk and the next-door neighbor's driveway. Four small children played in the middle of the street, two of them on bikes. Three teenage boys leaned over the hood of a car on blocks in a nearby driveway.

As Connie walked up to the house, she heard nothing.

But Benjamin, according to Mrs. Baker, had been screaming repeatedly, calling out her name.

Connie! Connie!

And now, silence.

She stepped onto the porch, its concrete surface spiderwebbed with subsidence cracks. The screen door was closed, probably locked. The front door itself stood open a foot or two, enough to let in air, but not enough for her to see into the living room.

She knew there would not be an entryway in a house this size.

She knocked on the screen. "Mrs. Baker? It's Dr. Stallman."
No sound came from inside the house.

She smelled it then—heavy, acrid, damp, stomach-turning.

She had been around enough emergency and operating rooms to know what it was.

Dark images flashed through her mind as she stood on the porch, smelling that smell. She saw Mrs. Baker, driven mad by Benjamin's constant screaming, taking a knife or a meat cleaver, and striking Benjamin with it, again and again, taking out her own frustrations on the helpless child, chopping him into a bloody, twitching mass of muscles, organs, skin, and bone. Sitting now at the kitchen table, head in her hands, deep into grief and denial about what she had done, not even hearing Connie knocking and calling at the front door. Or, if hearing her, unable to answer.

Connie pounded on the screen door. "Mrs. *Baker!*"

From inside, nothing. The children on their bikes laughed and screamed in the middle of the street. Rap blasted from a boom box next to the car on blocks.

She reached for the handle and pulled. The screen door swung open, rusted hinges squealing. She took a deep breath, tried to ignore the smell, and pushed the door the rest of the way open.

The inside of the house was dark, blinds shut, curtains drawn.

It took her eyes a few seconds to adjust from the brightness of late-afternoon sun to the darkness of Mrs. Baker's living room.

When they did, she saw where the smell was coming from.

A jumble of body organs lay scattered across a mildewed orange carpet. Heart, lungs, liver, kidneys, spleen, intestines, long glistening ropes of them—and blood, lots of it, even more than she had stepped in last night, surrounding the body of Emilia Santos.

On the other side of the small living room, propped against a frayed sofa, sat Mrs. Baker's body—if it could still be called that. Mrs. Baker had been a woman of ample dimensions.

What was left of her now looked shriveled and shrunken, like the husk of a humanoid insect. Her hollow eye sockets leaked blood. Her mouth had been torn open at the corners, all the way back to her ears, and wrenched wide to form a large, gaping hole instead of a face.

What had come out of that hole was a medical impossibility.

Connie knew this, as she leaned back against the doorjamb, breathing hard. But nothing else could explain what she saw before her now. Something had attacked Mrs. Baker, some strange and unknown force, sucking out her internal organs through her mouth, then flinging them across the orange carpet.

Liposuction with a vengeance.

Connie's face felt damp. "Benjamin?"

"Close the door," whispered the hoarse voice beside her.

She cried out, knocking a lamp off a side table. It bounced against the wall, then crashed down to the carpet, light bulb exploding with a sharp pop. She looked for the source of that voice, but could see no one near her.

"Close the door," the voice said again, coming now from somewhere farther back in the living room, beyond the charnel-house remains of the late Mrs. Amanda Baker.

She looked up, and backed away from what she saw.

He stood on the other side of that small, malodorous living room—old, wrinkled, hunched over, pale yellow cat's eyes, hands like twisted spider's claws, looking as he had always looked, here and in Venice, then and now.

Looking the way he had looked when the world began.

And the way he would look when the world came to an end.

"You seem surprised to see me," he said, "Dr. Stallman."

He had never used her name before, and the sound of it, hissing on the *s* like that, made her flesh crawl.

"Who did you think was responsible for—this?" He gestured at the scattered remains of Mrs. Baker. "Him?"

He pointed to Benjamin Simmons, crouched underneath a drop-leaf table, dark eyes wild with fear.

"Benjamin!" Connie moved toward him.

The child scurried out from underneath the table, avoiding the mess on the living-room floor. He ran into her arms, grabbing hold of her with a desperation that cut deep into her heart.

"It's okay, Benjamin," she said, hugging him, knowing that her words had no meaning for him, but he still needed to hear them.

Hugging Benjamin, with the remains of Mrs. Baker spread across the living-room floor, and the Angel of Death looking on like an obscene parody of a grandfather, Connie made a break for it.

She didn't stop to think. There wasn't time. Picking up Benjamin, she turned toward the screen door and grabbed for the latch with her free hand, hoping that if she could just get outside in time, into the sunlight, they might be safe, away from him, out where he couldn't harm them.

The front door slammed shut, almost cutting off the tips of her fingers. She pulled back her hand, shaking with fear and the sour aftertaste of a thwarted adrenaline rush. She grabbed at the doorknob. It would not turn. She twisted it, gritting her teeth with the effort, still holding Benjamin under one arm.

The doorknob fell off in her hand.

She stood blinking at it stupidly.

Something seized the back of her head and turned it around, forcing her to turn with it. She cried out, thinking that *he* had touched her with his filthy, death-scented claws. But when she finished turning around, she saw that he was still standing where she had last seen him, on the other side of the living room.

"That was foolish," he said. "Don't try it again."

Still holding on to Benjamin, she said, "Let the child go."

"The child is of no significance."

"Then let him *go!*"

"No." He paused. "Aren't you getting tired of holding him?"

She put Benjamin down. He did not want to let go. After she pried his small hands loose from her neck, he grabbed her leg with a death-grip. Connie smoothed his tousled dark hair.

She looked over at Mrs. Baker. "Why did you kill her?"

"Must there be a reason?"

He hates life so, she remembered Zenobia saying.

"Why did you kill her that way?"

"Does it make a difference? After all, to die is to die."

Quit answering me with riddles! she thought angrily.

High, evil laughter floated across the living room.

"Do you grieve for her? Are you sorry to see her dead?"

"She didn't deserve to die—not like that."

"What an original statement! Nobody deserves to die. But they all do, don't they?" His laughter echoed off the walls.

Then, suddenly, it stopped.

"I answer you with riddles because you ask me riddles."

Astonishment entered her eyes.

He can go inside your mind, she thought, *just like Jarrow.*

"Far more effectively, Contessa."

She put a check on her thoughts, aware of just how dangerous this was becoming.

"Ask me a real question, and I will give you a real answer."

"What do you want from me?"

The yellow eyes studied her thoughtfully. "Your powers."

"Why? Aren't your own good enough?"

She meant it as an insult, but he looked at her with an intensity that made her go cold inside.

"My powers are limitless," he said. "But no power wishes to exist in isolation. Eternity is such a long time to spend alone."

Maybe, she could hear Zenobia saying, *it is more like he loves life, with a dark and fatal love—*

She tried to keep her sudden nausea from adding to the

mess already on the carpet. She tried not to let him read her mind.

But she could not make herself look at him, and see what she knew would be, God help her, desire in those pale yellow eyes.

He sensed her revulsion.

"You will have all eternity in which to grow fond of me."

"Is that what you're using Tod Jarrow for? As your alter ego? So that you can put on human flesh and—"

She stopped, unable to go on.

The high, evil laughter drifted toward her.

"You did not enjoy your—encounter of two nights ago?"

The laughter stopped.

"No. I am not Tod Jarrow. I used him only to acquire you. He is a peasant, then and now. Weak, ineffectual, doomed to failure, always. But his great passion for you, pathetic though it may be, is entirely his own."

She looked up into the yellow eyes.

"I see that you do not believe me. So, let me tell you a story. A love story. Dear to the hearts of foolish mortals."

"Pretty damn dear to your heart, too," she said. "Crying your eyes out about having to spend eternity all alone."

The yellow eyes burned into her own then, making her step back, and turn her head to one side, flinching as though caught beneath the glare of an intense, penetrating light.

"Desire and the communication of power," he whispered, "have nothing whatsoever to do with love. *Nothing!*"

The last word exploded inside her mind, its echoes traveling down through her blood and bones.

"But, to my story. Once, many years ago, there was a young man, a peasant, who fell in love with a—countess. She was rich, admired, all the things that he was not. He loved her beyond measure, beyond reason and sanity. But in her lovely eyes, he did not even exist. Had he possessed the slightest amount of common sense, he would have forgotten about her and turned to other things. But he did not. He loved her with a love that consumed his entire world. He would have her, even if it cost him the world. Even if it cost him more than that.

"Some say that, in his desperation, he sold his soul to the devil. But he was not that fortunate. He came, instead, to me.

"A bargain was struck. A deal was made. He would bring me blood sacrifices. The deaths of young, beautiful women, exquisitely wrought, at a cost of long and enormous suffering, which made their deaths more rare, their beauty more intense, and so the more to be desired."

Something almost like passion touched the edges of that hoarse, whispering voice.

"And for this service, he would be rewarded. He would possess the one thing he desired—more than anything else in this world.

"But once he possessed his great love, it turned to dust before his eyes, and ashes in his mouth. The countess remained young and beautiful, her physical charms more alluring than ever. But his love became mere rutting lust, carried on in the shadows. He wanted more than this. And he got it. Because you see, this countess lived another life, reincarnate in another age—"

Connie looked up at him.

"—and the young peasant, with simple powers of his own, though nothing like those of the beautiful young countess, was allowed to cross the yawning gulf of time and make love to her in both the ages, both the worlds of time, then and now."

The horror passed through her, dropping deep into her soul.

"A pretty story, don't you think, Contessa?"

"Especially the ending, where they both get burned alive at St. Mark's Column. But you left out that part."

"Ah!" he whispered. "The end for him. But for her, only the beginning." He lifted his black-robed arm and beckoned with his spider's claws. "My countess. My eternal companion. Come."

She stalled for time—a way out, any way out.

"The child can't be left here alone."

She tightened her grip on Benjamin's shoulder. "He—"

"If the child is a problem," whispered the Dark Sorcerer, "then he can be disposed of now."

Benjamin was torn loose from her grasp and lifted, screaming, until his body pressed against the shallow ceiling.

"No!" Connie cried, reaching up for him.

She looked over at the yellow eyes, her fury building.

It's not his time! she thought, pushing it at the black-robed figure like a fist. *Get back! Get BACK!*

Benjamin dropped from the ceiling like a lead *piñata*.

Connie managed to catch him just before he hit the floor.

She felt the yellow eyes burning into her, and looked up.

She saw, for the first time, something like human emotion in those eyes. Rage. A rage that made the earth shake beneath her feet, rolling and shuddering.

She was thrown to the floor, on top of Benjamin.

Then it passed, with a sound like the fluttering of a thousand black wings in the night.

Still on the floor, holding Benjamin, she heard the hoarse voice whisper in her ear.

"Do not *dare* to set your powers in opposition to mine! A foolish old woman has taught you a bag of worn-out tricks. But they will not work against *me*. If you try this again—"

She looked up, trembling.

"I will destroy you, again and again, through all eternity."

The black robes were gone. He had grown huge and non-human, crouching beneath the shallow ceiling, spider's claws the talons of a beast, body covered with dark scales that dripped black liquid and flickered with coruscations of unearthly light.

Connie drew back, pulling Benjamin close.

She had never felt more frightened, more alone.

But deep inside, where The Gift maintained its silent vigil, a faint hope persisted.

His powers were great.

He could do what he threatened—destroy her again and again, life after life, through all the worlds of time.

But he had threatened her, and he had changed before her,

unmasking himself, to terrify her, to frighten her into submission, for one reason, and one reason only.

He was scared.

Out in the street, the children heard it first.

They looked up at the sound of a muffled explosion.

The windows blew out in a shower of glass, flashing in the late-afternoon sun. The front door skidded across the sidewalk and smashed into Connie's Acura, dinging the paint job.

From inside the house came a small boy's terrified voice.

"Connie!"

The kids in the street started running toward the house.

"Dark Man!"

Three teenage boys peered out from behind the car on blocks.

"Gone!"

46

Showdown

Tod Jarrow pulled into the Beckford parking lot driving a white Hyundai Sonata with two small children in the back. From a distance, he looked like any suburban daddy going shopping.

He had broken into the Hyundai on Franklin, using a slim jim to open the door, then hot-wiring the engine. He had dumped the van earlier. It was too conspicuous to keep using.

He turned to the backseat, where both Stevie and Trent sat belted in, hands taped behind them. Trent, nose running, eyes red, had cried himself into a blubbery, sniffling state.

"He should be in his car seat," Stevie said.

"Fuck his car seat," Jarrow said. "Listen up. This is the building where Mommy works, okay? We're gonna go see her. Since you two kids have been so good, I'm cutting off the tape."

He raised the long, curved knife, holding it delicately in his hand, like a surgeon's scalpel.

Stevie drew back at the sight of it.

"Either of you pull any shit on me—try to run away, yell for help. Anything. I'm bringing you back out here, and locking you in the trunk. And that's where you'll *stay* from now on. Okay?"

Stevie nodded, then closed her eyes as Jarrow reached into the backseat and cut the tape that bound her hands.

Up in the Hollywood Hills, Lieutenant Ed Dormer felt a sour taste at the back of his throat as he got out of the black and white patrol car in the Stallman driveway. Three other cruisers and a paramedic meat wagon had already arrived.

The housekeeper, a Russian-Jewish émigré, Galina Marenkov, had missed her own death by minutes, coming back just after Jarrow drove off with the two kids. She was the one who found Lisa Stallman's body in the entryway. The paramedics had sedated her. Dormer did not know how well Ken Stallman was taking this.

He was not eager to find out.

As he approached the front door, with uniformed officers keeping back the curious while a forensics team worked at chalking, measuring, and photographing the remains of Lisa Tate, Dormer saw Sergeant Mike Salazar standing off to one side.

"What've we got, Mike?"

"A fucking mess," Salazar said. "Go take a look at that woman in there, with the back of her head blown off."

"Okay, Mike. I understand." Dormer sighed. "I knew her."

Salazar looked surprised.

"She served me coffee, that night I waited for Dr. Stallman to come back from the near miss in Long Beach. It's a shame."

"A fucking goddamn shame," Salazar said.

Ken Stallman came toward them, stepping past the forensics team gathered around his sister's corpse, and through the police line, his eyes haunted, like those of a man who had watched his world disappear, only to find himself a lone, unwilling survivor.

"Do they know where Jarrow is?"

"We're working on that, Ken."

"He has to be *somewhere.*"

"We'll find him."

"Have they found Connie yet?"

"We called her office. Talked with her receptionist, Becky—"

"Martinez," Salazar said.

"Said your wife had an emergency call from one of her patients. Benjamin—" He looked at Salazar again.

"Simmons," Ken said. "Benjamin Simmons. Was he there?"

"No," Dormer said. "She drove over to his house, place in Culver City where he lives with a foster parent."

Ken turned and started for his car.

Dormer grabbed his arm. "We've got men on their way over, Ken. They'll get there before you do."

"Where's Jarrow now?"

"We don't know. He might be hiding out in some motel room. Or maybe he's already changed vehicles, and now he's trying to drive out of the city—into the mountains, the desert."

"When you find him," Ken said, "I want to be there. Okay?"

"I understand how you feel—"

"No you don't. I've never even *seen* him. I have to see who's gone after my wife, my kids, my sister. I don't want you killing him before I *see* him, alive. Understand now?"

"Sure, Ken. We understand."

Inside the Beckford Clinic, Becky Martinez dabbed at her eyes with a Kleenex, still thinking about her conversation with the police—the impersonal voice on the other end of the line, telling her what had happened to Connie's kids and Ken's sister, asking her where Connie was, because that's where Tod Jarrow might go next.

It was horrible. She knew something was bothering Connie.

But nothing like this. Nothing this—awful.

She crossed herself.

The door to the reception room opened.

She put on the smile she reserved for people with severe physical deformities, a smile that said she liked them, and wasn't shocked or offended by the way they looked.

But almost immediately, with the smile still taking shape on her face, she realized that something was wrong with this dark-eyed young man, something unrelated to his scars and bruises. And even as the smile continued to form on her face— even as she saw him reach into a Nordstrom's bag with one hand, a frightened-looking little boy riding on his other arm, and draw out a large, heavy silver revolver—she moved her own hand beneath the desk and pressed an alarm buzzer, the one connected to the Hollywood Station of the Los Angeles Police Department. She did this quickly, automatically, without thinking. Because if she had stopped to think, even for an instant, she would have started screaming.

"Becky!" Stevie said, the word almost a sob.

Jarrow said to Stevie, "You shut the fuck up."

He turned the .357 magnum on Becky. "Where is she?"

She kept her voice steady and professional. "With a patient."

"Don't bullshit me, Chiquita baby."

The anger she felt helped steady her nerves. "I'm telling you the truth, *Mis*ter Jarrow. If you don't believe me, you can go back to her office and check for yourself."

She hoped he would, after leaving the kids with her first.

Jarrow stood there, the gun balanced in his hand.

Then he told Stevie, "Say hi to Mommy. Tell her you're here."

"Mom?" Stevie's frightened voice carried down the short corridor from the front desk to her mother's office. "It's me, Stevie! And Trent!"

The corridor was silent.

"Shit!" Jarrow exploded.

Stevie jumped back from him. Trent started wailing again.

Becky opened her desk drawer and reached inside.

Jarrow moved forward with breathtaking speed, until the muzzle of the .357 magnum was less than an inch from her face.

Becky felt the sweat break out along her upper lip.

"That was fucking stupid of you, Chiquita. Now, you take your hand out of there, r-e-a-l slow, and put down whatever you're holding right in the middle of the goddamn desk."

She remained frozen for several seconds, the gun in her face.

Then she drew out her hand, and placed a Kleenex on the desk.

"Someone needs to wipe his nose," she said quietly.

A lopsided grin broke out on Jarrow's face. "Now that's real sweet of you, Chiquita Banana." He said to Stevie, "Come on and wipe your baby brother's snotty nose, sis."

Trent squirmed as Stevie tried to clean his face, and said, "Ba'room!" Then again, a little louder this time. *"Ba'room!"*

Jarrow frowned at Stevie. "What's this 'varoom' shit?"

"He has to go to the bathroom," Stevie said.

"Maybe he'll have to hold it. Or crap in his pants."

"He'll smell awful then. And he'll never stop crying."

"There's a staff bathroom right outside in the hall," Becky volunteered. "I can take him."

"All *right!*" Jarrow shouted, startling her. *"Take* the little shit bag!" He handed him over to her. "But we're *all* going out into the hall. And if you're not finished in about two minutes, I'm coming in after you. You *entiendo* me, Chiquita?"

"Sure," she said, carrying Trent toward the reception-room door. "I understand English almost as good as you speak Spanish."

"Fuck you, taco head!"

Out in the empty hall, Jarrow stood watching, gun back in

the Nordstrom bag, his other hand gripping Stevie's shoulder, as Becky turned the key and opened the door to the staff rest room.

"Okay," Jarrow said. "Now toss me the keys."

She closed the door, and locked it.

"Hey!" Jarrow crossed over to the rest-room door, dragging Stevie with him. "Open the fuck *up!*"

He kicked the door hard, then hissed under his breath, limping back a step or two. It was a heavy, solid wooden door.

He put his mouth close to the frame and said in a low voice, "Open it, Chiquita baby, before I get good and fucking mad, okay?"

"Can I help you with something, sir?"

Jarrow's head snapped up. He saw Dr. Louis Pelham walking down the hall toward him, dark African eyes grave.

Jarrow drew the .357 magnum out of the Nordstrom bag.

"Yeah, Sambo. You can open this goddamn fucking door."

Lou Pelham stopped, recognizing Stevie.

"I'm afraid I don't have a key to that room, sir."

"Like *shit* you don't! Open the fucking door!"

"Perhaps I didn't make myself clear—"

Jarrow stepped forward, sticking the gun in Lou's face.

"Don't fuck with me, Uncle Remus."

Lou Pelham did not frighten easily. But he knew something about guns, having been shot with one once. He knew even more about acute homicidal psychosis, a textbook example of which was on display for him here.

"Perhaps I was mistaken," Lou said, reaching slowly into his pocket, taking out a full key ring. "Maybe I do have the right one here, somewhere." He began to sort through the keys.

"*Move* it, asshole!" Jarrow glanced uneasily down the hall.

Lou offered him the key ring, his face expressionless.

"Perhaps you'd like to look for yourself, sir?"

Jarrow saw Lou glance at Stevie.

He looked down at her himself, following her gaze back to a tall plate-glass window in the stairwell behind them.

Three patrol cars blocked the street outside. Two more pulled up as Jarrow watched. Helmeted SWAT-team members began taking their positions behind the cars.

From inside the locked rest room, Trent started howling.

Jarrow turned back to the door. "You stupid *cunt!*" he screamed at Becky inside. "Open this goddamn door! *Now!*"

He fired into the door. The gun bucked in his hand, its blast echoing down the hall. Stevie clapped her hands to her ears. The .357 bullet tore a chunk out of the door, then ricocheted off a metal stall inside the rest room.

Jarrow got ready to fire again, aiming lower this time.

The stairwell window behind them exploded, followed by the echoing recoil of a heavy-gauge rifle. Glass fragments showered down on top of them, catching in their hair and clothes, popping and tinkling on the hall floor. Stevie began to scream.

Jarrow backed up toward the stairwell with her, scattering broken glass underfoot, the .357 magnum pointed at Lou Pelham.

"You called the cops on me! You goddamn black shit!"

"No I didn't. But given a chance, I would have—Mr. Jarrow."

A bullet cut through the air beside Jarrow, wide of Stevie, but only inches from his own head.

"You dirty fucking nigger!" He aimed and fired at Lou, then stumbled down the stairway, dragging Stevie with him.

Lou jumped to one side when he saw Jarrow aim. The impact hit him in the chest with the force of a kicking stallion, throwing him up against the wall, then down onto the floor, hammering the breath from his body. For several seconds he lay there, motionless, not knowing exactly where he had been hit.

Lou waited, lying on broken glass. He glanced at his body, saw the entry hole, and felt some relief, even as the pain began to register, dimly at first, along his shocked nerves. It was a shoulder wound, not a chest wound. That's why his lungs weren't filling up with blood, why he wasn't choking on it as the temporary cavity expanded, killing him. He could not tell whether the bullet had fractured bone or severed tendons. It might have hit the deltoid muscle.

He did not panic. He had been through this before.

Hit by machine-gun fire in Vietnam, more than twenty-five years ago, he not only survived, but made it through college and med school on the government's money, made something of himself. No psychotic punk with a handgun was going to take that away.

He heard footsteps crunching on broken glass and raised his head, fear gripping his heart, pain shooting through his shoulder.

Two paramedics hurried down the hall toward him.

"What happened to Jarrow?" Lou asked, as they began to examine his wound. "And the little girl with him?"

"Used her as a shield," the older paramedic said. "Police couldn't shoot. Son of a bitch got away."

47

Betrayal

Hands on a keyboard, bathed in the soft glow of flickering candlelight. Piano keyboard. No, not a piano. Much smaller. Enclosed in a gilded, painted case, more like a harpsichord, but not that, either. *Verginale.* A virginal, yes. A wonderful instrument, producing crisp, clear sounds from its plucked strings. Something she had learned to play as a small child before guests in her father's house, and still played now for the sheer pleasure of it in private, though not as well as she once had. A pretty piece of music by William Byrd, the Englishman, who had come to Venice once, years ago, to escape the dark, cold land of his birth.

She hit a wrong note, jarring in its dissonance.

She looked up into the mirror on the wall, framed by golden cupidons blowing long, angelic trumpets. She stared at herself—dark reddish-brown hair piled high, silver crucifix and diamonds glittering at her throat.

I can't really play this, she thought suddenly, taking her hands from the keyboard. *I don't belong here at all.*

A sharp pain flashed in her head—a blinding yellow light.

The guts of an animal, or a human being, lying spilled across an orange carpet. Yellow eyes burning into her brain, huge as lanterns in the night. A nonhuman form, scales dripping darkness.

Il stregóne morello. The Dark Sorcerer.

Her throat felt tight. She could not catch her breath.

Her heart beat frantically. She got to her feet, gold velvet gown trailing the tile floor. She put a hand to her breasts, exposed half-naked by the low-cut gown, and paced the floor, the sweet music of the virginal forgotten, the hem of her gown rustling across the tiles.

It was something of great importance. She could not forget it. She must not. But what *was* it? Something involving the other place. What she had learned there, in her other life.

She stopped, in the middle of the music room.

What other life? She *had* no other life. This was her life, the *Palazzo* Contarini. Her servants and attendants, her position in society as the Countess Contarini, wife of a powerful and respected man.

The pain burst inside her skull again, making her bend over in the center of the music room, clutching at her head with both hands, moaning like a sick child. She leaned on a velvet-cushioned chair for support, until her breathing returned to normal.

The thing that she must not forget, it had to do with a woman.

A woman's name. What was the name? *Z.* It began with a *z.* Zanni? Venetian dialect for Giovanni. Impossible! That was a man's name. She was searching for a woman's name, one that began with *z.* Zorena? No, that was close. But it was not the name she was looking for—the name she must remember.

Because my life depends upon it, she thought. *My own life, and the lives of all the others.*

What other lives? She and her husband had no children, which was much to her liking, and pray God it might continue, because his physical affections filled her with disgust. But who were the others, whose lives, like her own, depended upon this name?

Her heart beat even faster as she paced the tiles of the music room, trying to remember the woman's name that began with a *z*.

My own life, and the lives of all the others.

She heard footsteps coming up the outside stairs to the main entrance of the *Palazzo* Contarini, then the front door opening, and heavy boots echoing across the marble floor of the entryway.

She stopped in the middle of the music room, and listened.

"You are certain of this?" came her husband's deep, rumbling *basso* of a voice from the entryway.

Another man started to speak, but Contarini cut him off.

"Answer carefully," he warned him. "Before God and Saint Mark, your life depends upon it."

"We are betrayed," the man said, and she recognized the voice of the hawk-nosed *Signoria* member, the one who had been with her husband and the other conspirators in the dining hall that night she had listened at the double doors. "All is lost."

She looked up into the gold-framed mirror.

She drew back at what she saw. A woman's face, not unlike her own, but yet so different. Her hair shorter, falling only to her shoulders, like a boy's, pale brown streaked with gold. Skin burned dark by the sun, like the face of a peasant working in the mainland fields. What sorcery brought this strange face into the mirror of her music room? Could *this* be the one, the woman whose name began with a *z?*

But then she knew whose face it was, and her flesh grew cold.

It was the face of her other life.

The life that was still to come.

On the other side of that mirror, looking out now across the worlds of time, with the Dark Sorcerer's burning yellow eyes at her back, Connie Stallman, for a fleeting instant, saw herself in Venice in the Year of Grace 1594, a lovely young woman of twenty-three who would never reach twenty-four.

The moment passed. The strange face in the mirror of the music room dissolved back into her own, the Countess Alessandra Contarini. She heard the voices of her husband and the other *Signoria* member, closer now, having moved out from the entryway and into the grand hallway.

"Speak no more of it now," came the deep voice of her husband, "where there are ears everywhere to overhear us. Idle serving girls. My chamberlain, Pietro. Even my—wife."

"There are things I could tell you about your wife," said the other man, "that would turn you into a murderer."

"I know already the things you would speak of. I have no illusions about my *wife!*"

Alessandra crossed herself with a trembling hand.

"But no more of this talk!" Contarini said. "Come. We will go to my study. There we can safely discuss— No, decide. We can decide what must be done."

Alessandra sat down quickly at the keyboard of the virginal and began to play the piece by William Byrd, hitting many wrong notes. She felt a chill at the back of her neck as she heard, even above the dissonant notes of the virginal, the tread of heavy boots passing outside the music room. She bent over the keyboard.

Then, noticing a curious stillness in the room, as if the boots had passed on by, she turned around.

Her fingers froze on the keys.

Ludovico Contarini stood at the open door of the music room, his great bulk blocking her view of the other man out in the hallway with him, the hawk-nosed *Signoria* member.

"You play badly tonight. You are out of practice."

"Yes," she said, seizing the excuse. "I had hoped to regain my skills through diligence. I know how much you loved to hear me play, once, and I thought to please you again."

"You thought to please me," he repeated slowly.

A tear blinked from her eyelash down onto her cheek. She wanted to reach up and wipe it away. But she did not dare. Her hand would tremble with fear, betraying her.

We are all betrayed. Everything is lost.

Ludovico Contarini stared at her, as if about to speak again, then turned and walked away.

She waited until she heard them reach the far end of the grand hallway and begin to mount the stairs to her husband's study on the second floor. Then she stepped out of the music room and started walking quickly down the grand hallway herself, dark velvet slippers whispering across the tiles. More tears fell from her eyes, but she did not bother to wipe them away. She was thinking hard, about her life, and how to save it.

My own life, and the lives of all the others.

She must flee the *Palazzo* Contarini. Flee Venice itself. Tonight. Immediately. And go where? She did not know. Venice was her life, had always been her life, the most glorious city on the face of the earth. Outside it lay blood and darkness, filth and superstition, savage armies locked in perpetual conflict. But now, for her, the darkness had fallen on Venice, too. She thought of the deadly anger in her husband's voice, and then of the high, evil laughter of the Dark Sorcerer as her demon lover, Marcangelo, dismembered the body of the prostitute and poured the blood upon her own naked flesh. She shuddered at the memory.

Darkness. Corruption. Sorcery. Death.

She knew what she must do. Walk until she reached the kitchen at the end of the grand hallway, then keep walking, out through the back door, into the night. Sell the diamonds and small crucifix at her throat, the simple rings on her fingers, to some Jew from the Ghetto. Take the money, buy passage on a ship going—somewhere.

Anywhere. Away.

But she could not leave like that, not even with her life in danger. She would go upstairs to her own room first, tiptoeing past her husband's study in silent velvet slippers.

Then, in her own room, she would put into a traveling pouch the few precious things she could take with her, some to sell for money, others to keep close to her as mementos of a Venice she would never see again. Her mother's golden crucifix, the one that had been given to her after her mother died in childbirth, along with the baby that would have been Alessandra's younger sister. A marvelous winged lion, the symbol of Venice, carved of dark purple porphyry, brought to her by her father from Constantinople, Byzantium that once was. Other jewels, expensive but meaningless, given to her by Ludovico Contarini in their first year of marriage.

She hurried up the stairs to the second floor, lifting the hem of her gown so that it would not drag across the steps. Who had betrayed her to Ludovico? Tulia, the mutilated scullery maid, seeking revenge? Marcangelo himself, breaking under torture in the Doge's dungeons? Unspeakable tortures, diabolical machines that crushed skulls, tore out tongues, wrenched arms loose from sockets. She winced at the visions from her dream. It did not matter now. The betrayal was fact, the damage done.

All that mattered now was escape.

As she reached the second floor and turned toward her own room, she paused, looking at that part of the hallway, lost in dark shadow, where her husband and the other man sat in his study, deep in conversation. Light from the study fell out into the hallway in a distorted rectangle, crawling across the floor and up onto the opposite wall, framing two grotesque shadows—her husband, Ludovico Contarini, and the hawk-nosed member of the *Signoria*.

She could hear their voices, not everything they said, just individual words.

Stregóneria. Sorcery.

Il stregóne morello. The Dark Sorcerer.

She moved forward on her noiseless velvet slippers, breathing through a dry, open mouth. Closer now, she could hear their conversation more clearly.

"—accuse them both of practicing sorcery to kill you," the *Signoria* member was saying, "then turn them over to the Inquisition and have done with it."

Her heart stopped. The Inquisition. Torture, forced confession. Then, a public burning. Slow burning, as the fire roasted you alive, working from the feet up.

"I can deal with my wife's infidelities, in my own way."

Alessandra thought of Tulia, with her severed nose and ears.

"But you ignore an even greater danger," the *Signoria* member said. "Now that the plot is betrayed and in the open, the Ten will look for the guilty. Not, mind you, the truly guilty. The Doge would rather not know that members of his own *Signoria* are plotting to kill him. He suspects it, of course. But he would not *know*. And yet, he must have someone to punish for it, guilty or not. A *capro espiatorio,* a scapegoat. So, give him one. Give him two. Your *assassino* is in the service of this Dark Sorcerer. Why not your wife as well? Give Pasquale Cicogna three scapegoats. The hired murderer, your wife, the Dark Sorcerer. Not even the Lords of the Night will ever lay hands on that devil in human form. But the Ten will accept the guilt of the other two. The Inquisition, most certainly."

"Perhaps," Contarini said, considering it. "But although my wife is a faithless whore, I do not know that she practices sorcery. If accused, she may deny it."

"Let her! Why else would she turn from a man of your noble birth and Christian mercy? Then throw herself into the arms of a common hired murderer? Except that she was deceived by those Demons of Hell which she and her damned lover called forth. Besides—" The voice of the *Signoria* member took on a more practical tone. "After the torturers of the Ten finish with her, she'll confess to anything."

In the shadowy hallway, Alessandra raised a hand to her mouth.

"My lady!" called a voice near the stairs.

Alessandra turned, and saw her frightened serving girl.

"Are you ill, my lady? What's wrong?"

She saw the shadows move suddenly on the wall, heard the heavy steps of Ludovico Contarini coming to the door of his study.

She turned and ran, pushing past the girl, who tried to block her way. She ran to her own room, unlocked the heavy wooden door, hands trembling as she turned the key.

"Alessandra!" Her husband's deep voice carried down the dark hallway toward her. *"Stop! I command you!"*

She closed the door from the inside, locked it, fell back against it, breathing hard, trying to get air into her lungs again.

Now she was truly lost. He knew she had overheard them.

He might leave her in the room tonight, meaning to deal with her later. Or turn her over to the Lords of the Night, who would thunder up the stairs of the *Palazzo* Contarini, breaking down her bedroom door with raised pikes and halberds.

A violent knocking hammered against the door.

She cried out and drew back from it.

"Alessandra!" Ludovico Contarini shouted through the closed door, voice barely muted by the heavy wood. "Open this door! I, as your husband before God, command you!"

Another voice came from behind the door now, in opposition to Contarini's. High and angry, the voice of her serving girl. Then Contarini's voice again, interrupted by hers, now both of them together, in heated argument. Then a scream, the serving girl's, followed by a series of screams—sharp, shattering. Then low and guttural, as if the living heart was being torn from her body.

The screams stopped. Alessandra unlocked the door, opened it.

The girl's body fell forward, crumpled up against the door, her dead hands having clawed bloody tracks into the wood. Both eyes were punctured, face slashed into shreds of flesh, breasts and stomach ripped and gouged.

Ludovico Contarini stood out in the hallway, a beast instead of a man, blood flecking his great silver head. He breathed heavily through his hanging mouth, a Turkish dagger gripped hard in his right hand, blood on the blade, on his hand, on his arm all the way up to the elbow. Blood on his robe and doublet, on the tiles of the hallway. Whoever would have thought that such a small, thin, gentle-eyed girl could have had so much blood in her?

"The faithless servant," he wheezed, "of a faithless wife."

"Your heart," she said to him, "is blacker than Satan's."

"And you would know," he answered, bringing the dagger forward, "for you are his whore."

Let the pain come to your own black heart then. Let it come!

A piercing cry burst from Contarini's open mouth.

The Turkish dagger dropped from his hand, clattering onto the tile floor. He clutched his massive chest with both hands, stumbled backward, fell to his knees, gasping for breath, eyes glazed with pain, sweat breaking out over his heavy-featured face, glistening like a sheen of oil.

"Stréga!" he cried out in a strangled voice. "Sorceress!"

In the hallway behind him, the hawk-nosed *Signoria* member, his own dagger unsheathed, drew back in horror, crossing himself, eyes wild and frightened.

"God and Saint Mark protect us all," he whispered fervently, "from the Demons of Hell and their Master!"

He turned and ran.

"Help me!" Contarini called after him, reaching out with one palsied hand, the other still clutching his chest.

She went back inside her room and began to gather her things. Her mother's golden crucifix. The winged lion of Saint Mark. The most valuable jewels Ludovico had given her. She put them in a pouch and strapped it to her waist, beneath her gown. To these she added a small vial of the famed Venetian *teriaca,* antidote to all illnesses except the Plague. Who knew what sickness lurked in foreign lands?

Out in the hall, she stepped over the butchered body of her serving girl, then walked past the huge bulk of her husband, lying on the floor now, mouth open and gasping for air, like a fish at the fishmonger's stall. She stopped at the head of the stairs and looked back at him. He would not die just now. She knew this, as surely as if she looked into the future and saw it written in a book. He would suffer great pain, but he would not die until later, when his time came, like everyone's.

She left by the back door, through the kitchen, saying nothing to the scullery maids. She could not risk taking a Contarini gondola along the great public thoroughfare of the Grand Canal.

Outside, she walked through the narrow, twisting *calli,* keeping her wits about her, watching out for rats, and murderers. She glanced up now and then at the stone heads and figures carved above doorways, on walls, at the tops of columns. Gryphons, dragons, wolves, crocodiles, lions, monsters, snakes. Familiar figures, some of them, part of the bizarre visual richness of the city. But now, looking down at her as she fled for her life, they seemed dark and malevolent, stone gods bent on her destruction.

She came at last to a narrow, out-of-the-way canal, and saw what she was looking for. A gondola, black as death, glided silently along the dark waters of the canal. It seemed to be carrying cargo, boxes of different sizes, but no passengers other than its solitary gondolier. She hailed it.

"I wish to be taken to the docks," she said.

The gondolier, face hidden by a dark hat and mask, nodded in silence. She sat down in the narrow boat and made herself comfortable. The gondola cut slowly through the back canals toward the docks, and the unknown ship that would take her away to some other, distant port. For the first time since fleeing the *Palazzo* Contarini, she began to feel safe, as if she might escape the blood and darkness closing in on her.

Darkness. Corruption. Sorcery. Death.

She stared at the covered boxes in front of her, especially at one long, heavy crate that stood out from the others. Its cover slipped off, revealing a black coffin underneath. She gasped at the sight, then crossed herself, fearful now that she had made a horrible mistake, and hailed a funeral gondola on its way to the cemetery island of San Michele. Unnerved, she turned around to the silent gondolier.

The yellow eyes of the Dark Sorcerer stared deep into her own.

Her scream echoed off the buildings of the back canal.

"Open it," whispered the hoarse voice, wrinkled face nodding at the black coffin. "Open it, and look inside."

Like a dreamer in a nightmare, she obeyed, turning back to the coffin. She reached out fearfully to lift its lid. But the lid popped open on its own, startling her.

She leaned forward and looked inside the coffin.

At first, she could see only darkness. Then the darkness began to move, and swarm. Rats, dozens of them, crawled over the corpse. She felt the nausea rise in her throat and tried to look away. But she could not. The rats skittered back from the corpse's face. The blue eyes were gone, eaten away, hollow staring sockets in their place. The left hand, beneath the swarming rats, lay clenched and paralyzed, the fingertips of the right stained yellow with cigarette smoke. Dried blood covered the body, dark brown beneath the rats, like a crusted shroud.

The pain burst inside her head again. *"No!"*

The Dark Sorcerer's laughter floated above her anguished cry.

As she looked at her mother's savaged corpse, floating in a gondola on a back canal in Venice, four hundred years ago, Connie Stallman knew who she was, and where she was, trapped inside the body of the terrified Alessandra Contarini. She could remember everything now, everything Zenobia Horowitz had taught her. But it was too late. Her mother, Alice MacKendrick, was one of the other lives she was supposed to save, one of the lives from which she was to have drawn the strength she needed to save her own life.

My own life, and the lives of all the others.

She looked down at the coffin again. It was empty. The corpse, the rats, all had gone. She turned back to the Dark

Sorcerer. Gone. The gondola bumped into the side of the canal. She smelled wood smoke drifting across the damp night air.

She looked up.

They stood waiting for her along the stone bank of the narrow canal, the *Signori di Notte,* Lords of the Night, torches raised, hands on sword hilts, no mercy or compassion of any kind in their hard, staring eyes.

The leader stepped forward, grim-faced, with a dark beard.

"We arrest you," he announced, "in the name of the Doge and the Republic, for the crime of murder—"

A look of dread entered his hard eyes.

"And for the forbidden, un-Christian crime of sorcery."

48
High Wire

It was almost evening when Ken Stallman stood in the Beckford parking lot, holding his son Trent, unwilling to surrender him to anyone, even Babs Stallman, his own mother, who had driven up from Newport Beach on learning of Lisa's murder.

LAPD officers and paramedics swarmed over the lot, shadowed by television news reporters.

One of them asked Lieutenant Ed Dormer, "Where's Jarrow now?"

"Heading east on Sunset."

"What about the little girl he has with him?"

"Getting her out safe is our number-one priority, even if that means letting Jarrow go. No more questions right now."

Dormer turned from the reporter, and saw Ken watching him.

"Where's he taking Stevie?"

"Ken, if we knew that—"

"Don't bullshit me, Ed."

"I'm not. I just don't know. I doubt if Jarrow knows."

"What did your men find in Culver City?"

"Not what you're looking for."

"What did they *find,* goddamn it?"

"An eviscerated female corpse. But it wasn't your wife."

"How do you know?"

"We had the forensics people check it out."

"Did they find anything else?"

"Signs of an explosion. But not the usual signs. No burns or charring. No melted wires. Not even the smell of smoke."

"That's impossible!"

"We don't make up the evidence, Ken."

"Then what *happened* to my wife?"

"At the present time—"

"Lieutenant?" A uniformed officer approached Dormer. "I'm afraid we just got some bad news in from Long Beach."

Ken looked over at him.

"Jarrow's stopped!" called a plainclothes detective standing beside a patrol car with its door open, police-band radio turned up. "He's out of the car now, on foot. Little girl's with him."

The noisy parking lot fell silent.

"Location?" Dormer asked.

The detective gave him the address of a new high-rise under construction near Sunset and La Cienega.

"Is he talking?" Dormer asked. "Making any demands?"

The detective held up his hand while he listened to another quick report crackling across the police band, then turned and said, "Looks like he's trying to get into the man-lift cage."

"That's the crane they use on high-rise jobs," Ken explained, "to carry workers up to the steel girders."

"Could one person run something like that?" Dormer asked.

"Sure. You operate it from inside the cage."

Dormer called to Sergeant Mike Salazar. "Let's go!"

"I'm coming with you," Ken said.

Dormer paused, then said, "Get in back."

"Ken!" A woman's voice carried across the parking lot.

He looked up and saw his mother, Babs Stallman.

"Are you going to take him with you?" she asked, pointing to Trent in his arms.

Ken walked over and handed Trent to her. "I have to go with them, Mom. It's not like I have a choice."

Babs held her grandson close.

"Trent may not have a sister after this is over," she said. "Or a mother. He'll need someone, Ken."

He wanted to explain to her why he had to do this, but all he said was, "I'll be careful, Mom."

Jarrow stopped the stolen Hyundai in a gravel lot next to the construction equipment. Two black-and-whites pulled in behind him, keeping their distance. A noisy helicopter closed down overhead, searchlight switched on.

He said to Stevie, "See that big tall building up there?"

He pointed through the windshield with the .357 magnum.

"We're gonna take a ride *all* the way to the top, up to where those steel bars are. Sound like fun, sugar?"

"No."

"Well, *fuck* you and your lousy attitude, okay?"

He and Stevie got out of the car, slowly, the muzzle of the .357 against her throat, right underneath her chin.

He couldn't see beyond the glare of the construction company's security lights, but he knew that more black-and-whites would be pulling up by now, white-helmeted SWAT-team members scrambling quickly for positions. That was cool, as long as they could see him and the little bitch.

At first he thought they might have locked the man-lift, and he felt anger building inside him. Then he found the key in the ignition, just waiting to be turned on. He smiled.

Jarrow turned around, so that he and Stevie, the gun still to her throat, faced into the bright security lights. He opened the door to the man-lift cage, and backed them both inside.

"Tod Jarrow," a loudspeaker echoed from behind the lights. *"That's dangerous equipment. You're not trained to operate it. The child could get hurt. Let her go."*

"Fuck you, assholes!" Jarrow shouted, feeling secure inside the cage. "She's gonna *get* hurt, if you don't shut the fuck up!"

He pushed the lever to the UP position.

With a groan of creaking metal, the man-lift cage bucked once, then started to ascend. Stevie tried to pretend that this was a fun ride at Magic Mountain, or Knott's Berry Farm, or Disneyland. But it didn't work. She knew where she was— trapped inside a cage with the Thing in the Closet, an evil man with crazy eyes who had killed Aunt Lisa. Now he would kill her, too. There was nowhere else to go. He was only using her to make Mom come and find him.

But Mom wouldn't come. Not now. She couldn't.

Mom was in big trouble.

Stevie had no idea how she knew this. She just did, somehow.

She watched the ground and the bright lights drop slowly beneath them, bit by bit, while the cage moved higher and higher up the side of the dark building, carrying her to her death.

By the time the man-lift reached the upper level of the high-rise where the exposed steel girders began, the cruiser with Ed Dormer, Mike Salazar, and Ken Stallman had pulled in behind the security lights. They looked up as they got out of the car.

High-voltage spotlights had been aimed at the top of the building, illuminating the girders like metal sculpture against a black background. Officers out on Sunset tried to keep the traffic moving, but it was turning into gridlock, with drivers getting out of their cars, crowds gathering on the sidewalk, staring up at the spectacle in the night sky.

Ken looked down and asked one of the officers behind the lights, "Do they have the elevators turned on inside?"

"SWAT team's working on it."

Ken stepped forward, brushing off Dormer's restraining hand.

"I'm her father, goddamn it."

He moved out into the glare of the security lights, heading for the ground-floor entrance to the building.

"Stallman!" Dormer called after him.

"I'll go get him," Salazar said.

Dormer shook his head. "I'll handle this."

He caught up with Ken in front of the elevator wall inside, where he was trying to talk a SWAT-team member into letting him go up to the open level.

"I'm not authorized to okay something like that," the officer said. "And you're not supposed to be—"

"I'll take over," Dormer said. "Look, Ken, if I let you go up there, have I got your word you won't try anything stupid?"

"What if Jarrow freezes up? What if he loses his nerve?"

"Not too fucking likely."

"Ever been up on high steel?"

"No," Dormer said. "Have you?"

"Years ago, working one summer for a friend of my dad's. It's a real ball-buster. You're balanced on a beam hundreds of feet above the ground, thinking the wind's going to blow you off any second, even if you don't get dizzy first, and go over the edge."

Dormer thought of all the reasons why he should say no. Instead he looked at Ken, and said, "Okay."

Halfway up the high-steel section, three floors from the top, the man-lift stopped with a sudden jolt, rocking the cage back and forth. Stevie screamed. Jarrow frowned, and jammed the lever into the UP position, hard, with the heel of his hand. Nothing.

Then, the cage kicked into life again, and started to descend.

"Son of a fucking *bitch!"* Jarrow muttered under his breath, yanking the lever down to EMERGENCY STOP.

A shudder jolted through the cage once again. Stevie clung to its rusted metal side and gazed down with terrified eyes on

the brightly lighted scene far below—the police cars, the traffic, the people, all of them looking as tiny and doll-like as Los
Angeles itself viewed from the window of a departing 747.

Jarrow opened the door to the cage and looked down.

The man-lift had stopped almost in the middle of a floor.
The closest girder was a four-foot drop below them.

Jarrow stared at it. *"Shit!"*

He did not want to risk touching the controls again.

"Come on!" he said, grabbing hold of Stevie. "We'll just
have to climb down there. Let's get the fuck out of this thing,
before it starts to drop on us again."

"No," Stevie whimpered, gripping the side of the cage.

"Come on—sugar." Jarrow yanked on her arm, ripping
Stevie's hands loose from the metal.

"Ow!" she screamed. "You're *hurting* me!"

"You do like you're fuckin' told, or I'll kill you!"

Three floors down, Ken Stallman and Ed Dormer heard
Stevie's cry, and Jarrow's shouted response, echoing from the
girders above them. They stood on the last floor below the
open structure, and looked up into spotlighted darkness. A
SWAT-team member held a sniper rifle mounted with an infra-
red telescopic sight.

"No clear shot from down here, sir," he said. "When he
gets her out of that cage, he'll use her like a shield again. And
with all this steel overhead, we got ricochet problems out the
ass."

"Yeah," Dormer agreed. "Motherfucker knows what he's
doing, all right." He said to Ken, "This may be as close as we
get."

No response. Then, the rattle of boards on metal.

Dormer looked over toward the sound. He saw Ken Stallman standing on top of a scaffolding plank, lifting himself up
onto the first of the girders overhead.

"Stallman!" Dormer called. "What do you think you're
doing?"

"Giving Stevie a chance."

Ken looked up at the next girder above him, a good five

feet over his head. He jumped for it, stretching out his arms. He missed, and came down hard. He started to slip off the girder beneath him, catching his balance at the last minute.

Ken jumped again. This time he caught the girder above him, and hung there, gasping for breath. He pulled himself up onto it.

The SWAT-team member came over to Dormer, who was starting to climb the scaffolding himself.

"Want me to go up there for you, Lieutenant?"

"No. I want you to keep an eye on Jarrow and that little girl. If she moves away from him, or if he gives you a clear shot of any kind, go for it. With every goddamn thing you've got."

"Kill instead of disable, sir?"

"Blow the fucker away."

Stevie knew she was going to fall.

She stood there, frozen on the narrow girder, unable to move.

"Come *on!*" Jarrow pushed her. *"Move!"*

Stevie gave a frightened squeal, and inched forward.

"Move!" Jarrow shouted again.

Stevie started to sob. "I—*can't!*"

"Fuck, if you can't!" He shoved her, hard.

Stevie slipped and fell to one knee, her other leg sliding off the girder, and dangling over the edge. Distant screams rose from the crowd below. Stevie moaned, teeth clenched in terror.

"Get on your feet, you little shit!"

Jarrow had let go of her when she fell, but now he reached for her with one hand, the other covering her with the .357 magnum.

"What's the matter, Jarrow? Afraid of a little girl?"

Jarrow turned to the voice. Ken stood on a girder directly opposite him, one floor down, eyes steady in the spotlight's glare.

"Surfer boy!" Jarrow laughed. "Come to save the fucking day!"

He raised the .357 magnum.

On another girder down below, closer in, Ed Dormer used both hands to steady his own .357, a Colt Python, and took what he knew would be his first and last clear shot at Tod Jarrow.

He squeezed the trigger, and felt the recoil hit his hands.

The bullet came within inches of Jarrow's head. It hit an upright girder behind him, striking a burst of blue sparks. One of them landed in the pupil of his left eye.

"Shit!" Jarrow screamed, grabbing at his eye.

Thinking he had hit him, Dormer paused just for an instant.

Jarrow turned and emptied the .357 magnum at him.

The first shot cut wide of Dormer on the right. The second went too high. The third caught him in the neck. He staggered back, arms flung out, blood spraying from his throat. He slipped and fell, landing on one knee, shattering the kneecap, and slipped again. Dormer fell from the girder, leaking blood. He bounced off another girder on his way down, before crashing onto a temporary rooftop two stories below.

Jarrow raised the magnum and took careful aim at Ken.

A hand reached up and grabbed for the gun. Stevie's hand.

"You little *bitch!*"

Jarrow popped her on the head with the gun barrel, not hard enough to make her vomit or see double, but hard enough to hurt.

Stevie put her hands to her head and started wailing. Jarrow picked her up roughly, locking his left arm around her chest.

Then he turned the gun back on Ken.

"What the fuck—"

Ken was pulling himself up onto the girder where Jarrow stood with Stevie. His arms, weakened by earlier efforts, shook badly, but he was almost halfway up now, over halfway, lifting himself by sheer willpower more than anything else.

Jarrow steadied his aim with the .357, smiling.

"Bye-bye, asshole!" he whispered, and pulled the trigger.

The hammer snapped down with a crisp, metallic sound.

Jarrow stared at the gun, then remembered that he hadn't reloaded it since shooting that blond bitch at Connie's house.

"Aw, shit!" he mumbled, breaking open the magnum's cylinder, tightening his grip on Stevie, digging into his jeans pocket to scoop up a handful of .357 shells.

"You're crushin' my chest," Stevie whimpered.

"Shut up!" he hissed, holding a bullet between thumb and index finger, starting to drop it into an empty chamber.

He glanced up—and saw Ken almost on top of him.

"Fuck you!" Jarrow screamed.

He hurled the bullets at him, then the empty magnum itself.

Ken raised an arm to protect himself. The heavy revolver bounced off his forearm, sending a shock wave of pain up his arm.

Holding Stevie in a death grip, Jarrow reached back with his right hand, unsnapped a worn leather sheath, and drew out a combat knife with a curved blade over a foot long. It looked like a Renaissance dagger, the kind Macbeth might have murdered Banquo with, and Jarrow held it like one, the heavy handle balanced easily in the palm of his hand, blade pointing at Ken.

Ken glanced at it, then stared into Tod Jarrow's dark eyes, the left one half-blinded by the spark from the ricochet, starting to swell shut, some kind of fluid leaking from beneath the lid.

They were the eyes of someone who had killed his sister, raped his wife, kidnapped his kids, and now held his daughter's life, literally, in his hands.

But they were also the eyes of a damned thing, driven by a madness beyond his understanding or control.

"Put it away," Ken said to him, nodding at the knife. "Let her go. And I'll let you go. Which is more than you'd do for me in the same situation." He stared into the dark eyes. "More than you did for my sister."

"What if I say, shit on you and your fucking offer?"

"Then you're going to die."

"Fuck you, asshole!" Jarrow said cheerfully. "Think you're good enough to take me, surfer boy? Come on! Let's try it!"

Ken made a feint for the knife hand, then drew back, expecting Jarrow to lunge at him.

He slashed down with the knife instead, trying to cut a jagged line from Ken's mouth to his stomach and dump his guts out on the girder. The knife hit Ken's thigh, cutting through denim, skin, fat, muscle, missing the femoral artery by inches. Ken hissed as the blade sliced open his leg. He grabbed hold of Jarrow's knife arm with both hands, squeezing it hard enough to bruise the bone, hard enough to make those dark eyes flash with pain and alarm.

"Let me *go!*" Jarrow screamed. "Or I'll fucking *drop* her!"

He grabbed Stevie by her left arm, and threw her off the girder, hanging on to her as she dangled helplessly in midair.

Screams and shouts broke out from the crowd below.

Stevie hung there with her eyes shut, unable to look down, or even think about what would happen if Jarrow let her go.

The two men stood on the girder, face-to-face, neither one moving, Ken gripping Jarrow's knife arm with both hands, Jarrow holding Stevie out over empty space, everything suspended in time.

Ken grabbed for Stevie's arm.

Jarrow dropped her.

What happened next took only a few seconds in real time, but it seemed to Stevie as if time and motion had both slowed down.

The moment Jarrow dropped her, she opened her eyes. She saw the spotlights and the screaming crowds down below, and the lights of far-off buildings. She knew that if she turned around, she could probably even see the lights of their house in the Hollywood Hills one last time, before she fell to the ground and died.

Thinking that, she turned around, and stopped falling.

She hovered there in midair, seeing the astonished, unbelieving look in her father's wide blue eyes, and the open-mouthed horror on Tod Jarrow's scarred face. Stevie knew nothing of The Gift. Her grandmother was gone where she could not tell her about it, and her mother was trapped in another world of time. But some power seemed to link the dead Alice MacKendrick and the missing Connie Stallman with the living Stevie Stallman like a life force flowing through the body of one gigantic cosmic being, or one great universal tree, its roots and branches interconnecting throughout all the worlds and all the ages.

She thought that where she really wanted to be was back on the girder again, with Daddy, but away from Tod Jarrow. And thinking that, she reached for it inside her mind, stretching out for it.

...s...t...r...e...t...c...h...

She moved back onto the girder, down behind her father, grabbing tight to his leg, the one with all the blood on it, and then she held on for dear life, because she was not sure she could ever do that again, not if she lived to be one hundred years old.

Ken had no idea what had happened.

But Jarrow knew.

"Stréga!" he whispered, then, screaming, *"Witch child!"*

He thrust at her with the knife, trying to stab her between Ken's legs. But before he could get close, the knife popped out of his hand and began to spin in front of him like a propeller at maximum rpm. Automatically, without thinking, he reached for it. The whirling blade sliced off the four fingers of his right hand and part of his thumb. Blood spurted from the fresh stumps.

Jarrow threw back his head and howled like an animal.

The blade moved into his face, gouging out his good eye, shearing the flesh from his bones. He batted blindly at the whirling knife, and stumbled off the edge of the girder.

"Azrael!"

He screamed as he fell, trailing blood behind him.

Then he vanished, as if he had never been.

49
The Burning

On a late Friday afternoon, the twenty-third of July, 1594, all Venice assembled in the piazzetta off the Doge's Palace to watch the ungodly burn.

Rich and poor, high and low, they all came to see the burning.

Mountebanks, merchants, shipyard workers from the Arsenal, beggars, countesses, gondoliers, priests, prostitutes, foreign princes, soldiers, sailors, diplomats, Jews, bishops, actors, printers, mimes, apothecaries, fishmongers, thieves, murderers, magnificoes, Turks, *Signoria* members.

Count Ludovico Contarini stood among these last, heavy face pale and sagging, a permanent droop to his mouth, silver gray hair turned white and thin. He was an object of great curiosity now, of something almost like religious veneration, whispered about and pointed at.

For he had been the victim of their damnable sorcery, the two who were to burn today.

"They say she turned him into a snake," whispered the wife of a wealthy merchant to her friend. "And made him writhe on his belly in the hall of his own *palazzo!*"

A sickly little beggar girl came up and timidly touched the hem of Ludovico Contarini's red robe, hoping to receive some of the holy magic that must emanate from one who had survived sorcery.

The Countesses Laura Antenori, Maria Frascati, and Veronica Bragadin were among those present, standing almost at the front of the crowd, where they had made their servants wait from before first light that morning to save places for them.

"I wonder," Laura Antenori said, long face shrewd as ever behind the black veil. "Will they let her, as a countess, wear a smock for decency? Or burn her naked, as the law demands?"

"Naked, I hope," murmured the youthful Veronica Bragadin in her little girl's voice. "She has such a lovely body."

Maria Frascati cast a disapproving glance. "It is a deplorable tragedy. Think of the disgrace to the Contarinis!" She paused. "Think of the danger to ourselves! Mother of God, we were standing next to her aboard the *Bucintoro* just this last Ascension Day! She could have drowned us all!"

"Instead she fell into the water herself," Veronica Bragadin said, "but did not drown. She stayed afloat until one of the attendant ships picked her up. Remember? That was the first sign of her sorcery."

Laura Antenori shook her veiled head. "There have been other signs. Her servants say that she would sometimes speak of events in the impossibly distant future, centuries from now, as if they had already happened. As if she had experienced them herself. A scullery maid of hers, a deformed creature named Tulia, said that once she saw her use sorcery to turn herself into a black cat."

Maria Frascati crossed herself. "She always seemed like such a sensible girl! Quiet, but not one of those shy, withdrawn types you want to pack off to a nunnery. She could be quite charming at dinner parties and festivals. But then, to take up with some gutter-scum like that Marcangelo Mosca! Mosca, indeed. Well named! A common fly, feeding on garbage. A hired murderer, consorting with shipyard prostitutes from the Arsenal, then killing them for his amusement. It's a wonder she didn't catch the Plague from him! Whatever made her do it?"

"Power. Ultimate power."

"Come now, Laura! What kind of power was she going to get from a hired murderer?"

"A murderer in the service of the Dark Sorcerer."

"Oh, him again! Where is he today, by the way? You'd think he might at least come by to watch his two pupils burn for what he taught them. I wonder why he's so afraid to show his face?"

"He is never seen, unless he wishes to be seen."

"I guess that tells us something about his sense of social obligation then, doesn't it?"

"Do you think they were tortured by the Ten?" Veronica Bragadin asked, a hint of excitement in her childlike voice. "Will we be able to see the wounds on their bodies?"

"Oh, I doubt it!" Maria Frascati said. "After all, she *is* sensible. Or used to be, anyway. I'm sure she gave her confession right away and saved herself all that unpleasantness."

"It wouldn't matter." Laura Antenori smiled. "The Ten always torture you, whether you confess or not. They have their reputation to maintain."

"Really, Laura! Sometimes you dwell on the most unpleasant—"

"Shh!" Veronica Bragadin put a finger to her lips.

A hushed murmur rose from the crowd.

The prisoners were brought out from the Doge's Palace, up from the basement dungeons and into the light of day, toward St. Mark's Column. They walked slowly, the man limping, both of them dressed in dark sackcloth robes, hands and bare feet chained and shackled, led by guards with pikes and sharp halberds, preceded by a priest in ceremonial vestments, a heavy silver crucifix raised in his right hand, a gold-bound Bible clutched in his left.

The members of the crowd crossed themselves and bowed to the crucifix. Following close behind the condemned prisoners, like the Shadow of Death, came the executioners, large men in black masks, carrying ropes, wood kindling, torches, all the items necessary for a successful burning. Many members of the crowd crossed themselves again, then looked away to avoid the *malocchio,* the evil eye.

The procession stopped before St. Mark's Column. Even at a distance the onlookers could see that the man had been savagely tortured, his left eye a gaping hole, his mouth slack-jawed and toothless. A wind from the sea blew across the assembled crowd and the condemned prisoners, scattering the unbound reddish-brown locks of the young woman, and disappointing certain members of the crowd.

A strong wind meant a fast burning, and a quick death.

The priest opened his Bible and began to read from it in Latin, administering the Holy Sacrament of Extreme Unction. The prisoners had confessed their sins of diabolical sorcery, and could now be granted absolution by the Church, before being burned alive.

As the priest droned on in Latin, the young Countess Alessandra Contarini looked out through terrified eyes at the place where she had lived all her short life, and at the friends and relatives, and disinterested onlookers, who had come to watch her burn. Her terror was intensified by the Demon that possessed her now, taking control of her mind, making her think and feel things strange and unknown. It had entered her mind that night she tried to flee the city, there in the gondola with the black coffin and the rats. It had been sent to her by the Dark Sorcerer. He had triumphed, at last. He had taken Marcangelo's love for her, corrupted and perverted it, and used it to destroy them both. She wanted to weep, letting the tears flow down her face.

But the Demon would not let her.

From inside the body of Alessandra Contarini, Connie Stallman stared at the huge crowd of late-sixteenth-century witnesses to a witch burning. She felt contempt for their cruel, simpleminded innocence, but at the same time, she recognized a kinship. They were not that much different from their descendants four hundred years later. What they could not understand, they destroyed.

Besides, they were not her enemies. Even the sinister members of the Council of Ten, the brutal guards and sadistic torturers, none of these were her enemies. Her enemy was the Angel of Death. And he had not yet made his appearance. But he would. Today. Here, at the burning. She was sure of that.

The mind of the poor young girl whose body she inhabited now was a weak, defenseless thing, almost a child's mind, obsessed with clothes and jewels and friends and childhood memories, alternating between foolish dreams of escape and dreadful fears of what was to come. Connie had been forced to dominate Alessandra's mind completely, and crush it to one side. She needed full play for her own more complex thoughts, and for the detailed training Zenobia had given her, the only thing that now stood between her and the Angel of Death—the only thing that could save her life.

My own life, and the lives of all the others.

She and Marcangelo never had a chance to see the members of the Council of Ten face-to-face, for the Ten operated in strict and notorious secrecy. An emissary from the council had informed the lovers of the charges against them—attempted murder of a *Signoria* member, the forbidden practice of sorcery.

He had advised them of the penalties that would be applied.

Then, he had turned them over to the torturers.

She knew that Venetian torturers had a reputation for terror and cruelty undiminished by the passage of four hundred years.

Beneath the dungeons of the Doge's Palace, she found out why.

She and Marcangelo were thrown into separate cells. Hers consisted of a pit half-full of stinking black water, the only dry ground a narrow ledge shared by rats and spiders. Next to her, chained to the wall, a poor old woman, who should have been on some kind of chlorpromazine therapy, shouted and screamed herself hoarse, banging her head against the damp stone wall until she collapsed at last into blood-smeared unconsciousness.

The torture took place in a dry room filled with sinister machinery, and sufficient torchlight to insure technical precision.

The torturers awaited them, a Master and his assistants.

It was their job to get a signed confession from her and Marcangelo. She had been willing to sign hers at once.

An assistant placed a quill and parchment before her.

The Master Torturer laid his hand on top of the confession. "No," he said, pulling it back from her. "The crimes of sorcery were committed by both of you, acting in concert. They must be confessed and signed the same way."

She turned and looked at Marcangelo.

Nothing registered in his dark eyes, except defiance.

"She will sign," the Master Torturer said to him. "Will you?"

"Let her do as she wishes. I will sign nothing."

The Master Torturer stepped in front of him, holding up the confession and the quill for signing.

"I urge you," he said, "to reconsider."

Marcangelo stared at the confession, then at the quill.

He spit in the face of the Master Torturer.

His assistant gave a small, startled cry. He hurried over with a fine silken handkerchief. The Master took it from him and dabbed at the spittle on his face, keeping his eyes on Marcangelo.

"You will regret that," he said softly. "I promise you."

Then, to his assistant, "Prepare him for the ordeal at once."

"The interrogation first, my lord? And then the machines?"

"This one has no need of interrogation. He has given us his answer. Proceed directly with the machines."

"Yes, my lord."

Even as they began work on Marcangelo in the background—stretching his body slowly on the rack, eliciting first groans, then screams—the Master Torturer continued Connie's interrogation himself. She could see in his eyes the certainty of her guilt.

"You are aware of the accusations made against you?"

"Yes, my lord."

"Do you deny them?"

She knew that to do so would only confirm her guilt.

"No, my lord."

"You confess, then, to being a witch—*stréga?*"

"No, my lord. I confess to having been deceived, by one I thought I loved—by one I thought loved me in return."

She lowered her eyes.

"You lay the blame for these crimes upon his head?"

"My lord, I did only as he commanded me."

She looked up, and saw the disappointment in his eyes.

She had given the right answer, the one that would save her.

"You are the weaker vessel," the Master Torturer conceded, bitterness in his voice. "Your crimes are great and terrible. But insofar as you committed them only in obedience to him, your sin is the lesser—as shall be your punishment."

"Am I to be tortured, too?" she asked, the words catching like dry stones in her throat.

The Master Torturer did not answer at first.

Then he said, "You will be spared the ordeal. But you will be forced to watch him undergo his. You will be a witness to the price of pride, and damnation."

The mere watching had been enough to shrivel up her soul.

The visible signs of Marcangelo's torture as seen by the crowd in the piazetta—the missing eye, the broken jaw, the toothless mouth—these revealed only a small part of what had been done to him. The torturers of Venice were thorough, patient, and precise.

Their terrible machines, obscene parodies of modern medical technology, had been designed to destroy the body rather than heal it. They possessed machines for crushing testicles, one by one, machines for breaking every bone in the body not essential to upright support, machines for extracting teeth, fingernails, and toenails with inhuman slowness. They knew methods of injecting corrosive acids into body cavities, and inserting long, thin glass tubes up the urethra, then smashing them to pieces inside. They knew ways of reviving the victim from pain-induced unconsciousness and restoring his sensitivity, so that they might subject him to new, ever more intense tortures.

After gouging out one of Marcangelo's eyes with a sadistic ingenuity that made Connie close her own, they began to burn the other eye, by slow degrees, with acids and fire.

When he at last signed his confession, other hands had to

guide the broken bones of his own hand, producing a scrawled signature that his one eye could no longer see.

Watching was its own torture. The Master Torturer knew this well. More than once she had caught him looking in her direction, and smiling to see her face damp with sweat.

But one thing held more terror for her than any torture.

Throughout Marcangelo's long agony, she had not once seen any sign of Tod Jarrow's dark rage, his fierce hatred for her. He could not be inside Marcangelo now, as she was inside Alessandra. But where was he? The Dark Sorcerer had called her back for this burning. Surely, he had called back Jarrow, too.

Unless—

Unless he was using him for some other, specific purpose.

Such as killing off the members of her family, one by one.

The thought so terrified her that it eclipsed the horror of Marcangelo's tortures, even her own fear of being burned alive. She pushed it violently from her mind, terrifying what was left of poor, frightened little Alessandra Contarini's mind in the process.

As the priest continued to read the last rites for Marcangelo in Latin, making the sign of the cross over him, Tod Jarrow came back into that broken body with a sudden vengeance.

Snatched from a blinded, mutilated body falling hundreds of feet to its certain death in Los Angeles, his first reaction on finding himself blind and crippled in Venice was one of all-consuming rage. He tried to cry out, but discovered that he had no tongue and no teeth, and a broken jaw.

He spit instead, spraying saliva and clotted blood over the priest's face and ceremonial vestments.

The priest stepped back, making the sign of the cross to protect himself against the Demon, and whispered *"Exsecratus!"*

Accursed One.

Barely able to see out of his one acid- and fire-burned eye, he turned it on Connie as Alessandra and said, "You!"

But without a tongue, or jaw muscles, it came out more like the cry of a wild beast trying to imitate human speech.

Then she heard him speak to her in the old, familiar way. Inside her head, softly, like a lover's caress.

Don't worry, Contessa—he will give me a new body, and we will be together again, wed to one eternity.

The memories came back to her then, and along with them the passion—all the passion she had known for him in this life, here in Venice, as Marcangelo, and the dark passion that had drawn her to him as Tod Jarrow, in Los Angeles, now impossibly distant in space and time.

She saw their bodies moving together again, his inside hers, vividly, here in Venice, insubstantially, there in distant Los Angeles. She felt the fire of his flesh within hers, the union of body and soul. Her eyes filled with tears, cold against the strong wind blowing in from the Adriatic. And for a moment, brief as a heartbeat, she wanted him again, even loved him again, with the dark, violent love that had always been theirs.

But it was not a passion that could be sustained.

The body she had loved appeared before her now, broken and debased, the flesh stinking and corroded. Marcangelo in this life, Tod Jarrow in the other, he stood revealed to her now as he had always been—a creature of darkness, marked by death, in the service of the Angel of Death.

Contessa mia, she heard him whisper, *wed to one eternity.*

Her flesh turned cold. She knew who had designs on her for eternity. The very thought of it made her tremble inside the rough sackcloth robe that she wore.

The priest, having abruptly terminated the last rites for Marcangelo Mosca, stepped back and turned things over to the executioners. They cut the sackcloth from the prisoners' bodies, exposing them naked before the crowd, hands and feet still shackled. Gasps rose from the onlookers at the sight of Marcangelo's mutilated, broken body.

Some raised younger children onto their shoulders to get a better view. Others pointed out the details to older children, explaining their importance. This, after all, was a spectacle of profound moral and educational significance. It was why parents brought their children to witness a burning.

"Her body is so beautiful," Veronica Bragadin whispered. "Her skin is white as milk. And her breasts are exquisite!"

Maria Frascati squinted through her veil.

"She *has* lost some weight, hasn't she?"

"The Ten will do that to you," Laura Antenori said.

They bound the prisoners to St. Mark's Column, pulling hard on heavy ropes until they cut deep into their flesh. Connie sucked air through clenched teeth as the ropes cut her, hating the executioners for their cruelty. Then she realized how it must look from their point of view, inside this barbaric other world. The prisoners would be burned to ashes soon. It happened all the time. What difference could a bit more pain make, one way or the other?

The executioners began to pile up kindling wood around the prisoners' bare feet and legs, packing it in tight, yet not so tight as to affect air flow. One of the executioners tied back the woman's dark reddish-brown hair from her face with a leather thong. This was not a kindness. When the fire began to burn, drifting sparks could ignite her unbound hair. While that might delight certain members of the audience, it would also hasten the woman's unconsciousness, possibly resulting in her death. The idea of a burning was to keep the victims alive for as long as possible.

When the wood had been arranged to the executioners' liking, they set fire to it. Several men in black masks reached down with torches at the same time. The dry kindling caught, and crackled into flame. Smoke drifted up from the heap of wood, the pungent smell of burning pine, harvested from the forest-rich Dalmatian Coast, cut down and loaded onto ships by cheerful peasants with no thought of what it would be used for.

The wood smoke burned into Connie's lungs, worse than a first-stage smog alert back home. Soon, within minutes, she began to feel the heat of the fire on her bare feet and legs. At first it was nothing more than a generalized warmth, something a small electric heater might give out. Then, quickly, it began to burn. Not the fire itself. That had not reached her flesh yet. But the heat was beginning to burn her fiercely, the way it might have done had she stepped too close to an open fireplace, felt the painful heat scorch her legs, then quickly jumped back.

But here, tied to St. Mark's Column, she could not jump back.

The pain was growing worse, unbearably bad.

It's burning *me!* she wanted to cry aloud.

But she did not, because she could see that was what the fascinated crowd was waiting for her to do. Waiting patiently, like customers at Sea World watching the killer whales perform. This was what they had come for. The Big Climax of the afternoon. Something to be savored later tonight, along with the evening meal.

She tried to shift her feet away from the burning heat, but the ropes and the wood held her fast. Sweat dribbled down her naked, unwashed body. A sudden cry of pain escaped her clenched teeth. She coughed on the hot rising smoke.

The wood was burning faster near Marcangelo. Whether by chance, or because the executioners had set it up that way, it was hard to tell. His sweating body bucked against the ropes. He tried to kick at the burning wood near his feet. All he did was send up bursts of sparks onto his naked flesh. Because his body hair had been burned off by the methodical torturers, there was nothing dry for the sparks to ignite. But after the torturers had finished with him, a well-meaning doctor had applied healing oils to his many lacerations and open wounds. Some of the sparks caught the oil. His flesh began to burn.

Guttural cries broke loose from his toothless, slack-jawed mouth, echoing across the piazetta in the dying light of the day.

"AAAAAAGGGGGGGHHHHHHHHHH!" he screamed.

"AAAAAAAAAAAAAAAAAAAAAGGGGGGGGGGGGGGGGG-GGGGGGGHHHHHHHHHHHHHHHHHH!"

Connie turned her head, trembling against St. Mark's Column, the pain cutting into her feet and legs. Not the fire itself yet. Just the heat, burning her flesh like smoking acid.

Veronica Bragadin watched Marcangelo's burning in a state of frenzied passion, her mouth open, her own blood on fire. She wanted to reach down and caress her swollen nipples and damp maidenhead. But such things were not allowed in public. A pity.

Marcangelo continued to burn.

Connie knew it was only a matter of minutes now, maybe less time than that, before her own flesh caught fire and she started to burn alive, from the feet up, for the amusement and instruction of the crowd. She forced herself to ignore the pain blistering her legs and feet, and made herself concentrate on the treacherous 32nd Path of the *Otz Chiim,* the Tree of Life, the living heart, as Zenobia had called it, of the Great Kabbalah.

Don't let me get blocked on it, please! Not now!

She visualized the symbol of the Sphere to which the 32nd Path led. A muscular naked man. *Yesod.* The Foundation.

The first Sphere, Zenobia told her, *where we can work magic.*

She saw the naked man in her mind's eye, arms and legs spread wide, muscles rippling beneath taut skin.

The fire reached her flesh, destroying it, sending hot waves of pain shooting up into her stomach and groin.

Beside her, Marcangelo continued to burn.

"AAAAAHHHH—AAAAAHHHHHH—AAAAAAAAAAAA-AAGGGGGGGGGGHHHHHHHH!"

Out in the watching crowd, a new terror arose.

The close-packed ranks of onlookers parted, moving back, far back, bumping into people next to them, crossing themselves as they stared in horror at what had made them move back, a sight even more shocking than the bodies burning alive at St. Mark's Column.

Il stregóne morello. The Dark Sorcerer.

He moved forward slowly through the parting crowd,

dressed in black robes, wrinkled head bent forward, spider's claws at his side, yellow eyes fastened on the burning.

"My God, Laura!" Maria Frascati whispered. "He looks hideous! Like someone who caught the Plague, and then lived through it."

"He *is* the Plague," Laura Antenori said.

Inside her mind Connie visualized the naked, muscular man, *Yesod,* the Foundation, making him intensely real, more real than the fire or her pain. She could see inside his body now, with anatomical clarity and exactness. The muscles, organs, blood, nerves, cells. And now she felt the pain lifting from her own body, peeling back like a layer of wasted skin, leaving what remained whole and new, part of the Foundation.

She felt herself rising, moving up out of Alessandra Contarini's burning body, ascending St. Mark's Column with the greasy smoke of roasting human flesh. Looking down now on the swarming multitudes below, as they pointed up at her, faces transfixed with fear, or with openmouthed religious veneration.

"Lord protect us and save us from the Demons of Hell!" Maria Frascati gasped, crossing herself, as she watched the astral body rise above the piazetta. "She *is* a witch! *Stréga!*"

"Or a saint," whispered Veronica Bragadin.

The astral body was like dream-consciousness, without solid form or direction—matter controlled and animated entirely by the mind. It was not her own body, Connie Stallman's body, back in Los Angeles. But for right now, it was a good place to be, hovering over the piazetta and St. Mark's Column, where the bodies of Marcangelo Mosca and poor Alessandra Contarini burned alive.

It hit her like a shock wave then, smashing through the dream-consciousness, overshadowing her mind.

Do you think you can escape me *so easily?*

She tried to look down at the piazetta again, but she had lost all sense of direction and saw only darkness, distant lights, storm-tossed waves.

She looked again and saw it, the piazetta, farther off than ever now, and in its center, the crowd spreading out away from him like a human wave, the Dark Sorcerer.

Do you dare pit your human weakness against my *great power?*

Even at this height, his yellow eyes burned with a blinding malevolence that made her shut her own eyes and look away. And still she felt the yellow eyes on her, reaching inside her mind and heart, replacing courage with fear, hope with despair.

If you move against me, I will destroy you.

A black wind of death blew over her naked astral body.

You, and all you love, throughout all the worlds of time.

Her courage failed her. She could not do it.

Then she heard Zenobia say, *You must fight him, my dear.*

They were in the garden again, out in back of the office building. She was telling Zenobia that she just could not do this. She could understand *how* to do it, maybe. But even to think of confronting the Dark Sorcerer filled her with such terror that—

But you have no choice, my dear, Zenobia had said to her. *You must do this, to save your own life, and the lives of all the others who love you. It is the only way.*

She looked down at the blinding yellow eyes, shining up at her like beacons from the center of the piazetta. She thought of her family, of the friends who had helped her. She thought of her mother, dead, because of the thing standing there in the piazetta.

Soon they would all be dead, if she did nothing.

She stared down at him, looking directly into the blinding yellow eyes, and felt her contempt for him, her defiance, felt them grow inside her mind until they threatened to explode.

The yellow eyes dimmed, as if hit by a sudden power failure.

The Dark Sorcerer, startled, stepped back.

And the battle was joined.

A violent wind roared out of nowhere, sweeping over the

piazetta and all of Venice. Whipping at the flames of St. Mark's Column and turning the prisoners into human torches. Knocking over the guards, their pikes and halberds clattering down stone steps. Ripping black masks from the faces of the executioners.

The wind blew down children and rolled them across the stones of the piazetta. It scattered the crowd in all directions, screaming, arms stretched out blindly before them. Gondolas capsized on the Grand Canal. Huge waves broke over the outlying islands, crashing into the placid waters of the lagoon.

But another force, even more powerful than the raging wind, pushed Connie back from the piazetta, out above the open lagoon, as the golden domes of the Basilica, the pink marble of the Doge's Palace, all faded into the darkness of the oncoming night. The world seemed to tilt precariously to one side, so that Venice lay at a slant, lashed by winds in the distance. Below her and around her, dark, storm-tossed waters rolled.

Then, from beneath the waters, bursting forth like a new and monstrous creation, rising above the waves, immeasurably gigantic, like a mountain towering over the sea, something moving but not alive, sentient but nonhuman, dripping black liquid from rattling scales, continuing to rise, rising up above her astral body, and still rising, until it bent down over her like Demogorgon in the heart of chaos.

No longer the Dark Sorcerer of Venice.

But Azrael, the Angel of Death.

She broke free from the stunned paralysis that had made her watch helplessly as the monstrosity took final shape before her. She forced herself to visualize the body of a beautiful naked woman, shining in her beauty like a radiant angel. *Netzach.* The Sphere of Victory. Victory through Love.

She entered the triumphant protection of that Sphere.

Just in time. The yellow eyes opened wide, huge as double moons in a distant sky. They blazed with the obliterating brightness of a nuclear blast at ground zero. Had Connie not been protected by the Sphere of *Netzach,* she would have

been annihilated, swept out forever into intergalactic emptiness, like cosmic dust in the tail of a universe-orbiting comet.

As it was, both she and Azrael were hurled headlong
through the worlds of time, flashing across the ages. Days,
weeks, months, years, decades, centuries, millennia. Flashing
past like seconds, milliseconds, nanoseconds. Venice itself,
framed like a picture in the blackness of interdimensional
time, passed through its long and detailed decline in the blink
of an eye. The Turkish wars and internal conspiracies of the
seventeenth century. The sensual decadence of the eigh-
teenth. The tourists and revolutionaries of the nineteenth. The
coming of motorboats to the Grand Canal, trains to Mestre,
jumbo jets to Marco Polo. Then the final decay and dissolu-
tion. And, at last, the city's return to the sea from which it had
arisen. The waters covering the golden domes and marble
walls, the narrow *calli* and regal *piazze*.

Until Venice was no more, and only the sea remained.

The sea, and nothing else. Over all the vast expanse of
what had once been Earth, the dark waters rolled unimpeded.
The atmosphere grew thin and wavering. Cosmic radiation
poisoned all living things, and Earth became a dead planet.
The weather grew cold. Great sheets of ice, some large as
vanished continents, floated on the surface of the waters, col-
liding, cracking asunder, re-forming. The sun itself grew red
and pale, and drew near its own death.

And still, she and Azrael raced through the worlds of time,
the burning yellow eyes unable to touch her within the protective Sphere of *Netzach*.

But where his eyes did not pierce, his thoughts still could.

How long, he asked inside her head, *do you think you can
flee from me? Soon you must stop, and make your stand.*

She knew this was true. Somewhere, even the endlessness
of time might have an end. Besides, she wanted to go back.
Back home. If she had to face the Angel of Death, even if she
had to die, she wanted to do it in *her* world. Not on this dead
planet beneath a dying red sun.

But the way back was perilous. It led to a Sphere of great

and terrible power. One that could destroy her, along with Azrael.

It is like the double-edged sword, Zenobia had warned her, *that cuts you, even as it cuts your enemy. Unless it is approached with the greatest possible caution and self-control.*

It had to be approached from the Sphere of *Netzach,* where she was now. From Victory through Love to ultimate Power.

Are you afraid? asked Azrael. *Are you ready to submit to me?*

She closed her eyes, and began to visualize the next Sphere.

Overhead, the dying sun exploded in a nova-burst of such blinding radiance that the world turned inside out.

Meanwhile, back in late-twentieth-century Los Angeles, down in the south-central part of the city, two ten-year-old boys, Trevor Jackson and Christopher Jones, hurried through an alley, taking a shortcut to get home before Christopher's mother discovered that they were gone. They should not have been out this late, almost ten, and they knew it. There were gangbangers loose on the streets, and worse. But they had no choice. Christopher's cousin had said they could borrow his copy of the video game *Ninja Attack!*—if they came over and picked it up themselves.

They were running down the alley, watching for broken glass and bad dogs, when it plopped down onto the concrete in front of them, like something falling out of the sky. It was a little over three feet long and crispy black all over, like a large hot dog that had caught fire at a Fourth of July picnic.

With one big difference—this hot dog had two arms and legs.

"Dang!" Christopher said, skidding to a stop. "You see that?"

"Uh-huh," Trevor nodded. "What you think it is?"

"A bug."

"Man, you're a real genius, you know that?"

"What *you* think it is? A extra-crispy giant burrito?"

"Man, any fool can see it's a bug! What *kind* of bug?"

"A cockroach. A b-i-g cockroach that got its ass burned off."

"Cockroach, shit! That thing's a giant cricket."

"Aw, man!" Christopher objected.

"Go on pick it up. See for yourself."

"I ain't puttin' *my* hands on that thing!"

"Me either," Trevor said, looking around at the trash cans in the alley until he saw what he wanted.

He picked up a long, thin piece of wood and brought it back over to where the thing lay on the concrete.

"What you gonna do?" Christopher asked. "Poke it some?"

"Gonna see if it's still alive or not."

"Looks dead."

"You never can tell."

Trevor prodded the black shape with his stick.

It jumped into the air with a high, chittering sound.

"Dang!" Christopher said, stepping back.

Trevor raised the stick in case the thing decided to attack.

But it just hovered there, about five feet off the ground.

Then it burst into ashes, like an exploding paper bag.

Christopher and Trevor watched as the ashes blew down the alley and out into that windless summer night.

The ashes did not come to rest until they reached a distant part of the city, and the final human form of Tod Jarrow settled down softly onto the overgrown weeds of a vacant lot.

50
Back

The rain had been falling all that morning and into the afternoon, as if trying to wash away the past.

Ken sat by the back window, and watched the rain come down.

He had always heard that wounds acted up when it rained. But he had never had a wound to test the theory. He did now, and found that it was true. His thigh, where Jarrow had cut it, hurt like a son of a bitch.

It might help if he took some of those pain pills they had given him that night in the emergency room at Cedars Sinai. But he wanted his brain clear, even if that meant enduring the pain.

He needed to think about Connie.

About whether she was still alive.

Last night, he had tried to play a video game with Stevie. She had started to cry, and he held her.

Then she asked him, "You think Mom's dead?"

"I don't know, Stevie."

"Someone's tryin' to hurt her. Tryin' to hurt her real *bad.*"

"Tod Jarrow?"

Stevie shook her head. "Someone who *runs* him, just like I run this." She raised the video control. "Except, inside his *head.*"

She had a strange light in her eyes. "See what I mean, Dad?"

"I think so, Stevie."

Early this morning, a woman with an accent had called. She identified herself as Zenobia Horowitz, a friend of Jake's, and asked about Connie, about what had happened at Culver City.

"How do you know about that?"

"Please. This is not the time to tell everything. She was with me. A call came through. She left. What happened?"

Ken waited, wondering whether to call Jake, or the police.

Then he went with his gut feeling, and told her.

A long silence followed. He thought she had hung up on him.

"She is in mortal combat," Zenobia said at last, so softly he could barely hear her. "All the Spheres and Powers of the *Otz Chiim* be with her in this, her final struggle."

After that, he had believed Connie might still be alive.

But that was this morning. By now, reality had set in.

He no longer believed that the dead could come back to life.

He looked out at the pool and spa, the surface of the water rippled by rain, the whole world weeping for the death of his wife.

Trent lay fast asleep on the sofa. Stevie sat cross-legged on the living-room floor, staring out the picture window at the other half of the backyard, the part with the fruit trees and a wide expanse of grass. Raindrops trickled down the surface of the windowpane, etching shadows across her face.

She got to her feet. "Dad!"

Ken turned and looked at her.

"Dad! Mom's out there!"

"No, Stevie," he said gently, "she's not."

"She *is!*"

Stevie backed away from the picture window, eyes more frightened than they had been that night on the high-steel girder, in Tod Jarrow's deadly grasp.

Ken got up from his chair. "Stevie—"

She moved back farther, and bumped into a side table.

Trent woke up on the sofa and began to cry.

Stevie raised clenched fists to her mouth.

She started screaming then, shrieking hysterically.

"Something's out there with her!"

Ken rushed over to the window in a panic, not sure what he expected to see. Maybe Jarrow had come back for them, blind and mutilated, rain washing over his blood-soaked face, the .357 magnum in his left hand, pointing through the glass at Stevie.

Ken looked out the window, into the falling rain.

And there, he saw the impossible.

Falling back through the worlds of time, back from the death of the sun and the end of the Earth, Connie had become so completely disoriented, still locked within the safety of the Sphere of *Netzach,* that when the falling finally stopped and she came to earth again, solid earth, wet grass beneath her bare feet, she had no idea where she was.

Venice, four hundred years ago.

Or some strange land, four thousand years in the future.

Then she saw the fruit trees, the pool, the spa, the house Bryce Stallman had built for them, rain streaking its windows, the rooms behind the glass too dark to see inside. No one outside except herself, standing naked on the grass beneath a pouring rain.

She understood the power of the Sphere of *Netzach* then. She had wanted to come back home. It had taken her at her word.

But Azrael had come back with her.

By the time she realized this, it was almost too late.

The monstrous darkness towered over her once again, scales black and glistening in the rain, inhuman yellow eyes, pale and pitted like alien moonscapes, burning with enough malevolence to devour the living heart of the world.

He hates life so, she could hear Zenobia say.

Then, whispering inside her head, the voice of Azrael.

Surrender yourself to me. *We are wed to one eternity.*

The yellow eyes blazed bright with annihilation.

She visualized the symbol of the dreaded Sphere, the Sphere of Ultimate Power, and approached it carefully, from *Netzach,* Triumph through Love, aware that the Power could destroy her along with the terror of Azrael. The symbol flashed before her eyes. Then it wavered, and faded. She shut her eyes so tight that the muscles ached in her face. She tried again to see the symbol before her.

Inside the house, Ken Stallman stood watching the final confrontation with stunned and unbelieving eyes. His first thought, his reality thought, was that he must be dreaming, or hallucinating, imagining that he saw Connie out in the yard, naked, locked in a silent standoff with some—illusion. But it was the rational part of his mind that tried to think that, the part that closed deals and paid bills. The deeper part, where everything that mattered lived, knew what he saw outside there with her now was no illusion, no self-deceiving trick of the mind. It was something from Somewhere Else. The thing Stevie had talked about. The thing that ran Tod Jarrow like a character in a video game.

And it had come for all of them, not just for Connie.

The picture window exploded, glass shards blowing back into the living room, driven by heavy rain. Stevie screamed and covered her face. Trent howled on the sofa. Ken turned and reached for both his children, trying to protect them from the flying glass. The wound in his thigh came alive then with a pain that seemed to bring the whole world to a stop.

Geburah.

Connie thought the word, and tried to visualize the symbol, the image that unlocked the magic of the Sphere of Ultimate Power. But it would not come. Now, at the final moment, with everything on the line, *it would not come.*

Geburah. She repeated it, moving her lips silently.

Inside the house, a suction power of incredible force began to pull loose objects across the living room and out through the shattered picture window. It was no less intense than the suction created by breaking a window or opening a door in a pressurized cabin at over 30,000 feet. Lamps, tables, books, chairs, all went bouncing across the rain-swept floor, leaping out the window. Trent was sucked right off the sofa and up into the air. He wailed in bewildered terror. Ken grabbed hold of his son's leg and held on to him. The suction ripped off Trent's shirt and shorts, his socks and shoes. And still Ken continued to hang on.

Geburah.

Connie saw in her mind the actual Hebrew letters of the word, strange and intricate in their ancient patterns.

$$\text{ה ד ר ב ג}$$

Geburah.

A vast, empty plain stretched to the far horizon. But rain was falling now, pouring down, hammering upon the dry, cracked earth, turning it to mud. On the horizon a rolling flood, a tidal wave, spilled in across the plain. And moving ahead of it, his chariot drawn by four powerful horses, rode the mighty warrior from legend, hair and beard damp with rain, armor streaked with water. The eyes of his great horses were wild and savage, ready for battle, nostrils flaring in the rain. Mud splattered up from the chariot wheels and the horses' hooves.

In his hand he held a sword, flashing with white light.

On his lips, he bore a battle cry.

A roar of hatred and despair detonated overhead, tearing through the rain above her like the uprooting of mountains, or the shaking of the earth's foundations.

The ground trembled beneath her feet, with the force of a major earthquake, throwing her down onto the wet grass. She lay there, gasping for breath, as the roaring of rage and frustration, hatred and loss, echoed in her ears and inside her mind.

Then, a sound arose like the beating of a thousand dark wings in the night, moving away from this world and into some other.

And then, nothing.

She raised herself from the wet grass, and looked up.

The rain continued to fall. But he was gone.

Azrael. The Angel of Death. The Dark Sorcerer.

Gone. As if he had never existed.

Inside the house, the suction stopped. Trent started to drop to the floor. Ken caught him before he hit, holding him as Trent howled in bewilderment. Ken's own face was touched with terror and wonder. Once again, he had seen the impossible happen.

He looked over at his daughter.

She smiled back at him, blue eyes shining with tears.

He handed her Trent. Then he moved slowly across the floor, stepping over broken glass. He looked out through the shattered picture window, and saw Connie standing naked in the rain.

She stood with her arms spread out beside her, looking up as the rain fell down on her face and naked body, pouring over her like a great ablution, washing away the horrors of the past.

The world of Tod Jarrow and the Dark Sorcerer.

The blood and gold and death of Venice.

Her mother's death. Her own death as Alessandra.

And for the first time since her father's death, so many years ago, she was a whole person once again.

Back home. Where she belonged.

Ken came running across the wet grass toward her, the wound in his thigh making him limp. Behind him, next to the shattered picture window, Stevie stepped out into the rain, holding the naked Trent Stallman in her arms.

Ken stopped in front of his wife, the rain falling on them both, and reached out for her with an uncertain hand, afraid that if he touched her too suddenly, or seemed too anxious, she might disappear again, and return to wherever she had been.

He tried to say something, but the words would not come.

She looked at him, at Stevie and Trent, and said, "I'm back."